The Chemist

The Chemist is a work of fiction.
The story's location of San Francisco has only been visited by
the author and so begs the readers forgiveness if locations or
distances are not accurate. Events that motivated the content of this
book were twofold; one was the terrible occurrence of what
became known as the Sharon Tate murders that took place on Aug
9th 1969. Although the name Charles Manson, is referred to in this
book, it in no way links the real Charles Manson to events in this
fictitious tale and this applies to every other character in this story.

Prologue

My story has transpired from a combination of imagination and facts contained in two historic events, the first being the witch trials of Salem, Massachusetts. These took place in the 1600s. It occurred to me that this must have been a very dark and frightening time for the people living in that east coast locality. With this in mind I gave imagination a free rein, hence the following...

A number of villagers, afraid for their lives and the lives of their children, decide to uproot and leave the east coast. Other settlements, hearing of the hangings and of all the finger pointing hurry to join them. They form a wagon train and head west in search of a new land. Add to this band a preacher, a man that had been accused himself by the witch finders of colluding with the devil, a priest that has lost faith in the God that failed to protect him. This man has now turned to the very Icon he was accused of being in league with. Being a very persuasive priest, he works on the minds of his fellow travellers. By the time the wagons reach their destination, a prime piece of land in a valley which they name Peace, they have become a satanic cult.

As I said my story concerns two events, the second takes place in 1969 a time of the Sharon Tate murders. It was also a time of the flower children and many hippies were looking to get high. With these facts in mind imagination once again supplies the fiction, hence...

Aaron Yarn, is an ex-college student that has majored in Chemistry. Being part of beatnik set he's known as the chemist. While browsing in a library one day, Aaron comes across a rare book which sets him on a journey to find a town that doesn't want to be found: a town called Peace.

Table of Contents

Barry William Doughty

The Chemist

Chapter 1 Witchville

Brenda Spinner had been nervously aware of him since he arrived. Brenda considered the man to be handsome in a way, yet disturbing. In fact she thought him to be the most unsettling individual that had ever stepped foot in her little library in Witchville, Massachusetts. The man's features were square and sharp, like his skin had been stretched tight over the facial bones so that one could imagine his head as a skull. She could not determine the colour of his eyes except to notice how deep set and dark they were. Brenda felt that they had the ability to delve into her every thought. He was broad and very tall, Brenda guessed around 6'2" and his age to be in his mid 40s maybe, but the beard made it hard to determine. He wasn't what she would describe as muscular, but big boned, lean and physically upright. She wasn't sure if his legs were artificial but the two wooden crutches he used suggested they could be. His size, nevertheless, gave Brenda the impression of great strength while his black drape coat and matching shapeless derby reminded her of a 17th century Quaker, though unlike that friendly society; friendly was not a word Brenda would have associated with him. Young Jenny Blake, Brenda's assistant, remarked to her that she found him to be scary.

"I think he would make a credible Rasputin," she whispered to Brenda when he first arrived.

"Yes or maybe Bram Stoker's Dracula," Brenda replied.

The man had refused to give a name or an address saying he never intended to borrow a book, or join the library, but only wished to use their reading table for his studies. When Jenny thought he wasn't within hearing distance she jokingly referred to him as Mr Raspy the misanthrope.

The phone call had come a fortnight previous; the man on the phone said he was the chief librarian at Boston's central library and asked for Brenda Spinner the writer. Brenda wanted to inquire how he knew she was a writer, but the caller continued talking and she forgot to ask the question. He told her they had a man at the desk enquiring about a certain book and Brenda was delighted when he mentioned the title—A cargo of Hope. The book was a narrative and detailed account of Brenda's favourite subject: the history of the New England settlers. Brenda had written and self published her own book on that very subject which she entitled Escape to Peace.

A cargo of Hope was quite a large leather bound book. Brenda remembered the trouble she had acquiring it; records showed that there were only a few copies and all were owned by libraries throughout the states. Brenda used it to cross-reference and verify certain dates in her own work. The man on the phone told her that a man on crutches would be arriving in a week to browse through the book. The voice also said the visitor would like to see any other books that she might have appertaining to rare fungi and its habitat. Brenda had no trouble finding three books on the subject of mushrooms, and with regard to the New England book she knew exactly where it was kept. She did struggle getting it down from its resting place but Brenda didn't mind, she was so pleased that someone was arriving with whom she could converse on her favourite subject: Devil worship in the 17th century.

When the man arrived Brenda mistakenly called him Father. It was the beard, the Fedora and the black suit; anyone could have mistaken him for a priest. It was only when she realised he wasn't wearing a dog collar Brenda realised her mistake. She apologised with a giggle and asked him if he was Amish expecting him to, at least, smile whether he was or not. He didn't. Instead, he made her feel like she had insulted him; his eyes blazed and in that moment his whole being seemed to emit hatred. Later that same day as he sat in the reading aisle studying his New England book, Brenda decided to test his mood again. She took the three books on the subject of Fungi plus a copy of her own book over to him. She laid the books beside him and chose the moment to attempt repairing their first awkward introduction.

"I don't know if it will help with your research sir," she said, "but I thought you might like to browse through this book. It's one I wrote myself on the tribulations of the first New England settlers?"

The man responded with another hostile glare, "I'm well aware of what you've written, Miss Spinner," he said. "As a matter of fact I've read Escape to Peace and that is precisely why I will not need your assistance." With that he turned his back on her without even thanking her for finding the three books on fungi.

Every weekday he arrived at the library between 2 and 3pm. He sat at the reading table hidden down a central aisle between two high bookshelves. Brenda was now thankful that he was out of sight from their reception area. Jenny was also pleased she did not have to look at him. Each day he sat studying the same books and making notes until closing time. Brenda hoped each day would be the last and that he would not return, unfortunately he did, for two weeks. Each day Brenda avoided him. At closing time she prayed she would not have to remind him they were closing. She needn't have worried; at four minutes to five each day she would hear the heavy book slam shut. Brenda had never actually witnessed it, but with or without his crutches he always returned the heavy book to the history section and for that, at least, she was grateful. On the second Friday, Jenny had left for the weekend and it remained for Brenda to lock up.

"Goodnight Mr Corbin." She said, stamping the books of one of her regulars. She watched the eighty-year-old hobble out of the swing doors then looked up at the wall clock; it was one minute to five. Realising she had not heard the scary Mr Raspy's book slam shut, she opened the counter flap and walked over to the reading aisle. She had expected to see the crippled man still sitting there, and having to confront him about the time was something she dreaded. The aisle was deserted, and his crutches were gone from the table where he always laid them, but the large book was still lying open on the reading table. She peered down each aisle thinking he may be looking for another book but all the aisles were deserted. Brenda decided that maybe he had just forgotten to put the book away and that maybe he'd left when she was with another customer and never saw him leave. Yes that must be the case, she reasoned. The quietness of the empty hall suddenly sent a chill through her and it was a feeling she'd never experienced before. In all her years as head librarian she had never felt such an urgent need to get away from her beloved library.

She glanced again at the clock; it was almost five past five. She hurried to the entrance and bolted the main doors. As she made her way to the staff exit at the rear of the building she noticed a sudden draught of cold air and an icy tingle touch her cheek. She looked up to see snowflakes fluttering in through an open skylight. Why, she wondered, would Jenny leave it open when she was always first to complain about the cold. Brenda cursed quietly to herself then quickly unwound the nylon cord from its wall bracket and closed the skylight. She then made her way to the staff cloakroom. The cloakroom was also a means of exiting the building. Staff would enter here with a key in the morning and leave the same way if they were the last to lock up at closing time. Brenda looked out through the glass-panelled door, the thirty foot long path leading onto the sidewalk had thick hedgerows either side; She had always worried that on winter nights the hedgerows made an ideal cover for anyone waiting to leap out on a vulnerable middle-aged librarian while her back was turned to locked the door.

The temperature seemed to be dropping fast now and in the yellow glow of the nearest street lamp she could see it was snowing heavily. She donned her coat and changed into her fur lined boots thinking how she would soon be snuggling up to a warm fire at home with her typewriter and the fresh ideas she had for her latest book to keep her company. As she reached up to turn off all the lights, she remembered the open tome left on the reading table. Being afflicted by a mild degree of O.C.D Brenda could no more sleep at night knowing a valuable book was not put back in its place, than walk on water. Nervously she walked back to the non-fiction section of the main hall. She stopped once and held her breath believing she heard a voice whispering, but she quickly dismissed it as a silly case of the jitters. She peered again down each aisle as she went. At the reading table she reached out to close the book when, on the open page she notice a circle had been drawn. Peering closer she saw that the page held a list of names, names she had become familiar with when researching for her own book. The list was of people that had given evidence in some of the Salem witch trials. She peered closer at the name that had been circled then straightened up in disbelief, not only because the book had been defaced, but because the circle was around her own name: Spinner. Why, she wondered, would anyone damage such a valuable old book and was it coincidence that someone would choose her name when defacing it. As Brenda stood staring at it she felt a warm sensation on the back of her neck.

~~~~~~~~~

By Monday it had stopped snowing but the little town of Witchville was dressed in a foot of it. The first surprise that faced Jenny as she reached the library that morning was why there were no foot prints along the path to the staff entrance. She was well aware of Brenda's obsessive compulsions, it was the reason she was never late. Having to use her own keys to unlock the staff entrance and not finding Brenda's coat or boots in the lobby caused her to wonder if Brenda had been taken ill. I expect I'll get a call from her soon. She'll ask me to hold the fort I expect, Jenny mused, knowing Brenda usually did this whenever she had to pop out for something, or been delayed. Jenny used her own key, got changed and made her way into the library's main hall. As she opened the staff counter she saw a shadow move crossed the floor in front of the main glass door. Of course, she then remembered, it was the first Monday in the month, the day Mable Oakley came in. Mable was eighty two, she lived alone and came into the library once a month to do her accounts; for years Mable had ran a postal catalogue in the little town. The old lady was lonely and the catalogue gave her an excuse to call on neighbours to chat. Her sight was failing, but she refused to give it up. Jenny had once offered to help Mable fill in her return forms, now it had become routine.

"Morning Jenny," Mable said, stamping snow from her boots as Jenny unbolted and opened the door. "I never expected all this mucky stuff this morning did you?"

"No, but don't you think the trees look beautiful, in their white dresses?"

"I don't know about that, I think I'd rather see them naked." The old lady mumbled, looking at Jenny like she'd gone insane. "Where's Brenda this morning?"

"I don't know. I'm just hoping she's not been taken ill or something. I expect she'll phone soon, if not I'll ring her."

"So you are on your own this morning, Jenny. Does that mean you won't be able to help me?" The old lady said, looking concerned.

"Of course I will; we're never very busy on a Monday and I don't think many readers will be venturing out in this snow, do you? I'll get your paperwork sorted out don't you fret. You go get your forms all laid out on the reading table and I'll be over in a minute."

Mable hobbled off with her carrier bag of cash and remittance forms while Jenny got on the phone. She dialled Brenda's number and heard it ring only twice before the sound of a loud thump and a groan came from somewhere across the library. She looked up to see the old lady on the floor trying desperately to crawl out of the reading aisle. Jenny's first thought was heart attack.

"Mable!" Jenny dropped the phone and ran to the old woman. Mable's head was bleeding and Jenny guessed she'd hit it against one of the bookshelves. Mable's mouth was opening and closing yet emitted no sound. Jenny suspected Mable was having some kind of seizure but knowing little about strokes or heart attacks she was not sure what to do. She lifted the old lady's head and rested it in the crook of her arm. "Mable what happened, did you faint, is it your heart, do you have pills for it. Please tell me what to do." Mable lifted her arm shakily and pointed an index finger upward. Jenny's eyes followed its direction before letting out a piercing scream.

Brenda Spinner's own leather belt had been used to strap her ankles together. She had then been lifted feet-first and hung by the ankle strap over a large hook that had been screwed into a crossbeam above the reading table. Brenda was naked apart from her panties. It was as if her assailant was not content to just take the librarian's life, but only by inflicting complete and utter degradation would satisfy her killer. Brenda's blood had drained from two large incisions leaving her skin pale as milk. The vertical incision stretched from sternum to navel; while a horizontal cut six inches long had been added just above the navel producing a bloody inverted cross. Her arms, her face and especially her hair had retained much of the blood, but the excess had dripped down directly onto an open book, which was left beneath her. News of Brenda's murder sent the region in and around Witchville into a state of numbness and fear. The media wasn't helping. Journalists were having a field day with stories suggesting witchcraft and that devil worship had returned to the east coast. The town of Salem was certainly mentioned several times while every columnist jostled for the best pun. They led their columns with headings such as: The lights all went out in Massachusetts and Witch town will the devil strike next. Of course, for those seeking to gain power in office, it was a chance to gain political points by accusing their opposition of failing in their basic governing commitment, which was to keep their citizens safe. One popular TV personality suggested a link with the murders of a beautiful young starlet and her guests at her home in Los Angeles on the west coast. This was a news item that was still fresh in most people's minds and alluding to it only served to exacerbate public fear.

After two days of finger print experts scrutinising the Witchville library and the best detectives in the state of Massachusetts pooling opinions, police were no closer to finding or arresting the Bookworm Psycho: the nametag papers had attached to this elusive killer. After two weeks the little Witchville town was still in a state of shock. The local diner where teenagers normally hung out after school was now deserted and the library was still closed. Not that that bothered the local inhabitants; they were reluctant to enter the place anyway, and the dark winter nights kept the little town's streets deserted.

The police had nothing in the way of progress to give reporters, in fact they had not yet even figured out how the killer had left the building. Jenny Blake swears she had to unlock the rear door with her key when she arrived that morning and that the main door was bolted from the inside. The only logical theory offered was that he used Brenda's key to lock the rear door behind him, but this theory was dispelled when Brenda's keys were found still in her bag, thus adding to the confusion. But the police never made this public. They reasoned that it would only enhance the local community's hang-ups about witchcraft, devil worship, and spooks. Political pressure was building within the police hierarchy. They needed to be seen to be doing something and as a result they decided a fresh face might bring fresh ideas while helping keep news hounds off their backs.

They put a keen and handsome thirty-five-year-old on the case: a detective by the name of Jimmy Gardner, the son of a priest. Jimmy was originally from Vancouver where he started his career in the Canadian police force. He married an American girl and gave up the job to move to the states. Still only twenty-five, he then served for a spell in the American marines but it was while on a tour of duty, that his young wife did her own tour of the bars around the little town where they lived. Jimmy came back home to find her large as life in more ways than one; he knew the child wasn't his so that was it, marriage over. Jimmy moved to another town but rejoined the police and soon made DI. Jimmy relished being given such a high profile case. He needed something to keep his mind off the fact that his latest girlfriend had just dumped him, saying he spent too much time beyond the call of duty.

Being given such an important case as the Witchville Murder caused some resentment among his fellow detectives. Light-hearted jibes, pertaining to the Canadian police always getting their man, became more acute to the point of spite. But Jimmy tried not to let it interfere with his objective. He felt that his first priority should be to conduct his questioning of pretty Jenny Blake.

At first Jenny refused to be interviewed again. She knew that living through that terrible morning again would upset her; but Jimmy's charm and good looks finally won her over.

"It had to be him," Jenny was saying, while dabbing more tears from her eyes.

"Yes you said that in your statement. Why are you so sure?" Jimmy said.

"You wouldn't ask if you'd seen him."

"Yes I can see by this report you gave to the first D.I that interviewed you, but I'd like you to describe him again for me?"

"Why? He wrote it all down."

"Yes I know, but often witnesses remember something else when given time to collect their thoughts; ask someone to describe a person at different intervals and you'll often get a different answer."

"Okay, well like I said, evil, pure and simple." Jimmy made a face; Jenny took the hint, "Yes okay, description. Well, he was well over six feet tall, black beard, walked with the aid of crutches."

"Okay. Did he have a moustache?"

"No, just the beard; not long, but trimmed short and dark, very dark like his hair."

"There's nothing here about hair, only that he wore a hat," Jimmy said, checking his notes. "It's written here you said he wore a hat?"

"Yes, but not when he was sat at the table, reading. Apart from his scary eyes, it was his hair that gave him that mad monk appearance, you know, Rasputin. It was almost black and down to his shoulders"

"Christ, who was the cop that took your statement?"

"I think he said his name was..."

"Never mind; it doesn't matter. This Rasputin guy, it states here that he never gave a name?"

"No, he refused to give a name and we didn't push it because as far as we knew he wasn't actually borrowing a book to take out. Like I said to the other detective, he might have given his name to the Boston central library; they were the ones that phoned Brenda...poor Bren. She was such a gentle woman. All she wanted was a quiet life with her little dog, Pickles, and her book."

"Brenda was a librarian; don't you mean books?"

"No, I mean the one she was writing."

"She was an author?" Jimmy said thumbing through the file on his lap. "There's nothing here about her being anything other than a librarian."

"Well it wasn't something she talked much about. She was very modest about her writing I think she treated it like a hobby."

"Oh, so she wasn't published."

"Yes, her first book was…" Jenny paused.

"What? Have you thought of something?"

"Yes, her book I looked for them before you came, we had two copies. They're not booked out, yet they're both gone."

"What made you decide to look for her book; did someone ask you for it?"

"No it was something I recalled Brenda saying after we got that phone call. As she replaced the receiver she said: *At last, someone who's interested in the early settlers; maybe we can exchange notes*".

"So she wrote history books?"

"She only wrote the one, all about the plight of the first settlers to arrive. How they dealt with the native Indians and I think there was quite a lot about the Salem witch trials. I don't know how many copies were in circulation but we had two until your forensic people took one away. Isn't it there in your report?"

"It doesn't mention any book."

"Really? It sounds like someone doesn't want you to solve this case."

"That doesn't surprise me."

"Brenda's book was on this table when the police came. It was covered in her…Oh! Maybe they didn't get the connection as Brenda wrote it under a pseudonym."

"Is that normal?"

"It's fairly common. An author may not want friends or neighbours linking him or her to their fictional characters, especially if they've aired too many of their own inhibitions within the pages."

"Oh, you're talking about porn…"

"Yes exactly."

"Okay but if this was just a history book why hide behind a false name? If I'd written a history book I'd be proud to put my name to it."

"Yes I asked Brenda that very question. She said many of the names in her book were associated with the occult and the New England witch trials."

"Christ that was four hundred years ago, was she joking?"

"I don't think so, Brenda was very superstitious. I remember asking her about a strange amulet she wore about her neck. She said it kept evil spirits away."

"Well there goes that theory." said Jimmy.

"Yes and I've just remembered something. The very book that Boston library asked us to find for the stranger was one that Brenda, herself, used in her research..."

"No they didn't."

"Sorry?"

"I checked. Boston central said none of their staff phoned this library, but one of them did remember a man phoning them to enquire about a particular book called Cargo of Hope. They checked the catalogues for him and told him Witchville library had one. Apparently only three or four libraries' in the whole country has one."

"Yes I remember Brenda telling me it was very hard to get hold of, but I was there when Brenda took the call and I heard their conversation."

"Maybe so, but it was not the Boston central. I think it was probably the psycho we're looking for. I've got a man checking that call now with the phone company. With any luck I should know by the end of the day where the call came from."

"But if Boston told this man we had the book, why would he bother to phone? Why not just walk in and ask for it."

"I don't know; but you said he came in a week later so maybe he wanted to be sure you didn't let anyone else sign the book out before he got here. Plus it would look less suspicious if you thought Boston central was involved in making the arrangement. Have you still got the book?"

"No it's gone along with Brenda's book: Escape to Peace, and three books on fungi."

"On what?"

"Fungi—mushrooms to you. That was something else the man was interested in."

"Oh, right. So to recap, this guy has performed some kind of sacrifice my murdering Brenda Spinner then made his escape through that skylight. That is bearing in mind he was either crippled or had one or two artificial legs and was carrying a bunch of books."

"Well you're the detective. I only know the place was locked when I came in the next day. And I agree that the skylight is the only logical explanation unless he had a key to the cloakroom exit."

Jimmy sat pondering for a while then he said, "Where do you put your keys after you unlock in the morning?"

"Most mornings Brenda is already here but I still have to bring my keys….Of course! I see what you're getting at. I leave my keys in my coat pocket and it hangs out back in the cloakroom. He often disappeared around lunchtime for an hour and there is a Cobbler's just down the road. They cut keys…"

"Now you're cooking with gas, Miss Marvel."

"Don't you mean Miss Marple?"

"I never said you were *that* clever." Jenny giggled. "Right, Miss clever clogs I've got one more important question. When are we going to have that dinner?"

~~~~~~~~

A week later, Jimmy Gardener received an early phone call from Jenny Blake.

"Hi Jenny, don't tell me. You want to know when you're going to get that dinner I promised you."

"Well it would give me the opportunity to give you something that I've just found. I think it might be important."

"Okay how about I pick you up at seven tonight?"

~~~~~~~~~

They came in their dark serge habits like silent monks in the night. They took no chances; there were six of them, which confirmed the serious consequences of failure in their quest to recapture the three escapees: John Cruickshank, his stepdaughter, Gina and FBI agent, Agnes Howe. Yes, failure by the six hunters was not an option. It was just before dawn when the six came upon the motel. It was Jake Tollman, sheriff of Peace, who spotted John's car outside their cabin. The smallest of the six abductors was the woman. John knew her as Sister Joy Harris. She entered the cabin through an unlocked window and let the men in while the three escapees slept. John Cruickshank and Agnes Howe were both bound and gagged even before they had time to knuckle the sleep from their eyes. Once fully awake, John saw that his stepdaughter, Gina, was already gone. He surmised that they had silenced Gina before she could cry out, and then they carried her out before she knew what was happening. Even if Gina had managed to scream out a warning it would have been too late. But John wasn't concerned for Gina's safety; he knew it would be more than Jake Tollman's life was worth to let any harm come to her or the mystery unborn child she carried. The six came prepared and John pretty much knew all was lost when he heard Tollman's words, "Sister Joy—the potion." The woman produced a red flask and a familiar medicine bottle. The five hooded men stood by, their expressions blank and sombre while Joy used an eyedropper to transfer a measured dose into the metal flask-cup before topping it up from the flask. John guessed she might use a weaker dose for

Agnes and guessed Aaron would have given her strict instructions on the quantities to mix. John knew because he himself had been forced to administer the liquid to a victim. John had witnessed that man's terrible fate and all because Aaron Yarn said the man's name was in the Peace Bible. That victim's ordeal had made him physically sick; he had seen drawings of people in medieval times being garrotted but never thought he would actually witness it for real. That had been the decider. With Aaron Yarn having left on his so called mission to the east coast, it had seemed the perfect time for them to make their escape. He had obviously underestimated the dedication of Aaron's disciples.

John now watched Agnes struggle as they pulled down her gag and forced her to drink before she had time to scream. They showed no compassion, cutting her lip as they forced the sharp rim of the metal cup into her mouth. They ignored her choking and spluttering and John wanted so much to help her, but could only watch her torment. They replaced her gag then turned to him. No doubt they were expecting an even greater struggle, but these were big men and John knew resisting was futile and would only result in a beating, which might hinder his chance to escape should the opportunity again arise. He drank the strange tasting liquid without a struggle, hoping the chance to escape might present itself before the drug took effect. As they escorted him outside John caught a glimpse of Gina's hair through the rear window of the big black Chevrolet pick-up truck. This was the vehicle the six had arrived in. He expected to be thrown in the back of it. This led him to think that if he could break free of his bonds it might be easier to get to a phone, but no, they bundled him in the trunk of his own car and slammed it shut. He lay there in the dark reflecting on the error he now realised he'd made. What a fool, forgetting to hide the car. Even though he never expected them to chase him this far it was stupid leaving it right outside the cabin, Christ, it could even be seen from the road. Stupid, stupid, stupid, might as well have hung a sign in the cabin window: We're all in here boys. Come and get us. The annoying thing was he thought about hiding the car even as they were signing in at the motel reception. He fully intended to drive it round the back of the cabin as soon as he had unloaded their cases, but then he remembered after bringing the cases in that he'd forgotten to ask the manager to call him, to warn him if anyone came asking about them. So he called the manager and during the phone conversation, hiding the car had slipped his mind. He lay there trying to plan their escape knowing time was short before Aaron Yarn's potion, as he called it, kicked in but lack of time made it hard to concentrate.

John's thoughts were suddenly severed by muffled screams, the car rocking on its springs and nerve jangling sounds of slamming doors. All told him they had tossed Agnes into the back seat of his car, which at least might be a plus. If he managed to escape his bonds he'd know where both Agnes and Gina were located. He heard both engines start up. It was a five-hour drive back to Peace, and he wondered if he could struggle out of his bonds before the drug rendered it impossible. If so, would he be able to open the trunk from the inside? Even if he could, they were bound to see it in the mirror. There were far too many ifs. He tried moving his hands but the thin cord cut into his wrist, Deputy Tollman knew his knots. He decided it was useless. He then became aware of a faint red glow inside the trunk; he lifted his head enough to see the light was coming from a misalignment in the rear lamp casement. It gave him an idea. He knew it was a long shot but if he was to kick out just one of the rear lamps, maybe a patrol car would pull them over, if that happened, all he had to do was create a noise or rock the car. Any cop worth his salt was bound to make them open the trunk. That was it. He decided that was his one and only chance of escape. He lifted his head again to see the light and where to aim his foot. He laid his head back down and took a breath before kicking hard. Nothing happened. Not only did the light not go out, but there was no sound of his foot kicking anything. He tried again this time lifting his head to see where his kick landed. Another deep breath then kick—nothing, his foot hadn't moved and he realised the concoction had already started to take effect. He'd seen it used on others and knew it only affected the muscles, leaving the senses unaffected. Aaron had explained it well; the brain still sends its messages through the nervous system but the concoction slowly paralyzes the muscles receivers. Yes Aaron had obviously experimented on himself to be able to describe the symptoms so accurately. It always started in the lower joints first, so John knew that in ten more minutes he would be completely immobile. He laid his head down and while a solitary tear trickled towards his ear he accepted what he knew would be his inevitable fate. First they would lock him and Agnes in the tunnels and wait for Aaron to return.

Chapter 2 Peace offering

I was late getting to my desk the morning Captain Winifred Howe sent for me. It was my partner, Neil Roster that told me she was already in her office and waiting to see me. As I entered and approached her desk I noticed that she had a list of names before her. Four of the names had been underlined and mine was next on the list. Her little polished nameplate read Chief Detective W. Howe. She looked up as I purposely gave a little false cough,

"Corwin, isn't it?"

I hate it when someone states the obvious. With only eight detectives in our precinct she didn't have that many names to remember and she did send for me. Mind you, she didn't mix with us detectives much, but pretty much stayed in her office.

Winifred Howe had been with the precinct for only a matter of days, in fact just after our last chief died when a drug deal went tits up and he took an 8mm slug in the chest. It was rumoured that Howe was brought out of retirement as an emergency stand in, but that was obviously a lie. Howe certainly was not old enough to retire, but I couldn't figure why the higher echelon didn't just upgrade one of us detectives, Karen Sykes, would have been perfect. But apparently it was down to a recommendation by some Chief Detective Inspector by the name of Dugan.

"Yes, Chief Howe is it?" I said in sarcastic retaliation, but then the thought of reversing those two words tickled me and she caught me grinning.

"What's funny, Corwin?"

"Chief Howe, Howe Chief...red Indians...get it?" She gave me a look that could turn milk sour and I could see she wasn't in the mood. "Okay, forget it. What did you want to see me about?"

"On the subject of names" she said. "Apart from your wife and daughter, have you any other relatives, a father, brothers or sisters,"

"No, my parents were killed in a road accident and I was an only child, why?"

"Oh never mind it's just that Corwin is a name that...well never mind, it's not important. Changing the subject, I want you to read that, Corwin." she said holding out a typed sheet.

"I do have a first name you know, its Spencer."

"Yeah whatever; just read it."

That's me, by the way, Spencer Corwin, Detective Inspector, Precinct Thirteen, San Francisco Police Department. Howe let go of the A4 sheet, it glided toward me across her desk. "Have a good look at that, it's been passed around the precinct. It's a real opportunity and I don't think the position will be open for very long. I want you to give it real consideration."

I glared at her as I picked it up. After scanning the memo, I grinned, "Is Roster up to his pranks again this looks like it's just been typed up?"

"Nope," she said, biting off a seemingly annoying part of a fingernail. "His stupid memos have stopped since I threatened to break his typing finger." I stared at her, she wasn't smiling and I got the feeling she could actually do it. My attention went back to the paper and after a more attentive scan, I said,

"You're suggesting I apply for this; are you serious?"

"Deadly."

"Surely this can't be right," I said, flicking the memo.

"What do you mean?" Howe said, filing the offending nail almost to a point.

"I mean, you've only been in this precinct a week, and here you are trying to poach cops for another town, I can't believe any CDI would do that. And besides, I've never heard of the place. Peace! What kind of a name is that; what is it, a fucking cemetery?"

"Yeah, funny," she said with as much mirth as an undertaker that's just been told he has a terminal illness. "It's just a small town up on the Oregon-Idaho border and I'm not poaching cops, just one cop and that's you." There was frost in her voice, which made me overdo the frown as I studied the memo again. It said a sheriff was needed in some place called Peace. I smiled as I pictured myself on a horse wearing a Stetson—yes okay—me, not the horse. I frowned at her again,

"Even if I did apply, what makes you think they'd take a city cop? Hell, I've never even been on a horse."

"Not a problem. They got roads. Apparently they've heard the wheel's been invented too. You'll get a motor and my uncle is the mayor there, so just say the word; I can swing it."

"So you want me gone. Is that what you're telling me? Would this have something to do with the last car I crunched? I explained about that, I had no choice; well actually I had two choices, either I kept chasing the felon with some old lady spread all over the grill like road kill, or hit the street lamp and let the felon escape. What would you do?"

"Corwin—this might surprise you, but General Motors can still turn them out faster than you can crunch them—just! But apparently it's not just squad cars you like to crunch."

"Oh! So they told you about that! Hell, that couldn't be helped. Call Internal Affairs, they'll confirm it. The guy came running out of this precinct just as I was turning into the motor pool. He just ran into the road while looking over his shoulder. It was like the guy was expecting someone to come chasing out of the precinct after him. Who runs off a sidewalk while looking behind them? He was either high on something, or scared of something, or just tired of life. Hell, there was even a witness. Strange though—just before my car hit him, he turned and saw me and I got the impression the guy was smiling. That is until he bounced of my hood. Anyway, I reckon I may have inadvertently done the city a favour."

"How will running someone down in a squad car be doing the city a favour?"

"It'll save the tax payer by avoiding a costly manhunt, and court case."

"Elaborate?"

"Okay, try this; No one has been able to find the guy I hit and two days after the accident another guy, who no one in the precinct seems to know, is found in this building in a basement maintenance cupboard with a second mouth carved under his chin. Didn't you hear about it?"

"No I didn't. So I suppose you're thinking..."

"Yes exactly! I think the guy I hit cut the throat of the guy in the cupboard and was making his getaway when he ran into my car."

"So you're saying the man you hit died?"

"Yes—No, I mean I don't know."

"How could you not know?"

"Well after I knocked him down I dashed into the precinct and got the desk sergeant to phone for an ambulance. When I ran back out to help him; someone was just closing the door to a big black pickup. Before I could get to it they drove off and the man I hit was gone. There was a witness though, one of the uniforms here. Maybe whoever was in the Chevy was just a Good Samaritan. Maybe he just found the guy on the sidewalk and decided to take him to hospital. Or was he an accomplice to the murder." Howe said nothing but just sat staring at me. I tried reading the expression on her face, but couldn't, the silence then became embarrassing so I said, "Anyway, your predecessor, Chief Danvers told me he died but I found that hard to believe. I was pulling in to the motor pool when he ran in front of the car. I couldn't have been going that fast. I requested to see the report on that incident, but it has never reached my desk."

"Why did you want to see the report? You ran the guy down and he died, no one has pressed charges so why chase it?"

"Because something smells and I'd like to know who the guy was and why he was in the precinct. If he had some ID on him it might have linked him to the guy in the cupboard. If he didn't murder the guy then did he have a family, was he married, was he from around here? If so the least I could have done was break the news to his wife."

"Really; I think the last thing a widow wants is to meet the cop that just killed her husband. Just forget it, Corwin."

I was still visualising the guy's face, which was why my next words were more my own thoughts than part of the conversation, even though they came out that way. "I'm sure I'd seen him more than once before. In fact, I think I saw him wandering around in this precinct as I was on my way out that morning. Little did I know I was going to run the guy down on my return; what was he doing here? I asked around the precinct and no one seemed to know him or the dead guy in the cupboard and I can't understand why the lab never answered my request for a post-mortem report. What's more, even the dead guy in the cupboard disappeared. Someone must have authorized the body to be removed yet no one seems to know anything about it."

"I told you to forget about it, Corwin, and it has nothing to do with why I sent for you."

"Okay, so why bring it up?"

"It doesn't matter. Let's get back to the matter in hand."

In the few days that Winnie Howe had been with us she seemed to have done some serious checking on the detectives in our precinct. None of the guys knew much about her and it seemed none of them had a good word for her because she'd already trodden on a few toes. I guessed she was around ten years younger than me, mid-thirty's maybe. She had a great figure, nice legs and attractive in a stern way; I wondered if this was the reason she'd made chief at such a young age, maybe she passed all her exams horizontally. Excuse the smut, but I was hoping she had; it would have made me feel less inferior. Anyway, she had just moved up on my shitty-people list, especially after the General Motors crack; but that's me, bitchy I guess. I scanned the leaflet again.

"No, this can't be right," I said. "You got to be kidding. I'd have to give up my house. I couldn't do that. I grew up in that house; my parents left it to me."

"I know."

"You know?"

"Yes, I make it my business to know as much about the officers working for me, like their strengths and weaknesses; anything in their private life that might influence their performance. Okay, you own a house; so what," her mouth drooped nonchalantly at the corners, "The Peace job comes with a substantial salary and a house, and I mean a real house that goes with the job. You can sell your house, bank the money, and think about the interest it'll make for your retirement." That kind of took my breath. I could feel my eyeballs turn into $ signs and the interest on the money securing my daughter's future. But I was still curious. I felt like I was being run out of town and I wanted to know why.

"Sounds too good to be true," I said. But if my driving isn't the reason you want me gone, the department must be cutting down! Am I the first one in the department that you've approached about this job?"

"You're the only one I intend to approach." She said indifferently, while starting on another nail. It was me that now wanted to break fingers.

"Why?" I said, at a volume now raised to the level of my blood pressure. "How come you're so keen for me to apply for this post? Why not Roster or Shadwell? Come to that, why not Karen Sykes? Women can make sheriff can't they?" As I said it, I glanced through the window to the outer office. Karen looked up from her desk and winked at me. It calmed me down and gave me a warm feeling; it shouldn't, I'm married, but it did: Karen had something that stirred me.

Karen Sykes had joined the team after moving into the district from some other state. She told me her husband had got himself killed trying to foil a bank raid; wrong place wrong time I guess. Howe's voice tore my attention away from Karen,

"I didn't pick you on merit, Corwin or even lack of it."

"Oh! Then why did you pick me?"

"It's your age."

"Ouch, that hurt."

"Well it's true. You're getting too old to police a big city, not to mention too heavy. How much do you weigh?"

"Hey! You said not to mention."

"I'm serious, there are too many guns on San Francisco's streets and you're too big a target. What was your last score on the target range?"

"One rooky and a sergeant I shot in the arse—just kidding. I don't remember."

She ignored that completely. "Do it for your wife: Charlotte, and think about your daughter; what would Avril do if you suddenly weren't around? Anyway, I want you to think about it, hard."

~~~~~~~~~

To a hiker or lost traveller that might pass the Pike and Heron on the old dirt road, the establishment was precisely what it was intended to be: a picturesque old English-style Inn or tavern perched on the edge of a lake. Yet from the surrounding hills above, one could see that it was very much bigger. This was due to the Inn's recent extension built onto the rear of the place, a large hall that stretched out over the lake on stilts. Pike Lake and the town of Peace are situated close to the Salmon River Mountains in the middle of logging country. Because Peace rests in a picturesque valley between the states of Oregon and Idaho controversy between nearby towns occasionally flare. This was usually over road maintenance or policing responsibility. The Inn's barkeep is Horace Rider, a long time Peace resident and one-time owner of the Inn. Bad luck had befallen Horace when a modern road had bypassed Peace Valley. After that he was lucky to serve the occasional hiker. He tried to sell the place, but to no avail. Then a stranger by the name of Aaron Yarn came to Peace. He made Horace an offer on the Inn. Although Yarn purchased the place for a giveaway price, he spent a great deal on the extension that was built to overhang the lake. This was an undertaking that caused the construction company more than a few headaches which involved imbedding metal stilts in the bottom of the lake. It also excited the town's curiosity.

Although Horace Rider was pleased with the Inn's sale, there were a number of provisos that Yarn insisted were met. Condition one was that he would occupy one guest room and Horace and his daughter were to stay on as Inn-keepers. By agreeing to this they were assured their poor monthly takings would be made up to a manageable wage. Condition two was that they would deter anyone from fishing in the lake and that warnings of prosecutions be emblazoned on posts around the lake.

~~~~~~~~~~

It is now December 1974 and snow lay heavy on the Douglas fir trees that surround Pike Lake, which was now a mile in diameter of snow covered ice.

It is almost midnight. The sky is cloudless with almost a full moon and had someone been around to witness it they would have been curious as to why two figures, resembling monks, were using pickaxes to dig a large hole in the ice beneath the Inn's extension.

Inside, the extension is like an American style courthouse complete with Judges Bench, Jurors enclosure, witness box and prisoner's enclosure. The main viewing area holds enough seats for around a hundred people. The courtroom is cold with an unwelcoming bareness. Around the dark wood panelled walls little alcoves contain black candles; a feature compatible to the town's satanic leaning. A few paintings adorn the place: pictures that portray men in stovepipe hats and buckled shoes, women in long smocks and white cotton caps or bonnets. The paintings depict an age characteristic of New England in the 1600s. Some paintings feature an Inn, remarkable in its similarity to the Pike and Heron. Only the characters period dress set the picture aside from the present day. One painting illustrated a small jetty beside a lake. In the painting the artist has painted a roughly constructed ducking chair: a medieval contraption used sadistically in witchcraft trials. In the scene an old woman is holding a clay pipe and she's grinning into the terrified face of a young girl being strapped into the chair.

In a back room of the original section of the inn, Horace Rider is sat reading a book when he is suddenly aroused by a faint sound of voices chanting.

"Prudence, they're coming. Better light the candles, girl." Prudence, Horace's pretty twenty-year-old daughter hurries to light the black candles in the courtroom as the chanting becomes louder. At the same time two men dressed in snow covered Monk habits enter the Inn and hand two pickaxes over the bar to Horace. They then follow Prudence through double doors into the courtroom where they sit in the juror's enclosure and wait as the chanting becomes louder.

Now, also dressed in habits, fifty members of ESOR approach the Inn each of them carrying a lantern; they have walked in a single file along a half mile trail through woods from the town's church. These men and women are all residents of Peace and most of them can trace their names back to the New England settlers. As they walk they chant words that had been forgotten for many years, now recently restored by their leader Aaron Yarn.

The congregation, have almost filled the hall now. Twelve of them have filled the juror's enclosure and the last five figures dressed in contrasting black, step onto the judges staging and stand before five high backed chairs. The centre figure is Aaron Yarn and apart from his six-foot-two stature, his black silken habit sets him apart by the gold embroidered letters: *ESOR* on his breast pocket. His accompanying Elders now take their seats while Aaron remains standing. Before him on the bench is a large leather bound book. From inside a drawer he produces a long barrelled navy colt which he places beside the book. He then lays a hand on the book before speaking,

"Brothers and Sisters of Esor, You have been summoned here tonight for two reasons. One, for me to present you with the gift I promised you on my very first sermon in your town: the replacement of your lost bible." With that Aaron stood the book up to show its gold embossed title: Cargo of Hope. A loud murmur of approval followed by much applause until Aaron raised his hand in a motion to calm their elation. As their excitement subsides Aaron continues,

"Unfortunately your jubilation has been marred by the second reason we are here and that is to determine the treachery of the prisoner, John Cruikshank, who is accused of plotting against the residents of Peace and the attempted abduction of one of our cult members." Aaron then raises his voice: "Bring in the prisoner."

A door opens at the entrance and all eyes are drawn to two big men escorting a man wearing only a long white shift. His wrists are bound by a leather strap. They half carry, half drag him into the prisoners enclosure. The man appears semi-conscious and his limbs appear limp. A chain attached to the back of the prisoner's enclosure is locked onto a leather strap about his waist preventing him from collapsing. As his two escorts retreat to their seats Aaron Yarn gets to his feet.

"Brother Tollman, please enter the witness box." A hooded figure immediately leaves the front row of the congregation and steps into the witness box beside the bench. "Brother Tollman, lower your hood." The man complies, revealing his age to be in the sixties. He is of average height and his head is a mass of red hair. "I'm sure you are well known to our community, brother, but for the purpose of procedure enlighten the court as to your position in our community."

There is nervousness in the sheriff's voice as he speaks. "My name is Jake Tollman and I am acting sheriff in the town of Peace."

~~~~~~~~~~

Jake Tollman had been a resident of Peace all his life. He remembers, not so long ago, when the town justified its name. A small peaceful hamlet trapped in a time warp, a town that had ignored the bustle of progress. Jake knew what it was like to live in Peace before Aaron Yarn and his disciples came.

Jake, like many other Peace residents had become a member of Aaron Yarn's cult because of the man's electrifying way of preaching. It was like he had breathed new life into their town.

Little did the town imagine how much their lives would change when they turned their backs on their regular priest and allowed Aaron Yarn to take over the town? Many had signed up to Aaron's cult which he named *Eternal Seekers of Retribution: ESOR.*

By the time the town had come to realise their error it was too late. Aaron Yarn had established a hold so strong and threatening that any attempt to leave ESOR was just too frightening to contemplate. Yes, Jake would have given anything to take his son, Orville and get far away from this town where fear controlled it's community, but there lies the rub; fear itself kept Jake captive as it did all the cult members. Others had tried to leave and had paid the price like John Cruickshank was about to. Jake, however, feared not only the power and influence of Aaron Yarn but the law outside of their town. Aaron had deviously subjected every member of his cult to take part in his so called acts of justified retribution. This made it impossible for any cult member to distance themselves from these crimes morally or in the eyes of state or federal law.

Jake Tollman is not at this moment looking at the judges or the jury. He is staring at the man in the prisoner's box. John Cruickshank's eyes are open and staring accusingly at Jake. Jake flinches; he is startled by Aaron's voice as it cuts into his trance.

"Tell the jury what led you to suspect the accused in the first instance?" Tollman was surprised by the question knowing it was Aaron himself that had first brought his attention to Cruikshank's questionable activities. Most of Jake's following statement had been orchestrated by Aaron Yarn.

"Err…well; Deputy Cruikshank had been acting suspicious for some time. A week ago, I walked into the sheriff's office to find him and a woman I now know as Agnes Howe, whispering to each other I think they had been using the switchboard. You see, it was midday and Miss Joy Harris was away from her desk taking her break. I saw John quickly pull a pin out of the switchboard."

"Yes" said Aaron, addressing the court, "Why would he do that if he weren't using an outside line? This is breaking one of our basic rules designed to safeguard our community. Everyone in Peace knows the rules: No outside communication unless it's authorised by duty switchboard operator."

"That's correct. Go on sheriff."

"That night we had a storm. The town's phone line went down. John Cruikshank didn't turn up at the office the next day so I drove over to the Grange to see him and find out what was wrong. I got there about 1pm. He told me he wasn't aware the phones were down. He said he had a cold and that he had been home all morning, but as I left, I put a hand on the hood of his car. It was still warm, I knew he was lying."

"And you knew where he had been?" said a woman elder.

"Not, right away, but I made a guess and I was right, he'd been to Cranford. I decided to find out why. I drove over there; I spoke to a deputy, a guy by the name of Trent Phillips."

"And?"

"John had been there. He told Phillips our phone line was down and he needed to make an urgent call. Phillips let him make the call, said he heard someone answer and John asked if he was talking to a retired C.D.I Winifred Howe."

At this point, a low murmur filled the hall. "Silence!" said Aaron. The response was immediate. "Go on sheriff Tollman." Jake continued with increased nervousness.

"Phillips told me the call was to San Francisco."

"Are you telling the court that this Winifred Howe has influence with the San Francisco police and that she's related to the woman helping the prisoner to abscond with a cult member?"

"Yes, I think they must be related. After the line was repaired and Deputy Cruikshank was out of the office, I got Sister Harris to put in a call to the police dept in San Francisco."

Aaron turned to face a woman on his left. "Is that correct Sister Harris?"

"Yes, they told me the only person named Howe on their list of employees was a retired Chief Detective Winifred Howe." Concerned and nervous murmurs again filled the hall until Aaron Yarn said,

"I believe this throws a new light on the reason for our presence here today," said Aaron. "It is unfortunate my people, but it appears that there is a threat that these Howe women pose. This will be dealt with at the earliest opportunity."

Aaron then turned his attention back to the witness, "Sheriff, can we be safe in the knowledge that the information you received from this deputy Trent in the hamlet of Cranford was obtained without disclosing our community affairs?"

"Yes Sir I was very discreet,"

"Very good and did you confront Cruikshank with your findings?"

"Yes, but he denied everything. Especially about breaking his oath, but I must have spooked him because when I called at his home the following day I saw luggage in the hall. That's when I guessed he and Agnes Howe were getting ready to leave the valley. I was right, although I wasn't expecting them to take the girl or leave so soon. Anyway they didn't get too far before we caught up with them."

"Knowing the severe punishment one incurs for the act of treachery, Deputy Tollman, do you regret bringing your findings to the courts attention?" The question came from another female Elder who was staring accusingly at Jake Tollman's son: Orville now sitting next to his father's empty chair in the front row.

"No Ma'am," said Jake. "John Cruickshank took the pledge, he was aware of our laws, and the penalty for breaking them. He betrayed SOR and the people who befriended him. Besides, I was just doing my job." This seemed to satisfy the woman and murmurs of agreement could be heard rippling through the congregation along with the nodding of hoods.

All eyes then focused on the bench. The central figure, in black stood and addressed the community.

"Loyal followers, we are all indebted to Brother Jake and his son, Orville, for their vigilance and dedication to the security and well being of our community. Deputy you may be seated." Jake Tollman left the witness box as Aaron turned to the jury, "Members of the jury, who is acting foreman?" A man nearest the bench stood,

"I will speak."

"Brother Rider, having heard the evidence, will you and your fellow jurors need time to converse in private before delivering your verdict?"

The man, turned to his fellow jurors, and a murmur of voices was heard amongst them. Much mumbling and head nodding followed before the foreman turned back to address the leading judge again.

"Brother Aaron, we have no need for a closed debate, our opinion is of one accord. We find the accused guilty." A murmur conveying mixed opinions filled the hall. Some called for the prisoner to be banished from Peace while less forgiving members were baying for the ultimate punishment. Several of them repeated the phrase: *The Lake awaits,* even before the foreman had sat back down. Aaron was about to address the court again until one of the women who sat beside him turned to him and spoke. Her words were little more than a whisper and obviously not meant to be heard by the congregation, but the few words that were audible and her body language implied that she was pleading for leniency for the accused. Aaron listened, his frown deepening. When she finished he spoke sharply to her and she settled back in her seat with a dejected look. Aaron then seemed to scan the congregation before laying his hand on the book. "The Book is our guide, my children, and for the act of treason it depicts only one punishment and the master demands that we do not deviate." With that Yarn's arm stretched across his bench and almost immediately a loud whirling sound came from above and all eyes watched as a steel hook attached to a chain descended from the rafters. As the whirring stopped the hook hung approximately 6 feet from the floor and directly over a trap door. As Aaron was about to speak again a female adjudicator on his left leaned toward him and whispered a few words to which Aaron nodded and looked toward the front row and the young giant of a young man sitting next to his father.

"Orville Tollman, you have now come of age and are the most recent to be sworn into the brotherhood. You have witnessed the punishment of others that have betrayed our cult. To cement your allegiance we feel you should take an active part in carrying out the sentence." There was a silent pause and for thirty seconds nobody moved. "Orville!" Aaron repeated the young man's name with impatience. The anger in Aaron's voice prompted Orville's father to elbow his son viciously and whisper angrily from the side of his mouth,

"Orville, do it. They're waiting." Orville slowly emerged from his seat as the man next to him handed Orville a key. He then walked unsteadily toward the prisoner's enclosure where he unlocked John's Cruickshank's chain. He then effortlessly lifted John and carried him to the centre aisle where the chain dangled ominously. As Orville slipped Johns wrist strap onto the hook Orville looked into John's accusing eyes and whispered,

"Forgive me John." Even before Orville had returned to his seat Aaron had pressed another button on the bench. The whirring started again and this time two trap doors below John's bare feet slowly opened while John's body slowly descended through the floor. Jubilation could be felt throughout the commune. One woman clapped her hands and giggled excitedly as the threshing of water could be heard below the floor as the body of John Cruickshank entered the icy waters. The sound lasted two minutes before all went quiet and once again Aaron pressed a button and the congregation watched as the bare hook reappeared and returned to the rafters.

"The master's pets have done their work and another of our enemies has paid for his crime," Yarn announced. "I am confident that his accomplice, Agnes Howe will soon join him. The seriousness of their treachery, however, has yet to be determined. For this reason a trustworthy team of our people is at this very minute in San Francisco dealing with whatever threats these infiltrators may have brought upon our way of life. I have lived many lifetimes, just as you will; my brothers and sisters, and everlasting life will be Satan's gift for your allegiance. In my past lives I have inspired and nurtured many sects to potential greatness only to have them destroyed by internal betrayal. I will not let it happen here in Peace. The master is watching over us and I'm sure he will give us the strength to prevail."

Chapter 03 Marriage

When Winifred Howe told me to think about the Peace job she made it sound like an ultimatum. Think about your daughter, she said; I hate it when people play the guilt card on you; it's kind of cheating. Anyway, I did. I thought about the Peace job. I thought about my kid's welfare and Howe's crack about my weight too—the bitch! Just because she had an hourglass figure, maybe she thought she'd have a poke at my lunch-hour one. But she was right. When my first wife died I stopped working out, in fact I stopped everything except eating and drinking. I suppose I found comfort in it. Everyone deals with grief in one's own way, mine was to eat drink and get fat. But anyway, I hadn't really regarded myself as old, not at forty-six, and I sure couldn't see myself working in some backwoods town where nothing ever happened. Let's face it, what could happen in a town with a name like Peace, besides, I had to consider Avril; she was my beautiful daughter from Lucy my first wife. How would a 14-year-old adjust to living in some back-woods town? Chief bitch Howe said I should do it for Charlotte's sake; now that did surprise me. I was sure I'd never spoken to Howe about my private life. And I know I had never mentioned Charlotte, my second wife, or my daughter, Avril. I didn't think that depth of detail was in one's file, so I presumed she'd been discussing me with one of the other DI's in the office. Anyway, I suspected the bitch had her own reasons for wanting me gone. Maybe filling in paperwork for wrecked squad cars was part of it. Some women just have no sense of fun. Anyway, it's not like my driving killed many pedestrians; at least, not to my knowledge, but then, this was Francisco; whatever havoc takes place in the wake of a speeding squad car is anyone's guess. There was that one guy Howe had alluded to, but there was no way I could have avoided him. I was told by one source, a Chief Detective Dugan, that the guy died and that no ID was found on him. I didn't believe it; I know I didn't hit him that hard. I checked with the hospitals and the morgue; no male road deaths in my precinct had been booked in, not on the day of the accident or any day up to a week later. Anyway that must have been over a year ago and infernal affairs, they hate it when you call them that, cleared me. They had to; a witness saw the whole thing. It wasn't long after that Charlotte Potter rented a place in our neighbourhood. It was also around that time that Lucy became ill and complained about headaches. I told her she may need glasses but she was convinced it was more serious, saying she was also having hallucinations. The headaches got worse and Lucy became convinced she had a tumour. Charlotte or Charlie as we had come to know her had become a friend. Charlie told us she'd lived alone since her husband died, and I got the impression she was lonely. With me having to spend so much time at the precinct, Lucy was also in need of a friend and Charlie helped her through those last painful months. Lucy's final breath came as a blessing when she secretly took an overdose; I discovered how hard it is to watch someone you love slowly die. In the last month, Lucy's pain became unbearable and I suppose I will never know whether it was her pain that made her take her life or fear of her hallucinations. She told me about a huge rat that spoke to her. As she told me she appeared terrified and held on to me until she fell asleep. I told the doc and he increased her medication. For that reason I felt that I had played a part in Lucy's suicide. Had she not had those extra pills maybe her overdose would not have had the strength to kill her. Her doctor seemed perplexed by the rapid progression of her illness and talked me into allowing a post mortem. It may help others with similar conditions, he said, and at least give some purpose to her demise. I was too stricken with grief and tanked up with bourbon to think or argue the point. I just waved him away, saying do what you have to.

After the funeral, Charlie took Avril to live with her for a while. It gave me a chance to do some heavy grieving and even heavier drinking. I figured as long as I stayed drunk the hurt couldn't get me. After a couple of weeks, Karen Sykes called at the house to find an unshaven drunk. I can still remember her kind words to me. They went something like: You self-pitying bastard, you fat selfish excuse for a father. Get your fucking act together and think about your kid. Anger always did seem to broaden Karen's vocabulary, but I admired her and not just for her looks, she's thirty-eight years young and a good detective, a match for any of the guys in the precinct, and definitely far prettier. She told me she'd married very young and that she and her husband, Steve Sykes who was also a cop, lived in Oregon somewhere. Apparently he had got himself killed attempting to be a hero foiling a bank raid. Wrong place, wrong time I guess. That is what Karen told me with surprisingly little remorse in her voice.

Lucy had been gone a respectable time when one day I invited Karen to dinner at my house. I wanted to show off my culinary expertise. I loved cooking, and I was gastronomically adventurous. I also wanted Karen to meet my daughter, Avril.

I was still feeling kind of down I guess, and I suppose I was hoping Karen and I might get it together, it being the operable word. I couldn't remember the last time I'd had any *it*. Unfortunately, and even though I told her I was having a guest for dinner that night, Charlie turned up and can you believe it, she actually brought her cat; weird looking thing. I swear if it wasn't for its enormous size I'd have said somewhere along its bloodline a rat must have been involved. Anyway she said the cat wasn't well and didn't like being left alone. Consequently *it* didn't happen. Our date had turned into a threesome. Later that evening, I left the two women alone while I put Avril to bed. Avril was having concerns; she saw Charlie and Karen as contenders, trying to fill her mother's shoes. In her room, she and I got into a long difference of opinion over why Karen was there. It was a rift we never resolved that night. When I returned to join the two women, Karen was gone. Charlie gave a somewhat flippant explanation saying Karen must have come over ill or something, because she just got up and left. The next day when I saw Karen she looked ill. I asked her if she thought the meal had made her ill. She said no, but refused to discuss it further. The following day I was told she was off sick. She'd been off work for a fortnight when I called on her, only to be told she didn't live at that address anymore. I never saw Karen again for almost a year.

During the time Karen was away, Charlie and I remained friends until one evening after Avril was asleep, our friendship matured into a steamy night of it. Not long after that, one of us suggested marriage and I'm not even sure that love played any part in the decision. The marriage was done and dusted so quick, no church no fuss. Charlie arranged everything, a private wedding performed by some registrar. It was all so quick. We had a small party reception where Charlotte introduced a young friend of hers to my partner D.I. Neil Roster.

Anyway I did appear to be getting the best of the deal with this marriage. Along with an overweight husband, Charlie was taking on a twelve-year-old schoolgirl with attitude, fuelled by the loss of her mother. I, on the other hand, was getting a good-looking wife and an excellent cook, whose only baggage was Carla: her green-eyed cat.

~~~~~~~~~~

About a week after I'd dismissed Howe's suggestion of applying for the Peace job, some kid decides to duck out of a drug store without paying. How about that! And me a cop, stood right next to him waiting to pay for a bottle of wine. So what did I do? Forgetting that I was close to hip-replacement-age and even closer to two hundred pounds, I left the bottle on the counter and took off after him like a demented whippet, Okay, an overweight whippet.

A couple of minutes later I was hanging over a hydrant gasping for breath. By the time I'd sucked in enough air to pump my head up straight, I expected the kid to be out of sight. Imagine my surprise when I looked up to see him leaning against a dumpster a few feet away, grinning at me.

As if in slow motion, I watched him raise his arm until I was looking down the barrel of a 38mm. My hand instinctively shot inside my coat and felt an empty holster. I suddenly remembered the awkward way he'd bumped into me in the shop and realized I was staring at my own 38.

It was checkmate. I stood frozen to the spot; I imagined any second to be sitting on a cloud with my Lucy. Then the strangest thing happened. The kids face gradually lost its grin. He placed the gun on the lid of the dumpster, turned and commenced his run. It was then that I decided maybe Howe's idea wasn't so stupid.

It was at dinner that same evening as Charlie, Avril and I sat at the dining table that I decided to poke a toe in the water to see what nibbled.

"I've been offered a Job!" Avril stopped chewing and Charlie looked up.

"You've got a job!" Avril said.

"Not like this one. It comes with a house."

"You're joking, Dad, and we've got a house. Anyway what kind of a job comes with a house?" Charlie stopped cutting her food, and maybe I should have waited for Avril to swallow the contents of her mouth before I answered,

"Sheriff."

Everything went back to Avril's plate except a piece of ham that got lodged. I quickly left my chair to give her a few slaps on the back to dislodge it. She eventually managed: "Dad, are you serious?"

"You're darned tooting!" I said in my best Walter Brennan voice.

"Oh God," Avril said. "You're not going to start talking like that are you?"

Charlie, obviously unimpressed with my impersonation and needle sharp wit, intervened with, "Where is this Job?"

"Some God forsaken place called Peace,"

"What about school, Dad," said Avril, "and what about all my friends?"

"They can't come. There's not room in the car."

"Stop messing about, Dad. You know what I mean."

"Now don't go jumping the gun, Hon, I might not even get the job, bound to be others applying for it, probably more qualified." Avril left her chair, came around the table and sat on my lap. She hugged me, then poking a finger in my oversized paunch said,

"No way, Dad; just look at how much they'd get for their money."

"Charlie! Who's teaching this kid to smart-mouth?" I said, hugging my little girl.

"She gets that from you. Anyway, I like the idea. I've always wanted to live in the country and I've heard Oregon's very nice."

"How did you...have you heard of this town called Peace?" I gave Charlie a sideways glance. "Have you been talking to this CDI Winnie Howe behind my back?" I thought I detected a slight reddening on Charlie's face. But she recovered quickly with,

"Who?"

"No not who... Howe!" It was one of those repeated wise cracks that had become a habit around the office, ever since our new bitch, I mean boss, arrived. Anyway the witticism was wasted on Charlie; she was not big on humour.

"No, of course not," Charlie said. "I've never met the woman. I just happen to know that Peace is on the border of Oregon and Idaho. I've always been pretty good at geography"

"Really? Well I've never heard of it. I hear Oregon's had some rough weather of late. Some say six feet of snow in places."

"Exaggeration," said Charlie. "You know what people are like."

"Yeah, anyway I'm due a couple of weeks break. What-say when the snow clears up we take a little holiday and check it out. It can't be any more than about a thousand miles and I've always fancied one of these log-cabin type holidays."

"Great I'll make all the arrangements," said Charlie. I think it was the first time I'd seen her become so energized. "There are some great holiday cabins around there. I've got a map of the area somewhere."

"What about your cat?"

There was a pause while Charlie pondered, "She'll be okay; I know someone that will look after her."

Chapter 4 Punishment

As daylight started to fade over the state of Oregon, the view from the hills surrounding the Pike and Heron Inn would have made the most beautiful of Christmas cards. The orange glow from the Inn's windows, the snow covered fir trees set beyond the frozen snow covered lake, all reflecting a reddish tint of a setting sun. What few scenes on a card could not capture was the silent serenity of falling snow or the slow-moving trail of yellow lanterns carried by fifty cloaked figures. Only the crunch of frozen grass beneath sandaled feet broke the silence or the spiritual ambience of the scene. The event that is about to unfold is, however, far removed from any modern day Christian service.

The moving lanterns come to a halt as the line form a part circle around the edge of the lake. A solitary woman's voice is suddenly heard speaking in a serious low monotone and for each line she recites, the rank of hooded figures around the edge of the lake chant a solemn and repetitive three-word response.

Enemies of the past
The lake waits.
Enemies of the future
The lake waits.
Enemies of the cult
The lake waits
Enemies of the master
The lake waits.
Enemies of Peace
The lake waits.

As the repetitive and harmonic drone breaks the silence, four figures step onto the snow covered ice while carrying coffin sized wooden box. They trudge slowly toward the centre of the lake where the lone figure of Aaron Yarn stands near the edge of a two-foot diameter hole in the ice. As the men reach him, Aaron is heard to voice instructions to the four men. They obey without faltering. Two of the men lift the woman's stiff and heavily drugged form out of the box. While Aaron Yarn recites a loud incantation the two men lift Agnes by her arms and standing each side of the black aperture in the ice they suspend Agnes above it. Yarns voice rises in volume, but the words belong to a long forgotten language that is indistinguishable. Gradually his voice becomes the epitome of rage as from the shore-line came a combined gasp of horror as they saw an enormous creature leap up through the ice, clamp its teeth on Agnes legs to snatch her from the two men's grasp before disappearing back into the icy water with its prize.

~~~~~~~~~~

I had no trouble getting Howe to phone this uncle she mentioned: some guy by the name of Cloyce, the mayor of Peace. He apparently confirmed the sheriff's job was still vacant. I thought Howe might have given me an earache over getting her to accept my application for vacation time off. It was kind of short notice, even though I was owed the time. But not a bit of it, she seemed pleased with the prospect of maybe getting rid of me, even though I believed at the time that it would only be temporary. To me this trip was more of a holiday than a serious job interview and I felt, for sure, I'd be back to resume my place as a thorn in Howe's side.

Avril on the other hand was not happy. She became the source of a headache on the outward journey. It was understandable; she was not overly keen on the prospect of leaving her school friends back in NY and therefore spent most of the trip giving us a catalogue of reasons why we were making a big mistake by even contemplating moving to Oregon or anywhere else.

In our 4x4 Jeep, we did the trip in three days, stopping over night at motels. The ride went practically incident free, except for the little run-in with the driver of an R.V. (recreation vehicle). He'd been tailgating us almost from the outset. I tried waving him on, but each time he just dropped back a little, only to be close on our tail a few minutes later. Eventually my nerves gave way and my temper took over; I just had to do something about him. Up ahead the road narrowed where it crossed a small bridge I accelerated suddenly to put some distance between us, I then swerved the Jeep to stop diagonally across the road at the bridge. There was no way he could cross the bridge to pass me, the RV had to stop.

I got out of the car, ignoring protests from Charlie going on about people getting shot in highway arguments. Avril, however, shouted encouragement, albeit sarcastically.

"Go on Dad teach him a lesson, driving that close is dangerous. Tell him he's dealing with a would-be Sheriff." she said giggling.

I tried not to laugh or let her derisive remark mellow my hostility. I was trying to maintain my anger for the coming altercation. (I just got to remember that word; the guys back at the precinct will be so impressed.) I walked slowly back towards his rig. It was one of those big expensive GMC jobs with blacked out windows. I couldn't even see the driver and had no idea if it was a man or woman. I hoped it was a guy I just can't get mad at a woman. I stood for a moment looking up at the driver's window wondering if it was a guy and how big he would be. Nothing happened so I made an anticlockwise motion with my finger. The window came down just enough to see it was a guy and he was wearing sunglasses. I shouted above the deep rumble of his engine,

"Sixty three thousand, do you want to make me an offer?" his head tilted reminding me of a confused Jack Russell. I enlightened him, "You've been driving close enough to read my instrument panel, and I'm guessing you wanted to see the mileage. I figured you must be interested in buying it."

The corners of his eyes wrinkled so I knew he was smiling. "Yeah, sorry mister it's a bad habit of mine. You made your point, it won't happen again." I'd been expecting, at least, some kind of retort; and my temper was such that I was ready to pull him down from his cab. I was almost disappointed and slightly embarrassed by his apologetic manner, but it had a calming effect on me. I walked back to the car and drove on. Good as his word, he stayed far behind and at some point he finally disappeared and I assumed I had seen the last of him. For some time after our encounter with the RV guy I had a nagging suspicion that he and I had met somewhere; but even an observant cop needs more than just sunglasses for a positive I.D.

The following evening we reached our last motel stop and I was ready to sleep.

"It's only another fifty miles to Pine Needle Camp, couldn't you just stick with it for another couple of hours?" Charlie protested.

"No way, I've been driving for eight hours and we've got a whole week to check it out. We'll go tomorrow, but I've just got to sleep." I must have sounded determined, because Charlie would usually argue the point, and most times win. Anyway, she let me sleep while she fixed the evening meal, one of her special soups, which I do find tasty. The following morning after a hearty breakfast of bacon eggs and mushrooms she must have picked locally, we set off early. Just a few miles before our destination we came across a fork in the road. Someone had vandalized a signpost. Charlie perused her map.

"Go left, she said, confidently folding up the map."

"Are you sure?" I said. "It seems like we're going in circles. Let me look at the map."

"No!" she said sharply, slotting it away in her bag. "We're nearly there. It's that way," she said, pointing. "Just go!"

"Why can't I just look at the map?"

"Trust—now drive." For some time after that, Avril and I jokingly called her the keeper of the map.

According to the keeper of the map the town of Peace was less than two miles from Pine Needle Camp, and she was right. The camp's entrance was at the top of a hill; I'm guessing a few hundred feet above the town of Peace, which appeared like a kiddie's toy town in the valley below. I was keen to see our cabin and was ready to book in but as Charlie pointed out it was Friday afternoon. We would need provisions for the weekend so she talked me into driving straight on down the hill and into the town.

Just before we reached the bottom of the hill Avril let out a yell, and Charlie gasped. I slammed my foot on the brake, the car screeched to a halt. I assumed the girls had seen, as I did, what looked like a small cougar dart out of the trees directly in front of us.

"Oh! Dad, you didn't hit it, did you?" Avril was upset and Charlie sat for some time covering her face.

"I don't think so." I lied, having felt a slight bump that I hoped the girls had not. A thick forest of firs and undergrowth lined both sides of the deserted road. I turned off the engine, stepped down from the Jeep and crept cautiously towards the rear of the car. There was not even the murmur of a breeze, and having spent my life in the big city, the silence around me felt unreal. There was nothing in the road. I looked under the Jeep. Again nothing, I walked back to the driver's door and was about to open it when I heard the faint sound of rustling. I turned just in time to see…well I wasn't sure what I saw; I only caught a glimpse before it disappeared into the woods. The thing had a more rounded back like a—yes more like a rat-like appearance, yet far too big to be a rat, and what made me question my sanity was that I'd have swore this thing appeared to run upright on its hind legs. I of course dismissed the idea and put it down to too many hours driving. When I returned to my seat the girl's expressions gave no clue as to whether they had seen anything.

"Nope, must have run right between the wheels," I said, trying to hide the edginess in my voice. "Talk about nine lives eh."

"Cats have nine lives, Dad! Dogs don't." Avril said, frowning at me in my driving mirror.

"Don't get mad at me hon. It ran right out in front of me and it was a cat, a big cat I'll admit but definitely a cat."

I could feel Charlie staring at me and I detected just the hint of a smile. I'm not sure what was going through her mind, but nothing more was said.

A minute later, we came to narrow stream where I stopped on a small wooden bridge. Here a sign beside the road stated that this was the town limit of Peace and its Population was 499. I wondered if the job offer was to replace number 500. This was timber country, and even more quiet than the town's name suggested. Charlie said she liked the look of the place, and I had always had a hankering to try my hand at fishing. Rivers and lakes were all around us and it seemed the ideal place to learn. Avril's monotonous faultfinding was starting to weaken. As we sat there We heard a young girlish giggle as I spotted some dozen young girls among the trees. At a glance, one could see they were all at a various stage of pregnancy. One looked no older than twelve and they all carried wicker baskets. As I watched, one girl stooped to retrieve something from the ground and dropped it in her basket. Avril asked,

"What do you think they're collecting Dad?"

I didn't find the question odd, only the fact that neither Avril nor Charlotte mentioned how young the girls appeared to be, considering the close proximity to their impending motherhood.

"I would say babies, among other things. What would I know about life outside of the city? Charlie, Avril wants to know what those kids are collecting in those baskets." Charlie turned back to her book with a nonchalant,

"What you had for breakfast, I expect: Mushrooms."

"Charlie, have you looked at those kids out there."

"Do you mean those young ladies?"

"No, I mean those *kids*. Some of them look no older than Avril. I would say fourteen is their average age. That can't be right, what the hell is going on, and where have they come from. There must be some home around here for promiscuous girls." Charlie started to laugh,

"Just listen to yourself, you are so brainwashed, so indoctrinated by generations of ignorance and stupid beliefs."

"What do you mean? Don't you find it disturbing that some of those girls look like they should still be playing with dolls? Doesn't it bother you that these girls are having their childhood torn away?"

Charlie lowered her book and let out an exasperated sigh, saying "It is not age that determines womanhood; it is the female body itself. It knows when she is ready." With that, Charlie turned back to her book; as if to say, here endeth the lesson.

Chapter 5 The Church

The town didn't look much. In fact it left one wondering how it could accommodate 500 people. We found what appeared to be the main street. We could see a church and a few shops, a gas station come general store and an eatery. From here the houses spanned out in a thinning expanse, but I found it hard to believe 5oo residents lived here. I saw a signpost pointing at a pathway between a small diner and a kiddie's play area which was packed with toddlers. A young girl was leaning against the post and I assumed it was her boyfriend that was pressed up against her. Two things crossed my mind as I glanced in their direction: should she be letting him do that, and what would her father say. The sign above them said "*To the lake 1/2 mile*". Another amorous teenage couple were walking along the path in the direction of the lake. I watched them until the path became hidden by more forest.

As I looked about me, I thought to myself why the hell would this insignificant town need a sheriff, unless it was to stop all these under aged kids fornicating. This was our first stop: the town's main street. We looked at a few shops and filled up with gas. We then found a general store to pick up some supplies. It was here we asked directions to the school. The place seemed like any other backwoods town, apart from an abundance of cats. Some of the locals were a strange looking bunch. I won't try to describe any of them but suffice to say I expected to hear the plucked strings of a banjo and guitar any moment; they, on the other hand, seemed to find me just as curious. In the store another young boy whom I took to be the proprietor's son started to eye Avril in a way I could see was making her uncomfortable so we left Charlie to finish her shopping while Avril and I retired back out to the car.

We sat there watching twenty or so infants enjoying themselves in their activity playground. There appeared to be only one middle-aged woman watching over them and I jokingly I said to Avril,

"It must be murder for that mother on bath night." But Avril's mind was elsewhere. As she stared at the kiddies, she said,

"That's strange dad."

"What is?"

"All these kids, yet how many young mothers have you seen since we got here?"

"Maybe they're all working, that's the idea of having a nursery."

"Hmm, I suppose," she said as her attention was distracted by something else, "And what do you make of that Dad?" She said, pointing toward the church facing us at the end of the Street.

"The church?"

"No, not the church,"

"You mean the town well; yes kind of quaint don't you think? But you didn't expect to find the luxuries of modern plumbing this far out did you?"

"I suppose not, but I was talking about that thing in front of the church."

"It looks like some kind of hitching post. Let's go take a look." We left the car and strolled past the well towards the curious fixture, as we got closer I realised it was an old set of stocks set in the ground. Sat within speaking distance on a sidewalk bench an old timer was sat smoking a pipe. I nodded to him. He smiled and nodded back.

"What's it used for Dad?"

"Well I would hope it's just there as an ancient curiosity. But in medieval England before they had any law they used these things to punish folk for, oh anything from stealing to just causing a disturbance. You see, the head would protrude through here and the hands through the smaller holes." As Avril and I stood discussing crime prevention of bygone ages, I could tell the old man was listening. As I imparted to Avril what little knowledge I had of fourteenth century crime and punishment I had the feeling the old man was grinning.

"Wow they really knew how to kick arse in them days. How long were they made to stay locked in that thing."

"I guess it depended on the crime. If it were something the town's people thought warranted it, they would be pelted with rotten tomatoes and such."

"Not always tomatoes," the old man chimed in. I guess the old feller felt he wanted to contribute something to the lesson, or thought I sounded too cocky and wanted to bring me down a peg. I ignored him and continued,

"Look at this Hon, would you believe it," I reached up, and peeled something from the wood with my thumbnail. "After all this time a piece of tomato skin." As I said it, the old guy laughed out loud and shuffled off down the street. As he left I just caught his last words, *"I guess you got it half right"*. I watched the old man until he disappeared down the lake path and into the woods.

"Nasty contraption," said Avril, "Can we go look in the old church?" I looked back down the street. Charlie was still nowhere in sight.

"Why not, Charlie can sit in the car if we're not back." We entered the church. It was much as I expected a timber built single hall with enough seating capacity to hold around a hundred or more. The place appeared to be seriously lacking in religious trappings. Although there were stained glass windows but the cross that took pride of place on the far wall overlooking the altar looked more like a giant dagger than a crucifix. Over the altar was draped a red cloth and on it stood three black candles the significance of, I had no idea. But what intrigued me was the lectern that stood to the front and right of the altar. Apart from its sinister looking design, the altar held what I thought was probably once a leather bound church bible, but it had obviously been in a fire because it's leather cover was shrivelled and it's title unreadable. I was trying to make out the embossed letters on the front when Avril broke the silence with,

"What's up dad never seen a bible before?"

"Not one like this." I pointed to the shrivelled cover. "Can you make out the title? I was thinking this word was Holy but it looks more like Hope to me." I opened the cover and although most of the words were illegible some were still intact. "Where on this page does it say bible? And what the hell is this all about." I said, pointing to the open passage. "I'm no expert on the bible but I always thought it started with the words: *In the beginning,"*

"Yes that's weird, Dad. What kind of Bible is it?"

"Not one that you are ever likely to have read." The booming voice seemed to echo around the great hall. Then we saw him, he was standing high above us in a raised pulpit. Even at that angle I could see he was very tall. The man was dressed in a black monastery type habit; his face hidden by the shadow of the hood, although it didn't hide his sinister glaring eyes. I immediately assumed him to be a preacher, and I guessed he must have been up there when we came in because we didn't see him climb the stairs As I addressed him my eyes scanned the rear wall assuming he may have entered from some door back there, but I couldn't see one.

"I'm sorry; my daughter and I were just..."

The scary guy interrupted rudely with, "Who are you, and what business brings you here to Peace?" The guy for some reason sounded angry and I could see no possible reason why he should be. I was not happy with the way he spoke to me especially in front of Avril and I knew she would be expecting me to retaliate in some way. I wasn't about to let her down.

"I thought this was a church, where everyone was welcome, I was obviously wrong. As to my business in this town, it's none of your dammed business." With that I put an arm around Avril and guided her toward the exit. As we reached the door Charlie appeared at the threshold.

"What are you two doing in there? I've been looking everywhere." She sounded almost as terse as the preacher. But before she could utter another word I cut her short,

"Just don't fucking go there." I rarely swore in Avril's presence but circumstances called for it. "And if the rest of this town is as friendly that guy," I said, jabbing a thumb over my shoulder, "then you can forget about living anywhere near this fucking place." With that I turned to give a last scowl at the guy but he was gone, which posed another mystery.

We reached the car and by then my blood pressure had dropped. Ten minutes later we approached the school. Kids were coming out of the main gate. Sat on the perimeter wall beside the gate was a good-looking boy whom I took to be a little too old to still be attending school. The boy's stare seemed less than friendly as I brought the car to a halt. His frown, however, faded when he saw Avril and Charlie emerge from the car. The boy's eyes followed Avril as we made our way across the schoolyard towards the main entrance of the building; I made a mental wager that Avril would look back at him before we reached the main entrance; she was that kind of age. We weren't half way there when I wished I'd had money on it.

Inside the school, we found the principal's office, a Miss Proctor, a jovial middle-aged woman. My first impression of her was a typical straight-laced tweedy schoolmarm. She appeared pleased to see us considering she was getting ready to go to lunch. Nevertheless, she seemed keen to show us around.

It appeared to be a well-equipped school and Miss Proctor's manner showed her to be proud of her student's, especially their artistic achievements. Along the main corridor, the walls were festooned with children's paintings. She exhausted a lot of time pointing out the refinements of each painting. She remembered each pupil; linking the child's name to the paintings we showed an interest in. She talked at length about each of them individually;

almost as if we should have a personal interest in children we had never met. Most of the time, Miss Proctor seemed to be addressing Charlie. It was like Avril and I were just tagging along.

"This is our fifth year student's art class," She said as she opened the last classroom door. It revealed about twenty easels set up with paintings in various stages of completion. It took me by surprise when I saw the subject being painted was not only a nude, but was in the late stages of pregnancy. From the artistic efforts on show, the subject appeared not much older than the students painting her. It immediately brought to mind the mushroom pickers I'd seen on the edge of town.

As I strolled through the line of easels, I had the feeling Miss Proctor was studying my reaction to the paintings. I also had the feeling that she was delighting in the discomfort some of the works were having on me. The young model had posed, or been placed in a most undignified position, and from the viewpoint of one or two painters nothing was left to imagination.

"What do you think of this one Mr Corwin?" she said pointing to the most degrading and undignified painting in the room. The picture could almost have been used as a gynaecologist's presentation chart.

"Not very much," I said, without giving it much consideration and trying to block Avril's view of it. Unfortunately, Avril peered over my shoulder and I heard her giggle. I ignored her and said, "I consider the subject matter to be inappropriate, especially considering the age of the class, and didn't you say twelve-year-olds?"

"Twelve to fourteen, but I was referring to the artist's artistic flair," she said. "What about this. With that, she pulled another painting out from behind the nude and placed it in front. "Gabriel Proctor is my son and he is only twelve." I tried to look surprised, saying,

"Sorry, I thought you said you're name was Miss Proctor."

The teacher's face suddenly took on a physical change and for a moment, I saw hatred blaze in her eyes, but she recovered quickly, trying to hide that unguarded moment with a false smile.

"Yes I did," she said, "We don't teach that religious claptrap in this school Mr Corwin."

"What claptrap would that be, Miss Proctor?"

"The claptrap of so called sanctity of marriage, all that rubbish." That kind of raised my hackles and I couldn't let it lie.

"I suppose that's understandable, as one shouldn't preach what one doesn't practice, so whatever turns you on, Miss Proctor; but as far as your boy's painting is concerned, I guess his ability as an artist, far exceeds his age, but what message is he trying to convey? I can't help thinking that if a shrink looked at that picture; he'd say the artist had some serious sociological problems." This appeared to amuse the middle-aged headmistress. Grinning, she said,

"The pictures are all the result of different projects the children has been set. This is one my son painted when the class was asked to paint a picture depicting a type of medieval torture or one that they might design themselves. Gabriel's picture is of a woman wearing his own adaptation of a Scold's Bridal."

"A cold what?" I said, playing to Avril's sense of humour. Avril giggled, until Charlie gave her a disapproving stare. I knew what a scold's bridal was; I'd seen one in a waxwork museum while on holiday in England. I decided, however, to let Miss Proctor give us the full explanatory excursion.

"A scold's bridal, Mr Corwin, was a medieval but relatively mild form of torture. An invention that I believe was conceived in the 16th century in Scotland. It was designed to punish its wearer for spreading gossip and slander. A metal or leather cage was clamped about the wearer's head. Attached to the mouth cover was a protuberance that held down the tongue, therefore literally stopping the victim's tongue from wagging?"

"Mild, you say! Well, the woman in that picture appears to be going through hell." I stared at the painting. Gabriel Procter had certainly captured a look of terror in the eyes of the victim. When I turned back, Miss Proctor was staring at Charlie and it was just a feeling, but I thought they both had the diminishing traces of a smile.

"Well like I said, the children were given marks for using their own interpretation of the various inventions. Gabriel explained to the class that the mouth plate was replaced with a hollow tube. He explained the reason there is fear on the face of the woman, Mr Corwin, is because boiling wax is being poured into the tube, thus changing a mild deterrent into an execution."

"Oh that's charming! Your boy has a rare talent, Miss Proctor." Avril giggled again.

The rest of the school tour was uneventful and while Avril and I discussed the pros and cons of resettling in Peace, Miss Proctor appeared to be trying to impress Charlie with her own achievements, rather than the teaching curriculum of her school. On the plus side of the tour, Avril had nothing negative to say about the place. Of course, that may have had something to do with the fact that, through one of the windows, we could still see cat-boy sitting outside on the wall.

When we left the last of the stragglers were gone. The campus was deserted. Only the boy remained. I got the feeling he'd waited for us to come out. As we approached the gate, his attention once again fell on Avril. His face broadened into that same smile. It was the smile and the seductive way he fondled a black cat that was nestling up to him made me feel uncomfortable. We got back in the car and drove away, but for the second time that day, something in the wing mirror disturbed me. Cat boy was still on the wall, and his hand was still busy fondling, but there was no cat. Instead it was a young girl; however, he was still smiling at our departing car. Avril was looking at me in the interior mirror, so I knew she could not have seen this. I glanced at Charlie; she was smiling, but staring at an open book on her lap. I wondered why I was the only one experiencing or seeing these strange occurrences. Was it possible that they never really happened? Had I driven too long the previous day, or could it be that I was coming down with some kind of malady? I was feeling quite bilious but I told myself it was due to yesterday's long spell at the wheel. Forget it Spencer, I told myself, before you crack up completely.

I parked right against the wall of the town hall which also doubled for the County Sheriff's dept. Charlie and Avril chose to stay in the car while I went in. I found a door marked County Sheriff. I knocked and entered.

There were four desks placed in no particular pattern around the office. A thirty-something bespectacled schoolmarm type sat at one, while wedged in what must have been a bespoke chair behind another desk was a baby-faced mountain of a boy with red hair. He wore a uniform fashioned out of enough material to make me two and it was still tight on him. He appeared very young. Almost too young to be carrying a weapon as powerful as a colt 45, although on him it looked like a toy. He looked at me with a vacant expression that suggested: if you ask me anything more complicated than my name I may have to shoot you.

I took a minute to look around the mahogany cluttered room. A padlocked gun case of assorted weapons was affixed to a wall. This assured me I was definitely in the law enforcement section of the building. I chose the schoolmarm to give my name to.

"Hi, my name's Corwin. I'm here to see a Mr Cloyce; I believe he's the Mayor." The name plaque on her desk said Miss Joy Harris. I'd have bet the "Joy" was an exaggeration, and the Miss probably meant some guy had yet to discover if she really was a joy.

"Oh yes, you're the new sheriff! The Mayor is expecting you." Naturally, I now had an extra question for the mayor, like: how come, just by arriving in Catsville, I was automatically qualified to be sheriff.

I was ushered into an office where a small balding guy sat behind a desk the size of another office. A particular word sprang to mind: compensating. As I entered I had the strange feeling that someone left in a hurry through a door on the other side of his office. But you know that feeling; did you see it or didn't you? Anyway I dismissed it. As I was saying, Cloyce was small, gaunt, almost emaciated. His all too large, swivel chair was spun at an angle, allowing him to gaze out of his window. We were on the ground floor, and I guessed by the layout of the building, the girls were in the Jeep, right outside his window. Without even turning to acknowledge me, he gestured for me to sit within shouting distance across his desk.

"Mr. Corwin, did you have a pleasant trip?" Now he spun round to face me…his eyes were chilling, dark and piercing.

"Yes, pretty much I guess."

"Good, excellent! What do you think of our little town of Peace?"

"Too many cats" I said, expecting him to make some comment or even explain why the place was seemingly overrun with them, but I never expected him to break into a coughing fit, which lasted a good thirty seconds. Gaining his composure he said,

"Sorry about that. Well I suppose you're wondering just what the job entails."

"Oh! I'm wondering about a little more than that! For instance I'm wondering why your receptionist spoke to me like I was already sheriff."

"Yes well Miss Harris's new to the job, a little nervous around men. You know how some women are." He said, spinning back to stare out of the window again. "She knew your name and why you were here, I expect she was just getting ahead of herself." He quickly spun his chair back again and said worriedly, "You are going to take the job, aren't you?"

"Well like you said, I'm wondering what the job entails. I'm also wondering what the pay is and there's a little matter of accommodation I was told came with the job. You can't really expect a guy to take a job without knowing more about these things? Besides, so far you've not asked me anything about myself. Don't you think that's a little odd?"

"Not really, I have your references. My niece has recommended you and your application tells us all we need to know. Of course, there's a little matter of a ballot, just to make the post official you understand, but that's just a formality."

"What do you mean?"

"Well our towns committee will have to approve you. It's our way of doing things in Peace but they have already decided that your credentials qualify you for the job. Besides, the dead line for applications is almost up and so far, your name is the only one on the ballet slips. No one else has applied,"

He turned to resume his window pose, and by now I was thinking he was just a dirty old man and I was slowly getting more annoyed.

"I take it, that's your wife and daughter out in the car?" he said.

"Yes. Would you like me to go get them; I wouldn't want you to end up in a neck brace." He turned red again, and quickly spun his chair back to face me.

"Forgive me Mr. Corwin. We don't get too many pretty ladies visiting our town."

"Yes, I was beginning to wonder if you'd ever seen one!" I said, cynically. "Look—Mister Mayor, maybe this has been a mistake. Maybe this is not the job for me. My daughter is already giving me grief about missing her friends and your town seems…"

"Oh don't say that Mr. Corwin. I promise you won't be sorry. I can tell you now that the committee has authorized me to offer you a hundred and twenty per annum."

"Thousand?"

"Of course."

He was right. I wasn't sorry; I was mentally doing a jig on top of his desk, though I was rather surprised. I wondered why a small community would pay such high wages to police their county, which I presumed would suffer very little in the way of crime.

"How wide an area does the policing cover, Mr. Cloyce?"

"I think there are fifteen small towns in Chasem County, Peace being the most populated."

"You think?"

"Yes, no I'm sure it's fifteen. Some of them are no more than settlements with few small farms. But don't worry; you'll be based here in Peace. There are a few bars around the area. I expect most of your problems will come from high spirited loggers as it's the only large industry around here. There are other part-time deputies just over the border and they're more than able to handle their own problems. They would only call on you if something major occurred. You'll have two deputies in Peace under your authority, one of which is very experienced and…"

"You see! That's what I find strange, Mr. Cloyce. You have an able deputy. So why has he not been offered the job? And how much help can I expect from a guy that's been passed over?"

Cloyce laughed but it was kind of false and overdone. After years of interrogating hoodlums, I'm adept at spotting little cover-ups.

"Oh don't worry about Jake Tollman." Cloyce said. "He's too close to retirement. He's been standing in as sheriff but he knew it was only temporary and he's too old to worry about promotion, but he'll stay on because he likes his job and he wouldn't know what to do if we made him give it up."

"And the guy out in reception; I'm guessing he's too young to retire?"

"You mean Jake's son: Orville, he's only just out of his teens. He's only been a deputy for a year, so he's not likely to think he's been passed over." With that, Cloyce let out a laugh that would have been best suited to some hag riding a broomstick. "Fact is I'm not sure thinking is one of Orville's strong points." Cloyce picked up his phone. "Miss Harris, If Jake is back, would you tell him that the new sheriff and his family are here and I'd like him to drive them over to see the Grange. Oh! And Miss Harris, E.C.M. tonight; would you arrange the necessary please."

~~~~~~~~~

We waited for Jake Tollman to arrive. In the meantime I tried to fit words to E.C.M. that might make sense, but nothing came to mind. Jake arrived in his deputy uniform, complete with scout hat. He looked a much slimmer and very much older, version of Orville. He was a sour faced guy and from the amount of hair poking out from under his hat I'd say it was as red as his boy's mass of red hair. The sour face might have just been for my benefit or had something to do with his arm being in a sling. It did appear to be giving him some pain. With little more than a nod of acknowledgement he led me out through the reception past Joy Harris who was busy making phone calls. Outside I gestured to the girls to leave the Jeep and join us. Charlie and Avril sat at the back of Jakes squad car. I offered to drive but he insisted he could manage so I was front passenger. It was a fifteen-minute ride and five minutes into the journey, I remembered something I had meant to ask Cloyce. With the intention of cheering up the girls and lightening the air, I half turned in my seat, winked at Avril, and suddenly aimed my question at Jake,

"Who shot the sheriff?" Now I know funny, and I thought everyone had heard the song; so considering the circumstances I thought that was funny, but Jake never smiled. In fact, he stared at me like I'd really accused him of murdering the last sheriff. Maybe he'd just not heard the hit song.

"What do you mean," he snapped?

"Hey man, it was just a joke. I just meant what happened to him. If you've been filling in I assume this place did have a sheriff before you, didn't it."

"Oh—Err, yes—a while back." Jake was staring in his driving mirror and sounding nervous. I was surprised when Charlie suddenly intervened with,

"Something fell on him, didn't it Jake. Didn't he get crushed?"

"How the hell would you know that?" I broke in.

"The man in the general store we stopped at. I told him my husband was going to be the new sheriff. And he said the last sheriff was crushed in an accident."

"Yes that's right, a tree," Jake said. "I'd forgotten about that; he was crushed by a tree. Not surprising with all the logging going on in these parts."

How does someone forget something like that I asked myself especially when you're the sheriff's deputy. I wanted to chase the subject, especially when I saw a trace of a smile around Jake's mouth, but he suddenly pulled into the driveway of a house, one that took my breath away. Avril and I stared at each other. It was like we'd stumbled into the eighteenth century and had arrived at a governor's colonial mansion.

"What is this place Jake? I thought you were taking us to some house called the Grange. This can't be the place!"

"Sure is! It's the only Grange we got." Jake sat in his car while we did our own thing. Charlie and Avril disappeared upstairs. I could hear Avril excitedly discussing curtains and decor so I thought it a good time to explore the grounds. There was a Chevy saloon parked in front of a double garage at the side of the house. It had the markings of a police patrol car with the name Chasem County on the doors. I assumed this would be my personal patrol car. I tried the doors and found them locked so I thought I'd check out the garage and just as I tried the door I heard Jakes footsteps on the gravel behind me,

"Have you got the keys to the car Jake?"

"No I expect they're back at the office. Anyway I expect it will be cleaned before you move in."

"What about the garage?"

"Not sure about the garage keys, the last sheriff never used it. Who's going to steal a police car anyway?" with that he sauntered back to his car and I went back inside the house. I could hear Avril excitingly giving Charlie her ideas for her room's decor and I guess any doubts I had about taking the job soon faded. We finished exploring the house, which I found surprisingly dust free, considering the time Jake said it had been empty. The next surprise came when the phone rang. Jake picked it up. "It's for you," he said handing it to me. I was fully expecting it to be the mayor as he was the only person that would have known where I was.

"Yes?"

"It's Howe!"

"Jesus! How did you know I was here?"

"I didn't. I phoned my uncle, the Mayor. His switchboard put me through. I just want to know if you're taking the job."

"Hell, you're a pushy broad, why the rush?" There was a pause.

"If it's yes, I got to get a replacement and I just want things sorted. Well?"

With that, the girls came down the stairs, Avril was jabbering excitedly about having two bathrooms. "Well I guess that's a yes."

"Good. No need for you to come back to the office. I'll have your desk cleared and sent to your house." I started to protest. There were so many things to discuss, but I heard a click and then nothing.

We returned to the Mayor's office to pick up the Jeep and to settle on an amicable date for my inauguration, one that would give us time to put our affairs in order back home. From there we drove up a long winding hill back to Pine Needle Camp. I was looking forward to spending a relaxing week trying out the fishing gear I'd bought especially for the trip. I also wanted to spend some quality time with Avril; we did enjoy each other's company, I believe she's developed my warped sense of humour. I imagined Charlie might even enjoy a little fishing too. Unfortunately she seemed to have another agenda.

"I'm not happy with the décor at the Grange", she said. "I want to find a handyman and arrange some changes to the new house. Don't wait up for me, you get an early night after all that driving you must be tired out." She took the car and drove into Peace without telling me how long she'd be gone. Avril decided to shower and wash her hair while I sat in a comfortable chair and read a book, but I must have fallen asleep because when I woke up it was 11.30 pm and there was a blanket on me. I opened Avril's door to find she was sleeping soundly. I found our bed empty when I entered our room and realised it must have been Avril who put the blanket on me. I wondered where Charlotte had got to, but I did not feel the kind of worried concern that I know I would have for my Lucy or Avril. This thought made me question, for the first time, the value of our marriage and our true feelings for each other. I undressed and got into bed but I suppose having slept already I found it difficult to sleep. What kept me awake should have been worrying where Charlotte had got to but no, it was all the unusual happenings of the past month, and why, since the start of our trip, they'd become more frequent. As I dismissed one strange event, such as the incident back in San Francisco with the teenager pointing my own gun at me, another would take its place. And so, the minutes passed until I became conscious of a sound that had gradually become intrusive.

I lifted my head off the pillow; two ears are better than one, and yes, it was slightly clearer. Was Avril humming to herself in the middle of the night, I asked myself. I reached out feeling for the torch that I'd placed on my bedside cabinet. I shone it on my watch. It was still only midnight. I got up and opened Avril's door.

The sound wasn't coming from her; she was fast asleep. I closed her door and funnelled all my senses into aural. Yes, the sound was still there, a creepy melodious chanting. I opened the cabin door and the sound became louder. I went out onto the cabin's veranda. It was a cloudless night and our cabin was situated only yards from the top of a hill. I climbed to the top and looked down, that's when I saw lights moving as in a procession; first, just one or two but then more came into view and I realized they were winding their way through a forest of trees towards...yes that must be the lake that the sign was pointing to I could see moonlight glinting on the water. As I stood watching, it reminded me of the Catholic processions they hold down in Mexico. I recalled the Mayor's words to Miss Harris and the letters: E.C.M. was that to do with what I was watching? I wondered if Charlie would have any notions about it and decided to mention it in the morning. Gradually the lights faded along with the sound. I felt a few specs of rain against my face and decided sleep might now be possible.

When we got up the next morning rain had set in for the day. We played scrabble then cards. After a while I could sense the girls becoming bored. I suddenly remembered the events of my sleepless night and not really giving much thought to why I said it, I laid down a card, picked up another and as I studied my hand, I just blurted out,

"How did the procession go?" It was Charlie's turn to pick up but moments passed and she'd still not moved. I raised my eyes over my hand to see her staring at me. Was it a look of hate, I'm not sure but a look I'll never forget. Avril glanced from me to Charlie, obviously not having a clue as to what I was referring. Charlie finally said,

"Were you talking to me?"

"Yes, wasn't there some kind of celebration going on in the town last night?"

"How would you know that, Dad?" Avril chimed in with interest.

"I had trouble sleeping. I heard some kind of chanting around midnight. I went outside, and climbed to the top of the hill. I saw the lanterns, or whatever kind of lights they were carrying." Charlie played her hand, saying,

"Well I never saw or heard anything and being in the town, I must have been closer than you. Maybe you were dreaming."

The intervention of that short distraction seemed to induce more boredom into the card game. Then the two of them started to argue about soft furnishings for the house. After that they decided to gang up on me about being bored, saying they wanted to get back to San Francisco and start packing. Rain still fell steadily, making it difficult for me to argue my case. I had to admit; I had learned why board games were so called. They became boring, and if the rain ever stopped, fishing was pretty much the only alternative and Charlie had even less interest in fishing than in board games. The girls now had the keys to the new house and were champing at the bit to move in. I eventually agreed to cut short the holiday and start back to San Francisco to squeals of delight from Avril and a smirk of triumph from Charlie,

Chapter 6 The move

As good as her word, Howe had stripped my desk and had my personal belongings delivered to the house. I expected them to be left with a neighbour but was kind of surprised and somewhat annoyed to see they had been placed on the floor inside the front door. As far as I knew no one in the department had a key to my place. It annoyed me, but Charlie brushed my grousing aside with,

"Doesn't matter, nothing's missing." Anyway, that night we discussed plans for the big move.

"I think you should go see the haulage people, and settle on a date, make it as soon as possible," said Charlie. "Oh, and get them to deliver some packing cases. I'll take Avril to settle things at her school, and arrange things with the realty people about selling the house."

"Don't you think we're rushing things a bit?"

"What do you mean? You've already given the Mayor your word."

"I know but there are things to sort out."

"Like what?"

"Like selling the house,"

"I've just said I'll deal with it. I'll hand it over to an estate agent I know. They'll get the best deal, it's not a problem, it'll all be sorted and you won't have to worry your head about it."

"Well what about all my years on the force, what about pension, severance pay, like…"

"That can all be done by phone or mail!"

She had all the answers. "Yeah I suppose. Okay well I'll drop in the precinct just to say bye to…"

"No!" Charlie snapped. I was surprised. It was out of character for Charlie to become aroused over anything, and this seemed such a trivial matter. She detected my sour change of mood as my temper started to rise. I'd spent twenty years with the SFPD, and some of the D.Is I worked with had been there as long as me. There was no way I was going to let Charlie tell me I had to leave without a farewell drink with them. She realised she'd over stepped the mark and quickly changed her tone. "Sorry I just meant that you won't have time," she said, easing up on the haughty attitude. "And besides, didn't this Howe woman tell you there was no need to call in."

"Yes, but only because my desk would already be cleared out, but I spent years working with these guys, they'll think me a bit sour not to have a drink with them, just to say good bye." Charlie looked thoughtful.

"Well I thought it sounded like she didn't want you going back there. I've heard how disrupting retirement parties can be in a police precinct!"

"I'm not retiring!"

"Well you know what I mean." Her tone suddenly changed to one of accusation. "I heard that Karen woman is back."

"How did you...oh! I get it."

"What?"

"She's the reason for all this…"

"Oh don't be ridiculous! Go say your goodbyes if that's what you want, I don't care, but wait until we have everything settled and we're ready to leave."

I still wasn't sure why Charlie had made a big deal out of it, but I agreed and for the next week or so the three of us prepared for the move; however, without telling Charlie, I picked a day to visit the precinct and bought a bottle of Jack Daniels on the way there.

Apart from the usual office staff shifting paperwork around and the odd uniformed officer popping in and out, the office appeared almost deserted, but my closest friend and partner, Neil Roster, was at his desk.

Roster was a lot younger than me, but he was a detective that I had a great deal of trust and respect for. There were only two detectives in the precinct that I would fully trust if I found myself in a tight spot and that was Karen Sykes and Neil Roster.

"Hey Spence, what are you doing here?" Neil said putting his phone back in its cradle. "Thought you were on vacation, and what's with the bottle?" Neil was a good-looking guy, a little less than the two metre mark in height, and unlike me he kept himself fit and his 170 pounds pretty constant. His dark wavy hair was the kind that behaved itself with just a sweep of a comb, greying a little at the sides, but never untidy. The grey was just enough to match his Errol Flynn style moustache and small goatee. I've noticed more than once how he'd get that extra departing glance from a pretty female whenever a case brought us in contact with one.

"Yes I was, but we cut it short. You knew I was leaving though?" Roster grinned like he didn't believe me. I jabbed a thumb over my shoulder towards Howe's office, "She must have told you guys?"

"Who?"

"Not who, Howe." Roster grinned but his expression told me the joke had run its course. "I'm not kidding Neil, I've only come in to buy you guys a farewell drink. We're leaving tomorrow. To be honest I wanted to spend a night at Mc Ginty's Bar with you all, but as I wouldn't have time to sober up for the trip in the morning, I thought the least I could do is buy you one before I go. By the way, where is she?" I said, staring at the empty chair in Howe's office.

"Gone?"

"What do you mean? Gone to a meeting; gone out on a job?"

"No, just gone. She cleared her desk and just went out of here with an arm full of papers and belongings. Oh that reminds me." Roster started to chuckle while pulling his desk drawer open. He took out a small envelope and handed it to me. On it someone had printed by hand: *For the attention of D.I Corwin.* The envelope had been opened.

"Where did this come from? Why has it been opened? And what's so funny?"

"To your second question I don't know," Neil said. "Maybe the bitch Howe opened it. Where it came from is what made me grin. I told you Howe went out of here with an armful of papers and such, but when she reached those swing doors Red Shadwell came barging through and knocked her on her arse." Neil's chuckle then turned to real laughter as he recalled the incident. It was good to hear Roster's laugh again, it was infectious and I knew I was going to miss it. "I'm sure Red did it on purpose. Like the rest of us, she'd been giving him a hard time. Anyway her papers went flying. Red was all apologetic and as we both helped her pick them up I spotted that envelope addressed to you, I managed to slip it in my back pocket without her noticing."

"Have you read what's inside?"

Neil gave a funny sideways grin, "Got to admit I was curious as to why the bitch had not given it to you."

"Forensic department?" I queried, seeing the F.D motif on the envelope. "I take it you've read it."

"Only because it had already been opened, but there's nothing to read, just a guy's name; he wants to see you. Maybe it's about that guy you ran down outside?"

"Yeah, okay pal don't rub it in." Neil laughed just as a hand appeared on my shoulder.

"Hi Spencer. Where have you been?" That warm feeling came over me as I slid the paper back into the envelope. I turned to see Karen smiling at me.

"Hi Karen, Oregon." she frowned and drew back like I'd been a naughty boy who'd done something real bad.

"Why? What the hell made you go to Oregon?"

"Hell Karen, there's no law against it."

"Yeah, sorry I just had a…well…never mind."

"Christ! Didn't Howe tell you guys anything." I said, but I could tell by the way they looked at each other that she hadn't. "Where is she anyway? I got a few questions I want to ask her."

"You're not alone," said Neil, "I got a few of my own when I meet that bitch." Ross sounded more than just peeved and I'd never heard him speak of a woman with such malice in his voice, he liked them too much, especially the lookers and Winnie Howe in my book was a looker. "But I told you, she's gone. Her office has been empty since not long after you left. The commissioner phoned to tell us a new guy was coming to replace her."

"Didn't he tell you where she was?"

"No just that she'd moved to another precinct, but he wouldn't say, where. Never known a precinct to change a CDI without a handover, but I think I know where the bitch lives. I walked in on her as she was giving someone her address on the phone, the bitch."

"Sounds like she's got you riled, Neil. What's she done to get you so mad?" Karen asked.

"She wrote some things in a report. She's dropped me in it with Internal Affairs. They got me labelled bent, said I've been on the take. You know what they're like; smoke without fire, they just won't let up. It's McCarthyism all over again with those bastards, once they take the bait. Anyway I'm not taking it lying down; I'll get it straightened out with her. I'll get the bitch to retract whatever she's told them."

"How are you going to do that if she's moved on to another precinct?" Karen said.

"I'll call at her house, that way I can have it out with her in private."

"Don't worry," I said. "It's got to be some kind of foul up; Christ, Neil, we all know you're straight to the point of boredom. I, for one, will testify in court that whenever I can't sleep I call your number and get you to recite the rule book to me. Anyway, if you guys got no boss at the moment, there's no reason you can't have a drink, and toast my new job." I pulled a bunch of plastic cups from alongside the water dispenser. As I started to pour the J.D, I heard the swing doors open and another detective came in the door. He was handcuffed to a seedy looking character; one that had seen the inside of a precinct almost as many times as me.

"Hey! Red," Neil called to him. "Spence says he's leaving, come and have a drink."

"No shit!" Red Shadwell said, reaching his desk and forcing his captive to kneel on the floor. He snapped the guy's handcuffs around the short leg of his desk saying,

"There you go, Santini. If you can lift the desk up and get the cuffs out, you can go." The three of us were laughing, knowing the desks were all screwed to the floor. Red came over and joined us, "Is that right Spence, you're leaving?"

Karen was staring at me. I saw on her face what might have been sorrow, but looked more like grave concern, as she waited for an explanation. Two more detectives came in, Pearce and Simpson, they saw me pouring the drinks and came over. All were waiting for me to explain.

"Yes, it's no secret, guys. I've been to Oregon looking into that sheriff's job, and I've decided to take it." I could see by the half smile on Pearce and Simpson's faces that they were waiting for the punch line. They had no idea what I was talking about.

"The Peace job," I said looking at each of them in turn while noting the blank look on their faces. "Is this a conspiracy? I'm talking about the sheriff's job in Oregon. Howe told me the advert had been handed around the office. It's a town called Peace!" I was expecting someone to say oh that job, but nobody did. It took a while explaining to them how my decision to take the job had come about. Deacon and Bancroft left their desks to come over and listen to my explanation. Bancroft then downed his drink and slowly wandered back to his desk shaking his head.

"Well good luck pard," Deacon added, tossing back his whisky and adding "Give my best to John Wayne if you see him, and try not to get ambushed." Pearce gave my arm a friendly squeeze before wandering off with Shadwell and Simpson. I'm sure they all thought I'd gone completely insane. Then Roster's phone rang,

"I better get that," he said, looking pleased at not having to listen to anymore of my ramblings. He wandered off to his desk leaving only Karen. She stood looking at me like she should have me certified. It made me kind of angry. I looked around the office saying.

"Well I guess I've said goodbye to everyone."

"Yes, except the new guy," said Karen. "Mick O'Donnell, he must be out on a job."

"Mick O'Donnell, I know that name. Hell I've not seen Mick for years. He and I worked together on the Tate case. I thought he'd left the force. Oh well maybe I'll catch him next time." I took Karen by the hand and led her into Howe's empty office. I closed the door and shut the louver blinds to the outer office. This would not have surprised the other DI's. I think they always suspected something more than just a professional bond between Karen and me. When I turned around, Karen had a mischievous smile on her face.

"Don't you think we should lock the door?" she said.

"That's not why I brought you in here. Not that the idea doesn't appeal to me." Karen pouted child-like, and I grinned.

"Look, Karen, I'm serious. I'm not going crazy. Howe sat there in that chair and put a job offer in my hand, she said it had been going around the precinct."

"Well I've not seen it."

"No and judging by the reception I just received out there, no one else have." I looked at Howe's empty desk and started pulling out drawers. They were all empty.

"If you're serious, what makes you think you're sheriff material? And why would you want to move to Oregon, for Christ sake."

"I didn't, and I wouldn't, but the mayor of a little town called Peace seems to think I am. And Howe kind of pushed me into it." I stopped rummaging through the desk. "Karen, I took the girls to this place just for a holiday break, I never thought for one minute that this was going anywhere, but they want me, and the job pays more than I'll ever make here. Karen, they've offered me a hundred and twenty thou a year."

"Dollars?"

"Kaz, they don't use Francs in Oregon." Karen let out a whistle. "But that's not all. You should see the house that goes with it."

"You get a house! Aw, come on Spence, you got to be…"

"Karen I'm serious, and it's not just a shack, you should see the place." I could see that she'd stopped listening and was deep in thought. I brought her back with, "What?"

"Oh nothing, it's just that it all seems a bit sudden and—I don't know—weird. Are you sure about this?"

"I know what you mean and you're right. It all seems weird to me, but Avril and Charlie are sold on the place. I don't see there's any turning back now, but I do know one thing for sure, I'll miss you, Karen." Karen smiled and it filled me with such longing. She went up on her toes, and kissed me. It was the first time we'd really kissed and I mean the kind one should feel guilty about.

"I'm sorry I reacted when you mentioned Oregon," she said. "It just gave me bad vibes." She hesitated a while, then said, "Do you remember the story about my marriage?"

"Sure I do your old man was a hero, got himself killed trying to foil a bank job."

"Not true, I made that up. I guess the truth at the time was too hard to swallow."

"What do you mean?"

"The fact that I was rejected, he kicked me out of his life."

"Now I find that hard to believe."

"He was a young cop, just out of cadet school. We lived in a rented apartment in Berkeley, California. Money was tight, we argued a lot. Not long into our marriage his mother died, and being an only child, he got the house and all that his parents owned. It kind of opened up his chances of getting more out of life, but he decided he didn't need me hanging on his arm, so he just started dropping subtle little hints, about feeling claustrophobic. I soon caught on and left. I never saw him again."

"I understand, Karen, by making up that story you were just defending your pride. I expect you were still hurting at the time, but I fail to see what it has to do with me and Oregon?"

"I was coming to that. When I moved to San Francisco and met you, I thought I'd make a clean break. I set divorce proceedings in operation but couldn't find Brad. I made a lot of enquiries but all roads turned out to be a cul-de-sac. The strongest lead I had was that he had sold the house and moved to Oregon, that's where the search came to a dead end. When you said you were going to Oregon it was like that State was stealing the only two men..." I knew Karen had said too much, her bottom lip started to tremble and I could see she was feeling awkward. I wanted to alleviate her embarrassment so I held her close, saying,

"I only wish I'd known how you felt, Karen. It might surprise you to know, the night I asked you to come to my place to dinner I intended to tell you just how I felt.... Sadly, it all went wrong. Now I guess its all water under whatever." There was an uncomfortable silence until I realised Karen was staring at the envelope in my hand, "Did Neil show you this?" I took out the paper and unfolded it. "I've not looked at it myself yet."

"What is it?"

"Strange, it's just a hand written note. It says: *To D.I. Corwin. Come see me, soon as possible. Vic Rowan.* Do you know anyone at forensics by the name of Vic Rowan?"

"No, I've never heard of him, but then I don't know anyone in the forensic department."

"Well apparently he wanted to see me over there."

"Wanted?"

"Yes look at the date. This was written about the time I hit that guy in my car, and I'm guessing it's probably to do with either that guy or the one they found in the maintenance room. Anyway it's too late now; we're off first thing in the morning I haven't got the time. This letter has been sitting in this desk all this time, so it probably doesn't matter anymore. Maybe you or Neil could look into it, when one of you can find the time."

"Sure, I'll talk to Neil about it. Anyway I got reports to fill out so I suppose this is goodbye then Spencer."

I found it hard to interpret her expression or the look in her eyes but I wondered if Karen was feeling like me; like I was leaving someone who was more than just a friend.

As I drove home I found Karen's last words to me a little puzzling,

"Give my love to Avril, she said and keep an eye on Charlie".

Chapter 07 Roster goes missing

Our move to Peace went without a hitch and the girls seemed to quickly settle into the community. Either directly or indirectly most of the local folk made their living through the Foxgrove Logging and Paper Mill Company. That is to say, even the cafés and diners would not have existed without Foxgrove's. Maybe the townspeople found me curious: they seemed a little uneasy when I approached them, yet they were more than friendly toward Charlie. I'd heard how in some parts it was traditional to welcome new neighbours, but we lived quite a ways from the town centre yet people that we'd never seen were turning up at the door. All of them brought little gifts, for Charlie nothing grand, mostly just little knitted dolls or homemade preserves, yet I had the feeling the gifts were brought because it was expected and not all were given with a kind heart. But then I did find the people of Peace more than a little strange, and not just in appearance. Oh I knew we were in a remote part of the world and there had to be interbreeding so that didn't surprise me, but it was more than that. There was a kind of nervousness about them. Then there was the old fashioned way they dressed, I found it all strange as well as some of the daily happenings.

It had been a long time since I'd worn any kind of uniform, and the one I was expected to wear felt strange, like I was setting myself apart from the Peace residents, but then I suppose that was its purpose. I was also surprised that it was handed to me without even asking my size. When I questioned Miss Harris about it, she just smiled and said I was about the same size as the last sheriff and that it was a new one he'd ordered. The first day I patrolled the town, a car pulled up beside me. It was a young couple. The young lady waved a picture of a house at me. This is where we're going to live, she said excitedly, then asked directions to the town hall. This was my very first task in office. I directed them thinking maybe the town is growing. They seemed to be waiting for me to give an opinion as to why property was so cheap in the area. I didn't have one because I was as clueless as they were and I never saw them again. I thought maybe their house wasn't what they expected. A fortnight later, I was stopped again. This time the guy wanted directions to Avril's school. It had to be the uniform; it was attracting visitors like a moth to a flame. I liked the guy he was the bubbly friendly type who wanted to talk. He said he was applying for an opening with the school "Got to see a Miss Proctor he said." Then he asked if the town had trouble getting teachers. I told him I didn't know and what made him ask. He said because of the high wage they were offering. I shrugged; what did I know about teacher's wages. Anyway, he told me his name was Mathew Black. I remember thinking, shorten his Christian name and you got a nice finish in mat black. I gave him directions, we shook hands and he left. Nothing strange about that, you might think, but a fortnight later when I asked Avril what the kids thought of their new teacher: Mat Black, she said she had never heard of him and like the young couple, I never saw the man again. Maybe he'd turned the job down, I thought.

After a while, I got used to the odd little happenings around the place but I soon got bored and started to regret moving I told Charlie as much. I told her the job was boring and that I was missing the guy's back at the precinct. What I didn't tell her was that I was missing Karen.

Sure, we had a nice house, Avril said the school was okay but she missed her friends. Charlie was the only one that was really happy with the move and she seemed to fit in with the town and the locals. However the monotony for me got worse. Crime here was practically non-existent and there just seemed nothing for me to do. I started to think about how I could break it to Charlie that I wasn't happy and wanted to move back to San Francisco. I knew it would upset her; she was already in thick with the town committee and had been pestering me about signing the deed papers on the house. She wanted to finalize the sale of my San Francisco house but this boredom was the very thing that was stopping me from signing. Eventually I told her how I felt and we had our first big fight over it. This ended with her crying and me, being a sucker for a woman's tears; I agreed to give it a couple more weeks. Strangely enough two days after our fight I got involved in another one, this time it was a bar brawl. One thing I was happy about was the fact that I had Orville, Jake's son as a deputy. Orville had obviously found himself in the wrong queue when God was dishing out personal qualities. Luckily for me, Orville had mistaken the brain queue for the brawn queue. This proved to be a blessing for me when a couple of guys by the name of Calvin Phipps and Ben Alden started the brawl. I think I may have owed my life to Orville that day. Yes Calvin Phipps became my first serious official police matter and the reason the locals now stare at my broken nose.

Things might have been worse, if it wasn't for Orville sitting on a couple of guys that wanted to use my head to break chairs. Anyway, that ruckus got Cal a night in the cooler and a two hundred dollar fine; a price he could ill afford, having just been released from the state penitentiary. When Orville filled me in on the complete story, it explained the reason for the bar brawl. He told me that Cal and, his one time friend, Ben Alden was, apparently, the worst two rogues in the district and both worked at Foxgrove's. It seems Cal got himself put in the pen because a couple of deputies from the next county caught him breaking into a hardware store or to be more accurate, breaking out of the store. The officers just happened to see a moving torchlight through the store window. They waited and caught Calvin Phipps coming out the back of the store with a couple of hunting rifles. As they bundled Cal into the back of their patrol car the deputies said they saw a car make a fast getaway from the scene. It's believed it was

Ben Alden, as the two were rarely seen apart. However, Cal denied it and took the rap. I'm thinking Alden was probably the lookout on that job, but for some reason he fouled up and left Cal high and dry. Due to old man Foxgrove's good nature, he notified Cal's parole board that he was willing to let Cal have his job back. This got Cal off with serving less than a year. He'd only been out a few days when I got the call about the bar brawl.

A fortnight passed and then I got another strange call.

"Get over to Foxgrove's, there's going to be trouble," It sounded like some guy with a nasal affliction. Then click, he was gone. It took me no more than twenty minutes to drive there. I arrived in time to see a stretchered body being slid into an ambulance. I went over, it was Calvin Phipps. I touched one of the Paramedics on the arm,

"Is he...?"

"Just unconscious," he said. I left the crowd of loggers stood around watching the medics do their thing. Then I noticed one guy wearing a hard hat standing alone, I sidled up to him and said,

"What happened, Rick?" He looked confused.

"Do I know you?" he said.

"No but that's because, unlike you, I'm not wearing a helmet with my name daubed on the front." Enlightenment drifted across his face as he spotted the badge. He raised his arm and pointed. I followed the direction of his finger. He was pointing at the top of a steep hill. A hundred foot wide stretch of Douglas firs had been felled all the way to the top of a steep hill. At its summit, there stood a huge contraption on caterpillar tracks. This was the object of Rick's finger pointing. The machine had a massive hydraulic claw obviously capable of handling huge bundles of felled trees.

"A whole bunch of logs got away from that grabber and rolled down the hill," said Rick. "Cal just happened to be at the bottom. Can't understand why he's still alive."

"He's only been back at work a week or so, right?"

"Yeah, bet he wishes he'd stayed in the pen. He's one lucky son-f-bitch though. Anyone else would probably be dead. The logs must have bounced right over him."

"But did they? Something knocked him unconscious! So that's what you call the grabber is it."

"Yes, monster, ain't it?"

"Who was the driver?"

"Ben Alden." Now he really had my attention.

"Tell me! Any of your loggers got a cold." The guy looked at me like I'd forgotten to zip my fly.

"What the hell's that got to do with anything?" he said.

"The guy that called me sounded like he had a cold. You know—nasal like. Do any of your guys talk like that?"

"No, but then he could have been faking it. Does it really matter; sounds to me like he was just being a good citizen?"

"I might have agreed, but he didn't say there'd been an accident. His words were: *there's going to be trouble*. So if the call was made before those logs came down the hill maybe this wasn't an accident." Rick listened but just shrugged, so I went looking for Ben Alden.

I found Alden in the site office making out an accident report, while trying to charm the panties off a young office girl. Hoping to goad him into letting something slip, I laid straight into him with,

"What made you do it Ben; did Cal threaten you?"

"Why would he?" He answered casually after initially showing surprise.

"For letting him take the rap over that store job you bungled?" Ben wasn't biting.

"Like I told those stupid cops over in Cranford, I wasn't there. And this little episode was an accident." he said calmly. I tried a little more goading but I could see he wasn't going to bite. I waited until he left the office then got the girl to let me see his report. I then got back in my car and followed the ambulance to the hospital. I suspected there was some kind of feud still going on between Alden and Phipps and if I was right it could spell attempted murder. Word had it that the two had been friends since they were kids, but Orville told me that Alden didn't even visit Cal in prison. I suspected there was bad blood between them, and that Cal blamed Ben for his spell in prison.

I reached the hospital and was sat by Cal's bed when he started to come round. I watched him open his eyes and scan the unfamiliar ceiling. He was unaware of my presence until I said,

"So you're back from the dead Eh, Phipps? I knew it was too good to be true." Cal looked at me as his fingers probed the bandage around his head.

"Where am I?"

"Harwell Hospital, don't you remember what happened?" I said, while fiddling with the hard hat that I'd picked up from off his bedside locker.

"I—was working—I looked up—saw the claws open. I remember taking a running dive, must have hit my head on a stump. Anyway what do you want, Corwin? Hell! A patient shouldn't have to wake up to a face like yours hovering over him, it just ain't therapeutic, Christ! I thought I'd died and gone to hell. What do you want, anyway?"

I disregarded the insult. "Nothing, but I got a call. They tell me your pal Ben Alden was operating the grabber and that made me suspicious. Tried to kill you, did he?" I said, grinning. Cal's head was clearing; his two grey cells were starting to converse with each other.

"What are you talking about? It was an accident." He was staring at the hardhat. "And where did you get that, it's not mine?"

"That's very astute of you, considering it has Ben Alden's name on it. I expect the ambulance crew picked it up thinking it was yours. I came here because I learned that you and Alden were thick as thieves before they put you away. Let's face it you are thieves, and I've still got my suspicions that Alden was in on that break-in you did time for. Apparently, you and Alden's been thieving since you were kids, so what suddenly made him want to drop a small forest on you; did you threaten him or something?"

"I told you it was an accident, and old man Foxgrove is going to pay for it."

"You're one mean bastard, Phipps; the old man did you a favour, giving you your job back. You'd still be inside if not for him."

"Well that's life. You just got to grab your chance when you can."

"I guess that's up to you, Phipps, but if I were you I wouldn't go on a spending spree just yet."

"What do you mean? An accident like this ought to be good for a few G's"

"So that's it," I said. "You and Alden dreamed this up between you, just to take the old man to the cleaners." His hate filled eyes glared at me.

"Don't try to pull that one, Corwin. I told you. It was an accident. I could have been killed. Do you think I'm stupid enough to play dodge with five ton of trees?"

"Yes. And I also think you and Alden are crooked enough to try anything, but you're definitely on a loser with this one."

"Why?"

"Because I've just seen Alden's accident report, and if the pair of you did plan this little caper, then Alden has cocked up once again." I placed the helmet back on the cabinet and moved toward the door to leave. As I opened it I looked back and grinned. "You see, Alden's accident report states that the logs started rolling at ten past five. Ten minutes after working hours. According to the company rules you had no right to be there."

As I closed his door behind me I could feel his hatred trying to burn through it. Cal Phips was dangerous and I wasn't sure that ruffling his feathers was such a clever idea.

But that was it; I mean what else could I do? Even if Alden did drop the trees on purpose, as long as Phipps insisted it was an accident there was no case to answer. Six weeks passed without incident; then one morning I found a note on my desk with a name and phone number. I dialled it.

"Hello, Dr Kirby?"

"Yes."

"Sheriff Corwin here; you wanted to speak to me?"

"Yes, can you come over to Harwell Hospital, sheriff; and make it quick, it's important."

Chapter 13 Roster goes missing

Back in San Francisco Karen Sykes knocked hesitantly on her new boss's door before entering. Earlier that day she had overheard two uniformed cops talking; the topic was of someone she wasn't sure she caught the name of, but thought it sounded like Roster. For a moment her heart beat faster and she hoped she had heard wrong. They were talking about this person in the past tense and so she assumed that he had been hurt or even killed. The thought that it might have been Neil Roster worried her. Now that Spencer Corwin had left the precinct, Neil was now her closest friend and colleague. Frightened of the answer she might receive, she was loath to question the two officers. Instead, she consoled herself by the thought that San Francisco was a big city and there were lots of precincts, hundreds of cops and even if she had heard the name Roster there might be more than one. But now as a voice called out "enter" she wondered if there could be a link between her worrying thoughts of Roster and the reason her new Chief D.I had summoned her.

As Karen stood waiting to be spoken to she read the name plaque on the desk that spelled out Captain Andrew Dugan. She then stood staring at the top of Dugan's balding head as he sat, chin in hands, perusing a type written report on the desk before him. He ignored Karen for some moments and she started to wonder if it was part of a chiefs training to disparage their subordinates by making them wait to be spoken to. This was only his second week in the 13th precinct and already Karen decided she didn't like him. She became angry, and was about ready to ignore the consequences and castigate Dugan for his ignorance when he suddenly looked up and said,

"You knew Roster, didn't you Sykes." The said rumour suddenly became more meaningful with the word "knew". It caused a tightening in Karen's stomach.

"Yes sir. He was moved to another precinct just before you took over here." she said tentatively.

"He was a close friend?"

"Yes, I consider all my fellow officers as friends, but you said was?"

"Yes I'm sorry, he's missing. Has he—I mean do you know where he is" Dugan seemed to hang on pensively for Karen's answer. While Karen let Dugan's words penetrate.

"No! Missing since when?"

"Since his wife called me and said he never arrived home from his shift. They say he was once a good officer."

"He was, I mean is. Why are we discussing him like he was dead, how long has he been missing?"

"About a week."

"Hell—but why would his wife phone here? This is not his place of work anymore?"

The question seemed to take Dugan by surprise and Karen noted a distinctive pause before Dugan answered. "I suppose she thought his closest colleagues were still here and they'd be the ones he'd contact. Anyway you know how these things work, a domestic tiff and the guy walks out. We had to give it a reasonable time before we sent out a search party, but now it's time. I've asked you in here because you knew him and I thought you might know something that would throw some light on his whereabouts, like where he might be staying."

"Karen let out a sigh. Hell, I thought you were going to say he had committed suicide or something. I know he was peeved about the transfer."

"You mean demoted, to a desk job."

"Yes sir, he was more than a little upset about it. He told me Winifred Howe filed a report with the commissioner. I think it's what got him demoted. I remember Ross saying he knew where she lived. I had the impression he was going to call on her, find out her reasons for getting him demoted."

"Yes I saw the report. I can tell you now; the report implied that Roster was on the take."

"Bullshit—sorry sir, I mean that just doesn't fit Roster's profile, sir. In fact Roster was so by-the-book, it was a bit of a joke around here. Besides he's the last person in this precinct that needs to be on the take, his parents left him a fortune."

"Listen Sykes, I can vouch for Winnie Howe. We came up through the ranks together, and if she wanted this D.I Roster demoted then she must have had good reason. She's an honest cop. However, now you got me thinking there may be a link, because I've been trying to contact Winn for a couple of days now and got no answer."

"You know C.I Howe well, do you sir?" As if in answer, Dugan picked up a photo frame on his desk and stared lovingly at it.

"Sure do, since our academy days." Karen deduced by Dugan's voice and the way he was staring at the picture frame, that he was reminiscing.

Dugan replaced the frame in the same spot, facing him.

"May I see the photo sir?"

"Certainly," he said handing the frame to Karen. "That was taken at the party we had the same night of our leaving the academy."

The photo was of four young police cadets' three men and a woman. Karen studied the photo. She recognized Dugan even with a full head of hair, but none of the others.

"You were quite a looker sir." Dugan gave a little cough then coloured a little.

"Yes, amazing the difference hair can make,"

"Who's the woman?"

"It's Winifred Howe of course."

"No it isn't."

"Oh, I know she's a lot older. Twenty five years can make a big difference to…"

"No sir," Karen interrupted. "The Winifred Howe that sat at your desk was not much older than the woman in this photo and looked nothing like this."

Dugan frowned, "Christ, Sykes, this just gets worse. I took this position because I was told Howe was retiring. I expected her to stay long enough to hand over. I must admit I was surprised to find her office empty when I got here. Now you're telling me the woman that sat in this chair last, was not Winifred Howe?"

"It looks that way," said Karen

"Well I think I should visit Winnie to see if she can throw some light on this mystery. She may have been the last one to see Roster if you say he was going to call on her. I'd like you to come with me. It's best to have backup in these situations."

"Right Sir, do you have her address?"

"Yes, she lives over on Rowan Drive."

"What's this all about Doc?" I asked as Doc Kirby pointed to a chair. "That rogue, Phipps, hasn't died on you has he?" I said, and then kind of regretted my heartless remark when the doc gave me a disapproving frown.

"No nothing like that. Phipps was discharged six weeks ago. He only had a slight concussion. Odd, you should mention him though."

"Why."

"I'll come to that. No, this is about another patient: Ben Alden. Do you know him?"

"You bet. He and Phipps are trouble. What's wrong with Alden anyway?"

"That's the problem, we just don't know. Come with me." As I followed him along a corridor, he said, "How long since you last saw Alden?"

"Few weeks, I guess. I saw him the day they brought Phipps in here. In fact Alden was the guy who put Phipps in here, although he claimed it was an accident."

Kirby frowned, "Really?" It was Doc Kirby's only comment before stopping to unlock a door, which looked to me like just another private room but I've never known a patient to be locked in one's room. Kirby spotted the frown on my face and before opening the door he said, "It's just a precautionary measure," he said, "Just until we're sure it's not infectious. Here you better put this on," He said, handing me a surgeon's facemask. And don't get too close to him. He opened the door and stepped inside before beckoning me in but keeping his arm out as if to stop me from getting too close to the bed or the thing that occupied it. Kirby must have read the look of horror on my face as I stared across the room. "Not pretty is it?" he said. It took me a while before I could answer. I could not believe that the good-looking rogue, Ben Alden, who was no more than 35 years old, could be this same emaciated thing lying in a bed no more than four feet away.

"Hell doc! It's downright scary. What happened to him, he's like something out of a tomb?"

"Dehydration, the problem is we just don't know why. He was brought in here about six weeks ago, shouting and raving like a man possessed. He looked terrible then, but nothing like this. I've not seen or heard of anyone deteriorate to this extent in such a short time; we've tried every means of getting fluids into him but it either comes back as vomit, or goes straight through him."

"Are you sure he's still alive?"

"Unconscious, but I'll be surprised if he lasts the night." He said hurrying me out of the door and locking it again.

"Hell, what could cause something like this doc, poison? He looks to weigh about eighty pounds.

"Yes it's a real mystery. Poison is what we first suspected, and if it is then it's none that I've ever come across. We've run all the checks, blood, urine, every test we can think of. It all comes back negative. That's why I called you. I suspected some kind of foul play but what, and who? He lived alone. I'm told he had an elder brother, but that he moved away some while ago."

"You said Alden was raving when he came in. Can you remember anything he said?"

"Nothing that made much sense, he was shouting something about a watch or it could have been witch; I heard the name Phipps several times, kept shouting his name. That's another reason I was suspicious and why I said it was odd that you mentioned him."

"Okay, I'll make a few enquires but unless you can determine the cause. I don't see there's much I can do, Doc."

Chapter 08 Rowan Drive

When I got back to the office, it was gone 6pm Orville was manning the desk alone. It suddenly occurred to me that I'd not had a chance to talk to Orville without Miss Harris or Jake, his father, being there to answer for him. I took the opportunity to see if he would open up.

"Orville, you remember when we got that call from Duncan's Bar; saying two guys were busting up the place?"

"Sure do, reckon Cal Phipps was fixing to bust your head for stopping their fight, that day."

"You're right. If it hadn't been for you, I think those bastards might have killed me. Believe me Orville; I was glad you were there that day. Anyway, I was about to tell you that Ben Alden, is in the hospital. Doc thinks he'll be dead by the morning and nobody knows why." Orville said nothing but there was no mistaking the look of fear on his face. "You've lived in Peace all your life Orville; you must have seen some strange goings on. I know I have, and I've only just arrived."

"Yeah, I guess."

I thought Orville might loosen up if I addressed him as his father did. "What have you seen, Orville?"

"I can't say, Sheriff Corwin."

"Why can't you say?"

"Pa says I got to learn to keep my mouth shut or they'll take away the ..." With that Orville clamped a hand over his mouth.

"What Orv? Take what? Who might take it?"

"Can't say, mustn't say, don't make me Sheriff Corwin; Pa gets mad."

I could sense panic in Orville's voice and having witnessed his strength when someone hit him with a chair in that first bar brawl,

I thought it wise not to push him too far. It seemed like Orville didn't trust his own ability to keep a secret.

"Okay Orville, you get along home now. No more questions I promise."

~~~~~~~~~~~

Nine hundred miles away near the west coast, it was early evening and daylight had just started to fade when Karen Sykes and captain Dugan reached 13 Rowan Drive, the home of C.D.I Winifred Howe. This was a sought after area according to San Francisco's Realty firms and the first thing they noticed was the for sale board outside on the overgrown lawn. The house looked unoccupied.

"Hell I can't wait to make chief if this is the kind of place the pay gets you," Karen was looking up at the beautiful detached house.

"Forget it, Sykes, Win told me this place was left to her by her parents." Expensive plants and shrubs in the front garden said the property was recently loved and well maintained. However, grass and weeds had begun to label the place vacant. Tall unkempt hedges flanked the huge garden, keeping the house secluded in an otherwise open planned avenue. Karen stood staring at the for-sale board, while writing down its phone number.

"Something wrong Sykes?"

"No Sir, Just taking down the name and number of this Realty Company. I don't think I've ever seen this sale board before and I've certainly not seen the name, Danny Raug Realty. Strange name for an estate agents don't you think, sir? Anyway taking phone numbers when I'm on a case is kind of a habit."

"Oh, right, so you think this could turn out to be a case."

"I don't know but it could be." As they both turned back to stare at the property they heard what sounded like a muffled gunshot. They glanced at each other as Karen immediately unfastened the thong from her hip holster and Dugan produced a .38mm. The two separated, making for either side of the house. Karen took the nearest side, forcing her to take a narrow path between the house and the garage. Feeling for the butt of her 9mm, Karen inched along the side of the house. She stopped as she saw a shadow move across the lawn of the back garden. Again she inched quietly forward moving sideways like she'd been trained, giving any predator the smallest possible target.

Reaching the rear of the house, she peered cautiously around the corner at the back garden. She was just in time to see an elderly man in overalls levelling a rifle toward the far corner of the house where Dugan was due to show. He was standing with his back to her. Karen shouted just as Dugan appeared,

"Drop it!" Startled, the man twisted in an awkward movement just enough to see Karen aiming her gun at him. Slowly he crouched down and laid the rifle on the ground. He then stood with his hands raised. Karen and Dugan approached him. As they got closer, they could see the rifle was only a small .22 calibre. Not the kind of weapon one would chose to permanently eliminate an enemy. The man looked to be around sixty, possibly past retirement. He stared nervously at Dugan's 38 pointed at him and said,

"I'm s-sorry, are you police." Karen was surprised when Dugan suddenly hit the guy in the midriff. The man doubled up, fighting for breath. Karen felt sorry for him. She glared at Dugan. But the chief ignored her look of reproach, and shouted at the man,

"What the fuck do you think you're doing, aiming that rifle at me?" Karen flashed her badge and the man seemed to relax a little. Between gasps and the obvious pain from Dugan's punch, he explained,

"My name's Mathew Chandler. I wasn't pointing it at you. I came through the hedge. I live next door."

"Okay, but that doesn't excuse you being here. And just what were you aiming at?"

"A cat," he said, still grimacing with pain.

"Oh you like to kill cats do, you?"

"You don't understand. Ever since that relative of Win's came here I've been plagued by damned cats. I'm pretty sure they've left now but cats still come around." Karen picked up on a word,

"You said relative. Then you said they've left?"

"Yes, because Win and her sister must have left together. I've not seen either of them for over two weeks. Then that For-Sale board suddenly appeared in the front garden."

"Winifred Howe told you she had a sister staying with her?"

"No, the sister did. Matter of fact I haven't seen Win since before her sister arrived."

"Can you describe this sister." said Karen.

"She looked about your age, nice looking woman. I remember Win telling me she had a sister living somewhere in Oregon so I had no reason not to believe her." Karen looked at Dugan,

"Yes I think she did mention a younger sister once," Dugan said.

Karen didn't answer. Her attention was now on a freshly dug mound of earth at the rear of the garden. "Have you any idea what that is," The old man turned to look where Karen was pointing. He looked at the mound of earth with a puzzled frown. Then with a look of enlightenment he said,

"Oh no…I'm betting that's Sabre, Winnie's Alsatian. That's sad; he was a lovely dog. I didn't know he had died. I didn't think he was that old. Wait a minute…I remember hearing what sounded like a shot late one night, it woke me up but then I thought I might have been dreaming and just went back to sleep." The old man turned to gaze once more at the mound of earth.

"Maybe Sabre was ill and I wasn't dreaming."

"When was this?" Dugan said.

Chandler scratched his head. "I'm not too sure; memory's not what it was. I'm wondering why she didn't ask me to do it, though. I would have buried him for her, must have broke her heart."

"Mr Chandler, I don't suppose you've seen a man knocking Win's door recently. He'd be about 35 your height, dark hair little goatee and moustache?

"Matter of fact I did. He came back twice; the last time was two days ago, the guy seemed to have a problem. I recon by the way he was pounding her door he was pretty angry about something."

"Did you see who answered the door?"

"No Ma'am, I didn't want to get involved. I went in and shut my door,"

"So you never saw the guy leave?"

"No."

~~~~~~~~~~

It was as if Doc Kirby had an insight to God's own timetable. Kirby phoned me to say Ben Alden died just before daylight the following day. A week later I attended his burial.

It was the first time I had cause to visit the town's cemetery and was surprised by the amount of new graves there were, considering the size of the community. However, as I stared around at the fresh mounds of earth, something about them bothered me, but for that moment, I just wasn't sure what it was. My only reason for attending the burial was that I was curious to see who else would attend. As expected, Calvin Phipps did not show. Apart from the local preacher, there were two town's people there that I'd seen before, a young and very pretty girl that I hadn't, and a guy dressed in a long raincoat and black fedora. Even with the hat pulled low, I thought he looked a lot like Alden. After a short and impersonal eulogy in a language I didn't understand, the girl and priest left. This left just the raincoat man standing alone peering into the open grave. I approached him and decided to chance making a fool of myself.

"Sorry about your brother!" I'd guessed right, the guy spun around and looked about him as if I'd just asked him to buy some snort. "You're Alden, right?"

"I don't use that name anymore."

"Oh! Can I ask why?" I said as he continued scanning the cemetery. There was no mistaking his surly look, which was tinged with fear.

"No you can't. Are you on the..." He paused as he spotted my badge. He appeared to relax a little. "You're Corwin! Come here to gloat, have you?"

"I guessed you might think that, but no, I came to see if anyone else had, like the person responsible for his death, but you started to ask me something?"

"No I didn't!"

"Yes you did. You said, are you on the—then you stopped. Was I on what?"

"Forget it, I thought you might have been part of the town committee...doesn't matter, I know you're not."

"What if I had been?"

"Doesn't matter, forget it. And forget what I said about coming here to gloat. You got a job to do and my little brother probably didn't make it easy. If I'd tried harder to get him to leave this place, he might still be alive." He kept his left hand in his Mac pocket and having dealt with three-time losers that will shoot a cop rather than face prison, it was making me nervous, but then he held out his right to shake hands and I relaxed a little. He said his name was Don. His parents obviously had a thing for single syllable names. Then he told me he'd changed his surname to Smith, but still wouldn't say why.

"Did you see him?" he asked.

"Did I see who?"

"Ben. They wouldn't let me see him when I got here, said I was too late; said the casket was sealed and that it was bad luck to open it. Whose luck they meant, I don't know, Ben's had run out, that's for sure."

"I did see him the day before he died."

"How did he look, I mean physically, face, skin?"

"You don't want to know."

"Was it like this?" Without warning he pulled his left hand from his pocket. I stepped back startled and appalled by the sight of his hand, if hand is what it was, it was larger than a normal hand yet gnarled and blackened like it had been burned. It had the same leathery appearance that his brother had, like it had been unearthed from some Egyptian tomb.

"Not nice is it? I'm guessing Ben's skin might have had the same kind of appearance, am I right?"

I was speechless, mesmerized by the sight of this claw-like hand in front of me. He saw my reaction and thrust it back in his pocket.

"Yes but—how…"

"I was Ben's half brother on his mother's side, but Ben's father had ancestors that go back to the New England settlers, Salem, in fact. I didn't know that until about five years ago when I got interested in searching through our family tree. I found a link with the name Bishop, a family of early settlers in Massachusetts."

He was losing me now. I wanted to know about his hand, about what happened to Ben. All this about ancestors was telling me nothing.

"Can I ask why you left Peace?"

"I wouldn't have thought you needed to ask. You saw Ben before he died. And now this…" he said, glancing down at his pocket. I was glad I didn't have to look at his hand again.

"Yes but…"

"Did he look like he'd died of natural causes?"

"Well no, but…"

"How long have you been here?" He was talking to me, like I was the dumbest thing on the planet, and making me feel he was right.

"Not long."

"Have you never thought there was something strange about this place?"

"Yes, when I first arrived, quite a few things bothered me. But folk were pretty good to us, especially to my wife, didn't take her long to join their committee." It was here I thought I detected the wisp of a smile. But then his eyes took on that frightened look again with the mention of the word committee. "Mind you," I said. "Nothing has been as strange as the demise of your brother, but I've not given up on that mystery yet." He stared at me with narrowed eyes, then glanced around the deserted cemetery again before saying quietly,

"Be careful where and who you investigate, Sheriff. Things in Peace are not always what they seem. There are two communities living here: those with the gift and those without it, both have to be very careful about what they say or do." He paused for a moment, as if deliberating on whether to voice his next thoughts. Then with another quick scan around him he said, "What do you know about American history, about the New England settlers?"

"Oh Christ you're not going to give me a load of spiel about witches. I'm a little too old for that." It was my turn to talk like he was the dummy.

"Oh you think so! Do you deny that people were put to death for witchcraft in New Hampshire?"

"No, but that was through ignorance. Any rational thinking…"

"Okay," he interrupted, "but what if it was not just superstition. What if events happened in those communities that really couldn't be explained? I know they put it down to witchcraft or devil-worship let's face it any other explanation was beyond comprehension in those days."

"What do you mean?"

"Well, today, strange happenings like crop circles are more likely put down to aliens, Anyway, what if these witches—devil worshipers—call them what you like, did have some kind of power that people were afraid of, after all voodoo is still a reality among Haitians.

"Yes, I know but..."

"Well okay, you're a sceptic like most people, but let's just pretend for one moment that devil worship has some credence. What if some of those suspected devil worshipers of Massachusetts escaped the noose or whatever other means of execution was threatening them. We know the names of some of the people that were put to death, but what about their relatives. What if they reassembled and settled somewhere else, just waiting to avenge the torture and murder of their families?"

"But you're talking about people that were hanged in the 1600s."

"1692," he corrected. "Yes but only those that were kept on record. Only those we know about."

"Whatever; it's still too long ago for any direct descendents to be alive. And anyway why here? We're a hell of a ways from Massachusetts."

"It makes no difference. Who is to say they wouldn't know about using conflict tactics like, retreat, reform and live to fight another day? Of course, no direct relatives would be alive today but what if those relatives, and there had to be a number of them, carried their hatred of those who murdered their families to other parts like here for instance and what if their hatred was so strong that it festered until it became a religion in its own right. I agree we're a long way from the east coast, but do you know the Hebrew word for peace

"No. Is there one?" I said trying not to look bored.

A hint of a smile crossed his lips as he said, "Salem." Well I had to admit, that did surprise me, but not enough! I had no idea if he was spinning me a line and still thought this guy's nurse would be arriving any minute. Then he said, "If you ever find yourself back in any big city, take a trip to the local library. Search New England's history, search the names and look up the Massachusetts witch trials. You might find enough to change your mind."

Well, I'd heard enough, I accepted his phone number, made my excuses and started to leave, but as I started to walk away, he said,

"And sheriff, check your own name!"

As I left the cemetery it dawned on me what was odd about the new graves: there were no flowers.

Chapter 9 Howe

Chandler picked up his rifle and after Dugan told him not to take any notice if he heard the sound of breaking glass the old man retreated back through the hedge and into his own house.

Dugan and Sykes had no need to break in Howe's home, they tried a back door and it opened, the lock had been broken. This was the first thing to throw doubt on Chandler's theory that Winifred Howe had left for a holiday with her sister. Dugan tried a light switch and found the lights working.

"Check upstairs, Sykes I'll search down here." Karen took the stairs slowly She had a bad feeling about the place, a fear that she was about to discover something ghoulish. She didn't. The rooms upstairs were clean and tidy. The beds were made and the wardrobes were full. Suitcases were on top of the wardrobe, suggesting that no one had gone on vacation. There was not a clue to suggest the owner was about to sell up or move. Having checked the last bedroom and hearing nothing threatening from Dugan downstairs, Karen finally holstered her gun. As she emerged on to the landing, however, she was shocked see Dugan halfway up the stairs and his gun was pointing directly at her. In that instant they heard Mr Chandler call out before charging through the passage door and into the hall. Dugan swung his gun hand downward to point it at the old man before slowly relaxing and dropping his aim.

"Sorry for bursting in on you but the back door was left open and I wanted to catch you before you left," said the old man.

"What is it, Chandler," said Dugan. "What's that important you almost get yourself shot twice in one day?"

"Yeah sorry, it's just that I've remembered when I heard that shot fired, if it was a gun shot. It was the same night Win's sister arrived." When Dugan never responded the old man looked up at

Karen who was still staring at Dugan. "Did I do right miss? Will it help, Miss…Miss?"

"Yes Mr Chandler, you've been a great help." Karen said while moving her right hand closer to the butt of her gun and keeping Dugan in her line of sight.

"Yes we'll give you a call if we have any more questions." Dugan said, now holstering his gun. Chandler retreated out the back door leaving an uncomfortable silence between the two DIs until Karen said, "Why did you climb the stairs with your gun poised to shoot, when you must have realised I had time enough to secure all the rooms up here?"

"Well I thought I heard…Wait a minute…you didn't think that I was about to…being a little paranoid Sykes, aren't you."

"Better paranoid than dead. Considering we are here to check that someone is really who she claims to be. I'm wondering if others in the department is who they claim to be"

"I get your point, Sykes; I don't blame you for being a bit jumpy."

Karen descended the remaining stairs, "Did you check the rest of the house down here?"

"Yes, nothing," Dugan said "It looks like Win uses the cellar as a dark room; I remember she used to be a bit of an amateur photographer, reckon that's why she painted out that window."

"Nothing unusual upstairs either all her clothes are still in her wardrobe and her cases are still on top, nothing to suggest she's about to sell up, or take a holiday." They were standing in the hall. Karen was staring at the intermittent red light on the phone."

"Do I have your permission to check her calls sir?"

"Well I think under the…"

Karen didn't wait for him to finish, she pressed a button on the phone and a very nervous voice said,

"Hello Win, it's Agnes. Please, put me up for a few days. I will arrive in San Francisco next Friday that's the 15th at 10 am.

Would you please meet me at the station?" There was a pause on the recording then a beep before Karen recognised Roster's angry voice:

"Pick up Howe I know you're there, you spiteful bitch, I want to know what I've done to deserve the lies you wrote in that report to Internal Affairs. You must know you've destroyed a cop with a clean record not to mention the stress you've caused me and I want to know..."

There came a click and a long beep that signified the extent of tape on the machine.

"Sounds like a man with a grievance," said Dugan but Karen wasn't listening she appeared to be deep in thought. "Sykes, what's on your mind?"

"Sorry sir, my mind was somewhere else, San Francisco Amtrak Station to be exact. There was something on the local news about a fatality at the station and I'm sure the 15th was mentioned."

"Hey! I remember that, they said a woman fell under an incoming train. Aw forget it Sykes it's just a coincidence, if there had been any foul play we'd have heard about it. Don't forget, Chandler said he'd seen Win's sister, so she must have arrived safely." Karen was about to argue Dugan's point. She wanted to remind him of Chandler's words, that he had not seen Winifred Howe since her sister arrived; therefore it was possible the train fatality could be Win Howe herself. Karen, however, was convinced that Dugan had not vindicated himself of the stairs incident. Therefore she decided to keep her ideas to herself until she was sure Dugan was on the level. It seemed to Karen that Dugan was either not up to the job of solving what had become of Howe and Roster or he already knew and did not want her to find out.

"These things have a way of resolving themselves Sykes," Dugan said. "Let's get back to the office and see if there is any news about Roster." Karen was far from convinced things would resolve themselves and she was still worried about what had happened to Neil Roster.

~~~~~~~~~~

I knew I'd get no answers from Calvin Phipps, but for the next few days I visited the loggers' encampment to try talking to some of the men. I didn't find them very responsive and I'm sure the reason was more than just an aversion to cops; word about the Alden's fate had obviously reached them. Maybe one or two loggers had visited the hospital and Kirby had shown them Alden's body, but they certainly acted nervous. It was like they were afraid to be seen talking to me. I'm sure the men believed that Cal Phipps was responsible for Aden's death. Because of this, I had to make sure Cal was not around when trying to question them. I tried calling on some of them at their homes but they closed their doors on me. For a few days, and at different times, I turned up at the site hoping to catch one of them alone. On the third day I bumped into a straggler called Griggs. He was about to step out of the loggers changing cabin. I crowded him by first barring his exit, then I stepped up through the door forcing him back inside. I kicked the door closed behind me. Griggs looked nervous.

"Okay Griggs, no one knows we're here so what about it, talk to me. Did you see any animosity between Alden and Phipps?"

Griggs had turned up late that morning and was the last to get his working gear on. He wasn't a resident of Peace, but like a lot of the loggers, he came from one of the neighbouring small towns. The rest of the men had gone to their worksites. Griggs looked frightened but knowing we couldn't be seen he seemed willing to talk,

"What have you heard," he said

"Nothing, that's the trouble, nobody's talking to me."

"Yeah, I'm not surprised, they're all spooked, but then that's not unusual when it involves folk from Peace. There's a lot of strange goings on over there. They think Phipps is some kind of bloody demon."

"What do you mean?"

"You know like a man-witch, or whatever you call 'em." Here we go again I said to myself as I recalled my chat with Alden's brother. I grinned at the thought of grown men believing in childish fantasies.

"And what started them thinking that?"

"Well what do you think? Ben Alden dying that's what! It started when Cal came out of clink. They wouldn't even talk to each other. You could cut the air in here with a knife. I guess we knew there was gonna be trouble." Something in the way he said *gonna be trouble,* made me say,

"It was you that phoned me?"

"Shit! How could you tell? I was pinching my nose?"

"Never mind, go on."

"Well—then, the accident happened, if it was an accident."

"You don't think so?"

"Not for me to say; none of us were around when it happened but when Cal came out of hospital things really got out of hand; that was when Cal tried to give Ben his safety helmet back." I then recalled Cal's reminding me that I was holding Alden's hard hat.

"Tried?"

"Yeah, you should have seen Alden's face. He looked at that helmet like it was a rabid dog. We all thought he'd gone crazy. Keep it; he said to Phipps I got another one. But it's got your name on it; Cal said jabbing it toward him. But Alden wouldn't touch it. He backs out the door like he was afraid of it."

"Is that it? Is that what's got you all scared out of your wits?" I said.

"Well you haven't lived around here as long as some of us, sheriff. I've seen some weird happenings, but no, it wasn't just the business with the helmet. The next few days Alden came in early, before the rest of us. He got his gear on and locked himself in the cab of the Grabber before the rest of us arrived. I'm sure this was to avoid facing Phipps. At the end of each shift he would wait until we were all out of here before coming back to his locker to get changed. It was about the end of the week when it happened."

"What?"

"I was in Phipps's gang so I saw it firsthand."

"Saw what, for Christ sake!" I said, starting to get up tight.

"Well, that morning we got to the site, Alden was already operating the cat. Four of us began cutting trees, but not Cal. Cal climbs up the hill to the Cat and just stands there, looking up at Ben's cab. It was hard to see from where we stood but I had the impression Cal was grinning up at Ben. I thought he'd flipped. Then I saw what he was grinning at, and I think the other guys noticed too. We were all staring up at Ben. He must have sensed why. Suddenly he pulled his helmet off and stared at his own name painted on the front of it. Phipps must have got into his locker and swapped the helmets over."

"But Alden would have seen it before putting it on, surely."

"Not unless he remembered to check it. Look!" Griggs went to his own locker, opened the door and He then lifted his own helmet with both hands and slid it onto the top shelf. "You see? We all do it like that, and we put them on the same way so we never see the front of our own hardhats. Unless we happen to look in a mirror, we only see each other's names"

"OK but this all sounds like stupid superstition. It doesn't prove that Phipps had anything to do with Alden's death."

"Maybe not, but no one was as close to Phipps as Alden. Who would know more about his...well...capabilities for want of a better word? You should have seen Alden's face that last morning; man, he dropped that helmet like it was burning his hands, jumped from his cab, and ran like a frightened rabbit out of here. Yeah if you'd seen, you might think different."

"Does anyone talk to Phipps? I mean has he got any friends now that Alden's gone?"

"The only guys either of them is friendly with are residents of Peace. I've heard he drinks in the Pike and Heron." My frown prompted him to come up with its location.

"It's in the valley," he said pointing through the window. "It's on the other side of that hill we're working on at the moment." In the distance I could see the machine Rick had called the grabber still crowding the skyline on the top of the hill. "Taint that far, you could walk it from here, but to get to it by road is about five miles. It sits on the bank of Pike Lake, used to be good fishing there I've been told, but the water got poisoned killed everything in there. Now it got warning posts all around the lake to keep out. Phipps apparently drinks at the Inn with old Sean Finnegan. The pair of them used to get rowdy when they'd had a few. And one of the guys said they've seen him coming out of the church..." Griggs words faded and he seemed to become lost in thought.

"What?" I prompted.

"Well I don't know if it means anything, but I remember Ben Alden telling me he was sweet on the girl that spends time in..." Griggs paused again. "...Of course—it makes sense. Prudence visits the church, and she's the daughter of Horace Rider, the guy who runs the Pike and Heron. Do you get the picture?"

"Sorry Griggs, you've lost me."

"Think about it! We all thought this feud was over Phipps going to prison, but it could have been over the girl. Ben told me about Pru in confidence but I don't suppose it matters now."

I churned everything I'd learned, over in my mind, but eventually put the whole affair down to mass hysteria and decided that it was futile to put any more time into the Alden/Phipps episode. For the next week or so things went back to normal, with nothing odd or disturbing happening—then...

Chapter 10 Hit a and run

"What is it Spencer, cant you sleep?" Charlie had sensed by my breathing that I was having a bad night. She sat up and looked at the clock, it was nearly midnight. "Why are you still awake, my husband?"

If my head had not been full of worry and questions of where my Daughter could be, I would have questioned Charlie about why she seemed to sometimes slip into this strange old English dialect.

"Avril's still not home I can't sleep when she's out late, I wish she would ring when she decides to stay over with her school friends. I know—you're right. I shouldn't worry; I know she's sensible, but until I hear that key in the door I just can't settle."

Charlie said nothing. She just turned over and went back to sleep. I did eventually fall asleep that night, and without hearing Avril return home.

I awoke the next morning and found Charlie had already dressed and left the house, leaving a note to say she'd gone to the shops. I immediately checked Avril's room. As I stared at her undisturbed bed, the phone rang and even as I hurried downstairs to answer it, I sensed something was wrong.

"Corwin?" It was Jake's voice. His attitude toward me still retained enough hostility to prevent him from calling me by my first name or even sheriff. "I got bad news." He said without feeling. With the vision of Avril's empty bed fresh in my mind, my legs went weak. "It's your girl, she was found on the side of the road this morning. Hit and run."

"Is she…"

"I'm afraid so. We got the kid that did it though, it was…" Jakes voice became a meaningless drone as I slowly lowered the receiver onto its cradle. The details of the accident were unimportant at that moment. All I could think about was Avril's cheeky giggle, her sense of humour that was so far advanced for her age, and the way she tormented me with her wit. I grabbed the banister, as I felt my legs give way.

At that moment Charlie came through the door to find me sitting at the foot of the stairs, my face wet with tears. I told her about the call but she showed no surprise, and I thought at the time shock might be the reason she never shed a tear.

I spent the rest of that day shut in a room alone where I let grief once more tear me apart. However, this time, I did stay clear of the bottle.

The following day I forced myself to get to the office and listen to the details of Avril's death. Someone, however, had seen a kid steal the car, and it was not long before a local fifteen-year-old boy with a history of joy riding was picked up.

I went to see Avril's body at the hospital mortuary. Through the viewing window, she looked so beautiful, so angelic. She appeared unmarked by the accident. I wanted to hold her. I tried to open the door to the right of the window. It was locked. I was about to search for an attendant to let me in when Doctor Kirby turned up.

"Can you unlock the door; Doc I'd like to hold her hand once more when I say my goodbyes."

"I wouldn't advise it sheriff. You see I arranged for you to see her like this. I thought you'd rather remember her as she was. You see it's the left side of her face that took the impact and I'm afraid it's not a sight you'd want lodged in your memory."

I took his advice and came away from the hospital. It was the first time I'd ever felt grief that actually caused physical pain in my chest and stomach, a terrible dark sadness that would not abate. I'd lay awake at night for weeks, silently soaking my pillow. I was sure Charlie must also have been grieving, though I never saw her shed a tear. My nights were spent restlessly tossing and turning until our bedroom became a place of loathing. Charlie seemed unaffected and slept soundlessly as she always had. One might assume that this was because Avril was not of Charlie's blood, but

I didn't believe that. I was sure that Avril had come to accept Charlie as her own mother, and I thought their feelings were reciprocated. Gradually my grief turned to hate, hate for this young hoodlum that had torn my life apart.

When fatigue did finally succumb to sleep my nights became a repetitive dream. In it I am sat in a strange courthouse watching the boy joy rider's trial. It is strange, because for some reason Avril is there. Her coffin has no lid and she is on display her casket is stood on end and leaning back against the Judges bench. I look around me; all are wearing habits with cowls covering their heads. I hear myself begging for someone to close Avril's eyes, but as they turn toward me I see their hoods are empty. Unruly townsfolk fill the gallery their chatter sometimes interrupted by bouts of laughter like they had come to see a farcical show. The trial procedure varied each night, but the outcome was always the same with the boy, grinning at me as the Judge gave his précis. As far as the judge was concerned, the boy's age seemed to override all other consideration. Too young to be punished and therefore free to commit more crime and cause more misery to innocent folk. Each night the dream ended with the boy wringing his hands above his head like a prize fighter who'd just KO'd his opponent. The crowded courtroom, clamoured with applause while black empty hoods studied my obvious torment.

Each morning I would tell myself it was only a dream, but my own past experience in the force told me this could and almost certainly would be the only outcome of the boy's trial unless....

As the date for the boy's trial approached visions of Ben Alden's wizened body and his brother's words became part of my dreams. With them came dark and ridiculous thoughts; ideas so fantastic they could only be justified in fairy stories yet each day they became more credible.

One night, I lay awake plotting a method of avenging Avril's death. My mind filled with bitter and vengeful thoughts and my fists clenched so tight I didn't even feel my fingernails drawing blood from the palms of my hands until Charlie suddenly sat upright and spoke with a strange and distant echo in her voice.

"No! This one is mine." was all she said before lying down again. I asked what she meant, but realized she hadn't really awakened. I questioned her about it the next morning. She said she remembered nothing of the incident and didn't seem to want to talk about it. I didn't push too hard for an explanation. I was keen to put my night's plotting into action.

I discovered Cal Phipps's parents were deceased and that he lived alone. When I banged on his door he greeted me with,

"Aw hell, not you again!" Cal weighed around 180lb and stood no taller than 5ft 8". He'd drawn a short straw in the looks department with his greasy long hair and badly pockmarked face, so when he said,

"Christ you look terrible," I wanted to hit him. But I knew what he meant. I needed sleep, lots of it. "What am I supposed to have done this time?" he said. I glanced in both directions making sure I wasn't being watched before roughly pushing him back inside. I followed him in and closed the door behind me.

~~~~~~~~~~

It was Friday, 2pm and San Francisco's downtown Hospital was not normally that busy but today it was buzzing, because this was the Accident & Emergency wing and it had just received an intake from a major auto pile up. The reception desk was six people deep. Karen Sykes opened the leather wallet containing her police shield and elbowed her way up towards the reception desk. She had almost made it when a large hairy hand grabbed her arm.

"Hey lady, did someone tell you to ignore the queue?" The guy was huge and obviously stressed from the amount of congealed blood covering his face and neck. Karen flipped open her wallet and shoved it under his nose. The SFPD badge clearly did not impress him.

"So you got a piece of shiny metal but I don't see the word priority stamped on it."

Karen slipped the black Beretta-Storm out from under her coat, "How about this shiny piece of metal?" she said.

"Yeah okay lady, that's a strong argument," the man said, holding his hands up and backing through the crowd. Karen now had the attention of the receptionist who was smiling.

"You had a woman fatality brought in here on the 15th, that was three days ago. Where can I find the body?"

"If it was DOA it would go straight down to level A, the mortuary. They'll have the details." The elevator door opened just as Karen reached it, she stepped inside and hit the A button. The doors started to close just as a man's body squeezed between them. The guy was wearing a baseball cap with the peek pulled low. The sunglasses also made it hard to put a face to him, but his voice made it easier."

"Hi Karen!" he looked up and the sight of the goatee cinched it. It was Neil Roster. Karen had never seen him looking so jittery and unkempt.

"Neil! Where the hell have you been? Christ, did you sleep in a dumpster? You look terrible and you don't seem to be using that deodorant I bought you last Christmas."

"You saying I smell?"

"Well at least you're just as sharp. Where have you been, are you okay?"

"No, far from it; I've been following you since this morning. I haven't had much sleep and it's the first chance I've had to speak to you alone. Who's that guy you were with this morning?" The darkness under his eyes confirmed his lack of sleep.

"Dugan, our new CDI. You say you've been following me? Well, so much for my powers of detection. Do you know the whole department is searching for you, not to mention your wife? Where have you been and what's this all about Neil?"

"I'm not sure yet. I'm too scared to go home and as for what's going on, you're the only one I can trust to help me find out. I'm guessing you played the message on Howe's phone, that's why you're here."

"Was it you that broke the window in her house?"

"Yeah, and I guess I should have wiped the tape."

"Too right, Dugan was with me when I hit the play button."

"Dugan...Dugan, I've never heard of him!"

"Don't mean he ain't real. Look Neil something weird is going on and I'm trying to get to the bottom of it." The lift had stopped and the door was open.

"Weird is a bit tame Karen, fucking scary is more fitting. You don't know half of it yet. Look I've already been down here Karen. I can tell you anything you want to know." They stepped out into a deserted corridor. This was where patient's files and hospital archives were kept. It also housed the boilers and generators. It was in fact the heart that pumped blood into the whole hospital services. It also contained the department that the public was spared from being reminded of: the mortuary. If one discounted the dead it was the most deserted level in the hospital. The two D.I.s stepped out of the elevator. To their right was a long corridor with several numbered doors either side, to the left they faced a double swing door, above it the word, Mortuary.

"I don't think you ought to go in there Karen," said Neil staring at the double doors. "The body you came to see is not all in one piece and..."

"The face, Neil, what about the face, I've got to know if it's Howe."

"It wasn't anyone I know, and it's definitely not the bitch, that had me demoted that's for sure."

"Did she jump?"

"Or was she pushed? If that's what you're asking, I don't know. The woman that showed me the body thinks she was pushed but said she can't be sure,"

"So why does she think she was pushed?"

"She said she's seen a lot of train related suicides and the jumpers usually turn their head away at the last second. She said it's like they don't want to spoil their face when the train hits. Now that is strange don't you think? Anyway if that *is* Howe in there, she met the train face first and believe me Karen it's not a vision you want in your head when you're trying to get to sleep at night. Anyway the bitch is blond; the head in there has red hair. Karen I just don't know who the hell that is in there." Behind them, a door banged shut and Roster's hand shot inside his coat as a young woman in a green smock brushed past them to enter the mortuary.

"What's got you spooked Neil? You're not normally this nervous."

"I know, but things...can we go somewhere private, Karen? There are things happening, something funny is going on and we need to find out who's behind it. Like I said, I don't know who that is on the slab in there, but she looks nothing like the woman that dropped me in it with that report."

"Okay Neil. We'll go to my place. I think you're right, there is something funny going on but I've seen a photo of the real Winifred Howe so I've got to go look at whoever that is on the slab. If I don't identify the body in there we'll be no further advanced with this business."

"Ok but don't say I didn't warn you." They pushed through the mortuary swing doors to see the woman who brushed past them in the corridor; she was sat writing at a desk. She nodded at Karen. Recognition showed as her gaze shifted to Roster and Karen noted her smile was more than just friendly. After identifying themselves as SFPD and explaining that Karen may be able to identify the body of the train incident fatality, the woman ushered Karen and Neil toward a wall of cold storage drawers. The woman checked the inserted labels on the front of the drawers before unlocking one. Neil knew what to expect and he was watching Karen's face as the woman pulled out the drawer.

"Sorry," the young woman said, "This kind of accident can be messy and in this case there wasn't much for the cleanup team to collect. The face was a mess when you came in earlier Detective Roster but since then I've straightened out the bone structure in the face so you may find it easier to recognise."

"Why did you do that?" Karen asked.

"Hospital policy, relatives may come to identify the body"

Karen felt queasy as she looked at the small mound covered by a sheet. She looked at the Neil. He answered her quizzical stare with,

"After the initial impact, her body must have landed across one of the rails."

"Yes you're right," said the young pathologist. "I'm afraid there was too much damage to save anything below the rib cage."

"That's okay, I understand. I'm only interested in seeing the face." The woman nodded and pulled back the sheet only as far as the neck. But even that caused Karen to hold her breath. The back of the body's head had been smashed so that as it lay on the stainless steel tray it appeared to be only half a head. Karen felt a disturbance in her stomach and swallowed hard to avoid retching. She stared at the pale dead face for a good fifteen seconds before she nodded to the woman who replaced the sheet.

"Well?" Roster said.

"Is it someone you know?" asked the mortician.

"If the photo that Dugan showed me was C.D.I Howe, and I believe it was. Then I'd say this is probably her."

"Well I can't make that official unless you actually knew her. So unless someone comes along that did, she'll remain a Jane Doe."

As the two detectives stepped outside the hospital and onto the crowded sidewalk, Karen took a deep breath and tried to delete the picture of what she'd just seen from her mind. Roster started to show signs of agitation again by constantly peering over his shoulder.

"So if that was the real Winifred Howe, Karen, who is that bitch that dropped me in it with Internal Affairs and how come I heard her mention Rowan drive when I walked in on her phone call that day?"

"I don't know but I'd like to know who was on the other end of that call. The house definitely belonged to the real Winifred Howe that's for sure. Her neighbour confirmed it, He thinks the woman who's been living there since the day of the train fatality is Win's sister and I'm pretty sure she is the bitch that's been sitting in the Chief's office at precinct 13."

"So where is she now?"

"That's just what I intend to..." Karen's words broke off mid sentence, as they heard a woman scream followed by more shouting and screaming from farther along sidewalk. As Karen and Neil looked to see who had screamed, Pedestrians ahead of them started clearing the sidewalk. People were dashing in all directions. Some ran into the road while others flattened themselves against the wall of the hospital. Roster saw the cause moments before Karen. A large black 4x4 had mounted the sidewalk and was bearing down on them. One man was just too slow dodging its path. It caught him a glancing blow spinning him off his feet and into the road. Karen stood transfixed, unable to drag her eyes away from this surreal moment as the man rolled in the path of a yellow cab. Karen held her breath, her mind willing the cab to stop. She heard the screech of the cab's brakes but before she saw the outcome of the pedestrian's fate she suddenly had the wind knocked out of her as Neil, football tackled her off her feet and into the recess of the hospital entrance. His presence of mind saved them both from being run down by the huge pickup. Moments later they untangled themselves from others who had chosen the same means of escape from the insane driver.

"Are you okay?" Roster asked while staring at the fast disappearing truck as it swerved off the sidewalk to merge back into the busy traffic.

"Yes thanks to you. Can you believe that crazy bastard, losing control like that and then driving on without stopping?" Karen said as she dusted herself down."

"Sorry to be so rough."

"Don't be, Neil, you saved my life." They heard a child crying, the sound was coming from where the truck had mounted the kerb. A little girl no older than five was standing over her mother. She had hold of the young woman's hand and was trying to pull the woman up from her prone position on the sidewalk. One of the woman's legs appeared twisted at a strange angle beneath her. Someone dashed into the hospital to get help, others crowded around the man who still lay in the road. Others were still picking themselves up and examining their own injuries. Two stretcher-carrying porters came dashing out of the hospital entrance and almost knocked Karen over again, as they hurried to reach the guy in the road.

"Thank God you were alert, Neil."

"I think that was because I've been on edge since first thing this morning when that same bastard first tried to run me down."

"Christ, Neil, why didn't you say something?"

"Because I wasn't sure if it was intentional, but now I know it was. That's the same GMC Yukon that drove straight at me earlier when I attempted to cross a street. Come on Karen we're not safe out in the open. Let's get to your place, there's a lot more you don't know."

Chapter 11 Hocuspocus

"Hey what is this? You got a warrant?" Phipps said as he just managed to avoid falling backwards over a chair.

"Don't worry; it's not about you this time Phipps." Cal moved aside as I barged past him, kicking his door closed behind me. I glanced around the room and knew the daily help had not arrived that day. More from habit than purpose my cop's habitually trained eye immediately spotted something that brushed away any doubts about why I was there. Without being asked, I sat down at the room's well-chipped and worn dining table.

"You heard about the accident?" I said, making it sound more of a statement than a question. Cal hit the off button on a portable radio and sat nervously facing me at the table.

"Err—yeah, your kid wasn't it?"

"You know it was!" My stare became intense, and I could sense my knuckles turning white as I tightened my fists. Cal went on the defensive.

"Okay, Okay, calm down. No offence, but let's face it I never knew her, and you and I aren't exactly the best of friends so what do you want?"

"What you did to Alden... I want you to do it to the boy."

"What?" Phipps stared at me like I'd just asked him to marry me, but I knew it was an act. Phipps knew exactly what I meant.

"You know what I'm talking about; whatever you did to Alden I want you to do to the kid," I repeated.

"Well why don't you get...?"

"Why don't I get what?"

"Nothing; forget it. Anyway, I don't know what you're talking about." I tried to read his thoughts but couldn't. I stretched across to a corner table and struggled to lift the heavy leather-bound book that I'd spotted as I came in the room. I dropped it with a loud thud on the table so that the title stared up at him: "Witches of Salem." Cal looked at me, waiting for me to speak.

"I'm not stupid, Phipps, I know enough history to recognize a book on the occult." Cal gave a wry smile and took some time before saying,

"You don't believe all that crap about devil worship and witches, do you?"

"I didn't until I saw what you did to Alden, and if you don't believe in it what's the book doing here?"

Cal just stared at me. Again I tried to read his expression, what was he thinking? He got up and stared for some moments out of the window before he said, "Look, if I admitted I was able to—you know, do certain things, it would be like admitting I killed Alden." With that, I became even more convinced that he had, but my allegiance to law and order was not a priority any longer; avenging my little girl's murder was.

"So what?" I said. "Who would believe it anyway? Even the hospital has no idea why he died."

"OK, let's say I could do what you want. Why should I? The kid's done me no harm; but you've been breaking my balls ever since you arrived in Peace. It's you that I should be putting a... "

"A grand" I said, before he'd finished speaking. He went silent as he studied my face.

"Five," he said at last.

"Fifteen hundred and that's it. Turn it down and I'll hound you for the rest of your life."

"Hey! We're talking a kid's life here," Cal argued.

"As if you cared, but I'm not advocating murder. I don't want him dead, but I want him to pay for what he did to my daughter." I hissed the words through clenched teeth. Cal folded and unfolded his arms; his body language said he was getting uncomfortable. "I want him never to get behind a wheel again. I want you to use your... whatever it is you do to—take away his sight—permanent. I believe you can do it."

Cal stared at me for some moments before answering with an unconvincing, "Err—no—I mean yes." I studied Cal's expression, tried to probe his thoughts again, but gave up.

"Well what is it; can you do it, yes or no?"

"I meant it's not a problem, and yes I can do it. Christ, you know how to hold a grudge, but he's not even been tried yet; what if they put the kid away?"

"They won't, trust me the kid'll walk. Anyway it can wait until after the trial. Don't do anything until you hear from me."

Amos Carrier's trial was a joke. The runt of a boy walked, just as I knew he would. It was my nightmare all over again, even to the grin on the boy's face, but unbeknown to him his punishment had not yet started. For two weeks, I watched his movements, noting where he hung out, and on what days. I picked the ideal place to make my move: behind a pool hall where I knew he took a shortcut home through a small copes. It was here that I waited. The kid's abduction was a walk over. In the darkness he practically walked into me. His puny one hundred pounds weight was no match for my size. After slapping a plaster over his mouth, I pulled his woolly hat down over his eyes and bundled him in my cruiser. It was past midnight when Cal Phipps opened his front door to me. I pushed the kid in, knocking Cal to one side. Cal quickly closed the door and locked it. He looked shocked at the sight before him. I stood tightly grasping the collar of the Carrier kid. I'd taped his hands behind his back and I could feel him shaking. His woollen hat was still covering most of his face. The kid was scared. I'd hit him once and threatening him with more of the same if he made a sound. He stood there shaking and making whimpering noises. I had to force myself to picture my little girl lying on that cold hospital slab to stop myself from weakening.

"Okay," I said. "Do what you got to do." Cal seemed dazed. He stared at me with his mouth open for some time before he whispered to me,

"It won't work with his eyes covered." I pushed the kid backwards onto dining chair.

"Don't move a muscle." I hissed at him. I then pulled Phipps to the far side of the room. "Do you want him to see you?" I whispered, "He's got no idea where he is but if he sees you…"

"Turn the light out."

"What!"

"Just turn the light out, I'll pull the hat off, do my thing and put it back on. It'll only take a few seconds then you can get him out of here."

"How long will it take?"

"I told you, a few seconds. It's just a short an incantation."

"No! I mean how long before it works."

"Varies; might take a week, could take a couple of months."

"Okay—do it!" I grabbed the kid by the front of his jacket and yanked him to his feet ordering him to stand still. The boy had no idea what was about to happen to him, and I could see the wet stain at the front of his jeans growing. I motioned to Cal. He stood with his hands on the boy's shoulders as I moved toward the light switch. I stood waiting for Phipps's signal. Cal looked at me and nodded. I flicked the switch, and I heard a faint whimper from the boy as Cal pulled the hat from his head. I could faintly make out the shape of Cal stretching out his hand toward the boy. He appeared to be touching the boy's eyes. Then I heard the low murmur of Cal's voice…

"Eyes that saw fit to end a life, thus sending one to the grave. Savour the time that you have left for soon your light will fade."

My eyes had adjusted enough to see the pair clearly and as I watched I questioned my own sanity for believing what the laws of reality told me was impossible. I had to keep reminding myself of what had happened to Ben Alden. Cal slipped the bag back over the kid's head. I then switched the light on, took a roll of bank notes from my pocket, and tossed them on the table. My business with Cal Phipps was finished. I bundled the kid out the door and into my car. I drove him to the district where he lived and killed the car lights. I cut the tape from his hands and with the bag still on his head, pushed him out of the car. Before the kid had time to get the bag off his head I had turned a corner and was out of sight. When I got back to the Grange, I sat outside in the car for some time. I was trying to analyse my state of mind. Would I sleep any easier knowing what I'd done? Would blinding the boy, assuming Phipps's incantation wasn't just so much bullshit, bring my Avril back? No. I concluded that revenge was nothing like as sweet as it was supposed to be.

Karen had parked her car in an underground car park close to the hospital. It was quiet, the lighting was poor down there and had it not been for Roster, Karen would have felt vulnerable. However, Neil was the one acting nervous, but they reached the car without incident. As Karen drove to her apartment Neil constantly stared out of the rear window.

"Don't worry Neil, I'm checking the mirror. I would have said if I thought we were being followed."

"Yes, sorry Karen I should know better. Spence was always telling me what a good cop you are. I suppose you know he was kind of sweet on you."

"Obviously not sweet enough, he married someone else remember?"

"That's true, but you weren't around when he was still hurting from losing Lucy. Can't help thinking his second marriage was just a rebound thing, know what I mean? Lucy gone and you weren't there."

"Yes and I know I'm going to miss him."

"Yeah me too, and I'm more than a bit concerned." Karen gave Neil a sideways glance.

"Why? What are you saying, Neil?"

"I just can't help feeling his leaving is somehow linked to this trouble I'm getting of late. And why has he not been in touch? Not even a postcard."

Karen had been concerned about Spencer Corwin too. Ever since she met Charlotte Potter; the night Spencer invited her to dinner. Things she saw that night had haunted her ever since. She had tried to convince herself that the frightening apparitions she witnessed that night could have been attributed to her own weakened mental state. She was, after all, still getting over an unsettling divorce at the time. Karen regarded Spencer's Job offer as a sheriff strange enough, but the rest of it, the house the salary. These things were just too much to get ones head around; they just didn't seem plausible.

Now, with the strange things associated with the woman that had masqueraded as C.D.I Howe and the fact that it was she that had brought Spencer's attention to the position in Oregon; Karen doubly worried about him.

Karen pulled into her allotted parking space below her apartment block. Both she and Neil nervously surveyed the gloomy underground car park before entering the elevator. Karen pressed the button to her apartment on the seventh floor. Once inside the flat Karen locked the door. She fetched two cans from the fridge and handed one to Neil.

"I assume you've phoned your wife. Did you know she reported you missing, Neil?"

"Abigail? No I haven't phoned her but I had my credit cards and a little cash, I've been staying in a cheap rooming house. She doesn't know where I am."

"Hell! Neil, you should let her know you're alright."

Neil looked at Karen for a moment before dropping his head and gazing at the floor. "I can't—I don't trust her."

"What? Don't you think you're being a little paranoid?"

"Maybe—I just don't know anymore. I suppose you and Spencer are the only people left that I really do trust."

"Oh come on Neil! I mean, she is your wife?"

"Don't forget, we've only been married a short time, Karen. I've never told this to anyone and I hope you won't repeat it, but our marriage has never even been—you know—consummated."

"Hell, Neil! You or her?"

"Her. She always found an excuse, headaches, wrong time of, well you know; she came up with excuses I've never even heard of. I did confide in Spencer, him being a married man I thought he might have an answer, but all he could offer was: you shouldn't have got married so soon."

"That's a bit rich coming from him. How long had he known this Charlotte Potter before he jumped in her bed?"

"Whoops, little bit of green showing there Karen, but you're right he had no room to talk and that's what I told him. But anyway he was right I did jump in with blinkers on."

"So what else gives you reason not to trust her?"

"Oh I don't know, maybe it's me, but she just don't seem to be the same person I married. Come to that, I don't seem to be the same. It's like, as soon as we tied the knot, it was job done. All romance and tenderness got blown away with the confetti. Okay I'll admit she was very young but..." Neil paused when he noticed Karen's concentration had taken a detour.

"Tell me Neil, where did you meet her?"

"At Spencer's wedding reception. Why?"

"Are you talking about his marriage to Charlotte or Lucy?"

"Charlotte, of course."

"Hell that was a short engagement, Neil,"

"You can say that again. That's why it's so strange. She couldn't get me down the aisle fast enough. For a girl that was so keen to get married, she certainly went off the boil quick. It all happened just after you left the precinct. Where did you go, by the way? Never mind I guess you had your reasons. Anyway, at the time I met Abigail I was going through a miserable spell, my mother had not long died and my father's burial wreath was still in flower on his grave. Spencer knew I was depressed, I think that's why he asked me to be his best man. Anyway, it was Charlotte, who introduced me to Abigail. What she and Charlotte were to each other I'm not sure, but they seemed very close; Charlotte spent a lot of time at my house When Spence was on duty."

"Tell me, Neil, have you any other family?"

"No," Neil grinned and it was the first time Karen had seen any kind of smile on his face that day "I guess that's why I'm so spoilt, no brothers or sisters to compete with."

"Tell me to mind my own business if you like Neil, but did your parents have much to leave you?"

"About four hundred G; why do you think Mick O'Donnell keeps calling me poor little rich guy? And of course then there's the house, that's worth a fare amount."

"Hell Neil, why do you risk your life being a NY cop?"

"I like being a cop, at least I did. Anyway why has my inheritance come into this conversation?"

"The why depends on my next question: who gets it if anything happens to you?"

"My wife, I suppose…Hey, I'm not sure I like the picture you're trying to paint, Karen."

Karen stared at Neil for some time before she said, "When we were at the hospital, you said there were things you had to tell me. Were these things what had you so spooked?"

"Partly, but hey, don't forget the close call I told you I had earlier with that dammed 4x4. I don't normally come apart like that, Karen."

"I know that, tell me what else I'm missing."

"Okay. Do you remember the accident Spencer had outside our precinct?"

"Yes of course. The guy died."

"Did he though? That's what chief Danvers told Spencer, but Spencer asked him for a report on the guy's autopsy but he's never been shown one. All that has turned up is that note from the forensic department."

"That's right, I read it. The guy's name was Vic Rowan?"

"Hell, Karen you even remembered his name. Anyway, I'm wondering if this Rowan discovered more than he dared put in the report, things he didn't want to put in writing. Maybe it's why he wanted to see Spencer in person but Spence never got the note because I think it either got forgotten in Danvers desk drawer, or this Howe impostor kept it from him on purpose. If Red Shadwell hadn't knocked Howe on her arse that day we would never have discovered it."

"Yes he told me how you slipped it under your desk when she dropped it, but Spencer left for Oregon the morning after you gave him the letter so he never found out what this forensic guy wanted to see him about."

"That's right, but this desk job they've forced on me is in precinct 14, the same building as the forensic laboratory."

"And?"

"Well, I decided I'd do Spence a favour and find out what this guy, Rowan, wanted to see him about, but they bundled me out of that place faster than I went in."

"Why? I've been there before. I found them most helpful?"

"Well things have changed, as soon as I mentioned the name Rowan I got shown the door, but my showing up there did get a response." Roster slipped a hand in his inside breast pocket and pulled out a slip of paper. "The morning after they kicked me out of there, I found this sticking out from under my phone." Karen looked at the tiny slip of paper. *9.30 Thursday, at the Blue Bull* was all that was written on it. "What does it mean?"

"Not sure but a few people in that lab heard me mention Rowan and I think this note has resulted from it. Anyway today's Thursday and I know the Blue Bull is a quiet bar down near Fishermans Warf. I'm guessing whoever wrote that has something to tell me, but I'm loath to go anywhere near the place knowing some maniac wants me as a mascot on their fender. It could even be the same person that left me this note."

"Well I don't want to influence your decision to go there, Neil, I'd never live with the guilt if it went sour, but how can you resolve this if you don't find out what's going on; you'll always be looking over your shoulder."

"I know. Are you willing to watch my back, if I go, Karen? Remember, whoever tried to run me down saw you with me. That could make you a target." Karen was silent and appeared deep in thought. Neil took this to mean she was considering the risk, "I wouldn't blame you if you didn't want to play along Karen."

"That's not what's troubling me Neil. You know I'll back you it's just that, like you, I can't stop thinking about Spencer. Whatever's going on Spencer is also caught up in it."

"You could be right. He did say Howe practically forced him to take that sheriff job and now we discover that Howe isn't Howe; I'd say something's definitely weird about all this. So you'll go along with me tonight?"

"Of course, have you still got your weapon or did the department take that away from you too,"

"They did. I had to buy one."

"Good." Karen looked up at her wall clock. "Well we have six hours so I suggest you clean yourself up. You'll find my lady razor in the bathroom. You can take a shower while I fix us a sandwich. No, I'll rephrase that. You **will** take a shower while I fix us a sandwich some lunch." Neil smiled, aware that it had been more than a week since he'd showered. "Then I suggest you get some sleep, that way we'll both feel safer when we confront whoever this mystery person is. Meanwhile I'm going to try again to phone Spencer, but so far I've not had much luck. Some woman secretary usually tells me he's unavailable or his phone is out of order."

Chapter 12 Blind justice

Could take a couple of months—yes, I remember Phipps words. But only two weeks after the incident with Phipps and Carrier, I got a call; it was word about another accident.

"Is that you Corwin?" It was Jake Tollman sounding just as cold as ever.

"Yeah Jake, what's up?"

"It's that Carrier kid—he's done it again. He left a disco last night; saw a Toyota with the keys left in it. Guess he couldn't resist another ride."

"Where is he, have you brought him in? I want to see the little bastard."

"Not this time, he's in Harwell and they say it's bad. He's alive though, just; that's more than we can say for the guy he hit. Guess who?"

"Who was it?"

"Cal Phipps." Tollman's last words registered and my mind became fixed on a terrified kid stood in Phipps's house. My hand clamped around the back of the kid's neck, his body shaking and his jeans all wet. My head was suddenly full of conjecture; had the carrier kid seen Phipps face, or maybe recognised his voice and deliberately set out to run him down?

"Corwin! Did you hear what I said? It was Phipps! The guy the kid hit when he ran off the road—Phipps and old Sean Finnegan had just come out of the Pike and Heron. The accident happened quite late last night but there was almost a full moon, so the kid must have been blind not to have seen them. Maybe you ought to have a word with the Pike's owner his name is Rider, Horace Rider."

I asked Jake how to get there. Jake said there was a short cut but not by car. He explained how to drive there and I rang off with,

"Okay Jake I'll take a ride over there, I'll see you later at the office."

Did I imagine it or did Jake overemphasize the word blind? His words resounded in my head, could Jake possibly have known and was there a touch of derision in his voice. Is it possible that he found out about my meeting with Cal or was my feelings of guilt causing me to imagine it? I'd just gotten used to sleeping again with the help of a few strong pills I found in the bathroom cabinet we had brought from home; funny how I still thought of my house in San Francisco as home.

The memory of that night in Phipps house had now come back to haunt me. I couldn't get it out of my mind. Had I let hatred hijack my sense of justice? It was like my, play by the book, professionalism had left me. How could I have caused this terrible thing to happen? I was feeling real bad about what I'd done. I tried to think about Jake's call; I had never been to this Pike and Heron before. I'm not even sure what I hoped to gain by going there, but something compelled me to visit the place. Jake had given me directions but before setting out I changed the uniform and did my best to dress like a tourist, knowing not everyone is comfortable talking to a cop.

I found the big white rock Jake told me to look for and turned onto a dirt track. The track climbed steadily upward for about half a mile until I found myself on a rock-strewn hilltop. It was here I stopped the car and got out. The view from its summit was magnificent. From here I could see Pine Needles, the camp we first stopped at. I looked around, trees, trees and more trees, and midst them lying way below me I could see Pike Lake. It did not seem that far from Peace that could be seen to the left of it and I realised the road had led me in a wide circle. From here the lake looked beautiful, surrounded by a circle of grassland. On the shore of the lake was a picturesque thatched building. From the front of the building it certainly looked like an old English style pub that Jake had described but from above where I stood the place seemed more than that because the largest section of the building stretched out over the lake and for what purpose I couldn't fathom. The place seemed perfect for visitors to picnic and canoe on the lake, but it was now Saturday the weather was fine, yet the place was deserted. I got back in the car. The engine was still running but I slipped off the brake and let gravity coast me down the meandering dirt road to stop the car some hundred yards from the Inn I parked it on a grass verge where it was hidden from the Inn by trees. I got out and stretched my legs walking the last hundred yards to the Inn. As I reached the lake and took a deep breath, I understood why the place was deserted. The putrid smell tended to make me retch. I looked across the lake to where fir trees seemed to stop a hundred feet from the shore as if reluctant to come any closer to the foul smelling water. The pleasant grassland that I saw from the rim of the valley turned out to be thick and slimy algae. This was no place for a picnic and a notice board warning of *Toxic Algae* confirmed that fact. It was obvious the building was meant to replicate an English country pub with its thatched roof and traditional pub sign. The sign hung from a tall gallows-like prop and appeared to be freshly painted. It portrayed a Pike clinging to a Heron's leg by its teeth. The bird was trying to take flight and the artist had captured the terror in its eyes as it stared down at the Pike half out of the water. It crossed my mind that Gabriel Proctor could have painted it but he should have done more research on fish because I was certain Pike never grew to the enormous size he'd portrayed this one. I'm not sure how long I stood outside, mesmerized by the ghastly sign. Eventually a cold shiver stirred me out of my trance and I entered the Inn. It was like I'd stepped back in time but it was nothing like the cosy old pubs that I remembered on my visit to England, The chamber I found myself in was much larger than I imagined and more like a church hall than a cosy English pub bar. The floor was of rough sawn planks and the walls were of bare stone. The place was miserably dark due to the inadequate amount of windows which looked like they had never been cleaned. In an attempt to compensate for its dinginess, unlit candles were spaced out in little alcoves chiselled into the walls. Above me, misshapen wooden beams visibly supported the age old thatched roof. The most modern feature of the room was the double doors set in the wall opposite the entrance. These, I guessed would open onto the large extension I'd seen from the hilltop and I was intrigued to know of its purpose. I tried the doors but they were locked. I suddenly called to mind our first visit to Peace, the chanting and the trail of lights I saw from our holiday cabin at the top of the hill Was this their objective, the place they were heading? I tried the double doors again then heard someone fake a single cough. I turned and saw two elderly men sitting at a small corner bar. At the far end of the room. I could have sworn the room was deserted when I entered but maybe I just didn't notice them in the gloom. As I made my way toward them I glanced at the several old pictures adorning the walls: damp mildew stained paintings of men in stovepipe hats, knickerbockers and buckled shoes. Each painting contained several people attending a different trial and every picture depicted a different person pointing accusingly at a woman or a child. Maybe the place was built as a mock-up, a novelty to remind one of the first New England settlers. It certainly reminded me of Don Smith's ravings about witchcraft and more recently, of Phipps's leather bound book on the occult.

As I approached the two men at the bar I noticed another old-timer sat in the adjacent corner smoking a long stemmed pipe and reading what may have been a bible. I could see the two men at the bar were about my age. I guessed by their lack of concern, they had no idea who I was, and apparently cared less.

"Anyone serving," I asked, while peering into what looked like private living quarters behind the bar. It was in there I saw a pretty girl I guessed to be in her late teens. She was cleaning an old cast-iron range.

"That'll be me," said the most unshaven and scruffiest of the two men. This I assumed was Horace Rider; his accent was more suited to an English pub than the interior of this place. He made getting off his stool and opening the bar counter seem like a day's work as he mumbled,

"What'll it be, Mister?"

"Club and Seven-Up," I said, nodding friendly- like at the guy sat on the stool next to me. The two men looked at each other then the two of them suddenly erupted with laughter.

I gazed around the place again as I waited for them to either bust a rib or explain the gag.

"I got Buds, cider, or what's in the barrel!" said the unshaven barkeep after managing to control his humour.

"Oh right!" I said staring at the empty shelves behind the bar. "Well what's in the barrel?"

"Ain't quite sure, but we like it don't we Sean-boy." Maybe there was some hidden joke in his words because it seemed a signal for them both to shake with laughter again. When their laughter abated, the barkeep said, "You want to chance one from the barrel?"

I had to crane my neck to look over the bar before I could see the barrel he spoke of. "Why not, will you two have one with me?"

"That's right neighbourly of you, mister."

I unfolding my money and sensed their cordiality start to radiate, I turned to look at the old man in the corner and said "Give the gent in the corner whatever he wants."

"Old Elijah doesn't hear so well, but he likes a cider."

"Whatever."

"Just passing through, mister?" Sean asked as he pushed a pint glass of brown liquid toward me. "Most strangers do, mores the pity. Ain't that a fact Sean?" said the barman.

I knew there would be questions and I'd gotten quite used to the mysterious mistrust among the locals since we arrived in Peace, I therefore had my story ready. "No, matter of fact I'm staying at holiday cabin not too far from here. I heard about your lake and came out here to check on the fishing," I lied. "Mind you, I don't suppose there is much in the way of fish living in this lake of yours, looks pretty murky, not to mention the smell that seems to come from it."

"Ah well that'll be those pesky beavers slowing up the river," said the man I took to be Sean Finnegan. "Mind you, old Scissor Teeth don't seem to mind the smell, does he Horace?"

"Scissor teeth?" I questioned.

"Yeah old Peter Pike, as some likes to call him. Biggest damned pike you ever saw, been caught so many times but always chews through the line an gets away hence the name."

I guessed that I was now in the company of Sean Finnegan; when I set out that morning, my intention was to ask the old man some straight questions concerning Phipps's accidental demise. But realising he and the barkeep had no idea who I was, I decided it might be more productive to play the naïve tourist and see what information developed. "Yes I can't imagine much happening around here to start one's adrenalin flowing." I was hoping my observation might get the response that I came here for—it did. Horace went into another laughing tirade,

"That young Amos Carrier certainly had your adrenalin flowing the other night, Sean, ain't that right? Sean didn't look too amused at the barkeeps words.

"Oh why was that then?" I said, trying hard not to look too interested.

"There was a nasty accident just up the road from here. Old Sean here nearly bought it!"

"I keep telling you Horace, it was no bloody accident." Sean rasped, banging his fist on the bar.

"What happened," I asked, innocently.

"Some kid came out here on a joyride," Sean said angrily. "I suppose he thought that out here, there'd be no law around. Anyway, my mate and I were making our way home. We were almost to the top of the rise when this car comes over the hill like Satan himself was on the guy's tail. Now, as you'll know, if you came that way, the road ain't too wide and the first bend is a real hairpin. The kid lost it on the bend Cal and me made a dive for the verge. Next I hear a crash, when I looked up Cal is gone. The kid had hit a tree with Cal plastered to the front fender. Guess I was the lucky one. I took a look inside the car and saw the kid was still moving but I couldn't get the door open. One look at Cal crushed against the tree told me he was a goner. Best I could do was to get down to that filling station to a phone."

Horace jabbed a thumb at Sean while downing the last swig from his pewter jug, which prompted Sean to do the same. "Cal Phipps was Sean's drinking partner and one of my best customers."

"I reckon the kid didn't figure on meeting any wildlife out here. Sean here was lucky: the kid just missed him. I don't suppose the lad reckoned on meeting a deer on the road."

"Deer, my arse!" Sean snapped. "Last time anyone hit a deer on this road, Horace, You had your Prudence selling venison pies for weeks. If that kid hit a deer it'd be hanging butchered in your kitchen, or lying by the side of the road! I'm telling you, Horace, it weren't no animal forced that kid off the road."

"He's right!" The three turned to look at the old man, sat alone in the corner. "There's no deer, nor anything else living in this part of the forest; nothing natural anyway," said the old man."

"There! I told you Horace, didn't I? Deer got legs, and what I saw come out of those trees was not touching the ground and there ain't any birds that size around here."

"I thought you said the kid was just going too fast and couldn't make the bend?" I said.

Sean looked embarrassed as he explained, "Well, I wasn't going to mention it, seeing as no one believes me anyway, but just before the kid went into a skid, I swear I saw a dark shape hover in front of his windshield only for a moment then it was gone and in those last seconds the kids hands had left the wheel to cover his eyes."

Sean's story seemed to flatten the conversation so I thought I'd bring back a little humour to the dialogue, "This dark shape wasn't riding a broomstick was it?" They both looked at me like I'd lost my marbles. Even the old man in the corner was staring at me. Then Sean said, in a real serious tone,

"It wouldn't be the only strange thing that's happened around these parts." Then he turned to Horace,

"I reckon it had something to do with what Cal was telling us, you mark my words Horace."

I said "He was a good friend of yours was he, this guy, Cal Phipps?" Sean then gave Horace a knowing kind of look as he said,

"Not so much a friend but someone you sure didn't need for an enemy." Horace nodded in agreement.

"Bit of a tough nut eh?"

"Not so much tough, but we've lived here a long time, and we've seen things concerning Calvin Phipps that's not easily explained and I don't just mean his thieving." Sean saw the look of curiosity on my face. "Oh yes, that's what he was, a thief, him and Ben Alden, ever since they were kids. The last job got Cal put away, and he blamed Ben for that. Ben had seen the cops arrive but instead of warning Cal, Ben decided to save his own skin and made a run for it. Outcome was Cal Phipps went to prison. Within weeks of Cal being released Ben died, but from what no one knows."

"That is strange." I said pointing to their empty glasses, "Have another drink. I do like a good story."

"Well you'll like the one Cal told us the last time he was in here."

"Sean…" Horace snapped. Sean looked up to see Horace slowly shaking his head.

"It's okay Horace. What harm can it do now?" Horace thought about it and gave a please yourself shrug."

"After Ben died," Sean continued. "Cal had the new sheriff harassing him.

"New sheriff?"

"That's right, some guy from the west coast. San Francisco I think; a real greenhorn, so Cal reckoned. Anyway, this sheriff was sure that Cal was mixed up with some kind of black magic or witchcraft, and that he had somehow caused Bens death. He asked questions around the logging camp. Getting no answers, he eventually gave up. Then not long after that this sheriff's daughter gets hit by a joy rider: Same kid, Amos Carrier, not even old enough to own a driving licence."

"And you think this was Phipps way of getting back at this sheriff for hassling him, like he somehow willed this sheriff's daughter to be hit by the Kid?"

"Ain't for me to say, but after the way Ben bought it…"

"Sounds like it didn't pay to get on the wrong side of this Phipps character." I said, hoping for a reaction.

"That's just what I started to think!" said Sean. "It was like Cal was sticking pins in dolls or something. Anyway," Sean went on. "Not long after this the sheriff calls on Cal and offers Cal money to—and get this, put a spell on the kid that'll make him go blind." With that, Sean and Horace had another bout of hysterics. "I told Cal he should have brought him here and given him a few shots of Horace's special brew. That would do the trick"

"Ere, keep your voice down." Horace said while still laughing. I made a weak attempt to laugh along with them and tried to sound convincing but what they were telling me was not making me happy. Breaking into their merriment I said,

"So what happened?"

"Well—Cal told the cop he'd do it for a price. So, next thing the kid goes on trial over in Clear Water County. That's the closest Courthouse, at least one that's got a legal judge. Anyway the kid gets away with it, too young, see. It was just like the cop told Cal he would. Anyway, the cop ain't happy, so one night a little while after the trial this cop grabs Amos and turns up with him at Cal's place. That was when Cal did the spell thing on him."

"You mean he pretended to!" I said. With that, Sean gave Horace a look that I couldn't fathom but Sean's next words clarified its meaning.

"I saw the boy's mother this morning," he said. "I asked her how Amos was. She told me that the windshield on the car had shattered and lacerated his eyes."

"But I thought you said he took his hands off the wheel to shield his eyes? Besides, if he hit a tree the windshield would have shattered outward wouldn't it?"

"I suppose, but the doc told her he'd never see again so how else can you explain it?"

"Well!" I said, sounding intrigued. "If it was this Cal's curse that blinded the kid, sounds like his curse came back to bite him."

~~~~~~~~~

I'm not sure if spending any more time in the company of these two old sops would have furthered my investigation into the weird happenings in and around this now cursed town of Peace and the contents of Horace's barrel was starting to make me feel very queasy so I decided it was time to leave. As I drove back to the Grange my mind was a springboard of thoughts bouncing around in my head and none would settle on a sensible conclusion. I had no idea what was in Horace and Sean's barrel, but one thing was sure; it wasn't a barrel of laughs. My insides were doing somersaults. I pulled over at a secluded stretch of road, got out and heaved up in the undergrowth. As I turned back to the car a sudden rustling sound from close by caused me to snatch for my gun, which of course I'd left at the Grange. Then there followed a nerve tingling screech before a fox darted out from the undergrowth with some unfortunate furry creature hanging from its mouth, then in seconds it was gone. I felt the tightness in my chest relax, but I was still feeling ill and I wondered if, apart from feeling physically sick, I could be heading for a mental breakdown. So many strange things had filled my life since coming to Peace. I longed for a simple store or bank holdup; even a two-bit drug bust would do as long as it was normal. Sometimes I feel like any minute I'll wake up sweating, and Avril will be there sponging my brow and saying don't worry, Dad; it was all a nasty dream. All that was good about our move to Oregon had paled to insignificance; the house, the pay, none of it had any value without my little girl being here to share it with. Each day since we came here I found myself thinking more and more about Karen and wondering why I'd jumped into this present marriage so quick. I could only put it down to missing Lucy and Karen not being there when I needed someone. I pulled into my drive and as I opened the car door I heard the hall phone ringing. The day before news of Avril's demise I would have dashed up the veranda steps with key at the ready, but my stomach was growling and I was feeling depressed again. It was as much as I could do to just mount the veranda steps and find the keyhole in the front door. I reached the phone and as I picked it up I heard a click. I thought the caller had put their receiver down. But when I said hello, a voice answered. My suspicious mind caused me to think of the upstairs phone extension, I glanced upward to the landing and...did I see a moving shadow or was my imagination working overtime?

My attention went back to the receiver in my hand. "Hello, sorry about that, I thought someone had picked up the extension. Who is this?"

"It's Karen."

"Karen! Hell Karen, it's so good to hear your voice. Are you still in San Francisco? God, you sound so close. If ever I needed to hear a friendly voice…"

"Check it!"

"What!"

"Check the extension Spencer, please." I was intrigued, but complied. With new vigour I hurried up the stairs and peered into our bedroom, the bedside phone was in its cradle. Only Charlie's latest pet another cat sat beside it staring back at me. I hurried back down,

"It's clear Karen. There's no one else in the house. What's this all about?"

"I'm not sure yet but—how's things there?"

"You mean since Avril…"

"Spencer...are you still there—since Avril what?"

"Yes I'm sorry Karen you didn't know did you, I tried to phone you but I can never seem to get an outside line. She's gone, Karen. She was killed by some teenage joy-rider."

"Oh Jesus Spencer I'm so sorry. She was such a lovely girl."

"Yes, she was. I'm not exaggerating when I say there has been days since it happened, when I thought I'd go crazy."

"I can imagine. How are you holding up now?"

"They say that time heals but I'm not sure I'll live that long. There are things going on here…"

"Things, what things Spencer?"

"Yes weird things Karen; drugs back home I could handle, even the occasional shooter, but this…"

"That's why I phoned, Spencer. I have tried to phone you so many times before but some woman on your switchboard always comes up with some excuse not to put you through. For some reason she wasn't there today. It sounded like a young man that put me through. Where are you?"

"I'm at the Grange...It's the house I told you about that goes with the job...I'm not kidding Karen; this place is like something out of, *Gone with the Wind.* It's only about two miles west of the town...

"Spence...are you alright...you sound different."

"I'm talking too fast aren't I...yes it's something I do   when Avril gets mentioned, it stops me breaking down. It must have been Orville my young deputy that put you through that bitch Joy Harris must have been on a break..."

"Spencer, there are so many things I want to ask you and there are a couple of names I want you to mention to anyone in Peace that has any official standing. I want to know if you get a reaction. Listen Spencer, I don't want to say too much over the phone but I've been checking on a few things here. Some of it makes no sense and… do you remember the night you invited me to diner."

"Yes seems like a lifetime ago. Do you know why I asked you to dinner that night?"

"Yes you said you wanted me to meet Avril."

"Yes but I was also going to ask you to marry me...there I've said it. You never did tell me why you ran out that night."

"Oh Spencer—I was sick and not just too-much-wine sick, but real scary sick. I saw things in your house that couldn't possibly be there. My head started to spin and numbness in my fingers and toes started to creep into my limbs. Spence, I was so scared and Charlotte just stared at me. It was as if she knew what was happening to me. I know you would have thought I was crazy if I had tried to explain it...anyway the reason I phoned is because I think you're in danger. There are things happening here that..."

I heard a click and the line went dead, and my first thought was that Joy Harris had arrived back in the office. I tapped the phone cradle up and down, like they do in the old movies, got nothing. Why do they do that? Why did I do that? I've never seen a film where it did any good. Anyway I dialled the office and as I guessed Harris answered. I told her I'd been cut off and she said there must be a storm somewhere. "Oh sure," I said, sarcastically, "it's a big world and there's always a storm somewhere." Anyway, she insisted the line was down and she didn't know for how long. My head was spinning, partly from whatever was in Horace's barrel and partly from what Karen was trying to tell me. It was almost like she'd experienced some of the strange events that I'd been having since I arrived in Peace. I never got the names Karen was going to give me and I deliberated that as I put the phone back in its cradle. Then as I looked up into the hall mirror I froze. Stood in the open doorway behind me was Charlie, at least I assumed it was. Against the bright daylight of the open door behind her, she was a silhouette without a face. How long had she been there? Had she heard my conversation? I had no idea. Why she should put me on edge, I wasn't sure. I only knew that her silent pose gave me the creeps. Slowly she turned and closed the door.

"Hello Spencer," she said. You're home early, had a quiet day?" I waited, expecting her to mention the phone. She didn't.

"No quieter than usual. Had a bit of a headache, so I left early that's all. Oh and I finally got mayor Cloyce to give me a key that he said should fit the garage but it don't. I still can't get in there."

"Hmm, not been drinking have we." I thought I caught an inkling of a smile playing around her mouth and wondered if she could possibly know where I'd been. I've always had the feeling she knew my every move. She moved up close to me and kissed my cheek maybe she smelled my breath. "Some folk here, I'm told, brew their own ale. They say outsiders ought not to partake. It affects them differently." Now I was sure she knew where I'd been. I was also intrigued that her accent seemed to be changing. I could understand how she might have picked up a few words in the local dialect, but in the short time we were here she seemed to have picked up so much of the local inhabitants old English accent, and it seemed to be getting broader by the day.

"What do you mean by outsiders, and what's with the folk? That's not a word you use."

Her answer just came in the form of a pretentious smile, but feeling too ill to chase the subject; I climbed the stairs, fell on the bed and slept.

~~~~~~~~~

Karen decided to let Neil sleep as long as possible. She wanted him to be refreshed for his meeting. She woke him at 8:40pm and it didn't take long for Neil to notice the change in Karen's mood.

"What's wrong, Karen. Are you worried about this meeting?"

"No, it's just that...well you were Spencer's partner and I'm thinking you must have met his daughter, Avril."

"Yes I met her several times. She is such a witty and intelligent kid such a sense of hu..."

"She's dead Neil."

"What....How?"

"I phoned Spencer while you were asleep and for the first time I managed to speak to him. He told me Avril was run down by a young joy rider."

Neil put his hands up to his face and just shook his head. "Christ Karen this is like a nightmare how much more can go wrong."

"I don't know Neil. All we can do is try to deal with it as and when it happens."

There was still forty minutes until Roster was due to meet the mystery author of the note left on his desk. He and Karen had gone over the risk involved just getting to the meeting place. Rosters life had already been threatened twice that day and the possibility of this meeting being a trap was fully realised. At first the two of them planned for Roster to take a taxi and Karen to follow in her Ford, but they decided the front of Karen's apartment building may already be under surveillance and a taxi arriving outside could alert any would-be assassin that Roster could be about to leave the building. They decided on another plan. They took the lift down to the underground car park to Karen's car. They were half expecting trouble from the outset, so leaving nothing to chance they drew their weapons as the elevator slowed to a halt. The lift doors slid open to a cold and eerie quietness where even the slightest sound of a cooling engine echoed with amazing effect through the concrete expanse. The two D.I's nerves were on edge. They walked cautiously though the semi-darkness of the car park. The metallic echo of Karen's high heels annoyed Neil. He knew the sound would be a real giveaway to any assailant that could be laying in wait. A car door slammed somewhere on the far side of the building and Karen let out a small cry of pain as Roster reacted with an unintentional squeeze of her arm. He apologised as they neared Karen's Ford. Roster got in the back seat as planned and sank down out of sight. Karen slid behind the wheel, placing her gun on the seat beside her where she could quickly put a hand to it. Starting the engine, Karen flicked the headlights switch on and followed the exit arrows. She drove the big Ford at a snail's pace, while peering from side to side at the parked cars ahead of her. She was half expecting to see an unfriendly face staring back at her, or maybe hear an engine burst into life with the driver's intention of blocking her path; or even worse, spot a gun barrel too late. But whatever the eventuality she was ready to hit the brake and slam the car into reverse; any plan beyond that she'd not considered. Karen finally breathed a sigh of relief as she stopped at the bottom of the exit ramp and looked up to see the dark blue night sky. She could hear the sound of early evening traffic up on the street; as businessmen and women were making their way home from the office. Neil had the same view and as he peered through the gap between the front seats he voiced Karen's very thoughts,

"Better toe it Karen. If that bastard is up there on the street waiting for us to show, we don't want to give him time to wake up." Karen needed no further instruction. She waited for the shadow of a pedestrian to pass by at the top of the ramp then slammed the gas pedal down hard. The car's big six-cylinder engine lifted the ford up on its front springs like a cat making its deadly pounce. Karen prayed the sidewalk would remain deserted as the car roared up the ramp. Luckily she hit the road without collecting any pedestrians. She swerved right into a gap in the night traffic and ignored the blast of angry car horns from irate drivers. Then before tempers even had time to cool she threw the car into a left hand turn without signalling, causing an oncoming bus driver to stamp on his brake hard. Karen's driving manoeuvres sent Neil sprawling across the back seat from one direction to the other while hollering,

"Fucking hell Karen!"

"Sorry! Neil, it's the only way I know how to lose a tail. Didn't you see it? That black 4x4 pickup was parked opposite the ramp. Fortunately it was facing the wrong way."

"The problem is he's now seen your car even if he didn't have time to get the number." Neil sat up and peered out the back window to confirm Karen's driving had achieved her objective. It had, the street behind was empty.

Clouds accentuated the darkness of a new moon and spatters of rain started to dot the windscreen. Karen wasn't sure if this was a blessing or a hindrance. As they drove along Jefferson St, Neil's right hand shot past Karen's face,

"There it is, Karen" She looked down the side street and saw a neon blue sign depicting a snorting blue bull. "Maybe you should drive around Aquatic Park first, Karen, just to be sure." Neil said, being still concerned that they were possibly being followed.

Karen complied then pulled into the kerb about twenty feet from the neon sign.

"I think it best if I drop you here, Neil. I'll walk in five minutes after you; if the person or persons in that bar are the psychos who tried to run us down, we want them to think you're alone, right?"

"Right."

Chapter 13 Peace talks

Roster stepped out of the car and Karen watched him walk cautiously toward the Blue Bull. Opposite the bar were dark recessed shop fronts and Karen was concerned about how easy it would be for someone to be hiding in the shadows with a rifle. She watched Neil peer nervously over his shoulder and hesitate before passing each darkened doorway before reaching the bar entrance. Yellow light spilled across the sidewalk as Neil opened the door. As the light faded again she checked her watch and then the safety catch and magazine on her Beretta. She waited four minutes as agreed before stepping out of the car to make for the entrance. Karen was hoping to see the layout of the place before entering, but The Blue Bull's glass frontage had been blacked out to a height that made it impossible to view the interior layout. Having no other option she pushed the door open and was surprised to see so few people in the place. The interior was quite dark, maybe the reason it was chosen Karen thought. As she entered she heard the murmur of two voices directly to her left without turning her head she knew one voice was Neil's the other was female. At a swift glance Karen noted the two were sitting beneath the obscure window; this made sense she mused. Even if someone on the sidewalk was tall enough to peer over the obscure section of the window they would still not be able to see anyone sitting directly under it. Karen resisted the urge to get a good look in Neil's direction; instead she made straight for the bar while eyeing the rest of the clientele. She got as far as the jukebox where a scantily dressed, sixty-something woman was blocking the aisle. She was staring glassy-eyed into a jukebox window and swaying drunkenly to Julie London's Cry me a River. Karen sidestepped around her and made her way to the bar. She picked out a bar stool and sat facing the mirror at the back of the bar. If her time as a D.I had taught Karen anything, it was to take note of one's surroundings and possible danger areas. A middle-aged couple sat in a secluded booth directly behind her. Karen assessed they looked like regulars. They were eating chilli and crackers. The smell tickled Karen's taste buds, reminding her that a sandwich is not always enough. Two booths along from them were a couple of young white collar workers who were getting giggly. Karen guessed they had stayed too long for an after-work tipple. She saw none of these as a threat, but she kept an eye on them anyway via the mirror. At the far end of the bar an elderly man sat and appeared to be talking to his half empty glass, again no threat. The barkeep's free moments were absorbed by a game show taking place on the TV. That was the extent of the Blue Bull's clientele. The barkeeper turned toward Karen as she perched herself onto a high stool. She ordered a Bloody Mary and as she paid for her drink she was startled by the sound of the entrance door slamming. Her nervous reaction was to quickly feel the bulge of the Beretta concealed beneath her jacket. She turned to see a man standing just inside the entrance. He was tall and slim Karen estimated close to six foot. He wore dark glasses so that only by his head movements could Karen tell he was surveying the customers. He wore a baseball cap, tracksuit and trainers. His dark glasses made it hard to determine his age, although Karen guessed by his physique and posture to be only in his late twenties. His interest seemed to dwell in Neil's direction. Karen saw Neil slowly adjust his tie; another field practice of keeping a hand close to one's weapon without drawing attention to it. In this case Neil's shoulder holster. The newcomer turned back and started toward the bar, he got as far as the jukebox where the inebriated woman was now giving it her all to Dean Martin's Sway. As the newcomer tried to pass the inebriated woman she suddenly threw an arm around his neck in an attempt to make the stranger dance with her. It sickened Karen to watch the way he reacted. He grabbed the woman's arm, roughly pulled it from around his neck and viciously twisted her wrist. The woman arched her back in an attempt to relieve the pain. The newcomer grinned as woman's distorted features showed the agony he was causing her. He then covered the woman's face with his other hand and shoved her backwards while releasing her wrist. The woman crashed into the jukebox sending the stylist skidding across the disc. The whole clientele stared as the old woman slid to a sitting position on the floor where she sat sobbing and trying to rub her bruised back. Karen went to help the woman and as she barged past the assailant she hissed at him,

"You callous bastard!"

He grinned and responded with a light hearted, "Just not my kind of music." He then perched himself at the bar and ordered a beer. Karen helped the woman collect the items that had spilled from her handbag and used the moment to glance in Roster's direction; this time she got a good look at the woman with him. Just then Neil looked up, caught Karen's eye and signalled for her to join them.

"Karen, this is Gwen Cruickshank, the lady that left me the note. I've told her who you are." He then nodded toward the jukebox woman who was now hobbling toward the exit. "What was that all about?"

"Oh, just a nasty piece of work who likes to pick on the vulnerable," Karen said. She nodded an informal greeting at the woman sitting there, but Karen's cold stare left no doubt in the strangers mind as to her distrust. This woman's anonymous note and recent events had, for the last few days, put Karen's nerves on edge and for that reason Karen felt no cordiality toward her. She guessed Gwen to be around forty-five, very attractive and by the way Roster was gazing at her, she had already won him over. Her dress code was sombre yet expensive. She wore a tasteful dark grey two-piece suit over a black roll neck sweater accentuated by a delicate gold chain necklace. Karen had been expecting to meet an employee of the SFPDs forensic laboratories: the nerdy horn-rimmed glasses type, yet she'd have guessed this woman's occupation to be more like a secretary or headmistress of a private school. The woman did wear glasses, however, rimless and in Karen's estimate, expensive. Roster and the woman sat opposite each other at a small square table. The woman half stood to reach across and shake Karen's hand, but kept the left below the table. Karen reasoned that it could just be resting in her lap, but it could just as easily be holding a gun; either way it was not alleviating Karen's edginess. The woman had a glass of white wine in front of her while Neil had a beer and whisky chaser. Karen could see the woman also appeared nervous as she kept glancing toward the entrance as if expecting any minute for some gunman to burst in and start blasting away. As Gwen sat nervously spinning her wine glass Neil said,

"So, Gwen, you put a note on my desk, so why are we here? Is it to do with my visit to the forensic lab, I got a pretty cold reception from that bunch upstairs?"

"Yes. That's because you asked to see Vic Rowan. The reason I left the note by your phone is because I thought you were Spencer Corwin and that you came up to forensics to enquire about the memo I sent to his precinct."

"You sent Spencer the letter? So it didn't come from Vic Rowan—I don't get it?" said Neil."

"I can explain. I take it you're both acquainted with D.I Corwin otherwise you wouldn't know about the note?"

"Actually, it was me that gave Spencer the letter. If it wasn't for the fact that our C.D.I spilled her papers on the floor that it would not have reached him at all. It had been sitting in our Chiefs desk since it arrived at the precinct."

"I see, and Spencer Corwin asked you to deal with it?"

"Only because he didn't have the time, I just thought I'd do him a favour. I'd say Karen and I are his closest friends."

"Then I'll tell you what I came here to tell him, and maybe you can pass it on to Corwin, it really is more to do with him. I think maybe you should hear the whole story from the beginning."

Still, standing and observing the woman with a fixed stare, Karen slipped a hand inside her coat and gripped the handle of her Beretta before she spoke, with a surly,

"Okay, Gwen, but first would you mind putting your other hand where I can see it."

"Sorry?

"Are you carrying?"

"I don't know what…do you mean a gun? No I hate guns, but I can understand your mistrust. I know about your narrow escape today." this caused both D.I's to frown, but without asking how she knew they allowed Gwen to keep talking. "You see, since Neil walked into forensics and asked for Vic Rowan, he's been followed by a friend of mine. I had to be sure I wasn't going to walk into a trap tonight. Yes I know about the black pickup truck and I'm not altogether surprised. You'll understand why when you hear what I have to tell you, although I'm not sure you're going to believe me. I've had to question my own sanity over this business." Happy that both Gwen's hands now rested beside her drink, Karen pulled out a chair and sat down.

Leaning across the table Gwen spoke in little more than a whisper "My name is Gwyneth Cruikshank. Eighteen years ago I was a student in Cambridge College England I was still young enough to be naive and gullible. I fell for an American student who made me believe in his dreams and promises. To cut it short I became pregnant. We weren't married and he soon disappeared, I believe he came back here to the states. My parents helped me with my daughter, Gina, while I attained a physics degree and I went on to study pathology and biochemistry. I was eventually offered a position doing research with a prominent drug company here in the states."

"You were looking for the father?" Karen's response came as more of a statement than a question. Gwen smiled.

"Yes, I suppose. I was more than a little naive to think I'd find him and I never have. Anyway I got on well with the staff at Dex Herbatron..."

"You were researching weed killer?"

"So you've seen their products. Anyway Dex does more than just produce herbicides. The government also bankroll them to carry out genealogy experiments. They get through quite a few animals in their laboratories but that's something they like to keep confidential, Animal Rights and all that. Anyway, the job gave me a start and got me to the states where I wanted to be, although my passion was in pathology. Anyway I met and married my present husband John Cruickshank. John was, at the time, a police officer with the 7th precinct."

Roster put a mental plus sign to Gwen's credibility-scorecard, having taken note of her English accent.

"I won't go into technical jargon about amino acids, proteins or peptides," Gwen went on, "but our work was to test the properties of various plants and fungi ultimately to develop cures for ills and diseases. I liked working with plants and like I said it was a start that got me here to the states where I wanted to study. My qualifications were adequate enough for me to become a pathologist but I liked the work at Dex and because my daughter, Gina, wanted to follow in mum's footsteps I managed to get her a job there, as an assistant. This is something I've come to regret. My colleagues were a friendly bunch except for one, a man by the name of Aaron Yarn, a most unfriendly character. I've since discovered him to be a very dangerous man..." Gwen suddenly stopped talking and appeared to lapse into a trance. Neil and Karen stared at each other in wonder, until Karen reached over and gently grasped the woman's arm and murmured,

"Gwen!" the woman came out of her daze and carried on talking as if nothing had happened.

"Apart from his eyes and his piercing stare which most of the staff found unnerving, he was the most misanthropic character you could wish to…Oh I've already said that haven't I…"

"Ahem—Look—Gwen." Neil interrupted the woman because Karen had been throwing him glances that he took to mean, where is she going with this story. "I'm not sure that what you are telling us has any bearing on why we are here. You see, when I found that note asking me to come here, I expected to meet this Vic Rowan. Now you're telling us that you don't even work there?"

"But I do. I just wanted to give you a little background as to where this all started. I moved on from Dex when their government research contract came to an end, as did a few other chemists there. I wanted my daughter to leave with me. I could see she was becoming obsessed with this Aaron Yarn but she wouldn't leave Dex. She would scream and shout at me if I said anything derogatory regarding Yarn. So she stayed on at Dex while I joined the forensic team for the SFPD along with a couple of other close colleagues; one was Victor Rowan who is now deceased. He was the man found murdered at precinct 13."

"Vic Rowan was the guy in the cupboard—but how come…" Neil trailed off into silence.

"Yes, and I know your department tried to hush it up."

"You're right," said Karen, and I'm not condoning it but it's understandable, the media would have a field day; *mysterious murder committed under the noses of SFPD*. It would kind of make us look pretty stupid," said Karen.

Gwen's response was to nod in agreement. She then went on, "Anyway, the reason our friend Victor went to precinct 13 was to see a Chief Danvers. Victor was convinced the SFPD was being infiltrated by this secret cult and that Aaron Yarn was its leader. At that time I thought...

"Whoa, hold it there, lady." Neil suddenly interrupted Gwen while grinning at Karen. "Where did this secret cult come into the conversation? This is starting to sound like fantasy."

"I know," said Gwen "I told you, you may not believe what I had to tell you." Neil glanced at Karen expecting her to support his pessimism, but Karen wasn't smiling.

"Carry on, Gwen," Karen said. "I've seen things that have made me question my own sanity of late so I'm prepared to reserve judgment."

"Okay, well at the time my husband and I thought Victor was having psychological problems brought on by the death of his wife."

"Your husband also knew this Vic Rowan?"

"Yes, John and I liked to socialize and as I worked with Victor, he and his wife became good friends of ours; that is until, Victor's wife, took to her sickbed. She never recovered. It was about that time when Vic started to become paranoid and suspicious of everyone around him, Yarn in particular. I even heard him accuse Aaron Yarn of having something to do with his wife's illness. At the time, John and I could see no truth in his ramblings about cults or devil worship. We tried to talk him out of telling his story to Chief Danvers, but he was determined so we played along with him. To stop him making a fool of himself we suggested he did it anonymously by phone. We told him that if he was right he couldn't be sure who was a member of this cult and that it would be foolhardy to spill everything to Danvers, but he wouldn't listen. We don't even know if he got as far as Danvers office. It could be that he was followed and set upon in the building before he could get to Danvers, or maybe Danvers himself was mixed up with this cult and Vic was murdered after he spoke to him. All we know is he didn't come back. It was only then we believed there may have been some truth in his ramblings."

"I don't suppose you'd recall exactly what day he went to visit Precinct 13?"

"Yes, April 12th." the two D.Is looked at each other before Neil said,

"And you're sure of this because...?

"I'm sure because April 12th is my birthday." Neil glanced at Karen. He then delved into the inside pocket of his jacket and produced a folded sheet of paper; he handed it to Gwen, saying,

"This is the note that was left for Spencer Corwin. What is the date on that note Gwen?"

"June 4th. Yes, this is the note left with the desk sergeant at precinct 13 this is the reason you came asking to see Victor."

"Yes and according to the date on that paper Vic Rowan was already dead yet he's asking Spencer Corwin to come see him. How do you explain that," Neil said, looking smug.

"With that Gwen produced a pen. She quickly scribbled on the back of Neil's note and handed it back to him."

Neil stared at what Gwen had written then turned it over to see the name Vic Rowan was both written by the same hand. "You wrote the note to Spencer Corwin?

"Yes. I think I already said that. Victor died because I believe he was getting too close to these people. I wasn't about to make the same mistake by signing my own name on my note to Spencer Corwin. I wasn't sure how many people at your precinct would get to see it. I used Victor's name to stay anonymous and hopefully get the same result, which was to talk to D.I. Corwin. That's why I thought you were he when you walked into forensics and why I left another note under your phone."

"Why did you pick on Spencer Corwin to tell your story to?" said Karen. "It's not as if you knew him and you couldn't know if he was connected to this cult?"

"The first reason was because it was he that applied to see the autopsy report on a John Doe found outside Precinct 13. Of course there wasn't one because I don't believe he killed the person he hit. But I wanted him to describe the man because I suspected it was Yarn and I believe Yarn murdered Victor. The other reason I wanted to talk to D.I Corwin concerns his late wife."

"Lucy?" Karen and Neil almost said the name in unison.

"You knew her?"

"Yes," said Neil, "we both did. Spencer was really cut up when she died, but Spencer's not with the 13th precinct any longer, so whatever it is you want to discuss with him, you'll have to do it by phone."

"I see. Well as you are friends of his I don't suppose he will mind if I discuss it with you. Are you aware of what his wife, died of?"

"Yes an overdose of pain killers. She had a growth, a tumour on the brain." said Neil.

"That's what the death certificate reads. But her doctor is a college associate of mine, He was concerned about the speed at which Lucy's tumour progressed; he said it was far too rapid to be normal. I told him that if her husband would allow it, I would perform an autopsy which I did and found nothing."

"You found nothing suspicious?" said Karen.

"No, I found nothing. No swelling and no tumour. I found nothing that could physically cause her death. I took a blood sample and what I did find was a substance in her blood that should not have been there. I found trace elements from a species of fungi and other plant extracts that I recognised from my work at Dex."

Karen glanced at Neil and could see that, like her, he was making the connection. "What are you trying to tell us, Gwen?" Karen said. "Did Lucy die of natural causes or not?"

"I don't think so. I only know that what was in her blood should not have been there."

"Fungi you say?"

"Yes, among other substances, to give it its botanical name, Amanita muscaria, which you may know as magic mushroom."

"Sure I know about them," Neil said. "When I was a teen we used to get high on them. I've never known them it to kill anyone."

"Maybe not the way you ingested them, but Lucy Corwin was taking a concentrated version according to her stomach content. And there were other substances, which I could not identify. I believe it was either imbibed in liquid form or injected."

"So you are saying she was poisoned...that someone murdered her."

"No. Like you said, it was an overdose of painkillers that killed her, but if someone had been feeding her this hallucinogenic in a concentrated form I wouldn't like to guess the affects it might have on her mind."

"So this was the reason you came here," said Karen, "to tell Spence his wife was probably pushed into taking that overdose?"

"Yes and to maybe point him in the right direction to catch the man I believe did it. Do you think you could get this Spencer Corwin to come and see me?" Gwen said, glancing first at Neil, then at Karen.

"I'm sure he would if he wasn't about a thousand miles away," Karen answered.

"He's on holiday?"

"No, he's left San Francisco. He was offered another job in Oregon."

Gwen suddenly put a hand over her mouth and seemed lost for words. For some moments she just stared at Karen.

"What did I say?" said Karen, gazing from Neil to Gwen. "It's Oregon isn't it Gwen, it's something about Oregon."

"Yes."

"I knew it! Is Spencer Corwin in danger?" Gwen never answered but her expression was enough to worry Karen.

"Yes," said Neil. "Tell us what's behind all this business, Gwen, and what did you mean by needing help?"

"Okay, Well as I said, we thought Victor was becoming paranoid about everyone being a cult member, but we discovered he wasn't so very far from the truth. I believe there are people, cult members in the SFPD and when anyone gets close to learning of the cult's existence, they mysteriously disappear. Apart from coming here to tell Spencer Corwin about his wife's possible murder I was going to ask him to help me discover what has happened to..." Gwen couldn't finish her words, her eyes glazed over and her chin started to quiver before she delved into her purse to produce a handkerchief. Neil gave her a moment before asking,

"What has happened to who, Gwen?"

Gwen took a moment as if deciding how to express her next sentence. "Look—if I tell you what I know you can make of it what you will. In the state of Oregon there is a little known town called Peace." With that a quizzical expression passed between the two detectives and Gwen responded with "Yes, you're going to tell me this is where Corwin has gone."

Karen nodded. "Go on."

"Well this town—if you can call it a town—is miles from any major city. It's in the middle of timber country. This is where this secret cult began."

"Not so secret now," said Neil, grinning, Gwen responded by giving Neil a blank gaze until Karen frowned at Neil, saying,

"Carry on Gwen."

"Well, I believe keeping its secrecy is part of their problem," Gwen continued. "The cult is growing, and from what I've heard, not by recruitment alone. Pregnancy outside of marriage is rife and age doesn't matter even underage pregnancy is encouraged. I think Aaron Yarn is their Grand Master. He knows that like all religions including Satanists, the more followers he can entice the easier it is to convince its members that they are worshiping the only worthwhile deity."

"I'm not sure I follow," Neil said.

"Well If I told you there was an invisible alien from the planet Zop living in my garden shed you'd call for the men in white, and yet millions of people pray to a God they've never seen. It's the Emperors suit theory, the bigger the following the stronger the belief and the harder it becomes to discredit or dispute. I believe that apart from this Aaron's preaching, his cult is held together by fear. If he can maintain its secrecy long enough the cult will grow to a point where it cannot be stopped. Aaron is waging war on all beliefs but his own, and that is Satan. In his religion murder is not a sin. It is what his master expects of his disciples." Gwen paused and waited for a reaction while Neil and Karen absorbed her words. Karen was about to speak when Gwen continued with,

"You both visited the San Francisco General this morning didn't you?"

"How did you know that?"

"I told you, I have a friend who's been following you. Like I said I wanted to be sure you were not a cult member. You see some members of this cult are not confined to Peace. If they believe they are under threat of attack, by the FBI they will go to any lengths to protect themselves. I knew about your close call with the pickup truck this morning, my friend told me earlier today. Did you see the man that was hit, the man who was knocked into the road?"

"Yes we saw them carry him into the hospital."

"Well he was the one following you. He was watching your back as it were. Unfortunately no one was watching his. I visited him this afternoon in hospital. He's sure the driver of that truck tried to run you down and he wasn't fussy how many others he took with you. Luckily my friend will live, but he will spend some time in hospital, he has a broken hip." Both Karen and Neil continued to show their surprise with each revelation Gwen divulged. "This is what I meant when I said they will go to any lengths."

"I suppose you even know why Neil and I were at the San Francisco General today," said Karen.

Gwen smiled, "No there are limitations to what I know."

"Have you heard of a woman named Winifred Howe?" said Karen.

Gwen appeared surprised. "Yes; she was Chief DI in my husband's precinct until she retired. I not only know her, but a lot of what I've learnt about this secret cult has come from her. With Winnie working with my husband and me being part of the forensic department, our paths often crossed. She and I became friends. Win has a younger sister, named Agnes. Agnes left San Francisco recently to live in a little place close to Peace called Cranford. Why a young woman would want to bury herself in such a backwoods kind of place is a mystery to me. Win wouldn't say anymore about her sister than to say she had her reasons. Anyway Agnes has been sending information secretly to Winifred about the goings on in Peace. She is one brave lady. "Maybe you better tell us everything you know about this business Gwen then we'll pool what we know."

"Okay. My daughter, Gina was taken on as an improver; an apprentice if you like. That came about through my recommendation. Biggest mistake I ever made. Then Aaron joined the firm. He was just the type one could imagine being into demonology with his piercing eyes. Gina, however, was always hovering around him looking over his shoulder, watching his every experiment, test and trial. I tried my hardest to get her to stay away from him but it was no use, she wouldn't keep away. Yet if I, or any of the other scientists, came even close to him while he was working on something, he would throw a tantrum. If any of the others asked the girl to assist them she would find an excuse not to, yet Aaron only had to snap his fingers and she'd be there like an obedient dog. Most of the staff shared in any significant finds or breakthroughs and their notes were always accessible for management to examine, but not Aaron. Everything he worked on was secret. Only Gina was privileged to get close to his findings. He was falsifying results, hiding details of his work, refusing to divulge the full extent of his experiments. One of my old colleagues that stayed on at Dex told me that was the reason the management eventually got rid of him. They found a room in the building next to the Lab that was kept locked and no one could find a key for it. Eventually they got security to break the door down and what they found, apart from rows of glass aquariums, was equipment that suggested he'd been conducting genetic experiments and there are strict rules about getting into the realms of Frankenstein type experiments. Now like I said we did trials on several kinds of animals but never on fish so what Yarn was working on I've no idea but I'm guessing our Mr Yarn needed to finish whatever he'd started and maybe needed modern laboratory facilities to achieve his results. I think that is why he got a job with the police forensic department."

"So he was back working alongside you again?" said Neil.

"Yes he was, but not for long. After he left Dexter's, my daughter seemed to gradually start acting normal again, like she was getting him out of her system. That was until the day of your colleague's car accident. That was the last time I saw..." Gwen paused and became glassy eyed. Karen could see she was about to cry, she placed her hand on hers but as she was about to speak there came a loud commotion up at the bar. The barkeep started yelling at the young guy in the dark glasses before the guy used the same tactic he used on the woman earlier; he leaned across the bar, put a hand over the barkeep's face and shoved him backwards sending him crashing into the various bottles on the display shelf. The young man then got calmly off his stool and made for the exit. As he neared the door he stopped, turned and walked up to Karen's table. Neil's hand moved toward the inside of his coat but Karen raised her hand in a motion that stopped him drawing his gun. The young man stood for a moment staring at each of the three in turn before saying just three words,

"The lake awaits." Then he turned and strode out the door.

"Hell, Karen why did you stop me? We could have arrested the bastard for breaking up the bar. And what was all that about a lake? Gwen, do you know what he meant?"

"I have no..." Gwen's words were interrupted by the sound of a powerful engine starting right outside their window. Neil and Karen looked at each other and were struck by the same thought: 4x4. Neil quickly jumped up on his chair to peer out the window. He was just in time to see a big 4x4 pickup pull away from the kerb. When he sat back down, the women waited for Neil to speak but he seemed shaken and lost for words.

"Well!" said Karen, "was it the same truck?"

"I...I think...so."

"Hell! I'm starting to wish I'd let you shoot the bastard now, but I've a feeling we've not seen the last of him so you may still get a chance," Karen said staring at Neil who still appeared to look a little distant. "What's wrong Neil, are you feeling okay?"

"The rear window, it wasn't blacked out."

"So?"

"I saw Abigail," Neil said, snapping out of his stupor."

"Are you sure?"

"Positive, she looked straight at me. I was right not to trust her, Karen."

"Yes, it looks that way. I'm sorry Neil." With that Karen slipped her Beretta out of its holster and placed it on her lap." Neil looked quizzically at her. "If he comes through that door again, Neil, he goes out in a box."

It was Gwen that spoke next "Are you beginning to see how big a problem this is? I have no idea just how many are involved in this, but what really worries me is the history of these cults."

"Meaning what?" said Karen.

"Meaning suicide for one thing, in the last few weeks I have researched some dark religions and various past cults. History has seen quite a few of these fanatics like Aaron Yarn. Many of their followers have died in mass suicides, It's the greatest gift they can give to their God In Yarn's case, Satan. The leader orchestrates the ultimate sacrifice in the belief that Satan will grant him everlasting life. Some of these leaders have achieved their aim with no more than just their preaching. I believe Aaron has an even greater advantage and he's perfected it through his work as a chemist."

"You're talking about, drugs?"

"Yes, but not just the usual drugs but a more sophisticated adaption that reduces ones resistance to hypnotic suggestion. Can you imagine what chaos a psychopathic Satanist can create if he can command his followers to do whatever he wants without a second thought?"

"That doesn't bear thinking about," said Neil "I know little about these so called religious cults, but I did follow the Manson case. Did you know that he never killed anyone; his disciples carried out all the murders. The thought of that guy still leaves me cold. I can understand how one guy might be insane enough to do what they did, but how did Manson find so many with such murderous intent and then get them to follow his orders?"

"I suppose for any such organisation to flourish you first need a following with a certain amount of gullibility. Add to that drugs and participation, and the trap is sprung." Gwen answered.

"What do you mean by participation?" Karen queried.

"I mean once the disciples of people like Manson and Yarn can be induced to get their hands bloodied they're committed, there is no way out."

"But I'm curious about something," Neil said. "Why are you personally concerning yourself over this business? If you're right about all this, and there has been foul play concerning this guy, Aaron Yarn, why are you...?"

"It's Gina..."

"Your daughter, he's taken her hasn't he?" Karen said.

"Yes."

"I was afraid you were going to say that."

"Yes. I believe he's taken her to this town, Peace."

"You're sure?" said Karen.

"Well my husband was sure enough to accept a job there as a deputy with the intention of bringing her home. Winifred Howe has been getting messages from her sister Agnes about the terrible things she believed was taking place in Peace. She told us she was worried about Agnes. John's plan was to bring both Gina and Agnes back home with him, but it's been weeks since Winnie have heard from either of them."

With a sideways glance at Neil, Karen said, "When was the last time you had words with Winifred Howe?"

"Like I said, about two months ago, Win said Agnes had made contact with John, and the two of them were just waiting for the right opportunity to bring Gina home. Now you know why I needed help."

Karen glanced apprehensively at Neil who gave her a silent nod. "I'm sorry to be the one to tell you Gwen, but we believe Winifred Howe is dead." Gwen's jaw dropped and she appeared to be trying to say something but no sound was forthcoming. Karen continued,

"Your friend either jumped or was pushed in front of a train. That was the reason Neil and I was at the hospital this morning; to identify her body."

Gwen sat in silence for some time staring blankly at Karen, her eyes cloudy with tears. Neil caught the barkeeps attention and made a circular motion over the table indicating another round of drinks. The barkeep nodded his understanding and shortly arrived with a tray of refills. "Would you like something stronger Gwen?" Neil said. "This has been a shock for you."

Gwen declined Neil's offer saying, "Yes it has and I'm afraid it could mean Agnes and John's plan have been discovered. Now I don't know what to do. I don't even know if my husband is still alive."

"What is it with this place, sheriffs and deputies?" Neil said. Then to Karen, "It seems like they do have some kind of law in this town. I'm wondering if this was before they offered Spencer Corwin the sheriff's job."

"Maybe it's just a front to deter government interest in the place," said Gwen "They may figure that if a town is policing itself then it is unlikely to be flaunting federal law. Remember what happened to that religious cult in Waco, Texas?"

"But why Spencer, what made them pick him?" Karen said.

"I get the impression that this Spencer Corwin is more than just a colleague Detective Sykes," said Gwen. Karen felt herself blush; she looked at Neil who tried to look away but Karen caught his smile. Gwen decided to ease Karen's embarrassment by saying, "I'm not sure why some outside people are recruited although my husband and I had our suspicions. Before John was accepted for the job in Peace, he received a form which he had to fill out and post back. It was all to do with his finances. Is Spencer Corwin well off?"

"On a D.I's salary?" Karen said raising an eyebrow.

"Well does he own a house?"

"Yes a nice house. Why?"

"That was one of the questions on the form. What about relatives?"

"He recently married and he had a daughter but she died in a road accident, why, is there something else we should know."

"I'm not sure. I've told you all I know. Do you think you can help me?"

Neil answered with, "You must know, Gwen, that this is really a federal matter and that we have no jurisdiction to operate in another state, and let's face it Oregon isn't just over the California state line?"

"Yes of course, but I wasn't expecting you to become directly involved but if I had gone straight to the FBI they would have written me off as some delusionary crank. You, on the other hand, are respected police officers and are more likely to get the FBI to listen. That's why I chose to come to you. It needs the credibility of the SFPD to get them to listen."

~~~~~~~~

The first few minutes of the drive back to Karen's apartment block was in silence. Both D.I's were still trying to get their heads around Gwen's story. It was Neil who spoke first,

"What do you think Karen, do you believe any of that?"

"Every word."

"Really?"

"Yes, I've got good reason to. My only concern will be to convince Dugan."

"Dugan? Gwen thinks we are going to the FBI with this."

"Yes, but I can't go over Dugan's head. He would lynch me. I've got to go through the proper channels. I'm just hoping he'll believe what we've heard tonight. If so, I will stand a better chance of convincing the feds to take action against this Aaron Yarn and his cult."

~~~~~~~~

Karen pulled into the underground car park and found a space. "The problem with reporting this to Dugan is, assuming everything Gwen said is true, the more chance it has of reaching a member of this dammed cult."

"You keep saying I, Karen, like you intend to try dealing with this on your own. I thought we were in this together."

"We are, Neil, but you're forgetting there's an APB out on you plus this guy in the 4x4 is somewhere out there looking for you. I think it best if you keep a low profile, at least until we get them off your tail. I suggest you stay at my place for a day or two if you don't mind sleeping on the lounger. Meanwhile I'll see if I can get Dugan to run with what we got."

"Well thanks for caring, but aren't you forgetting the 4x4 guy has now seen you close up?"

"No I haven't and I will be watching my back."

"And what if Dugan don't buy all this devil worship business and refuses to involve the feds?"

"Then I'll go to the feds myself and try to convince them. I'll also try to get in touch with Spencer again, find out if he has any idea what's going on in his town. If he's unaware of anything, I can at least warn him by telling him what Gwen told us."

"And what if he's in trouble; what if he needs help?"

"Then I get to see a bit of Oregon."

"Not without me you don't."

"You'd come with me?"

"Spencer took me under his wing when I was just a green rookie, but he was always respectful and never made me feel inferior. He must be feeling bad enough after losing Avril and if you think he might also be in trouble then dammed sure I'll come."

Karen kissed his cheek. "Thanks, Neil, you're a true friend." They emerged from the car into the echoing expanse of the underground car park once more. This time they drew their weapons before cautiously making their way to the elevator. They reached and entered Karen's apartment without incident and both felt their tension dissipate. Karen engaged the door lock and safety chain.

"What did you mean, Karen, when you said you had good reason to believe Gwen's story." It was some moments before Karen answered,

"Make yourself at home Neil, I'll get you a drink and scramble up some eggs and toast then I'll explain." When Karen returned with a tray of food and two bottles of Budweiser Neil was sitting at the dining table by the window staring down at the city lights. Karen set the tray down and looked at Neil's solemn face. "Are you thinking about your wife, Neil?"

"Yes, you've never met Abigail, have you?"

"No, you say she was at Spencer's wedding, but I was in New Zealand about that time, something happened that caused me to think I might have been having some kind of mental break down. I needed to get away so I went abroad to visit family."

"But you're okay now?" Neil said with some concern.

"Yes."

"Good. Well I was going to say that Abigail is very attractive, I'd say beautiful. If you saw her you might wonder what she saw in me. I was smitten with her looks and never really got to know her before I agreed to marry her."

"You agreed? That sounds like she suggested it."

"Well—now you come to mention it, yes she did, but it wasn't long before she became dissatisfied with things the way they were."

"Like what?"

"Oh, everything I guess, mainly the house. She kept badgering me to sell up and move."

"But it's a lovely house, Neil. I've seen a photo."

"Yes, it was my parent's house. It's where I grew up. There is no way I would sell the house. And that's what I told her."

Karen was silent for a while before she said, "I've never spoken about this to anyone Neil, but you must now be feeling that your marriage is part of all these strange happenings."

"You can bet on it."

"Well if we are in this together I feel I should level with you, but if you repeat any of what I'm about to tell you and it gets back to Dugan, he will have me sectioned."

"Don't worry I know you're not crazy; no more than the rest of us anyway, and you're right; we're in this together so best that we don't have any secrets."

"Okay well do you remember when I left the force?"

"Sure, I remember, they said you were ill. We didn't know you'd gone abroad. The guy's all thought your illness must have been something pretty serious; you were gone a long time."

"I thought it was serious too, I believed I was losing my mind but now I'm fairly sure the problem was not in my head at all."

"Well Karen, I always thought you were one of the most rational D.I's in the department."

"Hmm, there was nothing rational about me at that time. Do you remember the day Spencer invited me to dinner?"

"I remember it took him a week to buck up the nerve to ask you." Neil said with a grin, "That was about the time you left wasn't it?"

"Yes, in fact I threw my hand in the very next day and the reason was because of what happened at Spencer's place."

"Are you saying Spencer stepped out of line—that he tried...?"

"If only it were that simple. No, you know Spencer better than that, Neil. He wanted me to meet his daughter, Avril. I had the impression he was going to pop the question that night and speaking to him on the phone today confirmed I was right."

"Spencer that sly bastard. And did he?"

"He never got the chance. Charlotte turned up and kind of invited herself to join us. And can you believe she brought her cat with her."

"You sound more than a bit peeved about it."

"You could say that, but it's more than that, I've never trusted that woman. I'd only met her once before; it was a few weeks before Lucy died. Charlotte and Spencer were wheeling Lucy through the park in her wheelchair. Oh I know it sounds trivial, maybe even bitchy, but as Spencer and Lucy were talking to me I noticed Charlotte staring at Spence behind his back, and if it's possible to interpret hate just by watching someone's eyes and body language, I saw it in Charlotte Potter that day."

"But then why would she marry him, and Spencer was always telling me what a terrific friend she was to Lucy."

"I know, I've heard him say that too, but Spencer's so trusting. Has it occurred to you that Lucy wasn't even sick before Charlie came on the scene? You heard what Gwen said about not finding the tumour that was supposed to have caused her death?"

"Yes but Charlie? I can't believe it; you're really laying it on, don't you think you're being paranoid?"

"Oh you think so? I've not finished telling you about that last night at Spencer's place."

"Okay. I'm listening."

"Right, so the four of us had dinner and I must say Spencer's not a bad cook. After dessert he put Avril to bed. He then decides to nip out to get some more wine leaving Charlie and I alone. I can tell you it was the most unpleasant silence I've ever experienced. Then to make matters worse I started to feel quite ill."

"Sounds like Spence is not such a good cook after all." Neil said, grinning.

"Oh, I don't think it was the food, at least not anything Spencer had done to it."

"Are you saying this Charlie could have laced the...whatever you were having?"

"She could have laced the wine. I remember when Charlie first arrived she went into the kitchen for a while and she brought the wine in already in glasses. Spencer was preparing the meal so I was left in the dining room with Charlie. Anyway, as I said, Spencer had put Avril to bed and left to get another bottle of wine leaving Charlie and I alone. God I've never felt so awkward. She just sat there staring at me while that bloody cat of hers kept rubbing itself around my legs and mewing loudly."

"Sounds like you had an unpleasant dinner date, especially if you have an aversion to cats."

"I don't, not normally, but like I said I started to feel quite ill and I had this strange numbness sensation in my feet. It was scary and like I said, Charlie kept staring at me, but now there was a smirk on her face like she knew what was happening to me. She had that same look on her face that day in the park when I saw her staring at Spence. I had to look away. I glanced down at the cat, the noise it was making was louder but the sound had changed. And Neil, this is the part that Dugan would have me sectioned for—the cat suddenly leapt onto the table and sat staring at me but it had now changed, its body was bigger and more...rat-like..."

"More what?"

"Rat-like, but it was still changing. Its face started to take on the appearance of a human...Neil it had a woman's face," Karen paused, expecting Neil to ridicule her bizarre account but instead he sat frowning so Karen continued, "This thing, this creature or whatever it was changed the sound it was making to one that seemed to reach right into my subconscious, a one word indelible message, *leave*. I've never been so scared in life, Neil. I got out of that house as fast as my numbed feet would take me and I didn't look back." Karen waited for Neil to make a comment but he just sat staring at Karen. She moved her head to the side but his eyes did not follow her and it was not until she waved a hand in front of his face that he came back from where ever Karen's narration had taken him. "Are you okay?" she said.

"Yes."

"At what point did you stop listening to me, because I clearly lost you somewhere along the way."

"Yes sorry." I think it was when you mentioned the word, Rat."

"Oh?"

"Yes, have you ever had a dream or in my case a nightmare that you have no memory of when you wake. Then one day you see something or hear something that suddenly reminds you of that dream."

"Yes I think I know what you mean."

"Well that just happened to me. I think I experience something similar to you, but I've always thought mine was a dream. It happened soon after Abby and I were married. I woke up—or dreamt that I woke up in the night—with this pain in my neck. Abigail's side of the bed was empty I was about to get out and go look for her. Then in the dark shadows of the room I noticed this even blacker shape like a huge rat just sitting facing me. At first I thought it was just a trick of the shadows and I still intended to get up. I remember swinging one leg out of bed, but as I did the shadow moved. Well that to me was the nightmare part, and I don't mind admitting, Karen, like a big kid I climbed under the covers and never came out until the morning when I didn't remember a thing. That is until just now when you mentioned seeing a rat. Suddenly it all came back to me, but not just the dream, because now I don't think it was a dream I remember the following day I was changing in the precinct locker room. I'd just taken my shirt off when Joe Bancroft, said hey Neil you enjoyed yourself last night, didn't you. That prompted me to go take a look in the mirror."

"And...?"

"I had what looked like bites all over my arms and back, but I still didn't remember the dream."

"So what did you put the marks down to?"

"I had no idea, still don't."

"Christ, Neil what the hell is going on. This whole thing is like a nightmare."

"Yes it is, but I think you were right not to mention it at the precinct. Dugan would definitely have had you put away. Is it possible that Abigail and Charlie Potter are mixed up with some kind of witch's coven?"

"No, of course not; what you and I have experienced must have all been in our heads. Remember what Gwyn was saying about those enhanced drugs. I'm now thinking I was subjected to something Charlie did to my food or my drink. Maybe your wife also has access to this substance."

"So you think Charlie is somehow tied up with this Aaron Yarn character and maybe this Peace cult?"

"Well it's starting to look that way, don't you agree? But if they are recruiting followers, then like Gwyn said, they would need gullible people to indoctrinate, I wouldn't put Spencer in that category, would you?"

"No I wouldn't," Neil agreed. "There has to be more to it. I mean, Christ! Even if this is one big conspiracy, who would go through the procedure of a marriage, and offer a guy a mountain of money and a house to take a post as sheriff. Christ! Any guy would take on the job for half the salary. This is too farfetched there has to be more to it."

Karen took some moments to think, before she said, the word "Funding!"

"What?"

"Funding—you remember we discussed the Waco siege with Gwyn, well how do you think a cult like that funds itself? David Koresh, their leader, had an arsenal of weapons not to mention buildings that housed his followers and they all had to be fed. Where did the money come from? Unless their leader, David Koresh was a millionaire he had to get his money from somewhere. I'm guessing it came from the cult members that he recruited. Now if this character, Aaron was working as some kind of chemist I hardly think he'd be rolling in the kind of money needed to fund anything like this. That setup at Mount Carmel must have cost a fortune."

"So what are you saying? Spencer didn't have a lot of money, so why would this Aaron cult want to indoctrinate him into their so called religion?"

"No you're right, he's not a rich man but like you, his parents left him a very nice house. I'm not sure they are interested in trying to enlist him; not as a believer anyway. I might be wrong, it could be that this Charlie Potter really did fall for him, but I rather think something more sinister is going on. I think it could be property they're after."

"Property, yes I see what you're getting at. So you think Abigail married me for..."

"Well who gets your house if anything happens to you?"

"I hadn't thought much about it. I haven't even made a will."

"It doesn't matter. Your wife will get it; she's next of kin now. Who gets Spencer's estate? If anything happens to Spencer now that his wife and daughter are gone Charlotte Potter gets everything! And if Winifred Howe's sister is her next of kin, then you can bet the cult has somehow got its hands on the deeds to Howe's place." Neil stared at Karen in disbelief for some time before he said,

"But if you're right, and this has been going on for who knows how long, you could be talking millions. You could also be talking about multiple murders."

"Well think about it, Win Howe, dead, her sister, probably dead and look who almost bought it today twice..."

"Me!"

"Right, and like I said you have a very nice house, Neil."

"Shit—what are we going to do, Karen?"

"First thing tomorrow we check out the Realty firm that's advertising Howe's place. If it confirms my theory, then we'll..."

Karen suddenly paused and stared at the door.

Neil turned in his chair to follow her line of sight. He was about to ask Karen what was wrong but she put a finger to her pursed lips as a shadow moved across the gap at the bottom of the door. Karen left her chair while silently mouthing instructions for Neil to move to where he couldn't be seen from the open door. She waited until he complied then grabbing her Beretta from its holster she moved quietly to the door and suddenly jerked the door open to the extent of its safety chain. She stood for some moments, shocked and transfixed by the sight of the woman that stood peering through the gap at her.

Chapter 14 The tunnel

I slept for no more than an hour or so but at least my head had cleared a little although my stomach was still complaining. Charlotte had gone out again, I've no idea where she spent so much time, and I never bothered to ask her, I think I'd stopped caring. Truth was, I had lost interest in her interests, like the song, we seemed like passing strangers. I decided to do a little patrolling in the car. I thought some fresh air might help. I was meant to be on duty but I didn't care, it was too hot to wear my uniform so in light summer clothes I walked the mile and a half into town. As I strolled slowly through the town's main street I looked at the little church where the medieval wooden stocks were prominently displayed. It was like looking at two opposing statements: God's house that suggested love and forgiveness and this ghastly contraption that was built specifically to punish. I found myself stood on the spot where Avril and I stepped out of the car to check out the stocks in front of the church. I knew it was stupid but it was like I needed to be where she and I were most recently together, I guess in some weird way I was hoping to feel her presence.

There were still a number of cats roaming the street and quite a few of the local inhabitants. It occurred to me that I had not seen any of the locals dressed in anything one might call modern or smart. Most of the men wore the old fashioned bib and brace type dungarees that made them all look like farmers and the few women that I saw, wore plain dresses much longer than the day's fashion. Although they all appeared to be going about their business, I had the feeling they were watching me. It was also the first time I noticed how many of them had a strange unsightliness about them. It brought to mind stories of remote settlements where, over many years excessive inbreeding had caused terrible disfigurements in its people. As I walked toward the stocks that Avril was so curious about, a young guy who looked like a tourist came out of the

General store with an arm full of provisions and accidentally bumped into me. He quickly apologized and headed across the street to a waiting car where a pretty girl sat in the passenger seat. Had I not been feeling so ill I might have politely confronted him and offered some assistance. I could see he was new to the town and I guessed he had probably been asking for directions, instead I carried on past the stocks and climbed the steps of the church. I pushed open the double doors just as Avril and I had that first day. My stomach felt like it was on fire as I walked slowly along the church's centre aisle. I climbed three steps onto the chancel where a large altar stood. I walked over to the lectern and laid a hand on its carving of a winged angel, closed my eyes and tried to will away the pain. I wanted only to feel the presence of my Avril. I stood there for some time then I heard the intermittent sound of a phone ringing. I could not determine where the sound was coming from, and then it stopped. I remembered the unfriendly priest that had spoken to us so sharply that day. I made my way to the base of the high pulpit and climbed the steps to where we saw him. I opened the waist high door and stepped inside. There was nothing there except a glass of water stood by the side of another lectern that overlooked the nave. I started tapping the wooden panels, searching for a hidden door but found nothing. I then made my way back to the chancel where I examined the rear wall. Again, I found no hidden door. I walked around staring at the floor and wondering if there could be a trap door but I found nothing. I leaned against the altar and stared out at the seating area, refusing to believe that any priest had the power to appear out of thin air. I stood with my hands resting on the edge of the altar: a huge oblong structure with its black lace table runner and ugly metal candelabra. I started to examine the ornate carvings around altar's edge when my fingers hit a projection, a button. Who can resist pressing a secret button? I pressed it and there was a faint humming noise before the altar started to move in an arc, like it was pivoted at one end. I was forced to move out of its way. The noise stopped along with the altar's movement and I stepped around to the front of the Altar and found myself staring down into a dark stairwell. I felt the urge to investigate; this could not have been the opening the mystery guy appeared from, of that I was sure. With a quick glance around the hall to make sure I was still alone, I started down the stairs while searching the walls for a light switch. I suppose I'd gone down about ten steps when I heard the droning sound start up again, fainter this time, suggesting its motor was above ground. I looked up and to my horror saw the opening above closing and the daylight fading. Panic caused me to start back up the steps before I realised I wouldn't make it, that I would be crushed before I was half way out. I felt beads of sweat multiplying on my forehead as the light faded. Fear started to shadow rational thinking. The meagre amount of light dimmed into complete darkness. Then as the drone stopped the stairwell suddenly became visible by a red glow of a low wattage lamp. I realised then that the altars resting place itself had activated the light switch and the tenth step activated the Altar's motor. I could now see the bottom of the stairs. I continued down, missing out the tenth step. On reaching the ground I found myself staring along what looked like a curved mine shaft with wooden props supporting its low roof. At the base of the altar steps a metal door was directly to my left but it was locked. I ventured forward for a few yards before coming to a wood panel door on my right. It opened but it was just a cupboard with towels, bedding and what looked like cotton nightgowns of the type worn in hospitals. I closed it and moved on to door number three, I opened it to find it was a huge food store or larder. High wooden racks filled the room and were filled with all manner of mostly tinned food. I closed the door and moved on. The next opening had no door but was a chamber full of more roof props. The next room I came to was just a cluttered broom or maintenance cupboard. It held buckets, mops, a stepladder, a wheel chair and a pair of wooden crutches. I moved on again following the bend and ignoring narrower tunnels that may have got me lost. As it was I'd already lost my bearings and had no idea which direction was north or south. I tried another door, it opened into what appeared to be a cloakroom and every clothes peg held an identical black serge garment. There were dozens of them. I took one off its peg and examined it. As far as I could tell it was a monk's habit complete with cowl. I returned it to the peg and left. It was the fifth door that I found most interesting because before I attempted to open it I heard what sounded like a female voice inside. I turned the handle gingerly but it was locked. Then I heard a man's voice and what sounded like the rattle of keys coming from farther around the bend in the passage. Without another word I quickly released the handle and retreated as far as the broom cupboard. I waited inside with the door almost closed. The footsteps grew louder, until I recognised the voice of the man that had annoyed me so much on my first visit, but I didn't hear or see the face of the other person. They stopped and as the man unlocked the same door I'd tried to open, I heard some of his words,

"He thinks Rockway will be gone soon. Well he better be right, the Miami family don't take kindly to having clients renege on an agreement."

Then as they opened the door I heard what sounded like a bunch of angry female voices before the door closed and all went quiet. As it turned out, the altar mechanism was the least of my worries. Treading on the tenth stair from the top tripped a switch automatically and with great relief I climbed out of there. Once out, I pressed the first button I'd found on the altar and watched it traverse back into place. As I drove back to the Grange I now had even more to dwell on. The Miami family; were they talking about the Mafia, and I desperately wanted to know what those other rooms and tunnels contained but the shooting pains in my stomach was giving me more concern. What was the story with these women and were they linked to the ones we saw in the woods on the day we first arrived? And the word Rockway was not unfamiliar, but where had I heard it. I toyed with the idea of calling on our lecherous Mayor, Mr Cloyce, but not until I'd taken something to ease these stomach pains and maybe had a little sleep.

~~~~~~~~~~

I got a surprise as I reached the Grange's circular driveway. The car that I'd already seen in Peace that day was parked behind my cruiser and the guy who bumped into me outside the general store less than an hour ago was standing on the porch. Before I mounted the porch I noticed the same pretty girl sitting in the passenger seat of their car. The guy gave a friendly,

"Hi there," I nodded, while putting on the most unfriendly face one could manage, nasty wasn't normally part of my nature; although my nature had taken a turn since losing Avril. The guy was smiling. I presumed he was ready to give me the big sell, and that was something my burning gut just wasn't in the mood for. "I'm glad I caught you I've been ringing your bell for a while. I was just about to give up."

"Maybe you should have, because whatever it is you're selling, mister, I've either got one, or don't want one."

"No prob, I ain't got one to sell."

The guy was still smiling and I got the notion he was trying to use humour on me and I wasn't in the mood for that either. I brushed past him and inserted my key in the front door and as I did I got the feeling the guy was closely studying me. "So if you're not here to sell me a bible or a vacuum cleaner what can I do for you?" I was watching the young girl, nice legs I thought as she swung them out of the car. She then stood watching me.

"I'd just like to ask a few questions?" That was my line, or used to be, back in San Francisco. "Who are you?" I said, "You sound like a cop, but I know that's not possible because my deputies and I are the only law in these parts."

"Gee mister, would you say that again, I'm a sucker for a good western."

"If you're joshing with me, mister, I'm not in the mood. I've asked nicely, now what the fuck do you want?" The guy was still grinning and the threat I tried to display was obviously not scaring him. He held out his hand.

"Jimmy Gardner, and you're wrong; I am a cop." He said flipping open a wallet with the other hand to display his I.D. "I'm on a kind of busman's holiday; this is my girlfriend, Jenny Blake." He said as he turned to smile at her. Curiosity eased my temper and I finally shook his hand as he said, "I'm sorry to bother you but you are the local sheriff aren't you?"

"Yes."

"Well I can assure you my reason for bothering you is important."

"Well can it wait? I've had a rough day and I need to get some sleep."

"Sure, Jenny and I are staying at Pine Needles Camp it's at the crest of the valley. We can come back tomorrow, no sweat. Just one question then we'll leave you to get your head down: have you ever been to Massachusetts."

"No never." As I said it he turned to look at his girl friend and I watched her slowly shake her head.

"Hey, what is this?" I said, feeling I was being setup for I don't know what.

"Forget it; we'll put you in the picture tomorrow. You get some sleep."

"Yeah right, sorry I was a bit sharp. The name's Spencer Corwii I've stayed at the Pine Needles Camp myself. It's okay and I'n told the fishing's good. I hope you both have a nice stay."

I was relieved to finally get inside the house and close the door on the world. I mixed myself a strong glass of liver salts and went straight to bed. I thought a couple of hours would straighten me out if I can only blank out my curious discovery in the church and the strange visit from this Jimmy Gardner and his girlfriend. I needn't have worried; I was asleep almost before getting horizontal. I guess all the sleepless nights had taken their toll because when I finally awoke it was 7am. I'd slept right round. I'd not heard Charlie come to bed or even get up. I wasn't even sure she had been home, but if she had I never heard her leave the house that morning, anyway, at least the pains in my stomach were gone. I got dressed and before I could fix breakfast the doorbell rang. I opened the door to the grinning face of Jimmy Gardner who introduced me to his girlfriend Jenny Blake.

"Christ you don't waste time do you?" I said, shaking Jenny's hand.

"Thou shalt not taketh the Lord's name in vain."

"Shit! You *are* selling bibles?"

"No, it's just a habit when I hear a profanity. My old man was a preacher and he did a fair share of preaching to me when I was a kid. Sorry if we're a bit early. I didn't get much sleep, what with the party going on in the town last night. Plus we got a bunch of kids getting ready to pack up in the next cabin to us. Their father started his car long before they had finished packing. Most inconsiderate, some people. Anyway, like I said, our reason for being here is important so I thought we might as well make an early start and catch you before you left for your office."

I led the way through to the Kitchen. "We can talk in here while I get some coffee on." I pointed to the chairs at the kitchen table, elves down while I fixed coffee. You mentioned a

Peace I suppose. You heard it Jen didn't you?" Jimmy

ard something," said Jenny. "I'm not sure I'd call it a party.
n it didn't exactly sound like revellers. More like mourners."
as suddenly reminded of our first nights stay in Pine Needle
amp; the chanting and the moving lanterns. As the couple sat
down at the table Jenny said,

"Can I ask a personal question, Mr Corwin?"

I felt apprehensive about what she was about to ask, but I just answered, "Sure, go ahead,"

"It's just that I noticed an urn on the telephone table as we came in. It has an inlay with a young girl's photo set in it..."

I was pouring coffee with my back to the couple, for this I was grateful, otherwise I might have bawled like a baby at having to tell these people how my little girl had died. I interrupted Jenny. "Yes, she was my daughter. Her name was Avril and she was run down recently by a hit and run driver."

"Oh—I am sorry," said Jenny with sincerity in her voice.

"Gee mister, I can't think of anything worse," said Jimmy.

"Yes and it still pains me. So I'd be grateful if you just ask your questions."

"Sure, I understand. Well like I said, I am a cop, to be exact, a D.I from Massachusetts. About eighteen months ago a sickening murder took place in a small town there called Witchville."

Suddenly bells started to ring in my head. "The Bookworm psycho," I said "Yes! I read about it, a pretty sick murder case as I remember; something to do with a library."

"That's right and that library is where Jenny here, was working at the time. The victim was her friend and colleague. The creep that we believe murdered her disappeared without a trace and we believe he may be here."

"Here in Peace? I doubt that. Do you know what the motive was?"

"That's what everyone was asking and drawing a blank, my colleagues thought it was just the opportune act of a psychotic killer but Jenny and I believe it was part of a satanic ritual and the reason he chose this woman was something to do with either her name or a book she'd written. We also think this guy is part of a cult that has its foundation here in Peace. The local boys were baffled; they gave up after a while and landed me with the case. With Jenny's help we found a possible link to the murder here in Oregon. As you know the police can't cross borders, and let's face it this place is several states away from Massachusetts. I tried phoning the police in Portland but when I mentioned Peace the guy I spoke to said he'd never heard of it. How could he not have heard of it? Anyway I drew a blank. As a result the case went cold, but one good thing came out of it for me, and that was Jenny and I getting together."

I still didn't know what this guy was after or what his business had to do with me, so I said,

"Good. I'm very happy for the both of you, but I still don't know how I can help you."

"We think the murder in Witchville has some connection to Peace or its residents. Jenny and I took our holiday together and because we both have a desire to see this evil bastard caught. We decided to spend it here on the off chance of finding someone who might take us serious. Jenny, maybe you can put Spencer in the picture from the beginning."

Jenny took a sip of her coffee, sat back in her seat and gave me the story of her colleague's murder just as she remembered it. When she finished I said to her,

"So you've seen the guy you're looking for. Is that why you were scrutinizing me out on the porch?"

"Yes it was,"

"Jenny's been scrutinizing every man she's seen ever since that guy came into her library, more so since we got here, I asked her to. So far she's not seen anyone that faintly resembles him. Of course the beard he had at the time could have been part of a disguise."

"Yes, but I won't forget his eyes."

"Okay but tell me if I'm missing something. Apart from this, Rasputin guy wanting to read a book and looking a bit scary, as you put it Jenny; you really have no proof that this guy actually did the deed. No fingerprints, nothing. You say the guy left the library by climbing through a roof skylight, yet he was on cru..." I paused as something I'd seen yesterday suddenly came to mind.

"What?" Jimmy said. "Have you seen someone fitting that profile?"

"No, I haven't," I said, but maybe I didn't sound convincing because Jimmy was looking slant-eyed at me. Then he surprised me with,

"Did you know I followed you yesterday?"

"What?"

"When I bumped into you outside the general store yesterday, the guy at the counter must have seen it. I'd just been asking him where I could find the sheriff. After I got back in the car he came across the road and pointed you out to me and by then you had reached the church and were just going inside. I waited knowing you would have to come back the same way, but you were in there a long time. I asked Jenny to stay in the car while I caught up with you. But when I got to the church it was empty there was no one there, Can you explain that?"

Jimmy had started to sound more and more like a cop probing a suspect. I'm not sure I liked it, but it kind of made me miss my old job and as much as I disliked the feeling that I was being interrogated in my own home, I took a liking to this Jimmy Gardner. He was a real crime fighter, a cop with a conscience. I felt I could trust him and I was about to tell him I'd help, but I heard Charlie's car pull up outside. I wasn't sure why, but I didn't want her to know why Jimmy and Jenny were there. I quickly told Jimmy there were things I wanted to discuss with him and arranged to meet them at their cabin later that day. I quickly asked them to say nothing about their reason for being there to Charlie, that's when she opened the front door. Charlie stood there staring with deep suspicion at the young couple.

"Hi Charlotte I wanted you to meet Jimmy and Jenny. Jimmy is the son of my old police instructor at the academy. They're staying at Pine Needle Lodge and decided to look me up. That was nice of them wasn't it? Unfortunately they can't stay, they're meeting friends up at the camp." Jimmy fell in line beautifully with,

"Yes, that's right they're arranging a barbeque but it was nice seeing you again Uncle Spence, we'll have to catch up again." I still wasn't sure Charlie was taken in by our little charade but I thought Jimmy was a natural, especially with his Uncle Spence line.

Chapter 15 Deja voo

"Karen Sykes?"

The question awoke Karen to the realisation that she hadn't spoken for some moments even to ask the woman at the door what she wanted. The moment Karen snatched open the door to the length of the chain, confusion and an unsettling feeling of de-ja-vu had struck Karen speechless. It almost caused her to drop the gun she held behind her back but she eventually found her voice with a simple,

"Yes?"

"My name is Abigail Roster; I believe you know my husband, Neil. I've come to ask if you've seen him recently."

"No sorry, I haven't." The woman's eyes narrowed in a manner that suggested Karen was lying.

"Are you sure he's not here, I thought I heard voices before you opened the door!"

"Yes it was the radio; I turned it off because I saw a shadow under the door and I don't like being called a liar." The woman never apologised, on the contrary, her posture together with the sneer on her face almost spelled out the words, *who gives a shit*, but instead she said,

"Well can I come in? There are questions concerning his disappearance I'd like to discuss with you."

"No! I'm sorry, it's not convenient and besides, there's nothing I can add," said Karen moving her head to one side to get a better view of the corridor. She could see as far as the elevator recess in the opposite wall. At first glance she was sure the corridor was empty but then a movement caught her eye. A man-sized trainer with the unmistakable Nike logo suddenly drew back out of view. The shoe suddenly drew back into the recess and Karen knew that at that distance the man could hear every word said.

"Are you saying you won't help me find my husband?"

"You got it in one, sister. Now if you'll excuse me I'm kind of busy."

The woman started to protest but Karen had seen the man's hand appear from behind the wall and in it she recognised a police issue revolver. Without hesitation she slammed the door in the woman's face and backed away from the door while watching the shadow fade from under the door, but at the same time she brought her gun from behind her to level it at the door. All the time Neil had been watching. He now grabbed his gun and moved up beside Karen as she whispered, "The guy from the Blue Bull was out there Neil, I saw his gun." The two stood there in silence for almost a minute staring at the light under the door, waiting for that warning shadow to appear. It didn't, Neil was the first to relax. He let out a sigh of relief and started to slip his gun back in his holster. Karen also lowered her gun. It was then that the blast came. The door lock shot across the room leaving a gaping hole in the door where the lock had been. The door swung open but only to the length of the chain. Karen realised the intruder was trying to push the door open not realising the safety chain was still secure. While Neil struggled to remove his gun again, Karen raised hers and fired at the centre of the door. She figured this would stand the best chance of hitting the intruder. She fired one round and the resounding scream from the corridor proved her right. Seconds later Neil had his weapon levelled. He quickly fired two more rounds through the door, this, however was met with silence and the two DI's stood fixed to the spot for some moments wondering if there was now a body lying in the corridor. The room was cloaked in blue smoke and the acrid smell from burnt cordite bit their throats. Neil inched slowly and cautiously up to the door and standing to the hinged side of the door reached across and unlatched the chain. Karen followed him into the passage. Both were surprised to find it deserted. The passage wall opposite the door was bespattered with blood proving that the scream they heard was genuine. Traces of blood also led to the elevator but they were satisfied the intruders were gone. Not one resident had opened their apartment doors to question the gunfire, but they guessed someone would probably have phoned the police.

"You better get out of here Neil." Karen said. "Cops will be all over this place in about five minutes. And until we can be sure that bastard won't be coming back with your so-called wife. I think it's best that you remain missing. There's a nice little eatery on the corner of twenty-fifth and Maple; called Lenny's. He's a friend. Get yourself a pizza and tell Lenny you're waiting for a phone call from Karen. I'll ring you when it's safe to come back. Oh just a second," Karen dashed back into the apartment and came back with a notebook in her hand. "Tomorrow I'd like you to check out this realty firm, Neil. I took down the name and number from the for-sale board on Winifred Howe's house." Karen tore the top page from the book and Neil glanced at it before slipping it in his top pocket.

"Danny Raug Realty. That's a new one on me, Karen?"

"Me too, that's why I'd like you to check it out." They heard the distant sound of police sirens prompting Karen to say,

"You better get going Neil. I'll ring Lenny's when it's clear and you can sleep on the couch tonight. I think I'll be a while explaining this to Dugan in the morning."

"Okay Karen but don't try dealing with this on your own. Don't forget Spencer was my friend and partner too and if he's in trouble I want to be part of any help he needs."

"Don't worry Neil, I got a feeling Spencer's going to need us both."

"There's one other thing, Karen. Before you tell this Dugan everything we know. Sound him out; remember what Gwen said. These bastards seem to be everywhere."

To Karen's surprise DCI Dugan appeared on the scene soon after two uniformed officers arrived from the nearest precinct. He pulled rank by showing them his I.D and told them Karen was one of his officers from precinct thirteen and they left.

"Hell Sykes, what the hell happened here?" Dugan gazed open mouthed from the blood spattered passage wall to Karen's shattered door. Several neighbours now lined the corridor, each colouring their individual version of the gunfight, which of course none of them had seen. "Have you been waging your own war up here?"

"It's a long story sir, and one that you might find hard to swallow. As you can see the bastard shot my lock out. That's when I opened fire from the inside."

"Well you didn't pull any punches Sykes, three shots through the door and by the amount of blood out here you really meant business. I think you better stick at your desk tomorrow and write out a detailed report."

"I'm sorry chief but what I've got to tell can't wait for you to get around to reading a report. I believe this matter needs federal intervention and that means someone with your seniority needs to get FBI involved as soon as possible." Dugan stared at her for some moments before he said,

"Are you serious, Sykes?"

"Yes Sir. This matter goes beyond this State. I think it would be better if I came into your office in the morning and told you what I've learnt since you and I were at the Rowan Drive house."

"Well it had better be pretty serious if you want me to involve the FBI, because so far a couple of young shooters trying to break into a cops apartment is just going to sound like a local drug related payback."

"No, I can assure you, sir, it's a lot more than that."

"Really, does it concern Roster? Have you heard from him? If you know where he is you better tell me, Sykes. His wife has been phoning me again, she's worried sick about him."

"I can understand that, but I can't tell you because I don't know. I'm feeling shook up, at the moment, sir, and I'd like to get some rest, you do understand?"

"Of course; you've had one hell of a fright. If you like I'll put a man on your door tonight in case those two come back."

"That won't be necessary sir. I won't be sleeping here tonight."

"I see—okay I'll leave you to it." Dugan got as far as the lift before he turned and said, "By the way, where did you go when you left me at Win's house?"

"San Francisco General, and I'm sorry to be the one to tell you, but it was your friend Winifred Howe that died under that train."

Dugan's head dropped and he stared at his feet for a moment before saying "Oh well, fill me in tomorrow." then he stepped into the elevator.

Neil Roster was just finishing his coffee when Lenny, the owner, tapped him on the shoulder,

"Is your name Roster?" Neil nodded. "Karen phoned to say the coast is clear, whatever that means."

"Thanks Lenny, great pizza by the way."

When Neil got back to Karen's apartment he found Karen's door ajar. This didn't surprise him knowing the lock was shot out but he *was* surprised to find the safety chain off. He knocked and entered to find Karen curled up on the settee with a blanket around her and looking disturbed.

"Karen, are you alright?" Neil said as he attached the safety latch.

"No I'm not. I'm frightened Neil."

"Hey, the way you handled yourself an hour ago, I wouldn't think anything could frighten you."

"Normally nothing does, but when things happen that I can't explain it does frighten me."

"You mean like your experience at Spencer's house?"

"Yes and again tonight when I opened the door to your wife."

"Abigail? Why what did she say?"

"It isn't anything she said, Neil. Remember what I told you about that night at Spencer's? When Spencer had gone to get wine I said the cat had taken on a human face?"

"Yes but I thought we put that down to Charlotte putting something in the food or your drink."

"And I was ready to accept that, but when I opened the door a while ago and saw your wife, it was the same face. It was Abigail. How is that possible when I had never seen her before? How could it have been just something I'd eaten or drank?" Neil thought Karen was about to cry as she said, "Am I going Mad?"

Neil sat down and put an arm around her. "Karen, I'm as confused as you as to what this is all about, but the one thing I'm positive about is that you are as sane as anyone I know, and we will sort this thing out together. Now let's get that door barricaded. If you got that blanket out for me, then I'd like to get some sleep."

Together they barricaded the door with heavy furniture. "I'm pretty sure they won't try again tonight, Neil."

"What makes you so sure?"

"Because if our 4x4 friend is still alive, he'll be laid up somewhere licking his wounds, and I told Dugan I wouldn't be staying here tonight."

"Dugan?"

"Yes, you were right Neil, he's one of them."

"Shit! How do you know?"

"Well for one thing he arrived here almost as fast as the uniformed guys from Precinct 7. Assuming someone phoned about the gun shots from this building, why pass the call on to the other side of town. And if the controller did pass the call on to pre 13 why was Dugan still at his desk at this time of night? No, I'm guessing your wife called him."

"You're right C.D.I's never work later than they have to."

"Right and remember you said to sound him out? Well I didn't have to; he blew it all by himself when he said, *"I'll put a man on your door, in case those two come back"*. "I never even told him there were two intruders."

"Christ. What do we do now?"

"He expects me to go in tomorrow and give him a full report on what we know. Well that's out. If I go in tomorrow and tell him what we've learnt he'll arrange to have me erased as soon as I leave the building, just like they've tried with you. No, tomorrow I'd like you to check out that realty firm. It's the company that selling The Winifred Howe place Neil, so be careful. I'm going to visit the Federal building. I don't know if I'll get them to listen but I've got to try. Then I suggest we meet up at Lenny's, let's say 1.30 and we'll compare notes. Just try not to get run down by that Chevy."

~~~~~~~~~

Apart from her practice time on the target range it had been a long time since Karen had fired her gun in public. The experience had unnerved her. That and the realisation that Dugan was part of this conspiracy made it hard for her to sleep. She lay awake long into night examining and cross-examining everything that had happened that day. She ran through her mind everyone she knew in her precinct trying to remember any details that could connect them to this strange and frightening cult. She also thought about the day ahead and before she finally dropped off to sleep she was clear in her mind; not only of the story she was going to put to the Feds, but also what her best opening line would be. Confident she could convince them to take action; she finally dropped off to sleep. The next day things didn't appear so clear cut; her confidence had somehow waned with the morning light but her schedule was set and she would not let negative thoughts deter her. Karen left the apartment that morning while Neil was still asleep. She decided that his stressful last few days would not make him a very efficient partner, so she left him to recharge his battery as it were.

Most people that had lived in and around San Francisco was familiar with the FBI building in Turk Street. Karen, being no exception drove as close as she could to its local. However, the nearest car park to the federal building still left her some distance to walk, which made her nervous. Glancing behind her caused a few disapproving stares from people she bumped into. She realised she was becoming almost paranoid about sidewalk-mounting pickup trucks. Relief came as she entered the Federal building. She was asked to give up her badge car-keys and weapon before walking through a metal detector. From there she was directed to the appropriate department. Karen was nervous, not because of the high ranking FBI officer she'd requested to see, but because she wasn't sure she could articulate her thought-out opening line without sounding like she'd managed to give her psychiatrist the slip. She knew that the very nature of her complaint may be her downfall. As she sat waiting outside the director's office she pondered the possible outcome of this meeting. As she saw it, there were three possibilities forthcoming from this interview. One: she will be regarded as some kind of deranged but harmless nut, and politely shown the door. Two: the interviewing officer could be another cult member, in which case her chance of getting home safely will become even more precarious. Three: they may actually listen and take the matter serious.

~~~~~~~~~~

At approximately 10.05am while Karen sat outside the director's office in the Federal building, Neil Roster, having showered and shaved sat alone in Karen's apartment dialling the number she had left him. A young female voice answered,

"Good morning, Danny Raug Realty."

"Oh good morning, my name is Craven," Neil lied. "You have a for-sale board on a property in Rowan Drive."

"Yes sir, it's a very nice house in a sought after district. We've had several inquiries in the short time it's become available. I'm sure it won't be on the market very long. Would you like to view it?"

"Yes if that's convenient."

"No problem. Can I ask if you will be seeking a mortgage?"

"No, if it turns out to be suitable it will be a cash sale."

"Really! In that case I can let you view the property today if you'd like to meet me there. I've been told it's now unoccupied."

"Well I'd rather visit your office first. No offence but I'd feel better if I know I'm dealing with a legitimate business, after all I'm not familiar with the name Danny Raug Realty and besides, you may have other properties I might be interested in."

"Of course I understand. Do you know where to find us?"

"No I only have your phone number."

"Okay, do you know Macy's in O'Farrel Street?"

"Yes."

"From there you go west until you come to Powel St you'll find our sign near the junction. I can assure you Mr Craven, we have been trading for some time."

"Fine, I'll find you. Expect me in about an hour."

~~~~~~~~~~

At the very moment Neil replaced the receiver another San Francisco number was being dialled from the town of Peace some eight hundred miles north. Seconds later the phone rang in CDI Dugan's office, he picked it up to hear a familiar voice.

"Am I speaking to DCI Dugan?"

"Aaron?"

"Yes."

"I thought we agreed I was not to be called on this line?"

"This is important. I need to know if Rockway or Rowan has sold yet. I got accounts to settle. The Miami family are making threats and funds are getting short."

"How's that possible with all the properties we've attained."

"It's possible because they're not all sold yet and I need cash now."

"Well I got nothing to cheer you up. The couple you sent has botched up on the Rockway place. I told you it was a mistake to go for another cop's house; not only is Roster still alive but Tobias has got himself shot up and his wife, Abigail, is threatening to take him to hospital if I don't get him a proper doctor. They're holed up in the Rockway house now."

"Did they get the book?"

"The what?"

"The book, remember the book we brought back from Massachusetts. I told Abigail and Tobias to steal the one from the San Francisco Library."

"Oh yes, Cargo of something, she did mention it. Isn't that the one we...

"Yes it is. Did they get it?"

"Yes, I don't know what she meant but she said it made interesting reading."

"Did she now?"

"Yes and she sounded angry, why? And why would you want another copy; you've replaced their burnt one?"

"I don't, I want you to destroy it. I have my reasons, and it seems Abigail and Tobias has become liabilities so it may be better if they didn't return to Peace if you get my meaning?"

"So you want me to...what about Charlotte? If she finds out..."

"I'll worry about her."

"Okay, Things are getting too hot here. I'd better wrap things up and come back to Peace, but I don't know if I'll get a chance at Roster this female D.I. Sykes is protecting him, so we may lose Rockway. This Sykes bitch is too clever for her own good."

"You said you were going to take care of her at the Howe place?"

"Yes I tried, but some old guy from next door came barging in the front door just as I was about to. Now I think Sykes suspects me."

"Well if you get the chance, you better do all four, we need those two sales. And burn that book do you hear. It's important."

Chapter 16 The School

After Jimmy and Jenny left the house, Charlie and I found ourselves sharing an awkward silence. She and I had, for some reason, grown less talkative since Avril's funeral I felt that Charlotte had not shown the amount of grief one would expect even though she was not Avril's biological mother, Avril had come to accept her as family and this lack of compassion in Charlotte had created in me a coldness toward her and a feeling of mistrust. Just for something to say I asked,

"Has there been any news about the house yet?" Her response surprised me; she answered like I'd just called her a dirty name,

"House, what house?"

"My house, or our house if you like; I was looking at the joint account you set up. I've not yet seen a bank statement since we came here. I just wanted to know if there had been any progress with its sale. You're the one that wanted to deal with it."

"Oh—yes, sorry, I'm not feeling too well this morning. Finding those strangers here has confused me. No I've not heard anything from the agents. Don't worry they will ring when they receive an offer. But you haven't signed those papers yet. The sale can't go through until you sign them." She opened a drawer in the cabinet behind her and brought out a folder that I knew held legal papers including the deeds to my San Francisco house. She took out three type-written papers and laid them out on the table before me.

"Do it now before you leave will you. There's only three papers just sign where they're marked with a cross."

I took the pen she handed me and scribbled beside each of the crosses without taking much notice of what was written on the forms. As I fed them back inside the envelope I said, "I think the price is too high that's why it hasn't sold. I think you should tell the agent to drop the price. Anyway I better get going or Jake will think I'm taking advantage of Orville. Oh, by the way, the preacher who did the service for Avril; is he the regular Peace preacher?"

"No, he was away at the time. I asked that one to come over from Frampton, Why?"

"Never mind, it's just that I thought he was a resident in Peace. I thought I'd seen him before. Anyway it's not important. What I don't understand is why so few came to the church. They're not a very friendly bunch in this town. Anyway I've got to get going I'll see you later."

I drove straight to the town hall. I knew Jake had a dental appointment that morning so I was hoping to catch Orville on his own. Unfortunately Joy Harris was at her desk and I couldn't tackle Orville with the questions I wanted answered. I thought he might know something about the church and its underground labyrinth, but mostly I wanted to know about these young pregnant girls I'd seen on our trip to Peace. As I sat at my desk pushing papers around, I sat there hoping Joy Harris would be called into the mayor's office so I could tackle Orville but it didn't happen. After a while I decided my questions would have to keep. It was too nice a day to be sitting in an office so I decided it was a good time to keep that appointment with Jimmy Gardner.

I got up from my desk and as soon as I donned my hat I immediately felt Joy and Orville's eyes on me. It was Joy that spoke,

"Are you going somewhere in particular," I found it odd that Harris should questioned my activities now. She's never asked before. "Jake likes to know where you are," she said, "just in case you need help you understand."

"Well when Jake comes in tell him I've just gone over to Pine Needle Camp. I hear they've had a bit of vandalism. It's probably just kids."

Orville started to leave his chair saying, "I'll come with you Sheriff."

"No Orville I'd rather you stayed and watched the shop, if I need you I'll call."

"But Pa said..."

"Sit!" The tone of my voice did the trick; reluctantly Orville sat back down, but I had the impression by his and Joy's behaviour that for some reason I was being kept an eye on.

It took me just ten minutes to drive to the camp. I asked reception where I could find Jimmy's cabin. I found some kids playing Frisbee outside Jimmy's cabin. They pointed down the hill and said Jimmy and his girl were down there fishing.

I found Jimmy sitting on a riverbank with one arm around Jenny and a fishing rod in the other hand. For some moments they were unaware I stood behind them. I watched them for a moment with envy. I realised something important was missing from my life and not just Avril.

"Hi there you two, it's nice to see you again, anything biting?"

"Hi Sheriff, I hope not, it took me ages to find that worm. I'm glad you came, wasn't sure you were going to show. You want to sit awhile?"

I sat down on the bank beside Jenny and she gave me a big smile like I used to get from Karen Sykes, God I miss her. "Seems like you two have been lucky with the weather."

"So far," said Jimmy. "Thanks for taking the trouble, Spencer."

"No trouble. To be honest I'm here as much for my sake as yours. I think I may need your help. Can I start by asking you a few questions?"

"Fire away."

"OK. Jenny, this man that you saw at your library the one you believe murdered your friend can you tell me anything more about him?"

"Not really, except that he was very tall and very unfriendly."

"You mean he said something to upset you?"

"No he never even spoke to me. It was just the way he looked at Brenda and me. It was his eyes; sharp piercing eyes that seemed to be accusing, threatening." Jimmy must have noticed something in my manner because he said.

"What is it? Have you seen someone like that in Peace," said Jimmy?

"Just once, it was when I first came out here. I saw him in the church in Peace. At first I took him to be the local priest, but there was nothing holy in the way he spoke to me. It made me feel as if I was trespassing. We stayed here in this camp when I came for an interview.

"Yes, I find that more than a little unusual, a San Francisco cop coming all the way out here to take up a post as sheriff," Jimmy said.

"If you stick around here I'm sure you'll find a lot of things unusual and my being here won't be top of the list. Jenny, this book you said the guy was reading, can you tell me what it was about."

"Which one?"

"I thought you said he wanted to read one particular book?"

"Yes but he also asked for anything we had on fungi."

"Fun what?"

"Fungi, mushrooms, toadstools, that kind of thing. We found him three books on the subject, and he must have taken them because I never found them after he'd gone." This started another nagging thought at the back of my mind, as Jenny continued, "Anyway the main book he asked for was a valuable old book about the first pilgrim settlers and how they coped with life after they got here. What they did to appease the Indians and..." This made me sit up straight and interrupt Jenny.

"Was there anything about witchcraft or devil worship?" Jenny turned to look at Jimmy and I knew I'd hit something pertinent.

"Look Spencer, I know this is going to make us sound like a couple of crazies," Jimmy said, "but there were things in that book that might have a bearing on Brenda's murder. Like lists of names people that gave evidence at witch trials and people that boarded wagon trains to reach Oregon. Brenda, the woman that was murdered, her name was circled in that book and Jenny thinks the killer did it. There was also a page of names missing. A page was carefully removed with a blade. Whoever removed it was trying to hide the fact that a page was missing but if the killer removed it, then he slipped up, because he screwed it up and left it in the library waste paper basket and Jenny found it. Jen have you got that page you found?" Jenny scrambled about in her bag before handing me a large folded sheet that had been crumpled at some time.

"Why are there so few names on such a large sheet?"

"End of the list, just a few W's and only three Y's

"Okay, but what do these names mean; what did the book say about these people?" Jenny now picked up the story with,

"Most of the names in the book read like a passenger list, Families booked on a wagon train to cross America they were headed for Oregon. There is another list, however. These are names linked with the persecution of the people that were put to death. These were either directly involved with the sentencing or they were the accusers. Jenny's words suddenly transported me back to the Peace cemetery where I recalled the last words Don Alden said to me. *"Find a book called: Cargo of Hope, Sheriff, and check your own name"*.

"We think this wagon train was carrying families that were fleeing from persecution because it was at the time of the Salem witch trials. The people in this town are the descendents of many of the people that were slain. I believe the names on this page left in the waste basket are some of the persecutors. It seems like every one that was arrested accused someone else. That was why so many were hanged. It was among these accusers that we found the name Spinner."

"You're not suggesting your friend was murdered for something maybe her ancestor did back in the 1600s,"

"We are open to suggestions," said Jimmy. "If you can come up with a better reason," Jimmy said. "Brenda was not sexually assaulted and she definitely had not seen the man before, so what other motive could he have."

"How was she killed?" As I asked the question Jenny turned her head away."

"It upsets Jenny to think about it. I felt it had a satanic connection, the way Jenny found her. She'd been stripped of her clothes, her ankles strapped together and from the strap he hung her upside down. Now if you think about it, when the body is in this position the shoulder joints keep the arms outstretched so that the whole body creates an inverted satanic cross. I'm guessing this was intentional. This nut was performing some kind of ritual. Having done this he then bled her by cutting another inverted cross from her sternum to her navel. Brenda literally bled to death."

"Christ, I hate these psycho cases," I said. "Give me an old fashioned gangland killing any day. At least they give one a sense of reason. With these religious freaks you have a job to fathom which way they're gonna jump."

"Yes and on whom. You never answered my earlier question, Spence. Where did you disappear when you entered that church?"

"Yes well, thereby hangs a tale." I said glancing at the two of them. Look, if I were to tell you, of all the strange things that I've seen or experienced since I came to this place, I swear you'd think I was ready for the happy farm. But to answer your question; the church is where I first saw the guy you could be looking for. He was tall, gaunt looking, with eyes that were kind of scary. My daughter and I had wandered into the church the first day we arrived, and we were discussing the book we found lying on the lectern. I was remarking to her as to why anyone put a lock on a holy book."

"Was it a bible?" Jimmy asked.

"I first assumed it was; we were in a church, but the book was in a mess, like it had been in a fire."

"Hmm, go on."

"Anyway that's when this guy suddenly appeared high up in the pulpit I could have swore he was not there when we entered the church. Anyway I naturally thought he was the local priest, but when he spoke he sounded real unfriendly, as if we were trespassing. I never went into that church again until the day you saw me enter it. I'm far from being a religious man, but losing someone real close does things to a person. They say there is no such thing as a dying atheist and I suppose the same principle applies when you lose someone close. I needed to believe my Avril had gone to a better place. When you saw me enter the church yesterday, I was feeling pretty low. I guess in my hypocritical way I was expecting to get some kind of comfort from the place."

"And did you speak to that same man."

"Wait for it Jimmy, it gets weird. I went in and found the church empty but I remembered where this priest appeared so I checked out the pulpit for a hidden door but I found no way out except the half dozen steps that I used to climb up to it. I then checked out the chancel behind the altar and that's when I accidently found a button behind the Altar. I pressed it and the whole altar slid in an arc to reveal steps leading down to a tunnel."

"And was that how the guy suddenly appeared the first time you saw him?"

"No. As I said Avril and I were looking at the burned book. If that Altar had moved we would have seen it. So how he appeared in that pulpit is still a mystery."

"So, tell us about this moving altar? You didn't find a magic lamp by any chance," said Jimmy grinning, until Jenny elbowed him in the ribs.

I ignored Jimmy's jibe saying, "Anyway the stairs led down to a passage."

"So that's why I couldn't find you, you went down there!"

"Yes and what I found makes me believe something strange and maybe dangerous is going on in Peace. Something federal law should be involved in. I didn't get a chance to investigate the whole place but what I did find was like an underground complex, I didn't want to be caught down there so I only saw a part of it but what I did find was a door where I heard the sound of young girls' voices behind a locked door. I heard someone approaching and I know it was the same guy I saw in the pulpit. I got out of there fast but I know there were more doors down there. I need to know what's behind them. And I'd like someone I can trust to watch my back. Have you brought a weapon with you?"

"Of course, but I thought you had deputies."

"Someone I can trust means someone who is not a resident of Peace."

"I see. Okay, count me in."

"Good, but I think we should check out the church when the town is sleeping and before we do that there's something else I'd like us to check out. Can you spare an hour tomorrow afternoon?"

"Sure."

"Good I'll pick you up at 2pm. I'll try not to keep him too long Jenny."

"Don't worry; I'll catch up on some reading. Just bring him back safe."

The next day was another scorcher. At 2pm on the dot I pulled up outside Jimmy and Jenny's cabin and found the couple waiting out on the veranda. I watched Jimmy kiss his girl goodbye and it crossed my mind that it was something I always did with Lucy and

Avril but couldn't remember ever having done so with Charlie. Jimmy got in the car while Jenny waved goodbye shouting,

"Play nice."

I smiled and pulled away, making for the open road. "She seems a very nice girl, your Jenny."

"She's the best and I love her to bits."

"But the two of you are not married?"

"Jenny wants to..."

"But?"

"But I tried it once."

"And?"

"Jesus! You ask a lot of questions."

"I'm a cop."

"Oh yeah. Well with my first marriage we were both too young and stupid at the time. I was put on a tour of duty after only a few weeks when I got back home she was two, if you know what I mean. I knew it wasn't mine and she didn't deny it. End of story, but Jen's different, I just know it."

"Then I best not let anything bad happen to you."

"Right, so where are we going?"

"We're nearly there already." I'd turned the car into a minor road, little more than a dirt track. It cut through dense forest. I pulled up beside a little footbridge that crossed a stream.

"I don't get it," said Jimmy. "There's nothing here."

"Maybe, but something your Jenny said makes me think there is. I've not been on this stretch of road since the first day we came here. Truth is I got lost, but I remember stopping on this bridge and we saw half a dozen young girls, I'm guessing as young as twelve no older than seventeen. They were among those trees and they were filling baskets with whatever they were collecting on the ground."

"Flowers?"

"No, what Jenny mentioned: fungi."

"I'm starting to see the connection."

"The point is there were no cars, buses or any other transport here waiting to pick them up so I'm thinking they came from somewhere nearby."

"Okay, but did I miss something. I mean, so what?"

"Oh yes, I forgot to mention some looked pregnant."

"I see, and what are you making of that? Could be there's a home around here for wayward girls?"

"I hope it's just that, and that's what we're here to find out." We left the car and headed into the trees where I'd seen the girls. We moved silently deeper into the trees when Jimmy said,

"Is that what you meant, Spence?"

I looked to where he was pointing; a bunch of reddish looking Fungi had amassed near the base of a tree.

"Could be, I remember my Charlie saying maybe they're collecting mushrooms." I crouched down to take a closer look at them. "Jenny said something about books your murder suspect stole? They were on fungi weren't they?"

"That's right! He must have had more than a slight interest in the subject."

I picked a few of the mushrooms and dropped them into my shirt pocket. "Check to see if there are any other types around Jimmy, I think we should get these checked out, I've heard some strange stories concerning mushrooms."

"Well Jenny might be the one to ask. Since her friend's murder and those books the guy took, she's been reading up on the subject of mushrooms, I'll take a couple to show her."

We moved further into the trees until we heard the faint sound of voices then what sounded like a young girl's laughter. It encouraged us to move faster. Suddenly we came upon it, a wall that must have been nearly ten foot high and the sound of young voices were much louder now. The wall seemed to extend in both directions. I didn't know how far or in which direction we'd have to walk before we found a gate and we both desperately wanted to know what those kids were up to behind that wall.

"Jimmy you're lighter than me, how about I give you a leg up."

"Everyone's lighter than you," he said grinning. "Okay, if you promise not to arrest me as a peeping tom." I linked my hands together and heaved Jimmy up until his hands grabbed the top of the wall. He then stood on my shoulders with me in a semi-crouch so that his head was just above the wall. "Hey I think it's a School," Jimmy whispered. "There's a big house on the far side of a cultivated lawn and there's lots of youngsters lying about on the gra...?" Jimmy suddenly ducked his head down behind the wall.

"What's up?"

"Young kids, they're lying around on the grass necking. Some are doing a little more than just necking. Hang on there's an older woman coming from the direction of the school; she looks like she could be a teacher." Jimmy whispered. "She's having words with what looks like a couple of sixteen-year-olds. Spencer, I've seen enough..."

I lowered Jimmy down on the ground. He stood there with his back against the wall shaking his head as in disbelief.

"What's up, what did you see?"

"I'm not a prude Spencer, I know what kids get up to and usually before they should, but they usually do it at night and in the back seat of a car. One doesn't expect to see them do it in the open with a teacher walking among them grinning like she was pleased. It was like she was encouraging them."

Jimmy's words still came as a shock although measuring what he'd just witnessed against seeing the young pregnant girls in the woods should have warned me that something like this was going on. Now it had me wondering about the female voices I heard in the tunnel.

"Come on Jimmy, next we check out that church."

~~~~~~~~~~

Karen glanced at her watch for the third time just as a pretty secretary approached her.

"Miss Sykes?"

"Mrs—divorced!" Karen corrected. The girl gave a polite but disinterested, *whatever* smile,

"The Director will see you now." Karen nervously entered the director's plush office without quite knowing how she was going to put her story across without sounding like a complete nut. She had imagined that this interview was going to be a one to one conversation. She was surprised and became even more nervous to find two men and a woman, all looked to be in their forties, sat behind one long desk. At one end of the desk was a much younger woman sat behind a monitor and keyboard. The man Karen assumed to be the director motioned to the empty chair facing them.

"Take a seat Miss Sykes."

"It's Mrs," Karen said and thinking how many more times.

"You're Married?" said the man to her left.

"Divorced."

"Ah," the director said, like divorce was something he approved of. "How long have you been with the SFPD, Karen?" asked the woman.

Hmm, first names Karen thought to herself. So they've been checking up on me. If that's the case they know very well how long I've been with the SFPD. "I'd say about ten years."

"Your record says it's only been months?"

"That's because I left and came back." Karen said letting out a sigh. She was starting to get annoyed with the questioning and it was evident in her manner, but it didn't deter the woman from asking,

"Where did you go when you left the force?"

"Russia." With that the woman looked surprised and turned her gaze to the director. He was about to comment, when Karen said, "Look, you know that's a lie. You've just said you've seen my records so you know that I went to New Zealand to visit with family. I've not come here to be interviewed for a job, so why don't you just hear me out."

The director glanced at the others and smiled before saying, "Yes Mrs Sykes you're right but we have to be sure you are the same person in our records, so what is it you want to tell us?"

Here goes, Karen thought, get the straight jacket ready. "I believe there is a major catastrophe building up in Oregon and I think it has the potential to turn into another Waco..."

~~~~~~~~~~

Neil Roster had no trouble finding the Realty office and he was sure, when entering the shop that it appeared to be a legitimate company. There were a dozen property photos on show in the window and the same photos on a display board inside. Roster stood staring at the inside board for some time before, Lily, the young lady with a name tag pinned to her blouse approached him. She seemed very businesslike as she looked up at the wall clock,

"How do you do. I'm guessing by the time that you are Mr Craven. You phoned about the house on Rowan?"

"Yes that's me," Neil said, still staring at the shop's photo display board. "Did you say the house is vacant?"

"Yes, I received a call from the owner to say that she had moved in with a relative so that the house could be marketed as vacant. It does make it easier to sell."

"Yes I can imagine." Neil said, now reading the young lady's name tag. "How long have you worked for this company, Lily?" A slight smile showed approval at the use of her name.

"I've been working in this office for more than five years but it's only three since the new owners took over."

"Danny Raug?"

"Yes. I believe he's the owner."

"He's your boss?"

"I suppose! I've never met him."

"I see. So who pays your wages?"

"They are paid directly into…Is this relevant Mr Craven? You seem more interested in…"

"Yes I must seem a little over zealous with my questions Lily but It wouldn't be the first time I've been duped over a business deal and I'd like to be sure your company is genuine and above board. When you said you had never seen your boss I found this to be a little odd."

"Yes I can see how it would seem like that. I've often wondered myself if I'm working for a real person."

"What do you mean?"

"Well I usually only get my instructions from a voice over the phone. That is until last week when I was handed a photo of a property that is shortly to go on sale."

"That is when you met your boss, was it?"

"No, this was a young woman. She said she owned the property in the photo. She said that Mr Raug had asked her to drop the photo in to me. I thought that was odd because property photos have always arrived through the post, or I've been given the address and been told to go photograph it myself. I must say she looked very young to have owned such a place but maybe she had it left to her in a will or something."

"Did this woman give her name?"

"Now you're starting to sound like a policeman," she said with a smile. "Just a minute," Lily opened a drawer and took out a photo. As she read the words on the back Roster gaped at the picture. "Yes her name was Mrs Roster."

"She asked you to include this on your list?"

"Yes as soon as I receive word from her. That was my instructions."

Neil glanced at his watch saying "Okay Lily well I would like to view this property on Rowan Drive, but I have another appointment that I'm already late for, so I'll phone you and arrange another time if that's okay?

~~~~~~~~~~~

Dugan parked his car at the north end of Rockway Avenue and carrying an aluminium briefcase he walked the two hundred yards to the Roster home. He swore under his breath when he saw the black 4x4 Chevrolet parked right outside the house. At the gate he quickly glanced around him making sure he had not been followed. He then walked up the drive and knocked the front door. As he expected, he saw a curtain furtively move in the front downstairs window. Seconds later the door opened and a very attractive young woman appeared, she acted extremely agitated and her blouse was stained with blood. She glanced over Dugan's shoulder before allowing him to enter. "Where is he?" she said excitedly. "You said you'd bring a doctor, where is he, where's the doctor?"

Dugan ignored the question and quickly closed the door before brushing past her. "Abigail, are you mad?" He said irritably. "You've parked the Chevy right outside the house, what if Roster or Sykes came back here?"

"I had no choice; I almost had to carry Tobias the length of the drive. Answer me! Where's the doctor? You said you'd bring a doctor. I'm frightened. My Tobias is in a real bad way—what's the case for?"

"I've brought some first aid dressings and something to ease his pain. I can't bring a local doctor here without him asking questions it's too risky."

"First aid! He needs proper hospital treatment—he's got two bullets in him. He's my husband,"

"At the moment you're still Mrs Roster thanks to you and your husband's incompetence."

Dugan was totally unprepared for the heavy slap he received square across the face. He staggered back against the hall telephone table nursing his face.

"Don't you dare criticize us." the woman said. "Tobias and I have shown more dedication to Esor than any other member of the cult, so you just take that back. Aaron has always preached that he would protect us and because of Toby's dedication he's now upstairs bleeding to death so you get a doctor now or I promise you Roster and Sykes will be the least of, your worries."

Dugan was still rubbing his reddening face as he said, "Okay okay, but I'm telling you the Elders are not happy. You promised this place would be on the market before the end of last month, but Roster's still the sole owner, still alive and with the help of Sykes, He's still making trouble. I'm just pointing out how risky..."

Dugan flinched and was cut short as the fraught woman suddenly screamed at him, "I don't care about the fucking risk and I don't care about Aaron Yarn any more. I discovered he is not one of us." It was at that moment her reflexes caused her to glance towards a large book resting on the hall table. She quickly looked back at Dugan but he had noted it and recognised the book "We've been tricked by Aaron. He came to Peace and preached of the great things he and the master would do for our people all we had to do was to let him guide us and he would eliminate our enemy and lift the curse on our town, but it was all lies. He is our enemy."

"Curse! What curse?"

"Never mind, you wouldn't understand, but I think Aaron's been lying all along. He's using our town for his own ends and I intend to expose him. When I do he'll suffer just as his victims have suffered."

"You should be more careful how you speak about Aaron."

"No, it's Aaron Yarn who should be careful."

"What do you mean?"

"Never mind, all I'm concerned about this minute is my husband. I want him seen by a doctor now, or I'm phoning for an ambulance."

"Take it easy and keep your voice down. We'll go take a look at him and see if he can be moved. Where have you put him?"

"I managed to get him upstairs in a bed, but he can't be moved without a stretcher."

"Show me." Dugan picked up his case and followed the woman up the stairs and along a semicircular landing before opening a bedroom door.

"Tobias is in here." They entered the room where a young man was half lying, half sitting in a blood-soaked bed, his skin was pallid looking and he appeared to be unconscious. The woman went to his bedside as Dugan laid his case on the dresser at the foot of the bed and clicked its clasps open. Abigail lifted the hand of her deathly white husband kissed it and whispered, "Toby, my husband, are you awake, Brother Dugan is here. He's got something to ease your pain then we'll get you to a hospital." She put a hand on his forehead. "He's burning with the fever I'll get some ice..." The young woman's sentence was curtailed by a sudden muffled thud. For a moment Abigail stood frozen as if in shock, at the blackened hole that had appeared in the back of her hand. Then as the blend of both hers and her husband's blood spurted through it, she turned to see the silencer attached to Dugan's gun. Her look of shock surprise and pain rapidly turned to one of rage as Dugan said,

"Sorry Sister but Aaron wants a clean break. Anyway I've stopped his pain." Fury took precedence over the woman's injury. Dugan's was amazed at Abigail's agility as she leaped at him, her wounded hand outstretched, her fingers like a blood soaked talons reaching for his throat; but Dugan was prepared. The gun thudded again and the young woman's body jerked in a twisting motion as the shell smashed into her right shoulder. Her right arm immediately flopped uselessly as she fell across the body of her dead husband. For some moments blasphemous words and non-coherent guttural sounds came from her mouth.

Dugan smiled to himself. He turned his back on her and kept talking as he opened his aluminium case and laid his gun inside. He then removed his trench coat and laid it carefully on a chair before returning to the case. The woman lay helpless as she watched Dugan rummage inside the case. He talked in a relaxed manner as he took out a roll of parcel tape and several rolls of bandages,

"Don't think for one moment I'm a bad marksman sister. That slug hit the exact mark I aimed for. You see I didn't want you dead, at least not yet because before I've finished with you, you will tell me just what it is you think you know about Aaron."

"I'll tell you nothing, you slimy bastard."

"I think you will, but there's no hurry, after all, you're a very attractive girl and I can think of other uses."

~~~~~~~~~

Although Andrew Dugan had become a member of ESOR, his reason for doing so had little to do with his belief in religious doctrine Satanic or otherwise. Dugan's roots were not associated with Peace or even Oregon. He and a few others had been approached and recruited by Aaron Yarn, mainly with promises of wealth but in Dugan's case Yarn had laced his promise with more than a hint of blackmail. Yarn knew Dugan personally from their past association with the flower people of the sixties. Dugan was always high on drugs and Aaron was constantly testing new ones on him. When they left the family of hippies they were attached to, Aaron was a true believer Satan was his deity: He was satanic through and through. They split up but Aaron kept tabs on those in the group with psychopathic and sexual tendencies. Deviants like

Dugan, Phipps and Ben Alden that had joined the flower cults for the free-love lifestyle. In particular he kept tabs on those that had escaped involvement with the Hollywood atrocities. Yarn knew that they were easily manipulated and one or two like Dugan showed psychotic tendencies that would blend nicely into Aarons ultimate plan; a plan that coexisted with his own satanic beliefs and eventual objective. He sent word to those former members. People that he believed he could control, that would fit into his plans. Among these were names such as Joy Harris, Sebastian Kirby, Cal Phipps and Ben Alden. He called them together and told them about the little town he'd discovered in the depths of the Oregon forests: a place unblemished by time; a place where state law didn't exist and federal law had no interest. He told them the local inhabitants of this town were ignorant inbred people that would be easily manipulated. With his knowledge of chemistry and hallucinogenic drugs in mind, He told them it was a place where he had indoctrinated the locals into his own satanic beliefs, a place where they could be a law and a religion unto themselves. Knowing many of them were sexual deviants he told them how he intended to import females for the specific purpose of populating his own satanic cult.

Having discovered that a cult associate named Dugan had been made Chief of detectives with the SFPD; Yarn saw him as a real prize. He offered Dugan a free partnership in his very profitable Realty business as an extra incentive to join his cult. Yarn omitted to explain the way his company operated. By the time Dugan realised that property owners were being systematically murdered his name was on the payroll as an executive. What Yarn saw in Dugan was having a hold over someone high in the SFPD. Dugan soon learnt the truth behind the realty business but by then his partnership was established and he was trapped.

"If you come anywhere near me the least it will cost you is an eye," Abigail hissed at Dugan.

"Hmm, I thought you might be difficult so I brought a little help." With that he reached behind him into the case. He grinned as he saw her expression change from one of defiance to one of fear as she saw the hypodermic syringe in his hand.

"Yes I see you're familiar with one of these, of course you know what it contains. They tell me you've used it yourself on many an uncooperative young girl. Now you'll have the chance to experience the degradation they suffer while I enjoy the experience that our young studs enjoy." Dugan moved toward the woman, his hand poised ready to plunge the hypodermic needle into the woman's neck, but he suddenly paused as the woman struggled to roll over onto her stomach. Dugan was amazed knowing the height of agony she must have endured to do this, but he was even more intrigued as to why. But then something started to happen. He stood fascinated by what he was witnessing. He saw the woman's back slowly arch upward while her head, hands and legs appeared to withdraw slowly beneath the bath robe until only the robe was visible. Dugan had heard rumours that some residents of Peace, direct decedents of the first settlers could shape shift. To Dugan this was a term only associated with fantasy. He put these ridiculous stories down to Yarn's hallucinogenic concoctions. As a teenager Dugan had been through the whole California flower scene and knew the effects some drugs could have on a person. What he couldn't understand was the fact that he had not used any for years, yet at this moment something... As suddenly as it had begun, all movement beneath the robe ceased and Dugan, cynical though he was, could plainly see that something had happened beneath the blood-soaked robe. Common sense was telling him to run, to get out, but his feet seemed glued to the spot. Fear gripped him, but curiosity would not let him leave. His heart was beating so hard he could have sworn it was audible. Without taking his eyes off the mound on the bed he reached behind him. Dropping the hypodermic in the case he then groped around until his hand gripped the gun again. Aiming it directly at the slowly moving mound he reached out with his left hand and snatched away the robe. Terror gripped him as a head emerged from beneath the robe. It was Abigail Yet it somehow wasn't. The eyes were Abigail's eyes but red, wild and evil. Dugan froze with fear and disbelief as he watched the thing arch its back and make ready to pounce. He took aim and tugged on the trigger but had forgotten that he'd put the safety catch on. He slipped the catch off but it was too late. The thing sprang directly at his face. He tried to take a step back but his heel caught in the thick rug and as he fell back hurting his back against the dresser. His gun arm flew upward in an attempt to protect his eyes from the beast's blooded talons. The gun flew from his hand as he crashed to the floor. The thing was on him in seconds clawing at every unprotected inch of bare flesh it could find. Then the creature bared its teeth and Dugan saw how the beast resembled, a huge rat. The thing clawed its way up his body, biting his fingers at every attempt he made to grab hold of it. He was screaming now as his face and neck became lacerated and his shirt collar became sticky with blood, but he'd gained his senses. He knew what he needed to do. His free arm quickly reached down to locate the hunting knife strapped to his calf. He quickly slid the knife from its scabbard and held it dagger fashion and poised to strike, but he had to see his target and to do so meant dropping his guard. The moment that his arm came away he was once again looking into the beautiful face of Sister Abigail. Had he imagined that change in her? In a flash she raked her nails across his face lacerating an eyelid but missing the eyeball by a hairs breadth. Dugan screamed while plunging the serrated blade into her side.

Chapter 17 Seeing the light

It was one of those hot and humid nights. The kind you know is going to keep you awake until the early hours, but I didn't intend to sleep anyway; not if all went to plan. Charlie sat reading as usual while I pondered over a crossword.

"Are you feeling alright?" Charlie said, looking up from her book. I knew what she meant; twice she had seen me glance at the clock.

"Yes, I suppose, why?"

"You keep looking at the clock?"

I had to think fast and came up with, "Yeah, habit I guess. I still keep thinking Avril is going to walk through that door."

"Well she won't; get over her? Is that the only thing that's bothering you?"

Since moving to Peace Charlie and I have grown so far apart that now we just tolerate each other living in the same house.

It seemed to me Charlie's sympathy over the death of Avril was short lived. Once Avril's funeral was over, Charlie never mentioned her again. I found this more than a little strange. And now just the mention of Avril seemed to annoy her, and this in turn annoyed me.

"She was my daughter, for fuck sake." I rarely swore in Charlie's presence, but if I did she knew my temper was aroused. "Avril was my daughter. You don't get over losing your own kid just like that. Christ, it's not like turning off a fucking faucet."

"Alright—alright calm down, I just thought it was something more; is everything working out with the job? Maybe you need a break. We could..."

The phone rang interrupting Charlie. I managed to reach it before she did.

I answered the caller with a "Yes that's me," before saying "What again! Not with a bottle. Okay I'll be right over." A second before I put the phone down I heard a faint click but I had no time to think about it as I said, "Another brawl over at Brady's Bar, I'll have to go sort it; I should be back in an hour."

~~~~~~~~~~

I drove to Peace with the window down due to a useless air conditioning unit and apart from the heat I was trying to blow that day's thoughts into some kind of order, but it wasn't working. I think maybe that would have taken a much longer journey. It was gone 11pm when I turned the lights off and slowly pulled into the alley beside the general store. I emerged from the car and closed the door as silently as I could. I walked back to Main Street and as I turned the corner a shadow moved out of the barber shop's doorway and approached me. Keeping my voice almost to a whisper, I said,

"Thanks for coming Jimmy, and for the call, I think the wife bought it and your call came right on time."

"Happy to oblige," said Jimmy. "I couldn't have slept anyway. Hell it's a warm night; what was all that about a bottle?"

"I wanted Charley to think I was being called out to a bar brawl, but now I'm wondering if asking you to phone me was such a good idea, as every call seems to go through a switch board and I don't trust anyone in this town."

"Yeah and I don't think your wife likes me. Did you see the way she looked at Jenny and me, real daggers?"

"I'm beginning to think she doesn't like anyone lately, Jimmy, least of all me."

"It sounds like married life doesn't suit you."

"It used to but I lost my first wife to cancer then remarried on a rebound. I've been thinking lately that it was a big mistake." Jimmy shrugged and changed the subject. "I see you brought a torch," he said. "Good thinking, so shall we go take a look at this church? We walked the length of the cu-de-sac and as we entered the church grounds, Jimmy said "What do we do if the church is locked we can't break a stained glass window it wouldn't be right."

"I haven't thought that far ahead. But I understood churches were never locked,"

On reaching the church I grabbed the handle of the huge arched door and twisted it. I felt the heavy latch inside lift before the door swung open. We stepped into the darkness and quietly closed the door behind us before I switched on the torch. We then moved silently up the centre aisle towards the altar. "Spence, are you sure you weren't dreaming. I can't believe there could be anything going on beneath us, it's far too quiet."

"Believe me Jimmy I know what I saw." We reached the Altar where I ran my fingers along the decorative top edging until I felt the slight protrusion. I pressed it and the familiar humming of the electric motor started and in the silence of the night it seemed much louder than before. The altar's movement started to push Jimmy aside and I thought at least Jimmy now knew that I wasn't dreaming. The humming stopped and I could only imagine the look on Jimmy's face as we peered into the even blacker void now uncovered. I shone the torch onto the steps leading downward. "Are you ready for this?" His answer was to slide the revolver from his belt. I led the way. Suddenly the humming started again and Jimmy had to crouch down low to avoid being crushed by the huge altar coming back to its resting place. "Don't worry," I whispered, "Just miss this step as you follow me down or it will open again." Before we reached the bottom of the steps there came a faint red glow of night-lights stretching along the passage. I remembered where and what was behind each door that I had opened on my last visit so I led the way passed these and tried the next one, it was locked.

"What do we do now?" said Jimmy.

"We just jump the hurdle, as my old man used to say." I pulled what jimmy thought was a penknife from my pocket and selected, for want of a better description, two appropriate hardened lock picks. In seconds I had the door open.

"Hey I got to have me a bunch of those." said Jimmy

"The set was a present from the guys at the SFPD."

"Really? So you were a key worker." Jimmy quipped.

The room was in darkness and I was reluctant to switch the torch on again. I was afraid it might be another dormitory full of young girls and that they might start screaming. I had to discover what was in there so I quietly closed the door before lighting the torch. I shone the beam around the room. Jimmy let out a low whistle. What we saw was a couple of racks that housed around a hundred or more army rifles and other items of weaponry. Jimmy and I stared open mouthed at each other. Jimmy picked a rifle out of a rack and examined it.

"Their quite old, Ex Army," he said. "M1 Garand holds 8 rounds and I'd say it's seen a lot of combat by the state of it."

"You seem to know a bit about guns." I said.

"I used to do a bit of hunting when I lived in Canada. You get to take an interest in them." Jimmy put it back and picked out a different rifle. "Springfield M1903 holds 5 rounds. There are a few AK47s but I'd say most are ex-army maybe brought home from the Second World War, maybe Korean."

I switched the torch off and hit the light switch.

"Christ is someone about to start a war here?" said Jimmy as the full array of weapons became visible.

"Maybe, does this remind you of anything Jimmy?"

"Yes, my spell in the Marines."

"The Marines?"

"Hey! There's an echo in here. Yes, I was in the marines. Why is that so surprising?"

"Only that you don't seem old enough to have had two careers."

"Oh! In that case I won't mention the Canadian Mounted Police."

"The Canadian Mounted police!"

"There's that echo again."

"Never mind, what I meant was, doesn't this remind you of Waco?"

"Hell yes, now you come to mention it but with this amount of guns can you imagine the scene when the FBI get wind of this place? It'll be a bigger bloodbath than Waco and this time it could be the marshals' blood."

"Come on let's see what else is hidden down here." We turned off the light and made our way further along the passage to the next door this had a number on the door 13. We entered and finding a switch that activated more low wattage red lamps, we found ourselves in what appeared to be a small chapel. There were no more than twenty chairs facing a small raised stage upon which stood another altar. Red drapes covered most of the walls, even the floor was carpeted in red. Apart from the occult look about the place it crossed my mind that it was probably fairly sound proof. There was no doubting the room's satanic purpose. A carved head of a goat highlighted the centre front panel of the altar and the black and gold runner that decorated its surface was stained with what appeared to be blood, however, the wicked looking dagger that lay on it seemed enough to confirm it. Jimmy looked at me without saying a word but I could see this discovery had affected him, he looked pale. I said,

"Jimmy, are you ok?"

"Not really. Knowing what happened to Brenda Spinner I should have been prepared to come across something like this, but I wasn't."

We left room 13 and moved on. Next we came to a glass panelled door. I opened it and switched on the light. This was an office complete with desk, exec chair and a phone, it even had an in and out tray. Jimmy started perusing though papers in the trays while I started looking through the desk drawers. There were several pictures of houses.

"Hey get a load of this Spencer. This is an invoice for an M2 or to give it its full title M2-2/M9A1dash7"

"Wow, I'm really impressed Jimmy. You know all those letters and numbers. Now impress me even more by telling me what the fuck you're talking about?"

"Flame thrower; this is an order for a one man flamethrower."

"Christ! Are you sure?"

"I did a course on weapons and when you see one of these in action you tend to remember what it was called. What the hell would these people want with a flame thrower? It's not the kind of weapon one would use to hold a siege. Spencer did you hear what I said...what's that you got there." Jimmy had seen me staring at what I had found in one of the desk drawers."

"Have you ever seen a crucifix like this Jimmy?" I held it up between two fingers so he could see it plainly.

"Sure lots. Can't say I've seen one in ebony though, is that what you meant?"

"Look again Jimmy." I held it closer to him. "Remember how you described to me how the Spinner woman's body was found, how it resembled an inverted cross?"

"Oh! I see what you mean. The eye is on the bottom so it's meant to hang upside down. I think I've seen enough Spencer. Let's get out of here and let the FBI deal with these nuts. If we get caught down here..."

"One more door Jimmy." I tried the handle of a glass panelled door that we had missed. This one had a Keep Out sign in large red letters, but it was locked. I'd like to know what's behind this one Jimmy but it will have to wait. Let's get out of here."

~~~~~~~~~~

Neil was on his third coffee and Lenny the owner kept giving him hostile looks. Neil expected to be asked to vacate his table if Karen didn't arrive soon. The restaurant was almost full and Neil was taking up profitable dining space. Twice Lenny had left his kitchen to come hovering around Neil's booth. Once again he saw Lenny heading his way when the sound of traffic became suddenly louder he looked up to see Karen had appeared at the open door. She spotted Neil and slid into his booth just before Lenny reached their table. With pen and note pad at the ready he said,

"Hi Karen, what's-it-a-gonna-be, babe?" Lenny said with a pretty good imitation of Chico Marx. "I was just-a gonna give-a your friend here a check for-a de rent."

Karen laughed, "Sorry Lenny; it was not his fault, I was delayed, but I'll have a small seafood pizza and a coffee please."

"Same again, Lenny," said Neil.

"Sorry to keep you waiting Neil. The traffic was a real pain. So you like Lenny's pizzas." Karen said as Lenny retreated back to the kitchen.

"Sure; you can't beat the Italians at their own game."

"I suppose, but Lenny was born in the Bronx. He and I went to the same high school, we were pretty close once. We were still in our teens when we both had visions of becoming movie stars. Can you believe we used to attend acting classes together?"

"You're kidding, but he sounds genuine Italian."

"Lenny does that for the customers,"

"He's been putting on that accent so long; I don't think he can turn it off. Anyway, back to business. What did you find out? I take it you found the realty firm."

"Yes and the place seemed genuine; at least the girl that I spoke to did. She was a doll. She obviously thought the sale of Winifred Howe's house was legitimate. And get this, She had a photo of my place with instructions to put it on the market as soon as she gets the nod from guess who, none other than my loving wife, Abigail."

"So that's why they're so keen to put you down Neil. Your house was probably the next one to go on the market. They can't very well sell it while you're still around. It must be how this Aaron is financing his cult; they're stealing property by rubbing out the owners. You've got me wondering now, just how long has it been going on and how many properties have they acquired by murdering the owners."

"That bitch must have been pretty sure her boyfriend was going to finish me to have put the house on the market so soon. Something else I discovered while I was looking at their array of properties for sale, Spencer's house."

"So while this girl at the realty office may think she's working for a legitimate company, it could be that this Danny Raug is in league with Aaron Yarn. Hell!"

"I don't think there is a Danny Raug," said Neil.

"Why?"

"Well—the name Raug for one thing, it just didn't seem genuine to me. As I sat in your apartment this morning I searched the phone book and couldn't find one person with that name, not spelt like that anyway. While I sat here waiting for you I played around with the two names Danny Raug and look!" Neil dropped a table napkin in front of Karen.

"It looks like you've been busy doodling Neil, but what am I looking at?"

"The two names at the bottom Yarn and Dugan—Danny Raug"

"Shit! Why didn't I see that?"

"Anyway, what about you, did the feds listen to your story."

"Oh they listened, and that was some experience. You know what these Feds are like with their clean-cut suits and ties. I had three of them glaring at me across a leather bound desk. The more I told them of what we discovered the more unbelievable I felt the story sounded. They didn't smile or interrupt though, but when I finished I honestly expected them to snap a rib laughing.

"And did they?"

"No, can you imagine my surprise when the director just looked at me and said, yes Miss Sykes, we know all about Peace."

"You're kidding. Was he just trying to humour you?"

"That's exactly what I thought, but no, they said they had an undercover agent in the town. They knew nothing about any cult though."

"So why would they be interested in a little town buried in the Oregon wilderness if they didn't know about this cult?"

"Weapons—they said some military base had been raided and a load of weapons were stolen. They knew the Mafia was mixed up in the raid and they've been watching to see where the stolen weapons were destined. They know that some went to Peace. What they knew was limited though, because they were only concerned with the guns and the possibility of a terrorist attack. They said they had never heard of Aaron Yarn and knew nothing about any religious cult."

"Did you tell them about Winifred Howe's link to Peace and how she died?"

"Yes, and when I mentioned her having a sister living near Peace it seemed to really get their attention. I'm not sure they believed everything though. I asked them if they had Dugan on file. I thought if Aaron Yarn and his band of crazies could replace Winifred Howe and get away with it maybe they had done the same with Dugan and guess what? They pulled Dugan's file up on screen while I sat there. It was so fast, Neil. I didn't realise that was possible. Anyway the girl on the key board turned her screen around to show me Dugan's photo and guess what? It was Dugan and there was me thinking there was another body somewhere, one that would prove Dugan wasn't Dugan."

"So he really is a cop, but they didn't know he bent and linked to Aaron Yarn. So what are the feds planning to do about him, come to that, what are they going to do about any of it?"

"That's what worries me. They seem pretty laid back about all this which leads me to think they didn't believe very much of what I told them. When I hinted that I was thinking of taking a trip to Peace myself they told me I shouldn't get involved and that they would deal with it. At the moment, though, they seem to be doing very little. They said they were waiting for an agent to report in, but then they let slip that he was late with his report. I asked them if they should be worried about him. They said no, he was often late because he had to make the call from another town to evade the local switch board operator. I told them Spencer was the sheriff in Peace and probably knew nothing about any guns or siege. I was thinking it might help if their agent knew that Spencer wasn't mixed up with these stolen weapons."

"What about us, Kaz, did you ask if we could help?"

"I never suggested it because they made it clear that any outside interference could put their agent in danger. They left me in no doubt that they didn't want any police involvement. After I left I had the feeling I was being followed. But the fact that their agent hasn't reported in, worries me and anyway, they can't stop us if we decide to take a trip to Oregon."

"If you're right about being followed I just hope it was FBI and not that Chevy driver. He could still be a threat."

"Yes that did cross my mind."

"If the Feds have put an agent in there, surely it would be an advantage for Spencer and him to work together. Do you think Spencer might know about him?"

"I don't know, Neil. What if this agent has already blown his own cover? If Vic Rowan is an example of how they deal with people who stand in their way he could already be dead. You know what the feds are likely to do if that were the case. If any harm comes to one of their agents they'll go in with guns blazing, and Spencer could be caught up in the middle of it."

"So what have you got in mind?"

"I'm not sure yet, but I think we should first wind up this business with your, shall we say, ex-wife and her joy-riding boyfriend. That is if they're still walking about. By the amount of blood left on the wall outside my apartment, I would say at least one of them is probably not a threat anymore."

"Okay so how do you want to handle it Karen?"

"First we get some backing from one of the guys back in precinct 13, a cop we feel we can trust, and one without a family. I was thinking maybe Red Shadwell."

"Yes but he looks after an elderly father. What about the new guy: O'Donnell? I think O'Donnell's probably a good cop, although let's face it, my judge of character has proved to be a little fallible, plus I don't think he likes me."

"I wouldn't take that too personal Neil. He told me he had it rough as a kid. Maybe he just has an aversion to anyone he thinks has had a privileged upbringing. Your parents had money Neil so that makes you a target. My only concern is that he hasn't been with precinct 13 very long and he does seem to spend a lot of time talking to Dugan."

"I wouldn't know, not being part of your team anymore."

"I guess not, anyway I'd be happier going with Shadwell if we can get him."

"Okay but if you're planning to call him at the precinct you better hope that he's sitting at his desk, otherwise Dugan may take the call and he'll know your voice," said Neil.

"You're right. Wait here!" With that Karen left the booth and Neil watched her walk to the rear of the restaurant and through the kitchen door. Minutes later she came back grinning. Neil waited until she was seated,

"What's the joke?"

"I got Lenny to help me with the call."

"Yes, so why the grin?"

The grin got wider as Karen said, "I couldn't get Shadwell. He's out on a job and I got put straight through to O'Donnell. It kind of settled the argument, so it'll have to be Mick O'Donnell."

"Okay, but the grin?"

"I got Lenny to do a little more acting on the phone while I played his wife about to have her throat cut. O'Donnell thinks he's on his way here to tackle a mad Italian cook holding a knife to his wife's throat."

"I guess that is pretty funny?"

"Let's hope he thinks so when he gets here. I thought it the best way to get him here without him reporting our whereabouts to Dugan, but wait until he discovers it was me having hysterics down the phone. Anyway, if he agrees to back us we'll go straight to your house. If Abigail and her boyfriend are not there I'll phone Dugan and tell him you're home. He doesn't know we're on to him yet. My guess is he'll come to finish you himself and we'll have the drop on him."

"So I'm the bait?" Neil said, looking decidedly worried.

"Yes, won't that be fun?" With that their pizza's arrived and before they had eaten half their meal Michael O'Donnell came rushing through the door while waving a 38mm in all directions. The restaurant tables were all taken and almost to a person the diners turned to stare, some cowered in fear as this six-foot-two Irishman checked them over with his gun in his hand. O'Donnell soon realised that nothing menacing was happening in the restaurant and he appeared embarrassed at his super hero style entrance. He then caught sight of Karen and Neil's grinning faces. He sidled over to their table while slipping his gun back inside his coat. His expression told them he was not amused as he greeted them with,

"Okay you two, I ain't happy so this better be good?"

"Take it easy Mick," said Neil. "Sit down and have some pizza. Karen will put you in the picture."

The big Irish detective slid in the booth beside Karen and grabbed two slices of Pizza saying "I think I earned this, Kaz." O'Donnell had always shortened Karen's name, but she didn't mind in fact she found it endearing. "Now what's this all about and who was that mad Italian on the phone?"

"Yes sorry about that," said Karen. "That was Lenny, a friend of mine. He owns this place and he did it as a favour to me. You see Mick, I was afraid Dugan would answer the phone and I had to get you here without him finding out Neil's whereabouts."

"Well you needn't have bothered Kaz; he wasn't even in the building. Matter of fact I saw him go out before you phoned. He's hardly spent five minutes in his office in the last couple of days it's like he got the world on his shoulders plus he looks like he's been attacked by a wildcat. Oh, and by the way, there's an APB out on you, Neil. What have you been up to?"

Karen gave O'Donnell the whole story including Neil's sham marriage and the shootout at Karen's apartment. Neil followed her version of accounts clarifying details he felt Karen had left ambiguous. When Karen finished Mick sat for some moments as if in a trance. Eventually he turned to Karen saying,

"This is not another one of your pranks? You say you've actually been to the Feds with this story?"

"That's right. We're not kidding this time Mick," Karen said. "We could really use some help. I believe this could turn out to be another Waco type siege and Spencer Corwin could be right in the middle of it. These people will kill at the drop of a hat to achieve their aim though just what that is, we haven't established. Neil seems to be the next on their hit list. They're after his house; we think it's the way they're financing this cult of theirs. From what we've learned they target house owners that have little or no family to challenge their claim on the property. My guess is, they either forge signatures or in Neal's case through a sham marriage, no offence Neil,"

"And you think Dugan is a member of this religious clan, what did you call them—Esor?" said Mick.

"He could be. Yes that's what our source called them, apparently it stands for eternal seekers of retribution, whatever that means," Neil said.

"It means revenge," offered Karen.

"I know what retribution means, Karen." said Neil, sounding peeved. "I meant retribution for what."

"Who knows?" said Karen.

O'Donnell then said impatiently, "By your source, I take it you mean this woman, Gwen. Do you think she's on the level?"

"Positive."

"Well If Spencer Corwin's in trouble what are we sitting here for. We should be on the first flight to Oregon?"

"We weren't asking you to go to that length Mick. We just wanted your backing to sort out these two bastards that are after my house."

"Look, just helping you sort these two oddballs out without official backing is enough to cost me my badge so if I get involved in that, I might as well go the whole nine yards but it'll have to wait until Friday. I'll be on leave then and Dugan won't be keeping tabs on me."

"Christ Mick, you'd do this for us?" said Neil.

"Well you are colleagues, but I'd be mainly doing it for Spencer. See that?" Mick held up his right hand which showed half the middle finger missing. "I got Spencer to thank for that."

Neil and Karen traded confused glances before Karen said,

"That makes sense Mick. Spencer cost you a finger so you'd travel a thousand miles to help get him out of a hole."

"That's right. You see Spence risked taking a bullet for me. If he hadn't rushed headlong at the low life that did this, the guy would have blown my head off. I owe him and the sooner we sort Neil's problem, the sooner we can work on Spencer's trouble. I'll be on leave in two days time. Meet me here at 6pm on Friday we'll take my car."

Chapter 18 Bodies

Two days later the three left Lenny's Diner and piled in O'Donnell's saloon, Mick drove with Neil sat up front beside him to give directions while Karen sat at the back.

As Mick turned at a snail's pace into Rockway Ave. Karen suddenly asked him to stop the car.

"Mick is that Dugan's car?"

"The grey Mustang? Yeah I think it is. Does he live around here?"

"No I don't think so," Neil said.

"So it kind of backs up your story Kaz, Dugan must be working with Neil's—shall we say ex-wife?"

"Yes, I think you can safely say ex, Mick."

"Okay, this is your show, so what do you want to do?"

"I don't know but I trust Karen's instincts. What do you think Karen?"

"Okay, drive slowly to the end of the road Mick. We'll be looking for a black 4x4 Chevrolet that's been trying to make road kill out of Neil. We will also be looking to see if there is any activity around Neil's house but don't stop; if they see a car stopping outside they will be suspicious and then on their guard. Park a little way past the house and we'll go it on foot. It's getting dark, that'll be in our favour." O'Donnell followed Karen's instructions to the letter. They saw no movement around Neil's house, and no 4x4 pick-up truck parked anywhere in the street. As O'Donnell parked the car and they started to walk toward Neil's house, he said,

"Dugan's car is still there. It could mean he's still in the house. Is there a rear entrance to your place?"

"Yes there's a path that runs along the back of the garden. I keep a key hidden at the back there so I think it best if I take the back while you and Mick cover the front lawn."

"Oh! The front lawn is it," said Mick. "What's it like, Neil, to have parents with money."

"I don't think much about their money Mick. I would rather they were both still alive."

"Shit! Sorry pal, no offence; foot in mouth as usual."

"None taken Mick, they've been gone a while."

"Right Neil," said Karen, "you take the back and we'll take the front, but be careful, this Dugan didn't make CDI for being stupid."

"Don't worry, I'm no gung-ho cop, but if I've got to have my place shot up I would rather do it myself. If you two want something to shoot at, you can shoot the lowlife's that's been trying to run me down if they come out the front door."

~~~~~~~~~~

As we retraced our steps and headed back to the altar Jimmy suddenly grabbed my arm,

"Did you hear that?"

"What?"

"I heard a bell, listen..."

"I stopped and listened but heard nothing." I started to think Jimmy was either suffering from claustrophobia or the satanic trappings we encountered had affected him, but I had the feeling he was crowding me in an attempt to hurry me along. His breathing became more noticeable as we neared the steps leading up to the church.

"Are you sure that Altar will move?" he said nervously as I put my foot on the first step.

"We'll soon find out," I said as I started to climb. The anticipation as my foot hit the tenth step was almost unbearable and my heart sank as I put my foot on the tenth step and nothing happened. I wondered if I'd miscounted but then to my relief we heard the low rumble as the step took my full weight. The welcome feeling of relief however, was quickly replaced by a muddle of surprise and uncertainty. Jimmy and I had entered the church thirty minutes earlier in complete darkness and only by torchlight did we find our way to the movable altar, but now as the altar slowly slid aside light shone down through the opening. As we waited for the rumble to cease and the opening above us to reach its full extent, I looked down at Jimmy and his frown told me he was as concerned about the light as I was. The rumble stopped and I recommenced climbing.

As my head rose above the floor opening the sight that greeted me stopped me dead. The first thing I saw was what looked like a size twelve boot only inches from my face, I recognized it immediately as belonging to Jake Tollman. I gazed about the church and at first I thought Jake was the only person there. Then I looked up and there high in the pulpit I saw the piercing eyes of the guy that annoyed me on my first visit to the church. I didn't recognise him right away because of the bandage he now wore around his head and it had me guessing as to how he had been injured. He was dressed in a silky hooded robe. It reminded me, somewhat, of a grand master of the KKK, but his breast pocket bore the letters ESOR. He stood there glaring and pointing a long barrelled colt at me as I heard Jimmy's loud whisper from below,

"What's up Spence, Why have you stopped?"

"Never mind," I answered. "Just keep coming, but stay calm and keep your hand away from your gun." Moments later Jake had Jimmy and I kneeling, our hands cuffed behind us. Jimmy gave me a slight nudge,

"Look at the eyes, Spence," He whispered from the corner of his mouth. There was no need; I was sure this was the same guy Jenny described. As I stared back at him I was reminded of Jenny's librarian friend and what this man, if it was him, had done to her. Two or three minutes had passed since Jake had forced us to kneel, but the man in the pulpit had still not spoken. His attention seemed to be focused on the large book opened on his lectern. Another minute ticked by and the pain in my knees were increasing my anger. I was about to blast a tirade of swear words in the direction of the pulpit when the silence was suddenly broken by the sound of a car door slamming. Seconds later another figure entered the church. My chest tightened, it was Charlotte. She was wearing the same black habit with the gold motif. She hardly glanced in my direction but went directly to the pulpit. She climbed the steps and handed the man what looked like the folder containing the papers she had given me to sign. He smiled and handed her a wooden box the size and shape of an average sized novel. Jimmy turned to me and whispered,

"Hey Spence, that's your wife!"

"Yeah, I noticed, don't rub it in." Jimmy and I watched Charlie make her way toward us. She stopped and stood over me for a few seconds. I had to turn my head sideways to look up at her and as I did I tried to fathom the meaning of her expression, was it hate, pity or triumph? I struggled to determine just what it was she was feeling. Then a slight upward movement at the corners of her mouth gave me the answer; it was the satisfaction of either seeing me shackled, or knowing what was in store for me. I wanted to say something but mere words could not express the loathing that I was feeling for this woman. She then stepped around me and I heard her place the box on the altar behind us. Jimmy tried turning to see what she was doing, but he received a vicious blow on his shoulder from Jake's gun with an order to keep facing the front.

It was then we heard the black monk speak for the first time. Oddly he addressed Jimmy and I as if we were attending a business meeting,

"Good evening gentlemen. My name is Aaron Yarn, not that you need to memorize it, there would be no point." Jimmy and I just stared at him. "Mister Corwin, I assume both you and your friend Mister Gardener have seen enough of our underground complex to satisfy your curiosity. I have to inform you that we do not take kindly to outsiders trespassing. As you will soon discover, the punishment is severe, but tell me, were you not impressed with what you found? The forefathers of some of our town's residents undertook the initial excavation of the tunnels. We believe its purpose was to hide them, should their pursuers discover their new location here in Oregon. Of course we have extended the complex to almost double the size and added the electrical power that you have now discovered. This suits my particular needs and helps protect the town and our way of life."

"And I suppose your way is to use underage girls to populate your sick little town? You're breaking federal law, Yarn. How long do you think you can get away with it?"

"We are the law here Mister Corwin. It's true we do not discourage copulation among our youth. We let nature decide whether a female is underage. Any threat to our laws by outside influence is dealt with severely as you will discover. We have our own special methods." With that Jimmy, still grimacing from the pain in his shoulder, said angrily,

"Just what kind of a threat was Brenda Spinner to your way of life you sick fuck." I saw Yarns eyes give a positive nod to Jake which earned Jimmy another blow from Jake, this time to his head sending him sprawling on his stomach. I saw a trickle of blood run down his neck. But I understood why Jimmy was provoking this mad monk. If Yarn had murdered Brenda Spinner he was more likely to confess to the deed knowing we were helpless and that he had the upper hand. Of course, by the same reasoning if he did confess it meant he never intended for us to ever leave this town.

"So that's the reason you've come here. Mister Gardner," said Yarn. In that case I congratulate you on your police work. I really thought I'd covered my tracks. Yes, the Spinner woman, she wrote a book divulging this towns existence. She was also one of our town's enemies. You see the people of Peace are sworn to eliminate any offspring of their onetime enemy. Spinner is a name on that list, not an important name; her ancestor was just a minor witness in the Salem witch trials. The name Corwin, However, is a legend among the residents of Peace, but not in a good way. Your ancestor, according to history was both accuser and executioner of many settlers whose bloodline is here in Peace. You, Mister Corwin, are a prize catch. It is the reason my people have had their game with you. You are here for one reason: retribution, the very crux of our cult's existence. You are here to pay for your ancestor's treachery and to appease our one true master. You see Mister Corwin, it is widely believed that the Salem witch trials were the product of superstition hyped up into mass hysteria; this is not true. Some did worship Satan just as some worshiped their Christian God. Most people today do not believe in witchcraft or the existence of Satan, yet they believe in a God they have never seen. Satan is our deity Mr Corwin and you will be our gift to him. It seems my followers have decided your fate and they will get their wish. This will be carried out with much rejoicing but in another location."

I couldn't believe what I was hearing, that I was about to be punished for something that happened over four hundred years ago. I couldn't contain my anger. "You think you're someone special, Yarn, and maybe you've got these poor deluded people believing your satanic claptrap, but I know what you are. You're not the first of your kind. Sick minds like yours unfortunately come along every so often. Sadly, though, you have a talent for manipulating gullible and vulnerable people like the people in this town. You are another Manson and even if you survive the FBI guns you will suffer the same fate you will either rot in prison or die by lethal injection."

"Ah yes the Helter Skelter man," said Yarn, "an early associate of mine who never really understood what Satan demanded of him.

He now suffers the consequences of failure. I have vowed that neither I nor my brothers and sisters here will suffer his fate."

Jimmy then decided to use some of his father's religious rhetoric on Yarn. I'm not sure what he hoped to achieve, even as Jimmy spoke I could tell his words had little influence.

"What has Satan promised you Yarn, eternal life, a place in his kingdom? You are delusional. Satan's loyalties lie only with himself, can't you understand that? He's using you the way you are using the people of Peace. Unless you turn away from this path, you will die in a hail of FBI bullets. I'm guessing you hear Satan's voice instructing you. Don't listen to his sick preaching's; read your bible, and think of the suffering the son of God endured for your sake."

With that Yarn let out a one syllable mocking laugh, "Huh, suffer? You're stupidity is only exceeded by your naivety Mr Gardener. If you believe a man, with the ability to perform miracles, would willingly allow mere mortals to stick thorns in his head and nail him to a wooden cross against his will, then you are a fool; if your bible's account were true then he allowed them to do this because he loved it! His suffering was the epitome of masochism. Yes, he knew the true meaning of real pleasure. As one who understands it as few humans do, I can confirm that pain is the ultimate sexual sensation, it surpasses all other pleasures. The two of you, however, have not the mindset to understand this. Therefore you will be unable to endure the kind of pain that's in store for you."

Whether Yarn's words had struck fear into Jimmy, or had shaken his faith, I'm not sure, but Jimmy's next words sounded increasingly desperate, "You think you are untouchable, Yarn, holed up out here, miles from a civilised city; I can promise you you're not. If the Feds don't fill your sick carcase full of lead, they'll drag you back to Massachusetts where you will die through lethal injection. I've left instructions with someone to report my disappearance if I don't return by a certain time, and that time has already past."

"You are obviously alluding to the young lady I once met in a library. You really should not have involved Miss Blake. Her name did not appear in our scriptures and prior to your arrival here ESOR had no interest in her. Now she has you to thank for whatever Esor decides her fate should be. Unfortunately Miss Blake has a tiresome habit of screaming, and so we had to take measures." With that Yarn directed his gaze toward Jake and nodded. Jake immediately left the hall only to appear seconds later escorting Jenny Blake. Her hands were tied behind her back and it was only by her dress that we knew it was her because strapped to her face was what looked like Gabriel Proctor's interpretation of the scold's bridal. Jimmy became agitated and started yelling when he saw her.

"Yarn you sick bastard, get that thing off her."

I could only imagine how Jenny must have been suffering with that leather protrusion pinning her tongue down. At the sight of her, Jimmy struggled in an attempt to get to his feet while directing a tirade of abuse at Yarn, but Jake directed Orville to restrain him and as Orville held him down with one hand Charlotte came up from behind Jimmy and plunged a hypodermic needle in his neck. It took less than a minute for Jimmy to stop struggling.

I felt bad. I'd seen Jimmy take two beatings, now seeing his girl trussed up with terror mirrored in her eyes, made me feel physically sick and responsible for dragging them into this mess; I also felt anger as I watched Charlie approach me with another hypo. If only my hands were free, I'd have grabbed Jakes gun and put a bullet between her eyes or died in the attempt. As the needle entered my neck I saw the smirk on Yarn's face and the evil behind his black eyes. I could feel the content of the hypodermic gradually   taking affect, and with my last rational thoughts I pictured a middle-aged librarian hanging up by her ankles and imagined the sound of her screams as Yarn's knife sliced into her.

~~~~~~~~~~

Andrew Dugan clutched an attaché case in one hand and a small suitcase in the other as he stepped onto Oregon soil from the steps of a Lear Jet. He was now on a secluded airstrip carved out of dense forest. It was nearly midnight as he scanned the dark deserted aerodrome for his arranged pickup. There attached to a rickety control tower a single lamp shone down on a woman leaning against a small family saloon. Dugan smiled as he recognised his wife, April Dugan, alias DCI Winifred Howe. April opened the car's trunk and took the case from him as Dugan reached her. April closed the trunk and as Dugan leaned in to kiss her she pulled away and frowned at him. "What happened?"

"What do you mean—oh yes," he said remembering then running a hand over the deep lacerations across his face. That bitch Abigail Potter. I made the mistake of thinking I'd killed her with the first shot."

"April said nothing but her eyes narrowed indicating her lack of trust."

"I've really missed you babe," he said as April wiped away the wetness on her face with the back of her hand. She stared at the briefcase in her husband's hand, "Is it in there?"

"Yes, but just the missing page. But that is all we need. Anyway, what do you think the penalty is for defacing a rare library book?" he said with a grin.

The woman never smiled and as they got in the car she asked, "So did you carry out Yarn's request?"

"Yes I did them both just like the Chemist told me to."

"You better get out of the habit of calling him the Chemist; you know Aaron never liked it. He used to get annoyed with Manson for calling him that."

"I don't care, I wouldn't mind betting it was one of his concoctions that caused those lunatics to go on the rampage in California."

"Anyway I can't wait to see Charlotte's face when she learns her cousin is dead and with this evidence," he said brandishing his case, "I reckon Aaron's days are numbered." Starting the car, April said, "It's almost one and a half hours drive to Peace so I think we should get going." She pulled the gear lever into D and pulled away. Once they were on the road April said. "By the way you'll be pleased to know there's a trial coming up—Trial— that's a laugh. Anyway you're always saying how you've never had the chance to see a cult sacrifice because you're always in San Francisco; well this time there's four to go."

"Four! Why?"

"Well things are coming to a head with Corwin. Apparently he discovered the tunnels and they caught him exploring down there. He must have been getting close to the truth. Apparently a cop and his girlfriend arrived from out east. They went to the Grange looking for Corwin. Aaron found out he was assigned to the Brenda Spinner case in Witchville."

"Oh Fuck!"

"Exactly, you were part of that."

"I only helped him so he could cover his tracks."

"So you say!"

"He said he would have done it himself if Corwin hadn't smashed his legs."

"Rubbish, Yarn was back on his feet long before you two took that trip." April said. She knew of Yarn and Dugan's trip to Massachusetts and she guessed that he and Yarn had carried out the Witchville murder. She guessed that it would have taken the strength of two big men to hang the victim's body in such a humiliating way but the barbaric act they then carried out shocked even her. Of course she had fallen for Dugan long before she learnt of his psychopathic tendencies. Her life, however, had revolved around him too long for her to change and she didn't have the strength or confidence to survive on her own. "Anyway they've stopped playing their games with Corwin; I think Charlotte got him to sign those joint ownership papers. So, like I said. There is going to be another midnight trial in the next day or so."

"You said four—who's the fourth one."

"You remember the Guy that showed up saying he was a teacher."

"I remember. He said his name was Black."

"That's him. Jake caught him trying to make a phone call to an Agnes Howe in Cranford."

"Oh Christ!"

"He wouldn't talk, but I think he could be FBI."

"Shit, things are getting too hot, April, we've got to wrap this up." Their journey carried on in silence for a while before April suddenly said.

"What about Abigail? Did you..."

"I told you, I took care of them both. How many properties have we acquired now? I thought the coffers was pretty healthy but to listen to Yarn, going on about the Miami family breathing down his neck, you'd think we were broke."

"I don't know, but Aaron was mad about losing the Rockley house I suppose that is why he told you to rub those two out."

Dugan patted the small case on his lap, "Yes but we know the main reason he wanted them gone don't we? Anyway fuck him! I'm getting sick of what makes him mad. I wish you hadn't told him about Roster's house, it was stupid and dangerous going for another cop's property." said Dugan.

"I agree but you know Aaron's feelings concerning the law, the only good cop is a dead one. Corwin broke his legs so he couldn't pass that one up. He preaches that any act against the establishment, gives his master more pleasure. He convinced

Charlotte Potter with his preaching. She's hated playing wife to Corwin. Can you imagine playing wife to a cop that you hate?"

"No but then I'm not a woman. Anyway what gripes me is that while we take all the chances, Aaron does what he likes with the proceeds. We're taking all the chances acquiring these properties and all we get is promises. Now he says the Miami family is threatening over payment on those weapons. We will never see the money he promised us. All the proceeds seem to be spent on that laboratory of his and whatever it is he's doing down there. I hate being under his thumb and now I can't go back to San Francisco they've probably got an APB out on me already. I've had enough; we've got to finish him. It's the only way we'll get what's due to us."

"I know, Andy, I feel the same, but we won't have to. When the town learns the truth about Yarn they'll do the job for us, then all we have to do is step in." She turned and smiled at Andrew Dugan then patted the suitcase on his lap, "This maybe the answer to our prayers."

"I hope so, anyway, I've been meaning to ask you, since you originally came from Peace, what's the story on these backwoods hillbillies, I'm sure there's more to them than just looking a bit weird."

"You've never asked about them before, why the sudden interest?" Dugan could feel she'd taken her eyes off the road and was now staring at the cuts on his face and had the light been better in the car he was sure she would have also read the guilt lurking there.

"No particular reason."

April stared at him for a while before she finally said, "Just how did you take care of Abigail?"

"Does it matter?"

"Yes it does. Abigail was the exception to the rest of the Peace townsfolk. She was very beautiful and I know you of old, Andy

Dugan, you were not known among the Manson gang as Randy Andy for nothing. There wasn't a girl in among that crowd you didn't try it on with."

"That was many years ago, I had hair then and I've not been with any other woman since you."

"Maybe that's because your appeal disappeared with your hair, but I know about leopards and spots. How come you let her get close enough to lacerate your face? Did you try...?"

"No I didn't."

"Dont play the innocent, we're talking about Abigail....Oh, never mind, just remember what I told you I'd do to this," she took her right hand off the steering wheel, grabbed his testicles and squeezed until he winced, "If I find out you've stuck this in another female you're gonna lose it, do I make myself clear?"

Dugan's pain made his answer slow in coming, causing April to squeeze harder. This resulted in a high pitched, "Yes." April released him to the sound of a relieved gasp and for the next few miles they drove in silence until Dugan said,

"You never answered my question. What's with this Peace crowd? I've not spent that much time in Peace to get to know them. Some of them look a bit weird. I only know what Aaron told me the day we accidently bumped into each other. That's when he talked me into joining his cult, by promising me the earth. I'm regretting it now."

"It was no accident you met Aaron when you did. He came looking for you when he heard you had joined the police and had made C.D.I. He knew you were a fucking psycho..."

"Hey, careful!"

"Well you are, just like him. And he knew you'd be useful. As for the residents of Peace, It's all in that book he keeps locked away. Their ancestors were from New Hampshire. It's said that their forefathers came to escape the witch trials. They're a strange lot. I came from Cranford, a little town not too far from Peace and

I remember my parents telling me to stay away from them. They told me the original settlers in Peace were witches and some of the residents that live there today still practice the art." Dugan let out a false laugh, but he was reminded of the last fateful encounter with Abigail Fisher and in the gloom of the car's interior his expression was anything but jovial.

"Yeah, sounds funny don't it, but the Salem witch trials were all about people consorting with Satan that's what attracted Aaron to the town. The people see Satan as their saviour and Aaron has made them believe he is Satan's messenger. This is the cult that you have signed up to Andy, and unless we do something about Aaron, there's no way out."

"Yeah, whatever; I don't give a fuck. I'm in it for the money Yarn's promised us. If I have to get my hands a bit bloody in the process so be it. You and I blew any chance of getting to heaven anyway."

"You can say that again."

~~~~~~~~~~

Daylight was fading when Neil stepped quietly along the path leading to the rear of his house. Meanwhile Karen and O'Donnell, crouching low, reached the front door and waited. Karen's nerves were on edge. She held her breath as she listened, in anticipation, sure that Neil would meet trouble and they were about to hear gunfire coming from inside the house. O'Donnell stood ready to kick the door in. After two minutes the front door quietly opened and Neil stood there with a finger to his lips while standing aside for them to enter.

"I think they're gone," he whispered. "I've not checked the bedrooms but I've not heard a sound from upstairs" Karen was nearest to the stairs, holding her gun stiffly out in front of her she started up the stairs. Mick and Neil followed, also with weapons at the ready. On the landing they split up each nervously opening different doors until Karen called out,

"In here." Neil was first to reach the bedroom Karen had entered. There was no disguising the shock on his face as he took in the sight of two blood-soaked bodies occupying his bed.

"Oh! God" Was all he said before dashing to the bathroom to vomit. Karen was covering Abigail's nakedness as Mick came to the door. Unlike Neil, Mick didn't seem perturbed by the bodies on the bed, but remarked,

"Christ that's Neil's wife. Is this Dugan's work?"

"I'd put this month's cheque on it." Karen said. "I don't know how long they've been dead, maybe soon after they left my apartment. Dugan's car being left in this street makes me think he's taken the Chevy we've been looking for and I'll lay odds he's on his way to Oregon." As Neil came back in the room Karen said. "Neil, Abigail's been cut up real bad. It's like she's been tortured, but why. The guy died quick, one round straight through the head, so what had Abigail done to deserve all this and why didn't he just finish her like the guy."

"Who knows?" said Neil as he looked sadly down at his dead wife. "Maybe he had a reason for wanting her to suffer."

"I'm sorry Neil; after all, she was still your wife."

"Yes but I'm not even sure of that now. I'm beginning to think it was all a sham, but whatever she tried to do to me I wouldn't have wished this on her."

"No, I'm sure Neil. We'll leave you to have a quiet minute. Mick and I can wait downstairs." The two DI's left the room closing the door quietly behind them. In the silence of the room Neil reached down and touched his dead wife's hand and as he did her eyes suddenly opened. Neil dropped her hand in fright. He stumbled backwards until his back was pressed up against a wardrobe. The dead and lifeless eyes of the woman started to glow with a brightness glaring at him. Neil shouted to Mick and Karen, seconds later thy burst into the room to find Neil sat on the floor, his back against the wardrobe. His face was almost white and while his arms rested on his knees his hands were shaking.

"Are you okay?" asked Mick "What was that you shouted out?"

"I shouted she's alive." Mick frowned and looked at Karen. She looked back at Mick and shook her head, much as to say, leave it. She went to the bed and felt Abigail's pulse again. "No way, Neil she's been dead at least twenty four hours, look at the congealed blood and she's cold."

"But she opened her eyes, scared the shit out of me."

"You did shout out, Neil but it wasn't *She's alive*."

"Didn't I...? No you're right, but I meant to," Neal stared at his wife's body. "It was her...she was in my head. What did I shout?"

"You shouted *kill the chemist*," said Mick. Neil and Karen stared at each other then at the woman's body for a moment then in one voice they said, "Yarn."

"Hell Karen, what a mess," said Neil, staring at the bodies.

"Yes," said Mick, "I hope you have a good idea how we get Neil out of this fix Karen, because when they find his wife and a stranger in bed, riddled full of holes, I know who I'd be looking for."

"Thanks Mick," Neil said, "you really know how to cheer a colleague."

"Okay, well *we* know who did this," said Karen. "So I figure we make the clues point to him."

"How?" said Neil.

"Dugan's car is just down the road. We hotwire it and back it up the drive."

"I can do that," said Mick.

"Good." Karen glanced at the window. "It's dark enough outside now, so we put the two bodies in it and leave it somewhere for the police to find. Have you ever been in Dugan's car Neil?"

"No never."

"Good, no trace of you ever being in his car will confuse matters for them. They'll initially think you did it, jealous husband finds wife with a lover, but then they'll ask themselves what they are doing in Dugan's car that hasn't even got your fingerprints in it."

"What about the bed; another day in this heat and it'll be crawling with maggots."

"We drag the mattress down the back garden and burn it."

"And what about ballistics; some of that guys wounds are probably from my gun, remember we fired through the door."

"That'll take them a while and by the time they figure things out I hope we'll be back here with all the answers to their questions."

"Back?" queried Neil.

"From Oregon."

"We *are* going then?"

"Well I certainly am, even if I have to go it alone. I'm convinced Spencer's in trouble, and I'm guessing that is where we'll catch up with Dugan. Things are too hot for him to remain here. He must know we are on to him."

"I'm in," Mick said.

"Right, Neil are you in." said Karen

"Well if I stay here I'll be arrested. Yes let's do it."

Chapter 19 Escape

Within seconds of waking in darkness I had a feeling of dread followed by panic. It wasn't just that I couldn't open my eyes; in fact I could not even tell if they were open. None of my muscles would function, not even my eyelids. No, it was also fear linked to a childhood memory and it was brought on by the smell. It was a dank, earthy smell that took me back to my seventh birthday.

~~~~~~~~~~

I'd been given my first new bike and been allowed to stay out late as a treat. A bunch of boys, six of them as I remember, took me on a ride for a woodland picnic. It was the farthest I'd ever been without my parents. I remembered one boy in particular: Brad Denham. I still remember his name even though he was not one of my regular friends. Brad was probably the biggest of the bunch and a bully. I remember on the ride there, how he kept pressing me to swop bikes even though he was too big for mine. Of course I refused. After the picnic they started a game of hide and seek. As one boy counted to a hundred the rest of us ran off to hide. Not having too much by way of an imagination I stood behind a tree. It went quiet as all the boys spread out, and all that could be heard was the boy some distance away, counting. Then I heard,

"Psst, Spencer." I looked around for the source of the voice. For a while I couldn't see anyone until, a few feet away, a section of ground lifted and the face of Brad Denham peered out from under a sheet of corrugated steel. "Come on quick," he said. "Get in here."

Someone had, for whatever reason, dug a pit in the forest floor; they had covered it with a sheet of corrugated steel then laid leaves and bracken over it. Brad must have known about it, possibly had a hand in digging it on some other past adventure. My initial thought was what a brilliant hiding place. Without a second thought I ran over and jumped in. Brad and I sat in that hole and listened to the sounds of the boys searching for us until their voices faded. "I think they're gone," Brad whispered. "Wait here." In an instant he slid the steel cover to one side and scrambled out. He quickly replaced the cover and I waited, expecting him to come straight back to say the boys had gone to look for us. Suddenly there was a loud thump on the steel above me. Seconds later there was another metallic bang on the roof of the pit. This time it dented the steel just an inch or so above my head. Then all went quiet. I'm not sure what had just taken place or how long I waited in that hole before attempting to lift that steel sheet, I only know it wouldn't move, I was trapped and as night fell I'd never felt so alone and scared. Now that fear was back, accompanied by the same dank damp smell that told me I was under ground and this time there would be no search party, no friendly face, or the strong arms of my father that eventually lifted me out of that would-be musty grave.

~~~~~~~~~

Were my eyes still closed? I couldn't tell. Maybe my surroundings were so dark that I couldn't determine. What could possibly be this dark...a coffin! My mind switched to panic mode and my heart started to race until I heard something like a door opening, suddenly light filled my left eye. It hurt yet I was unable to close it. Then I saw a hand withdraw from my face and I realised someone had pulled back my eyelid and left it open, strange I never felt it being touched. I must have looked comical staring through one eye. I saw Jake and Orville standing over me. Orville had that, *Sorry Sheriff Corwin they made me do it,* look on his face, but his dad's expression was more, *Serves you fucking right, Corwin, you shouldn't have come to our town and taken my job.* My brain instructed my voice to say hello boys what are you doing here, how about opening the other eye; I'd like to see you treacherous bastards in 3D. But no such words were forthcoming.

Then I heard Charlie's voice, she sounded apathetic even hostile. It was hard to believe this woman had shared my bed. This last thought set off another train of thought such as when was the last time she and I actually did *it*. Strange, I couldn't remember ever doing *it*, at least not with her.

"He'll be coming round soon," she said. "Orville go check on Gardener and his girlfriend. I heard her choking as I came past her cell. Better get that thing off her face. If she suffocates Aaron won't be pleased, but warn her if she starts screaming again it goes back on." With that Orville moved out of my vision and I heard the door open and close before Charlie's voice dropped to a whisper. "Jake, you must talk to Orville. Aaron doesn't think his loyalty is with the cult and you know that no one leaves the cult, Jake. Do you understand what I'm saying?"

"Yes, but he's soft like his mother, I'm not sure he'll take heed."

"Well you had better try if you don't want to lose him. Aaron thinks Orville's faith is weak and he wants only full commitment. Aaron needs to know he can be trusted to carry out orders if Esor is threatened, even if it means firing on government agents."

Jake suddenly looked down at me. "Can he hear us?"

"Don't worry about him; he'll soon be fish food."

Fish food! Did I hear right? Then I remembered the words in the church, *The Lake awaits.* Now I was really starting to worry. "Keep checking on him, come and tell me when he's revived enough to be responsive. There are some things I will enjoy telling him."

The light faded and I heard what sounded like a heavy metallic door close. I was alone with my thoughts, thoughts such as, what could that underhanded bitch have to tell me that I haven't worked out for myself? I still couldn't move, but I was starting to get a tingling sensation in my toes and the tips of my fingers. There was nothing wrong with my hearing though, and there was no denying I was scared. I'd seen room 13 it was no Christian chapel. These people were members of a satanic cult; to them taking a life was the act of allegiance to their deity. Guilt or any sense of wrong doing was alien to this cult.

~~~~~~~~~~~

Whether my inner feeling of panic had produced adrenalin that weakened the potency of whatever was in that hypodermic, I don't know, but suddenly I could move my head slightly. I started to think about escape even though I could not yet stand up. Then I heard a noise, a commotion coming from close by, maybe the next cell if there was one. Then I hear a female cry out was it Jenny I thought but then I remembered the female voices behind one of the locked doors. It could have been one of them, and it made me recollect Room 13. This made me angry and the angrier I became the more it seemed to stimulate my limbs. I could now open my right eye. I tried to sit up and tumbled sideways off the bunk and onto the stone floor but at least my partial numbness eliminated any pain. Again I tried to sit up, this was when I realised I still had the cuffs on. The numbness was disappearing rapidly now, I had feeling in my limbs. I felt something wet and slippery against my thigh. I looked down and was shocked to see blood down one side of my pants. The cuffs made it difficult to reach into my trouser pocket but I managed it and that's when I felt one of my steel lock-picks sticking in my leg. Two things crossed my mind, one, call someone to fix my leg and two, hide the lock-picks before anyone came back.

I hauled myself back up onto the bunk and pulled the pick out of my leg before hiding the tools under the bunks mattress. I could have used them to lose the handcuffs but I didn't want to rush things until I'd thought out some kind of plan, and so far I wasn't even sure where I was. I looked around my cell, the walls were just rough plaster and some had fallen away and beneath it was just earth. I had the feeling my cell was deeper underground than the corridors that Jimmy and I had explored I felt there had to be more cells. I sat on that bunk thinking about escape and wondering how much time I had. Then I heard the rattle of keys.

~~~~~~~~~~

It was decided Mick would do the driving to Oakland Airport as he was familiar with the route. It turned out to be less than an hour's drive and he seemed to know his way around the airport which was not surprising. Mick never stopped talking about the flying lessons he'd been taking. He guided them to the departure lounge and told them to grab a coffee and a sandwich while he found his flying instructor to try to get the three of them a deal on the cost of a flight.

Oakland was not the largest of airports but it was extremely busy. Mick told them his instructor catered for business people on short internal flights in the two Lear jets he owned. For a while Neil had been content to sit in the departure lounge and eye the females that drifted past him, especially the pretty flight attendants, but Mick had been gone twenty minutes and Neil was getting restless.

"I'm going to find him Karen he should have been back by now." With that he wandered off in the direction Mick had taken before Karen noticed he had gone. Her attention had been on two men sat at the bar; she had not seen them enter the lounge and was sure they never came through the main entrance. The two men made her uncomfortable not because they had been watching her, it was more their obvious effort not to. The shorter man carried a small black case while the younger and taller man appeared to have the look of a bodyguard. Karen noticed a slight bulge under the tall man's breast pocket suggesting a shoulder holster, the usual preference of an FBI agent. Suddenly Neil was back in his seat and interrupting Karen's thoughts with a nudge,

"Here comes Mick, Karen." Karen looked up to see Mick weaving through the tables towards them, closely followed by a red-haired man who easily matched Mick in size. The man wore clean white coveralls and as they approached, Mick grinned and held his thumbs up in a gesture of success.

"This is Sean Crawford my instructor, guys," said Mick. The man smiled and nodded politely shaking Karen and Neil's hand with the strength of a bear. "Sean has a flight leaving for the west coast in an hour."

In a distinct, Scottish accent Sean followed Mick's introduction with, "Mick tells me you want to get to a town in Oregon, place they call Peace. You won't find it on any map. It's as if the place doesn't want to be found, but I know it exists because I've been there."

"You've actually been to Peace!" Karen said sounding surprised.

"Only once: I have a brother who worked for logging company close to the town. He had a bit of an accident, nothing too serious but his lumberjack days were over, I went there to fetch him and bring him home. I didn't stop in Peace long. It's not a very friendly place and as I remember it's about an hour or so from the air strip, but you can hire a car there. There is a small hotel in the town— well, it's more a boarding house. But I'd give that a miss, even the woman that owned the place made like she didn't want me there. There's a holiday campsite that practically overlooks the town. I've heard the cabins are pretty good. Funny how, just lately, everyone wants to go to Peace."

"What do you mean?" said Neil.

"Those two guys at the bar they'll be coming with us. And this'll be my second landing on the Memaloose airstrip this week." Karen and Neil guessed he might be talking about Dugan and the two DIs glance at each other conveyed as much.

"Better tell them about the cost, Sean," Mick said while making a face that conveyed to Neil and Karen that it was not going to be cheap."

"Okay, well like Mick said, I've got four seats left and I'm fixing to leave in an hour. I'll take the three of you for a grand, for that I'll give you a return flight whenever you are ready to come back." He put a card in Karen's hand. "Just phone that number to say your business is finished and I'll give you an approximate time to be at the same airstrip. How does that sound?"

"Sounds steep," said Neil.

"Aye but you don't get to maintain aircraft like mine by charging Greyhound prices. You can always take the bus; it'll only take you a couple of days to get there. There's one problem, though," Sean said. With that he took hold of both Mick and Neil's coat lapels and flipped them open to reveal their shoulder holsters. "I know you're cops but we'll be crossing state lines. I can't allow guns on my plane."

"What!" Mick said, frowning at Karen and Neil. "There's no way, I'm walking into that town unarmed."

"I know how you feel Mick," said Karen, "and I don't blame you, but I still feel I've got to do something, even if I have to go unarmed and alone."

Mick tried pleading with the pilot. "Sean, can't you make an exception? This is not a holiday trip, its police business we got a friend and colleague in this town, his life may be on the line."

"Look you guys, this no-weapons rule is not just a whim on my part. The law, says I'm not allowed to carry weapons, Christ you can understand that can't you this is a private plane not a jet fighter....Okay, I'll tell you what I'll do. When you board my plane I'll take your weapons and lock them up front with me in the flight compartment. That will make me feel easier, but it's going to cost you an extra $100 for the risk I'm taking. Customs sometimes come on board to do a spot search. That's the deal, no compromise and as far as the fare goes, I'll only take the folding kind. No plastic. I'll give you five minutes to discuss it. When you've made up your mind I'll be at the bar."

"You drink before piloting a plane?" Karen said disapprovingly.

"Only to excess, and only when I'm taking a risk like carrying guns." Sean then added with a grin, "I'm from Glasgow, drinking is traditional." With that he strode off towards the bar.

"Guess there's nothing to discuss, we take his offer, or we don't go," said Neil.

"There is one snag," Mick said. "I don't have that kind of cash on hand."

"Shit." said Karen, delving into the inside pocket of her leather jacket, "I've got about two hundred bucks on me and ATM's just don't shed that kind of money."

"Put it away you two, this trip's on me," said Neil, "My bank has a branch here, just give me five minutes." Neil pulled a wallet from his inside pocket and hurried away.

"Is he serious?" said O'Donnell. "He can lay his hands on that kind of money, just like that?"

"I guess these poor little rich boys, as you call them, have their uses; wouldn't you say, Mick?" Mick coloured up, recalling his many prejudiced condemnations of Neil and with no more reason than Neil's privileged background. Karen read the awkwardness on Mick's face and to sever his embarrassment she looked at her watch, saying,

"Come on, you haven't eaten, let's go get a coffee and a sandwich. We'll tell our pilot he's got a deal."

~~~~~~~~~

The three DI's were the last to board the plane and no more than a friendly nod passed between them and the two strangers already strapped in their seats. Karen noticed the black case now rested on the lap of the man nearest the window, like he was loath to put it in the luggage rack above their seat. Unlike commercial flights, Sean had no flight attendants to pamper his passengers but starting at the rear of the plane he gave a friendly word of assurance to each of them individually while checking their seat belt was properly fastened. Karen's seat was next to the aisle while Neil had the window seat next to her. As Sean reached across Karen to check Neil's belt she whispered to him,

"The guy with the black case, how do you know he's not carrying a gun in there?" Sean quickly glanced back at the man in question,

"Because I made him open it, it just contains medical stuff. Bandages, bottles syringes, that kind of thing. The guy's obviously a doctor, now sit back and relax Miss Sykes. We'll be airborne inside ten minutes."

Chapter 20 The Truth

I was sat upright on the bunk when a metal insert in the door slid open and a pair of eyes glared at me before slamming it shut again. It was Jake checking to see if I was recovering from the injection. I was pretty sure Charlie would come calling soon. Meanwhile I stood up to stretch my legs and arms, though I still had the handcuffs on. I tried touching my toes, a lost art since I'd regained weight but I remembered where they were and attempted to reach them a few times. It seemed to help disperse the last of the stiffness. I vowed in that instant, that if anyone came near me again with a hypodermic I'd make them eat it. I spent the next minute or so checking the lock on the door and was pretty sure I could crack it. It was then I heard footsteps and the jangle of keys. I quickly sat back down and made like I was still groggy. I was hoping I'd get a chance to take advantage of whoever came through the door. When it did open, Jake entered cautiously. He held his gun at the ready while checking that I still appeared docile. He then nodded to someone standing outside the door. Charlie entered followed by Aaron Yarn then, and to my complete surprise, in walked Winifred Howe with some bald guy I'd never seen before. Baldy had his arm around her, so I guessed the two were an item. Yarn must have read the confused look on my face.

"I can almost hear the cogs turning Mr Corwin," Yarn said, grinning. "Of course, Charlotte you know, but I'd like you to meet two more members of Esor, April and Andrew Dugan. You know April as Winifred Howe, of course, but unfortunately the real Winifred Howe is no more. We needed her property you see just as we need yours, needs must, as they say. It may interest you to know that April, Andrew and myself were once part of another cult but we quit that when our leader started to become unstable and a danger to the rest of us."

"Well who better to know the meaning of unstable?" I said sarcastically.

The Dugan woman was filing a nail just like she was on the day she involved me with these lunatics. She only glanced at me long enough to smirk before resuming her task.

"Your mind must be crammed full of questions, Corwin," The bald guy said, joining in the fun. Then Yarn took the chair again.

"And considering the generous contribution you have made to our cause by donating your property the least we can do is to answer some of those questions before your demise."

"Bullshit, you came in here to gloat. I've already got your number, Yarn. You're just a sick psycho that'll either end up full of FBI lead or you'll fester in some prison just like your pal: Manson. As for any contribution, I've no idea what the fuck you're talking about."

"I'm talking about your estate, Mr Corwin," he said, seemingly unaffected by my aggressive insults. "You die and everything you own passes to Esor, your property your bank account, everything. It's all in here," he said waving the folder Charlie was so keen for me to sign before I left the grange. "Now you know why our Mayor Mr Cloyce could be so generous with your income, it all reverts back to Esor anyway," Charlie stood next to Yarn looking at him like she was a lovesick teenager and he was her idol. She then turned to me.

"I have longed for this day, Spencer Corwin," she said through gritted teeth. "However I have enjoyed the games that we have played with you. You were so naive, so unsuspecting. You think you know so much, but you have little knowledge of what Esor means, its growing numbers and our glorious objective." At this point she turned to Jake and took the gun from his hand. She pointed it at me and my heart raced as I waited for the blast. The shot never came. "Attach his handcuffs to the bunk Jake, then go get the new girls and take them to room thirteen for their initiation service." Jake unlocked one of my wrists and clamped the cuff to the metal bed end, while I had visions of young Jenny being strapped down on the black altar in room 13. Yarn and Charlie waited for Jake to leave my cell before either of them spoke and I got the feeling Jake was not entrusted to all that went on in Peace.

"Do you know why we went to such lengths to lure you here Mr Corwin?"

"Yeah, you told me." I said, trying to sound bored. "You didn't like my name."

"Oh, that was for the benefit of the town's folk. You see I'm fairly new to Peace but I have gained their confidence to such a degree that they have accepted me as father to their congregation. This in itself is an achievement as they don't normally welcome strangers in their town. I first discovered Peace by accident. In fact from reading a book, a copy of which the town folk here call their register. You see it holds two lists of names." It was at this point I noticed a secretive glance pass between Dugan and April. It occurred to me that Yarns followers were not completely trustworthy. "One list," Yarn continued, "is of their ancestors; people who were persecuted for being witches and colluding with the devil. Many were put to death..."

"Yes, yes. We've all heard the stories of the Salem witch trials and the stupid superstitions that were behind the barbaric ways of dealing with ..."

"But what you didn't know was that many people in this town were true believers and have worshiped Satan longer than we have. Some believe their ancestors had certain unusual physical abnormalities that they can change at will and that these anomalies were the reason their forefathers were being put to death. Personally I've not witnessed any of these unusual acts of morphing. I believe they are old wives tales."

Yarn's words seem to stir a physical reaction in Andrew Dugan, which made April shoot another glance at him. It also renewed in me a vision of something furry running upright through the trees on the first day we arrived. Was this Yarn's so called morphing or the effects of the mushrooms we found in the woods?

"But all this is irrelevant as far as I'm concerned." Yarn continued. "The second list in the register is of the informants, magistrates and executioners responsible for the deaths of the town's ancestors. The people of Peace swore to avenge their forbearers by executing any descendants that came to their town. One such descendant was a woman whose forefather was a renowned executioner in Salem."

"The librarian woman in Witchville," I said. Yarn smiled.

"Yes, so you see I have gained the town's trust and I, like them, have sworn to help eliminate anyone on that list. It just happens that Corwin is a very prominent name in that list. Corwin was the name of one of the magistrates responsible for many of the hangings in Salem."

"Yeah whatever, like I said you didn't like my name. If you've finished flapping your gums Yarn, would you get me a drink; all your talk is making my mouth dry?"

Now that did get to him because his brow furrowed and the anger on his face was unmistakable as he continued. "Your name just happens to be a coincidence that suits our purpose. As far as I'm concerned you are here because you broke my legs, Corwin, You put me in hospital for two months and on crutches for a further two months." I suddenly remembered Jenny describing the man on crutches that she believed murdered her librarian friend. I also recalled seeing crutches in a broom cupboard under the church. As he spoke a mist cleared in my head and I suddenly saw his face through the windshield of my car back in San Francisco. "Well of course that made my wife Charlotte and I very angry and as ESOR is all about retribution we were determined to make you pay."

"Wife?" I hated having to play his question and answer game but the word wife threw me.

"Yes, wife," Charlotte intervened, having read the surprise on my face and her voice became full of malice, "You thought that you and I were married, Corwin, but the man that performed the ceremony was a member of ESOR. You and I were never married, we never even copulated." She said it like the very thought was abhorrent to her. "No, it was all in the power of suggestion and a little help with my husband's potions."

I somehow knew she was telling the truth and I don't know why, considering the dire situation I was in, but for some reason her words made me feel cleaner. I nevertheless couldn't resist retaliating for the insulting way she delivered them. I also wondered what it would take to get Yarn riled.

"Well you certainly had me fooled Charlie." I said. "That potion really must be the dog's bollocks because as I remember, our first night was the wildest I've ever had. I remember we tried it in every position one could dream up." Yarn was staring at Charlie now and I could tell he was asking himself if his potion really was that good. "I find it hard to believe a drug can make sex seem that real because I particularly remember how you liked it from the back I could have swore you came at least..."

"Enough!" shouted Yarn, his face was like thunder and I knew he'd taken the bait."

"Yes! That's exactly what I said to her. Hell you were an animal Chas. Hell I've never known a woman to go at it like you did. But then you couldn't have because we didn't really do it, did we Chaz?" I overdid winking at her to make sure Yarn saw it. He did, and I think he wanted to strangle us both there and then. "Anyway, if you say it was all in my mind, I can't tell you what a relief that is, Chas, because I've always regarded bestiality as the most depraved act a woman could sink to. What I don't understand, is why a man, who thought anything of his wife, would let her be used like that." Now Charlie had that puzzled look. Was she asking herself the same question? "And to go to so much trouble just to pay me back for what was just an accident is beyond my comprehension. As I remember it, Yarn, you ran out in front of my car."

"I do not allow for accidents, Corwin." Yarn had dropped the mister so I knew I'd upset him. "Any offence against me is an offence against the master and any action against him must have a reaction."

The longer this guy prattled on, the more I thought he was totally insane.

"You ran me down in your car so you had to pay. That is the whole basis of our cult: retribution. I could have had you eliminated at the time, but then we discovered that you owned property. That meant a change of plans. First we had to get rid of any claimants to the house so I had Charlotte work on your wife by convincing her she had cancer. That had a positive result; it just left your daughter the only other claimant to your property."

I couldn't believe what I just heard. "Don't be stupid, Yarn. My wife committed suicide because of a brain tumour." Yarn responded to this by just grinning at me and it was then that I realised he was telling the truth and I knew just how sick these people were.

Tears clouded my eyes and Yarn could see he'd knocked the cockiness out of me but I wanted to know the extent of their crimes.

"And my daughter—you were behind that?" Again the three grinned. I cursed the shackles that were stopping me from tearing their throats out. "You're a sick bastard, Yarn. You murdered the man in my precinct and the librarian in Witchville Massachusetts, just how many more people have you murdered, Yarn?" I suddenly remembered Karen Sykes and how the search for her husband ended in Oregon. Oregon's a big state and it seemed a hell of a long shot to think Steve Sykes could also have ended up in Yarn's clutches, but I had nothing to lose in trying to find out if he did.

"You think you lured me here with money, Yarn but I had another reason for coming to Peace, do you remember Steve Sykes?"

"Ah yes, another profitable undertaking. Greed certainly proves to be a great means of entrapment."

It worked; if this Yarn had any weak points, arrogance was definitely one of them. He even confessed to murder with an air of superiority.

"So you murdered him for his property as well?"

"I do not personally murder anyone, Corwin, I just entice them here. I merely inform my disciples of the link to the accusers of their forefathers. They then pass sentence on them. The master's pets carry out the execution."

"You can mince words all you like, but you are still guilty of murder. Manson didn't physically murder any of the people at that Los Angeles address but he'll still spend the rest of his life behind bars because he was the instigator and you are no different."

"I do not regard the victims as people. I see them as souls in the shape of gifts for the master. However I do sometimes discriminate if my work is threatened I sometimes need to take steps. The man in precinct 13 was a past work associate who became a threat. He was about to make trouble for the cult so yes that was I. As for the woman in Witchville...she was obsessed with witches her writings were causing the town of Peace to become a curiosity for unwanted visitors and the like." Yarn paused for a moment as we all heard the sound of a female cry out as if in pain somewhere in close by. Yarn, however, continued talking, "People who read her books were becoming curious. Too many tourists were starting to visit the town so much so that a nearby campsite established itself to accommodate the curious. I promised the people of Peace I'd put a stop to their snooping and I did. Mr Dugan helped me deal with the authoress on the east coast. Then with the master guiding my hand a little genetic recoding to the fish in Pike Lake now deters visitors from coming anywhere near the place." I saw Dugan grin when Yarn mentioned his name and read the madness in his eyes. I knew he was as dangerous as Yarn. "I thought the crutches were a nice touch though," Yarn continued, "They certainly gave the police a hard time trying to fathom out how I escaped. You see they were not looking for two people."

"Just how many others have you murdered, Yarn?"

"Not enough Mr Corwin, I am a collector of souls but I've collected enough to keep the master happy and its early days. I can assure you we have something special awaiting you." It was at this point Jake came back in the room and seemed agitated as he quietly mumbled something to Charlie she frowned then turned to Yarn and repeated the whispered message. I had no idea what news Jake had brought, but I thought I heard the word birth.

~~~~~~~~~~

The weather was good and a favourable easterly wind helped the Lear arrive in good time. The landing strip was carved amid logging country and soon after Sean came over the intercom to tell his passengers they were making their descent, a single runway appeared as a thin white scar shaved through a vast sea of fir trees. Airstrip, as Sean called it was about right; the place did not merit the title: airport. A small hut sat atop a wooden construction was all it could boast for its control tower. The only sign that there was any kind of life around was a hangar which housed a water carrying chopper, a mobile diner and a small general store.

As the DI's left the plane Sean furtively handed them their weapons and reminded them to phone to arrange a return flight. He then nodded toward the general store next to a mobile diner, "That's where you'll hire your car. Good luck and I hope you find your friend." With that he closed the Lear's door and within two minutes they saw the plane taxiing for a takeoff.

As the three headed across the tarmac they had to pass a stationary patrol car where they saw the attaché case man and his companion conversing with a uniformed police officer sat in the driver's seat. As the DI's neared them they stopped talking and waited until the three were out of earshot.

"What do you make of those two?" Karen said as they neared the general store.

"They look like Feds," said Mick.

"The tall one, maybe," Neil said, "but I don't know about the little guy with the attaché case, he didn't look like a Fed to me. I caught the word, cops. I think they were talking about us."

They reached the store where two vehicles were parked outside: a beat up Toyota pickup truck and an equally dented Chevrolet saloon. Both vehicles were long past their scrap-by date. Sharon assumed the drivers were inside the store, but when they entered she was surprised to find only one unshaven fifty-something guy sitting behind a counter in a worn out armchair. He was reading a top shelf magazine, which he didn't bother to hide. In fact he seemed reluctant to drag his eyes over the top of it to even acknowledge them. Eventually, and with as much enthusiasm for their custom as a guy who'd just won a million on the lottery, he jerked his head up in a manner that Karen interpreted as, *what the fuck do you three want and how dare you disturb my perverted thoughts.*

Karen answered his lack of manners with, "We want to rent a car."

"They're all out except the two outside, the Chevy and the Pickup," was the man's terse reply. By the decrepit state of the store and the unkempt proprietor, Karen surmised that he probably owned three piles of junk and guessed that the two dented heaps outside were the worst of them. "It's fifty a day, plus a hundred for insurance up front which you get back if the vehicle comes back the same shape."

"Oh it will," said Mick, "We don't intend to straighten the dents out."

"Oo-oh there goes another rib," the man said with a mock chuckle before quickly reverting back to his miserable expression.

"Which one would you recommend?" said Mick scowling at him.

"Personally I'd recommend taking a bus but it depends where you want to get to."

"Peace," said Karen.

With that the man threw the magazine under the counter and stood up, "In that case you'll need the pickup and it'll cost you two hundred up front."

"Is that a joke!" exclaimed Neil we've been told it's only around fifty miles..."

"It's not the distance, it's the direction. I've already lost two cars to customers that claimed they were going there."

"Are you saying it's a dangerous road?" said Neil.

"No, I'm saying it's a dangerous destination. Sometimes they don't come back."

"The cars?"

"Not just the cars. I've been to Peace with a police escort. Not a sign of my cars or the drivers. It's a creepy town and the folk are a weird bunch; everyone we spoke to in that town said they never saw my cars or the drivers."

Karen produced her shield and held it out for him to see, "Look, we've also heard some strange things about that town, and we already suspect people have gone missing there. That's why we are here, to check out the place. Now this could be in your interest. You might even get your vehicles back." Karen then flipped Mick's coat open to reveal his gun. "As you can see, we don't intend to disappear like your other customers."

This seemed to spur enthusiasm into the proprietor; he turned and grabbed some keys from off a hook, "Here take the Toyota its four wheel drive, it's got a full tank and drives better than it looks. Forget the insurance just pay for the gas and hire cost when...if you get back,"

"Can you head us in the right direction for this place?"

"Sure, take the road behind this store and head north. I clocked the mileage to the town limits at exactly fifty miles, but when you've driven about forty miles you'll see a sign directing you to Harwell Hospital that means you're still on the right road. After that you'll start to see sign posts telling you to branch off, don't, you'll get lost. Villagers are suspicious; they hate strangers especially since someone opened a holiday camp that overlooks their town so they keep changing the signs. Stick with the same road all the way. You'll eventually come to a steep rise the camp is at the top. When you get there you'll be just a short distance from Peace. If the camp hasn't closed for the season you might want to stay the night. The cabins are good and it's safer than staying in the town."

When they left the store the patrol car was gone and so were the two men. Karen was keen to start their journey while it was still daylight but Mick was hungry and his stomach won the argument. They had a burger and a coffee at the diner and by the time they set off for Peace it was getting dark. Mick drove and the pickup handled better than expected. The cab was roomy but the road was none too smooth. They had driven for about an hour and covered forty miles without passing another vehicle, and in all that distance they saw nothing but fir trees on either side of the road. It was dark when the Toyota's engine started to labour as it started to climb a steep hill. Karen, who'd taken note of the mileage before they left said,

"Hey we've done forty five miles we must by close to that camp by now." Almost as Karen said this they came upon a notice board. Mick pulled up, found the switch for the adjustable search light to read the words: Pine Needle Camp, Log cabins for rent half a mile.

"Fingers crossed it's still open," said Neil. "I could really use some sleep."

"Yes, maybe we ought to do like the man said and stop for the night, we can't go knocking doors in the dark anyway," Mick said, "especially if the residents are as unfriendly as he said. Anyway we'll need a base to decide how we're going to tackle this."

"I agree," Karen said. "Okay, go for it." Slipping the Toyota back into drive Mick pulled away again. The road became Narrow and as they neared the top of the rise they entered a sharp bend where Mick suddenly hit the brakes hard. They could see the campsite entrance just up ahead and several armed men in suits. By the light of the exterior lamps each side of the entrance they recognised the tall man that was on their flight, but blocking their way was the patrol car and police officer they recognised from the aerodrome. The uniformed cop was leaning against his car with a pump rifle resting in the crook of his folded arm. The three waited for him to approach Mick's side of the truck.

"Good evening detectives, Mr Askey is expecting you. I'd like you to hand your weapons to me then vacate the vehicle please. You can leave the engine running sir I'll park it."

"We're police officers we have every right to carry our weapons" said Mick.

"You're in Oregon now and that changes your rights, so hand them over. Don't worry you'll get them back when Mr Askey say's so."

"What's going on? Who the hell's Mr Askey?" Mick said, sounding annoyed but handing over a model 22 Smith & Wesson as he stepped down from the Toyota. Karen and Neil followed suit, handing their weapons over as the deputy ordered.

"The tall man standing at the gate," said the Deputy, "He'll take you to meet Alex Askey. He will explain why you've been stopped."

The three did as they were ordered and as the police officer climbed into the Toyota's cab the tall man led the three inside the campsite. Log cabins could be seen generously spaced and stretching back into the trees. In the fading light there was no telling how many cabins there were or how far into the trees the camp stretched. The only people seen walking about, were men and all of them looked to be dressed like FBI agents.

The three detectives were taken to a large RV parked next to the nearest log cabin on which hung the sign: Pine Needle Camp Reception.

"Mister Askey is in this trailer. He wants to talk to the three of you," the sergeant said, opening the door. They looked around at the interior. It was immediately obvious to them that this was not part of the camp. This was a command centre. Electronic equipment lined the inside with one young man sitting at a computer monitor. A large aerial photo hung against one wall blanking out the windows; this was an aerial view of the camp site and a populated town in the valley beneath it. Sat behind a desk at the rear end of the camper was the attaché case man. He was conversing with a middle aged man that wore a baseball cap. The two of them looked up as the four entered, and the attaché case man motioned the three to the empty chairs facing his desk.

"Good evening detectives. Come and take a seat please. I know you'll have some questions. Thank you Greg I don't expect you'll be needed again tonight."

With that our big escort nodded and withdrew, closing the door behind him.

"I guessed it wouldn't take you long to get here." The three sat and Karen fired the first question,

"Who are you, and if you know we're cops why have we had our weapons taken away?"

"Whoa, one question at a time; first of all my name is Alex Askey and this gentleman is George Weston." Weston gave Karen a smile and nodded to Neil and Mick, "Mr Weston is the proprietor of Pine Needle Camp which as from today is closed for the season. George has kindly made his cabins available to the FBI, until we conclude our business in the area." Askey then addressed Mr Weston, "Thank you for your help George you will be compensated."

"Forget it. If you sort that town out, and customers start to come back, it will be all the compensation I need. I just hope you find that young couple." With that George nodded to Karen and as he left, the deputy marshal came in and unloaded the detectives' weapons on Askey's desk,

"I've parked your pickup on the grass verge outside the gate," he said to Mick. "It'll be safe enough there and out of the way. It will be chaos here when the police cars arrive tomorrow." As he handed the Toyota key back to Mick, Askey turned to the three detectives,

"Right," he said placing the hand guns in one of his desk drawers. "I will make sure you get these back before you leave. As far as your claim to being police officers is concerned, no you're not; at least not out here. I am connected to San Francisco's justice department and at present working with the FBI. You probably noticed several agents as you entered the camp. I have total jurisdiction over this region until our business here is completed. I believe, Miss Sykes, you were warned not to get involved with the investigations taking place in this area."

"Yes I was, but..."

"But you decided not to comply?" interrupted Askey.

"Well, I didn't think the FBI considered my story serious enough to act on. You see we have a colleague, a close friend in Peace and we believe he's in trouble. We're here to help bring him out. "Yes, you mean Spencer Corwin, the man posing as a sheriff in the town."

"Yes...what do you mean, posing?"

"Maybe that's the wrong word. Maybe this Spencer Corwin believes he is an official law officer doing a meaningful job, but he has no real authority. Ken Murray is the only official law officer here at the moment. We believe your Mr Corwin has been duped and we believe he's not the first. It's all smoke and mirrors in Peace and we are not sure what's real and what isn't but that is what I'm here to find out. Well detectives, you are practically in Peace the town is right at the bottom of this hill, in fact you can see the town from the top of the rise. I concur that Mr Corwin is in danger but then so is everyone in that town, because federal marshals and armed deputies will be crawling all over that town soon with instructions to shoot anyone who retaliates. I just hope it doesn't become another Waco siege."

Karen gave a worried glance at Mick and Neil before saying, "That sounds a bit heavy?"

"Maybe, but the information received from our source is that the members of this cult are more dangerous than the Manson family and we know what they did. We believe atrocities have been committed in Peace, acts in keeping with satanic rituals. What is more worrying is the arsenal they have been amassing and what their intentions are. Because of this I have orders to take whatever action is deemed necessary. Certain things have happened since your visit to the federal building. Did they inform you that two agents have gone missing from this region?"

"They only mentioned one and they never said he was missing."

"Well its two, a man and a woman and their reports have both stopped."

"A woman," Mick exclaimed. "You sent a woman in there?"

"Hey, I'm a woman!" said Karen.

"Oh yeah, sorry Kaz, I have to keep reminding myself," Mick said with a grin.

"Anyway," Askey added, "we believe the woman may have been discovered because her last message said she was coming in, meaning she was coming back to base. She may have been murdered if they discovered she was an informant working for the

FBI. That, we take serious and it's one of the reasons we've now moved on this."

"Not because you were following us?"

"No but we did arrive on the same plane so I can see why you'd think that. You said you didn't think our director took your report serious but he did. He listened to your concerns about who you thought was involved with this cult, you named Andrew Dugan for instance." Neil started to shift nervously in his chair. "We have had Dugan followed ever since you told us you suspected him." Mick glanced at Neil then at Karen. All three knew that if the FBI had been following Dugan they probably know about the two bodies in Neil's house? Alex Askey read the look of concern on Neil's face and his mouth curled into a smile as he said, "You really need not have put the bodies in Dugan's car. We already knew Dugan killed them. You have just caused the SFPD a headache. Dugan will pay for his crimes but we were hoping he'd lead us to others that were mixed up in this cult. For that reason we let him think he'd gotten away clean. As it turned out he led us straight to Oakland airport, where he booked a flight here."

"So you know about the bodies?" said Neil, sighing with relief.

"Yes, it's a pity that couldn't have been prevented. We were watching the house because of the APB issued on you, D.I Roster, but we had no idea Dugan intended to murder that couple. As to their identities, maybe you will be able to clear that up for us."

"Probably not," Karen said quickly, afraid that Neil might let on that he married Abigail and knowing it would just complicate matters further. "We only know they've been trying to murder D.I Roster, and we believe they murdered a retired Chief D.I by the name of Winifred Howe. I think they were into some kind of property stealing scam. Possibly to fund what's going on in Peace. We believe a man by the name of Aaron Yarn is behind all this. We don't know how many properties he has stolen or how many of the owners have been murdered but we believe Spencer Corwin's house is another they've set their sights on. We will tell you all we know Mr Askey, but right now we're concerned for Corwin's safety and we want to get into that town. Are you going to let us through?"

"No. At least not tonight I've got orders not to let you go down there until the marshals are ready. The town doesn't suspect anything and the raid has to be a surprise. Mr Weston has had a three bedroom cabin prepared for you. Its number 1 right opposite the reception cabin so I suggest you make yourselves comfortable and wait like the rest of us. Did you just say someone by the name of Howe had been murdered?"

"That's not definite, but we think so," said Neil. "She either fell or was pushed in front of a train."

"She?"

"Yes, is that relevant?"

"Maybe—Howe is not a common name and it's the name of our missing agent."

Neil suddenly recalled part of Gwen's story on his meeting at the Red Bull. "That wouldn't be Agnes Howe would it?" He said.

Askey's sudden frown suggested surprise. "How did you come by that info?"

"Our source told us Winifred Howe had a sister living in this area and that they often conversed by phone Agnes confided in her sister about this cult and some of what was going on in Peace. What we didn't know was that this sister Agnes was an FBI agent."

Mick O'Donnell, feeling the need to be more engaged said, "San Francisco cops are not just guts and guns Mr Askey."

"No I can see that. What else have you discovered from this source of yours?" Askey said. This was Karen's cue to take the lead again,

"Okay, so we also know that this Agnes was working with a man also posing as a law officer in Peace, a John Cruikshank. We know that this man went there in the hope of rescuing his daughter, Gina, from the influence of Aaron Yarn. If Agnes is missing maybe John and his daughter are both missing too."

"Well you certainly haven't let the grass grow under your feet with this case, I'll give you that," said Askey, "but I can tell you that when I realised where you were going I informed my boss expecting him to tell me to stop you and he did, but at least you won't have to wait long Armed Marshals and FBI agents are amassing now in Portland they are being briefed as we speak. I'm expecting them to arrive at first light tomorrow. They will have orders to go in hard if they meet resistance. So I'll give you two hours before the marshals go in. That'll give you time to get any innocents to safety including Corwin if you can. You'll be given FBI vests to take with you. Make sure you put them on before the SWAT team arrives; otherwise you'll just be three more targets. There is one more thing." Askey paused and lifted his briefcase onto his desk and as he snapped open the clasps he said, "I told you our agent sent us something before we lost contact, this is it," Askey took out a small glass vial of what looked like cloudy water and held it for them to see. "The agency's lab has analysed this and found it to be a very powerful and debilitating drug. I'm told when used, different strengths it gives differing results."

"Such as?" asked Neil

"Such as using it in its undiluted form a few grams will paralyse a person within a few minutes and incapacitate for an hour or two depending on certain factors, like the size of the person, whether they've eaten recently, that sort of thing. Too large a dose and the paralysis could be permanent."

"Is that it?" said Mick, sounding eager to move on.

Askey let out a sigh of exasperation before glaring angrily at Mick. "This is important Mr O'Donnell; if you go into that town without knowing what you're up against you may not come out."

Karen stepped in to alleviate the tension building through Mick's impatience.

"Sorry Mr Askey. Mick here is keen to get our friend out of that place."

"That I can understand, but what I have to impart could be what gets you or your friend out of that place alive. Let's say you find your Mr Corwin and maybe others in a drugged state, what would you do, carry them out? I don't think so; you'll have enough trouble just walking with those armoured vests on. So I think it's in your interest to hear me out. Now as I was saying, with some experimenting our lab found that in a weak solution this drug becomes a powerful hallucinogenic. I personally volunteered to be a guinea pig and wished I hadn't. I thought I was going crazy after they fed me that stuff." Karen's thoughts went immediately to the night she was invited to Spencer's house for dinner.

From his case Askey took a small leather wallet. He opened it to reveal a hypodermic syringe and a tiny vial of clear liquid.

"I want you to take this when you enter Peace. If you find any victims incapacitated through these drugs give him or her three millilitres from this bottle. It will stimulate their heart and produce adrenalin which will counteract the drug. Our laboratories have been working overtime to come up with this, but remember only three millilitres; any more could bring on a heart attack. Now cabin 8 is right behind the reception cabin and it has been made ready for you. You and my agents will be the only guests in the camp; Mr Weston said his last customers were a young couple that only spent two nights here. He said he thinks they went down into the town and that was the last he saw of them. I suggest you get some sleep and make an early start in the morning. If I don't see you again before this business is over, good luck." The three thanked him, shook his hand and left.

The lodge was nicely furnished and a potbelly stove had been lit for their comfort.

"Hey this is great," said Mick, opening the door to his room to see a comfortable bed. "I feel like I'm on vacation."

Neil answered with, "Hmm, let's hope you feel the same tomorrow when the cavalry arrives all waving their guns around and just itching to make holes in people."

Chapter 21 Chasing Shadows

I sat there shackled to the steel bed frame. I could hear muffled voices, sometimes a female voice crying out from somewhere within the tunnel, or maybe on another level. I thought about the circumstances that led me to Peace in the first place and ultimately to my present predicament. When I try to recall all the events and circumstances that led me to be in Peace; it's like trying to peer through a mist. I wondered how much of it could be blamed on influences beyond my control, i.e. drugs that had been slipped to me or was it something darker, something less explicable. Or was it due to my own stupidity which if I'm honest all amounted to the same thing. Now my mind seems to be clearing, and I realise why the guys back in the precinct treated me like I had lost it. In fact I had, but now I believe my sense of reasoning had been impaired though Charlotte keeping me semi-drugged on Yarn's concoctions. The important question now was whether I could get Jimmy, Julie and myself out of the immediate fix I'd gotten us into. Even if I managed to get out of this cell, how far would I get before someone tackled me and raised the alarm. I suddenly thought about the linen closet where I'd seen the habit style robes; now if I could get to that closet...it was worth a try. Jake had shackled my right hand to the steel bed end which made it difficult to reach the lock-picks that I'd stupidly hidden under the wrong end of the mattress before Jake cuffed me to the opposite end of the bed frame. My leg had stopped bleeding but felt sore as I stretched to reach the picks. I was sure the hole in my leg needed cleaning. I figured that in the gloom of the cell, Yarn had not noticed the blood. If he did he never questioned it, but why would he when he had much worse planned for me. I wondered if there were other cells on this level that Jimmy and Jenny could be confined. I tried to convince myself that the cries I heard were not from Jenny, that they were most likely from one some stranger that I'd never met or seen. I couldn't shake this sense of guilt for getting Jimmy and Jenny, mixed up in this.

I faced the cell door and called Jimmy's name in little more than a loud whisper, but I got no response and figured I was alone down there. I wondered if I'd be able to find steps that led up to the church altar. There were far too many things to go wrong but I had to try for Jimmy and Jenny's sake. I managed to reach the picks under the mattress, but more difficulty came in trying to pick the lock with my left hand and fearing that any minute the inspection plate would slide open and someone would catch me in the act.

Eventually the lock clicked open and I lay on the bed thinking about my next move. I found it hard to breathe and wondered if it was caused by my phobia of being trapped underground or just that my lack of exercise was finally taking its toll.

Next came the cell door, and I was surprised to find picking the door lock easier than the cuff links. I heard the lock open. I held my breath, listening intently before taking a chance on pushing the door open. The smell of the passageway outside was even mustier than the cell. Meagre lighting showed chalky earthen walls and the ceiling propped up at regular intervals with rough sawn wooden props. I wondered how far I was below the surface, how safe the wooden supports were and how many tons of earth were above just waiting to turn me into worm food. If this was what it felt like to work in a mine shaft, it was not a vocation I would envy. The glow from spaced out wall lamps was not really adequate, but just enough to see a few feet in front of me. The fact that these were ordinary lamps and not red told me this was a section of tunnel Jimmy and I had not explored. I had no idea which direction to take, so I took a guess and followed the passage to my right. It was the right choice; a few feet along I came to another cell door. Quietly I slid the inspection plate across and immediately recognised Jimmy's shirt but his back was to the door and I could not see if he was awake.

"Psst, Jimmy" There was no answer. And I called louder but still no response. I guessed he was still under the influence of Yarns drugs and unable to move. I was about to pick the lock on his cell but then realised I would not be able to get him out while he was still drugged. I thought about those hooded cloaks we'd seen behind and decided getting hold of one first might be a better idea. I moved on to the next cell and opened the inspection plate and wished I hadn't. I put my face close to it and just as I recognised Jenny a full plate of porridge oats hit the inspection slot. Her aim was perfect; it smashed against the inside of the opening covering my face and eyes in the thick sticky goo. This was my first introduction to Jenny's temper. I moved to the right of the inspection slot and wiped some of the warm porridge away from my face and eyes before I glared in the opening again.

"Thanks Jenny, you wouldn't have a spoon to go with that would you?" Only then did she realise it was me.

"Oh Spencer I'm sorry, I thought you were that horrible Jake. He's been spying on me. Please get me out of this terrible place. I've heard a girl screaming. And where's my Jimmy?"

"Jimmy's okay but save the questions Jen and keep your voice down, I'm going to try to get your cell open."

I had Jen's cell door open even faster than mine. The next problem was finding which direction would get us out. I grabbed Jenny's hand and let instinct choose the way. There were three more cells along the way and curiosity made me open their inspection plates. Two cells were empty but I immediately recognised the guy in the third one. It was the man that stopped to ask directions to the school, Mathew Black, the guy that had come to Peace as a teacher. By the growth around his face I'd guess he's been in that cell since the day I first saw him. He heard the inspection slot open and looked up, but I guess he needed to see more than a pair of eyes to recognise me. I decided not to get his hopes up by telling him who I was in case my escape attempt failed.

Black's was the last door, Jen and I hurried on and a few feet further along, the passage started to slope upwards; I could see a reddish glow up ahead and we could hear the sound of someone speaking in a loud voice. As we reached the top of the slope I realised we were in the section of passage that Jimmy and I had previously explored. The voice and words were now audible and the room that it came from had the number 13 on the door, I now had my bearings. Jen and I stood and listened for a moment. It was Yarn and he sounded like he was preaching.

"That's him Spencer" Jenny whispered excitedly. "That's the voice of the man in the library. What's going on in there Spencer?"

I was tempted to burst through that door without answering her. I expected to see some young girl giving birth, but without at least a side arm it would have been foolhardy, and my responsibility was to get Jenny to safety.

"You don't want to know Jenny," I whispered, "and without a weapon we'd best not try to find out." I pulled Jenny away and we continued on our way toward the exit. I remembered which room I'd seen robes stored and we found two black versions which we donned as we continued our way toward the exit. As we started to ascend the steps leading up to the church altar, I turned to Jenny,

"I've no idea what time of day it is, have you?"

"I don't care about the time. I'm only concerned about Jimmy." She sounded like she was about to cry.

"Take it easy—I care! There's a sliding floor at the top of these steps that's about to open. If it's daylight up there, our chance of getting out of here will be practically zero, that's why I care."

"Sorry, Spencer, but this place terrifies me."

"Yeah, me too, I know what those animals have put you through, and I'm beginning to understand what they're about, but try to hold it together, Jen. Once we get you somewhere safe I'll come back for Jimmy, but I'm not going back without a gun. I need to get to the sheriff's office first, I need a weapon." Suddenly we heard the familiar whirring sound of the church altar moving. We looked up and to my relief only darkness could be seen through the widening gap above us.

~~~~~~~~~

The main street of Peace seemed deserted. Rain clouds had formed threatening a storm. This was an advantage, it made the night even darker than I'd hoped. Most locals retired early and Jenny and I heard no generators and we saw no lights. We started to hurry while hugging the darkest of shadows. I had no idea of the hour but guessed that if there were any normal residents living in this town, they were all sleeping. It seemed longer, but I guessed it could only have been ten minutes since I opened my cell door. I expected that any minute, a crowd of shrieking Satanists might come charging from the church in pursuit of us. I prayed my car was still in the alley near the end of Main Street, beyond that thought my mind was blank. I had left the key in the ignition out of habit, after all who's going to steal a patrol car in a little town like Peace; Amos Carrier was blind and hospitalised. Suddenly there came exactly what I feared, the sound of voices from the direction of the church. We saw shadows moving in the church grounds and I felt Jenny squeeze my hand. Then we heard a shout and the sound of running feet before gun shots rang out and the audible sound of a bullet whistled passed us causing Jenny to let out a little squeak. The shot gave us another spurt of speed. There were several gaps and alleys between buildings and houses. We could have taken a chance and ducked down one of them in the hope the chasers would go past, but that would not have got Jenny away and the men would eventually find us. No, my car was in the last alley and our best chance was to try to get there but the pursuers were gaining. I prayed the car was still there, even if we made it to the car I calculated those cloaked devils would reach us before we could drive out of the alley. The hunters were still a distance away when we reached the alley and to my relief the car was still there and the keys were still in it. I had seconds to make a decision; I opened the back door, "Quick, Jenny, jump in here and get down on the floor." She did and I draped my yellow oilskin from off the back seat over her. "I'll lead them away from you and try to make it into the woods. Then I'll double back for Jimmy after I find a weapon. The key is in the ignition, as soon as it's clear get behind the wheel and drive as fast as you can up to Pine Needles Camp. Get someone to call the Portland police."

Without waiting for her to reply I quietly closed the back door and left Jenny there. I got to the entrance of the alley and peered around the corner towards the church. I was expecting to be shot at or jumped on as soon as I stepped out of the alley but I was surprised to find the street empty, then as I peered into the darkness a face appeared at the end of the block about a hundred feet away and I realised that our pursuers must have been searching for us down there. Whoever the man was, only his face made him visible and I was pleased my black cloak made the ideal camouflage. Providing I kept my face covered I might just make it to the woods. Another two faces then appeared behind the first. I sprinted across the road at a tangent as another shot rang out. The slug hit a wall some yards from me and I knew who ever fired was just taking pot luck at the sound of me running.

On the far side of the road I dived behind a hedgerow belonging to the kiddies nursery from here I watched and waited. I had to make sure the pursuers didn't enter the alley and discover Jenny in the car. It started to rain but as I waited my eyes were growing accustomed to the dark because I gradually made out the shapes of four shadows. They faltered at the opening to the alley and I guessed they were looking at the car and wondering if we were in it. Then I saw one of them enter the alley. When I heard the click of my car door being opened I knew it was time for plan B.

I sprang from behind the hedge shouting. "Keep running Jen! Get to the woods." with that I sprinted toward the signpost that read To the Lake, it was the quickest way to get into the woods. As I ran I heard more gunfire. I ran expecting any moment one of their shots to find its mark. I zigzagged without glancing back hoping that all four shadows were in pursuit and that Jen would see her chance to get away. I made it to the trees with a few yards to spare but not before feeling one shot tug at my hood as it whistled past me.

~~~~~~~~~~

Jenny, while hidden under the oilskin, waited and prayed that Spencer had made the right decision in telling her to hide there. Peering between the seats she checked to see if he was right about the keys; yes, the keys were there in the ignition, but as she looked at them a shadow fell across the windshield and she shrank further under the oilskin coat. She then heard the rear door click open and she held her breath expecting any moment for the oilskin to be snatched away from her. But through the open door came a distant, but clear, shout of, *"Keep running Jen! Get to the woods".* She felt the car door slam shut again and heard the diminishing sound of running feet before the sound of more gunfire Jenny let out a long sigh that formed the words, *"bless you Spence."* Jenny waited until the gunfire stopped while praying that Spencer had not been hit. She waited a few moments longer, listening and hoping she would not hear jubilant voices boasting of a kill, but all was silent. She emerged from under the oilskin jacket and climbed into the driver's seat. She sat looking at the cars controls and wishing that Spencer had first asked her if she could drive before leaving her. She'd watched jimmy drive almost the breadth of North America but as she looked at the controls she noted things were different. Why were there no letters at the base of the floor lever? She remembered Jimmy's car having the letters PND and numbers 123, but this had no markings and why were there three pedals when there should be only two? She started to bite her lip, thinking the hunters would be back to look for her any moment. She knew she had to do something fast. Stretching out her legs, she tried pressing the pedals down and found she had to sink down in her seat to be able to push them to the floor. This reminded her of when she was a twelve-year-old, sitting beside her father. He had let her drive his truck along the deserted beach sands near their home on the east coast. She remembered pushing that lever forward and the engine making that terrible grinding noise. Yes she suddenly remembered her father saying you got to use the clutch. Right this is it she said to herself as she turned the ignition key.

~~~~~~~~~

It was raining heavily now. I entered the woods with a hand outstretched in front of me lest I ran smack into a tree. I veered off at a tangent with the intention of moving in a wide circle, I figured I could then double back and get to the town hall and the office where the rifles were kept. I could hear bracken snapping in all directions and guessed the hunters had split up giving them a greater chance of finding me. I was suddenly put on my back when I ran into a low branch; it didn't knock me out, but instead knocked an idea into shape. I grabbed the culprit branch and hauled myself up.

I reasoned that if I could get high enough into a tree and hide they would eventually give up. I struggled to hoist myself onto the first branch but gained strength from the fear of being dragged back to that hole in the ground. The effort also reminded me of my weight problem and I promised myself that if I came out of this alive I'd diet. Having got my two feet onto the first branch the second was easier and I thought I might make tree-climbing part of my weight loss training. A loud thrashing of bracken made me suddenly hold my breath. I knew one of the shadows was close. I looked down and there he was in his monk's habit less than ten feet below me. It was like watching the grim reaper threshing about with his scythe but he was using the very thing I needed, a rifle. This was my chance, I could drop straight on top of him my weight alone would put him out of action. I just prayed the others were not too close by. I braced myself and made ready to drop when I heard the distant sound of a car engine. The shadow below froze too and I knew he was listening. Then there came a squeal of tyres and a shout from one of his fellow monks prompting him to dash off in the direction of the sound. I smiled, knowing Jenny was on her way.

I decided to wait until the sound of cracking twigs ceased. As I waited it occurred to me how cold the night had become, then I realised the serge cloak was now heavily soaked. After a generous time I climbed down and headed back towards the town when I saw a dim light through the trees. I moved in its direction and was surprised to see a house hidden away on the edge of the woods. I decided not to trust going any closer to it but to head for the sheriff's office. I would have to cut through to Main Street again and that was in itself worrying. I was hoping the four shadows believed that I had somehow doubled back to the car and escaped with Jenny. If that were the case they wouldn't be expecting me to return. I peered out towards the town and was about to step out into the clearing when I heard the faint rustle of a footstep behind me. I quickly turned to find myself feet away from an old man. He was not wearing a habit so I knew he was not one of my pursuers. I was about to speak when he held a finger up to his mouth in a gesture of silence. He then pointed to my right and that's when I saw the black shape of one of the hunters. I guessed his accomplices had already retreated back to their underground lair to report their failure. I quickly stooped to hide, and wondered if, Yarn might make an example of these men in room 13 for losing us.

The rain had dispersed now and unfortunately the clouds were clearing to give more visibility but it was as if the clouds had all dispersed. I shivered and pulled the wet hood across my lower face until the last of the monks had given up. I then turned to thank the old man, but he was some distance away now heading back into the woods. I quickly followed hoping he could furnish me with some kind of weapon. By the time I caught up with him he was just entering the garden gate of a small cottage that stood alone in a clearing. It reminded me of a story by the brothers Grimm, and sent another chill through me. But I still followed and as he hobble along his path toward the front door I suddenly realised he was the same old timer that spoke to Avril and me at the town stocks.

~~~~~~~~~~

As the old man reached the front door he turned and beckoned me to follow him inside. Why I trusted him I'm not sure, but my options were limited. I thought if the old man had some kind of weapon I may not have to risk going back to the town hall. Instead I could get straight back to the tunnel and try to rescue Jimmy. I checked to see if anyone had seen me enter the old man's house before closing his door behind me. I followed his shuffling walk into a cosy little lounge while breathing in a pleasant smell of pipe tobacco. It seemed odd that I now found myself in his home waiting for an explanation as to why he invited me in. As we started to converse I found myself liking the old man. There was something reassuring in his twinkling blue eyes and confident smile. Even more pleasing was the sight of his collection of old rifles decorating the wall above the old wood burning range. On the mantle below the riffles was an old-fashioned windup clock and as I looked at the time it emitted a single metallic clang.

"Is that clock right?"

"Pretty much," he confirmed.

"What day is it?"

"Thursday, does it matter? Why don't you get that wet cloak off, son, those things really hold water; spread it over that fire guard near the stove and come set yourself down. I figure all that shooting I heard had something to do with you."

"You could say that," I said, peering around the room, *old habits etc.* The darkest corners of the room didn't reveal much; oil lamps are not the best form of illumination, but on one wall was a painting of a cat stretched out on a cushion. *What's with these people and their dammed cats,* I thought to myself. Next to it was a faded sepia photo of a beautiful young woman in a high necked dress. I found something intriguing about her and realised it was her eyes, they were so much like those of the cat. The man brought me back to the present and captured my attention as he let out a worded chuckle,

"I wondered how long it would take them,"

"Who's them and how long to do what?"

"Never mind, son, just thinking aloud," he stooped down and opened a cabinet. I heard the clinking of glasses and bottles as he shifted things about in there. "You'll be pleased to know I saw your girlfriend get away."

"She's not my girlfriend, but thank God she did."

"Don't reckon he should take the credit, son. I was watching and I reckon you're the one she ought to thank."

"Did you know there are tunnels under the church?" I said, expecting a surprised reaction; there wasn't one. I tried something more poignant. "Do you know there are prison cells down there?" still his reaction was nil. I tried again. "Did you know Aaron Yarn is holding young women captive down there?" That didn't seem to move him much either but at least it got a response.

"I thought something like that might be going on, I've seen young-uns, some new born, appearing in the town with Peace women who certainly can't be young enough to breed. What better way to build a dedicated cult than to start with newborn babies?" This was all he said before changing the subject. "How did you discover the tunnels?"

"By accident; I touched a button on the church altar."

"Oh yes that one"

"You know about it? Are you saying there's more than one way in?"

"Yes, but few know about them. There's one in the cemetery behind the church, and another at the far end of the tunnel although I'm not sure that one counts anymore because there was a cave in at that end and it's never been cleared."

"You say there is one behind the church?"

"Yes there's a false grave close to the church wall. It has an x chiselled above the date. The epitaph stone is hinged at the bottom if you lower it to the ground it allows the base stone to be swivelled in an arc. This reveals a flight of stone steps leading down into the tunnels. Yarn found it and thinks he's the only one that knows it's there. He had a one man lift installed down there. He uses it to make a dramatic entrance when giving his sermons."

"So that's how he suddenly appeared in the pulpit."

"At the base of those stone steps is a short passage leading first to his elevator then further along to a metal door which Yarn keeps bolted. On the other side of that door is the bottom of the ladder that leads up to the church altar."

"Ah yes I remember trying that door. Like you said it wouldn't open."

"No, if it had you would have found Yarns secret lift."

"But why are you telling me this and how come you know about it."

"I've always known about the false grave. My grandfather had it excavated as an extra escape exit. You see, even then they were still concerned about persecutors. Yarn had men working at night to put the lift in secretly."

"Why, surely not just to make a magician's entrance?"

"It does seem a bit extreme, and one I've not figured out yet. Anyway I'm telling you this because it might come in handy if you find yourself in a tight spot. I trust you Mr Corwin. I could tell you weren't one of Yarns disciples the first day I saw you with your daughter. I said to myself, maybe this will be the one."

"What do you mean?"

"Mister, I got things to tell you. Things I've wanted to warn you about since the day I saw you looking at those stocks, but I couldn't—too many eyes watching. And by the way do you have any idea how long ago those stocks were put there?"

I rasped a hand around the growth on my chin and wondered if I'd lost more time than I thought.

"I'd guess about a couple of hundred years, maybe."

"Six months and they've been used half a dozen times already, but only in the dead of night and with the victim gagged."

"Why, what had they done to deserve being punished?"

"Breaking Yarn's rules, I guess. The last one was to get a man to confess being a government agent."

"Mat Black," I murmured almost to myself.

"What was that?" the old man said.

"Never mind, I was just thinking aloud."

"Yep that Aaron Yarn sure is a stickler for discipline guess he figures it keeps the others in line.

"How come you know all this, unless you're part of his cult?"

"I ain't part of no cult. Like I said he only uses the stocks in the dead of night and you ain't the only one with a black habit."

"Oh I see."

"Ain't you gonna set-a-spell son, I don't bite?"

I think he could still detect mistrust in me. He nodded in the direction of the two easy chairs arranged in front of the glowing old-fashioned range. "Still gets cold here at night you know. Valley, you see, cold air drops like a stone."

I could feel the stove's warmth from where I stood and I was shivering. I accepted his invitation and slipped the wet cloak off. As I spread the cloak out near the range and took a seat I saw the old man produce a stone bottle and two glasses from a cabinet. He set them on its surface and proceeded to pour an inch of liquid into each glass. As I watched him I remembered my visit to the Pike and Heron.

"If one of those is for me, thanks but no thanks; I've already sampled the local moonshine. It doesn't like me."

He chuckled. "I know what you mean, son, but what you got against Jack Daniels."

I couldn't stop myself from grinning, "Yeah sure, Rye whisky in a stone bottle. It must be the first batch old Jack produced." I said sarcastically. Again he chuckled.

"Maybe he did, but this ain't part of it," with that he pulled a half full Jack Daniels bottle of golden liquor out of the cabinet and emptied it into the stone bottle. "I have it delivered from Portland. Like you, I don't trust anything brewed in this valley, not since that fraudster arrived with his confounded elixirs. I don't know how he's doing it but I swear he's drugging everyone in these parts without them knowing it. In the old days I used to brew a little shine myself but the law kept raiding the town and confiscating it. They don't come any more though, too scared I guess. At least Yarn did that for us. Anyway I gave up the brewing, not worth the hassle, but I likes to pour it from my old bottle makes me think I'm young again. I keep it locked away so it can't be spiked." He handed me one of the glasses then eased himself down into one of his comfy chairs. "Go on drink up, son, taint in my interest to poison you, you're the one chance I got of getting my town back."

"How old are you old timer?"

"Ain't too sure, about eighty-five, I guess."

I took the drink in one gulp and felt its warmth radiate as I sat down to face him. "Cheers mister, sorry I doubted you. I didn't know there was anyone I could turn to in this town, but as much as I'd like to stay and chew the fat, I can't. There are people locked up in those tunnels, and I'm worried they won't be alive for long."

"And so you should be, but I'd wait a couple of hours if I were you. They will have given up looking for you by then. I'll get you a blanket and you can curl up on that couch if you like. In a while they'll think you've got clean away."

"Thanks but I wouldn't be able to sleep anyway." I stared up at the three rifles on the wall above the range "If you want to help me, I need a weapon. Do any of those old rifles still fire?"

"All of them, I've even got the shells. The name's Lukas Plimpton, folks that still talk to me call me Luke. Best not trust anyone though. I don't, not since that menace and his crew came to town. He's had this town under his thumb since the Potter girls and a good few others fell under his spell.

"You mean my so-called wife Charlotte Potter?"

"Yes and her cousin, Abigail."

"She never mentioned a cousin?"

"Mr, there is much Charlotte Potter never told you and much you have still to learn."

"Did you know she was not really my wife?"

"I never thought she was. She seemed to dislike all men, until Yarn came along. I've never seen a woman so trapped in a man's grip. I just can't figure how he does it, how he's managed to bring half the people of Peace so completely under his control, but I'm sure it's got to be something to do with those elixirs of his. Did you know he used to be a chemist?" I noticed Luke, like so many towns folk, used English rather than US terminology as did many of the town's folk.

"No but it doesn't surprise me." I was amused by the old man's use of the word elixir seemed such an old fashioned word. "How long have Aaron Yarn been here?"

"He first came here in 69, just after they arrested the gang that murdered those movie people. It's rumoured that Yarn was once one of the gang's disciples. I'd be more inclined to believe the gang was Yarn's disciples. Anyway the story goes that Yarn left the family because the leader and some of the others were losing it to drugs," Luke said, tapping his temple. "Judging by the massacre they carried out, I'd say it was likely."

"Yes, well it strikes me that Yarn is not exactly sane and did you know he's a Satanist?"

"Oh sure," Luke said nonchalantly, "but that's not the problem," the old man said, producing a pipe from out of the darkness and lighting it with a spill from the range.

"Really? I would have said it's the very crux of the problem. He has an altar down in one of those rooms and I believe he sacrifices humans on it."

"Animals."

"You can say that again."

"No! I mean animals are what they sacrifice, not people. What you saw down there is a satanic chapel. On special occasions it's used to sacrifice a small animal, something like a rabbit, or a chicken. It's traditional. It doesn't mean much. Mind you, I suppose it is a little more theatrical than some Christian rituals like drinking wine and calling it the blood of Christ,"

"But I heard a scream down there. It sounded like a young girl."

"You probably heard part of her inauguration, her enrolment into Yarn's cult. Let's face it, seeing a dagger plunged into a small animal for the first time will make most young girls scream."

"So it's animals that get sacrificed, not humans?" I said, sounding relieved

"Not humans—no—not down there..."

His words contained more than just their literal meaning and their delivery was edged with an unwillingness to elucidate. "Are you saying that people *have* been sacrificed in this valley...how many are we..."

"I don't know. I've only heard rumours." The old guy cut in like he was annoyed that I was chasing the subject. "Those that have joined Yarn's cult are too frightened to talk about it. If such things have taken place it would not happen in the church. There are still around seventy five per cent of the town that are not part of his cult. No I'm guessing it would take place at one of their midnight meetings at the Pike and Heron Inn. You asked how many," Luke's chin dropped to his chest like a kid scolded as he said; "You'd have to drag Pike Lake to find the answer to that."

There was a long pause and it appeared we were both churning over Luke's last sentence until I broke the silence with. "It defeats me how one man can come to a place like Peace and get a town to suddenly turn Satanist is beyond me, I just don't get it."

For the umpteenth time the old guy chuckled. "You really didn't check our town out before you came here did you? But to be fair the cards were stacked against you from day one. Day one being the day you first met Charlotte Potter. Mister, the people of this town have always been Satanists—That is what attracted Yarn to come here. But most of the people here are Satanists, but in name only."

"What does that mean?"

"Well when you are required to state your religion when filling in a form you probably answer, protestant or catholic, yet when did you last enter one of your churches?"

"Oh, I see what you mean."

"I watched you enter our church the day I first spoke to you, but you didn't really take in what you were looking at did you."

"I don't know what you mean? I saw room thirteen down in that catacomb if that's what you mean, but I assumed Yarn added that to the place."

"Yes he did. Some of the tunnels go back centuries and Yarn has spent a great deal of money having them extended and extra rooms added. Before he came here all services were held in the church proper because we had nothing to hide. What I was about to say was, if you had really looked at the outside of the church you would have noticed the cross on the roof is inverted and the stained glass windows depict Lucifer as the saviour not Jesus."

I sat for some moments just staring at the old man and trying to fathom the significance of his words. "So you're telling me the town was worshiping the Devil even before Yarn came here?"

"The people of Peace don't like the word devil; it's considered defamatory or bad manners. The town prefers to call him the forsaken one. Lucifer or Satan is acceptable and yes this town has always worshiped in the name of Lucifer, and like Christians they believe in God it's the reason the town came to be here in the first place.

"You're a believer in the dev...Lucifer?" I think the look of condemnation on my face made him smile and he surprised me with. "About as much as you do Mr Corwin."

"But I don't..."

"Are you not a Christian?"

"Well yes, although I'm not exactly a regular church goer,"

"Okay, but what I'm trying to say is that anyone who believes the scriptures in *your* bible cannot discount the existence of God's onetime favoured angel. It's all part of the Christian teachings. One cannot just pick out the bits one approves of, ignore the rest and still call themselves a Christian."

"You sound like a priest."

"That's because I was—here in this church a long time ago."

"So you preached Satanism?" Again, my tone alluded to disproval, his reaction to that was to let out a sigh as if struggling to make me understand.

"I used Satan in my preaching; there's a difference. I think you need enlightening Mister Corwin. I assume you know a little about the Salem witch trials."

"Yes some,"

"Okay, well our bible, that is to say the writings that have governed our way of life here in Peace started in the seventeenth century, 1690 to be exact; the time of the Salem executions. You see we believe that people who were put to death by the so-called puritan magistrates were not only innocent; some of them had the hearts of saints. If a child became sick they would use remedies that were probably no better than what nowadays we call a placebo, but the point is they believed in their remedies and some risked their lives attempting to cure people who were ill, even though they knew that if they were caught their actions would be perceived as witchcraft by so-called men of God. Work of the dev—Lucifer, they would say," he grinned then continued. "I suppose it's hard for anyone to imagine what a frightening time it was for the people of Salem at that time. Lynching's, stoning, drowning, whatever faith the condemned and their families had in Jesus and the Christian teachings was sorely tested. In their eyes God had forsaken them. Their prayers had no meaning and so in their defiance many turned to the Golden Calf, as it were, but in this case that calf was the very icon they were accused of worshipping—Satan. They fled from the witch finders and brought their new religion here where they found tranquillity, hence the name Peace."

"And after all this time you people have carried on that faith, worshipping the dev...Lucifer?"

"He has really been no more than a symbol as far I'm concerned Mister Corwin. Christians use Jesus and the cross as a symbol of their allegiance to God. The inverted cross is a symbol of Satan and to the people of this town it is a reminder of why this town came to be. I and my father before me, priests as far back as any town folk can remember have taught right from wrong just like any Christian religion. Just think of all the religious variations there are. Different nations have different ideas of what their God is to them. Then think of the wars and killings that have gone on, still go on in the name of those religions, those various conceptions of an almighty. Do you think a God with the name Lucifer could be any less compassionate? The truth is, Mister Corwin, I don't worship Lucifer or God or any other invisible myth. I am a nihilist, a sceptic. I believe all religions are hogwash and that is why I lost the confidence the town once had in me as their priest. That is why Yarn has been able to take over this town. My people need their idol and Yarn preaches Satanism the way they like it, with a vengeance.

"How do you mean?"

"Yarn has taught them to hate again. Turning the other cheek is the complete opposite of his preaching. Vengeance is ours sayeth Aaron Yarn. When a caravan of settlers fled the east coast, their hearts were full of hate for their persecutors. It is believed that they put to death anyone they came across whose name resembled known persecutors who had helped convict their friends or relatives. Yarn has rekindled that passion in them, a passion for revenge. Satan is more than just a symbol to Yarn. To him Satan is real and will return to wreak havoc on those who have spurned him. Yarn believes Satan will give everlasting life to those that do his bidding, but what my people do not understand is that Satan's bidding is really Yarns bidding. What really worries me is what Yarn believes his master, Satan, ultimately expects of him."

"What do you mean?"

"Well there are some that believe they can curry favour with Satan by collecting souls for him and I'm worried that Yarn has an ultimate plan. As you must know, through the ages there have been many mass suicides and all have been instigated by a leader or preacher. You remember how Charles Manson had this Helter Skelter thing in his head? If I'm right, all those that Yarn has under his influence are somehow going to regret joining this— *Eternal seekers of retribution,* cult of his."

"I get your meaning and I hope you're wrong. I think you must have been some preacher Luke, but you sound different."

"Different?"

"Yes. When I came in here you sounded—I don't know—like some back-woods hermit that's spent his life here. Now I get the impression you're much more astute than that."

"That might have something to do with my time at college."

"You had a college education! Oh, sorry I didn't mean that to sound..." Luke chuckled at me putting my foot in my mouth, but he didn't appear offended.

"Yes, let me explain how that came about. Some years ago a woman by the name of Spinner published a book about the early settlers, this town's forefathers. She named the town of Peace and this location in her book. She also wrote that we were all Satanists. I don't know where she found her information but most of it was fairly accurate. The book caused trouble for Peace.

"Sightseers started to arrive to ogle us. They even built a camp on the ridge of the valley. Folk in the neighbouring town of Cranford didn't like the idea of having a community of witches and devil worshipers as their neighbours. As a result, a bunch of so called Christians arrived here one night; they set fire to our church and the school. It didn't deter folk from rebuilding them but the thing that really upset them was the loss of their bible a rare book called Cargo of Hope."

"That's the book I saw in the church!"

"Yes the one that got burnt. Yarn promised the town he'd replace it, and he has mores the pity. It is that book that helped Yarn to establish his cult. As I said the book is rare and I've no idea how old it is. I only know it has rested on the churches lectern for as long as anyone can remember before and since the fire. The book has two lists of names, those of this town's ancestors and the names of the puritans that had a hand in putting so many to death. The fire, however, did result in my being sent to school in Portland, and to my father's amazement I won a scholarship. When I'm around city folk my collage days seem to take over. I didn't much like city life though. I couldn't wait to get back to Peace and the simple life with my own people."

"That makes sense although at the moment I don't share your affection for your people, they're giving me a hard time. Can you tell me anymore about this woman who wrote this troublesome book?"

"Only that she was a librarian who lived somewhere on the east coast. I believe it was her book: *Escape to Peace* that guided Yarn to our town. She is also partly the reason Yarn has been able to gain control here. I remember when he made his first sermon in our church. He made the congregation a promise. He predicted that Satan would punish the woman who wrote the book and caused the burning of our church. Strangely enough we heard about a terrible death that the woman had suffered. Yarn showed the news article to the congregation and told them Satan had kept his promise. The paper said that the police were mystified and that the perpetrator could not be found. He convinced the congregation that the Master, his term for Lucifer, carried out the act himself."

"Did he now! Well between you and me, Luke, I believe Yarn kept his promise personally. The woman that wrote that book was murdered but Satan had nothing to do with it. The murdered woman and the young lady that I helped escape tonight were colleagues. They worked in that same Witchville library. She has identified Yarn as the man who frequented that library every day for the two weeks leading up to the woman's murder."

"What you're saying doesn't surprise me; he is one deranged man, Mr Corwin. He controls the men that have been chasing you. The murdered woman described our town as a Satanic Cult which it was not, but this is why Yarn came here. As I said, I believe he has studied chemistry. I know he produces drugs and I believe he uses them to enlist his followers; I'm not sure what his ultimate aim is, but so far he seems to have enlisted the weakest and most vulnerable people in this town which amounts to a good many followers. Yarn is the most dangerous kind of Satanist because he truly believes Satan is as real as you or I and is all powerful."

"I'm surprised he hasn't tried to eliminate you, Luke."

"He probably thinks I'm too old to be a threat. Besides, too many people consider me a friend; he might think it risky for me to disappear."

"Well if I was you I'd be worried about those friends. History tells us these cults do not end well. Those that have not ended in mass suicide have ended in gunfights with government agents and I believe some of those have been drug related. Regarding the Salem trials, I can understand why some might have forsaken their God but I find it hard to believe these so called God-fearing people that drove your forefathers out could hang fellow citizens on such flimsy evidence of witchcraft or colluding with..." I stopped talking when I noticed Luke was holding both hands over his eyes. "Are you feeling okay?"

He took a while to answer but as he dropped his hands away from his face he said. "I have pondered this same question. History books have given us varying accounts of the Salem trials but I believe there was more to it than talk of people throwing fits and acting like they were possessed."

"Like What?"

"Genetic anomalies; I think there may have been people among those first settlers that were physically different, different enough for one to believe they were not of Gods making."

"I think you're talking about inbreeding; but surely..."

"No! Not Inbreeding. I understand about all that, and yes the evidence of it can be seen here in this valley. No, I'm talking about seeing humans physically change from normal to something abnormal." It was my turn to stare at the old man now. Was he trying to feed me something out of some Steven King story? Maybe he was, but all the same I was still mindful of some of the strange things I'd seen since coming to this town, "I see you're not laughing," the old man went on, "so I assume you don't think I've completely lost my marbles."

"I might have if it were not for the things that I have seen since I came here. My time as a cop taught me not to take anything for granted. I assume you got a theory about this so called anomaly."

"Sort of, do you want to hear it?" I nodded. "Okay well an incident happened here about ten years ago. It was a beautiful day; many of the villagers were out in the cornfield helping with the harvest. Things were friendlier around here then. There was an accident. Charlotte's young cousin Abigail Potter, who at the time a nine-year-old, was helping..."

"Wait a minute! Abigail Potter you said?"

"Yes."

"And this Abigail is the cousin of Charlotte?"

"Yes, though they are more like sisters, very close."

"Right—okay, it's just that—well never mind, sorry to interrupt."

"Well I was about to say Abigail was helping to bundle hay when she got too close to Jack Potter, her father, who was scything. The scythe caught her arm as she stooped to gather a bundle of hay. The cut was deep. We bound her arm and her father and I drove her all the way to Portland. The hospital managed to save Abigail's arm but when the surgeon came to tell us the good news he had another colleague with him. This guy seemed very interested in Abigail's family. I remember him asking Jack if Abigail had ever been bitten by a rat. Jack acted like he was surprised and said as far as he knew she had never been bitten. But I saw how Jack reacted and how that doctor looked at him. It was obvious he didn't believe Jack. Then he asked Jack if he would mind bringing his wife to the hospital for them both to have a blood test. Jack told him he would, but I'm sure he never did. What was it that hospital found when checking little Abigail's blood group. I had the feeling Jack knew what that doctor was alluding to. Later when I cornered Jack I questioned him about it. He broke down in tears, but all he would say was there had been a curse on his wife's side of the family that stretched as far back as she can remember. He also said Abigail was not the only one in our town that carried the curse.

"Okay but how does that give rise to..."

"For years fiction writers have told stories about humans changing their form through being bitten by some kind of animal, wolves, bats. I've always wondered where their ideas originated. Maybe their stories are not as fanciful as we believe, and it's possible there are still people in this town that carry the gene."

"You say this doctor asked about a rat bite?"

"Yes and when I asked if they had found any physical bite marks on young Abigail they said no. So I can only assume the hospital found something in her blood. Now in all my years here in Peace I've never seen a rat. Not a normal one anyway, too many cats around, I guess. Jack Potter said his wife's family had been cursed for years, suggesting ancestors were affected so it's something that is passed on. Now I got to thinking that Ships are notorious for being infested with rats especially old ships like the Mayflower or any of the early ships that followed."

"Well that would explain a lot, and give at least some justification to the actions of those barbaric witch-finders back in the 1600s. You said you had never seen a rat here, but then you said not a normal one. Does that mean you've seen something not quite human?"

The old man pondered for a few moments. I assumed he was deliberating whether to divulge something to me, and then he said,

"It was about five years or so after the scythe accident, the town was celebrating a good harvest with a hoedown and a feast in a picnic clearing in the forest. Everyone seemed to be having a good time until Jack Potter spotted young Abigail coming out of the woods looking dishevelled. Minutes later a young man by the name of Tobias Fisher...What?" Luke saw me response to the name Fisher.

"That was her name!" I said with total surprise.

"Who?"

"Never mind Luke, carry on with what you were telling me. I'll explain when you've finished."

"Well as I was saying, this young man, Tobias Fisher came out of the woods a few minutes later and entered the clearing from the same direction. Jack Potter went crazy. He didn't wait for an explanation, but gave Tobias a real beating. I think he would have done the same to Abigail, had Charlotte Potter not been there. Jack was afraid of Charlotte, never found out why but anyway Charlotte was very protective of young Abigail. As Jack was setting about Tobias I saw Abigail's face physically change from the pretty thing she is to an ugly—well I'm not sure what, but her eyes blazed red while her face seemed to elongate. Her body arched like a cat squaring up to a threatening dog. If Jack hadn't stopped the beating I swear Abigail would have pounced on her father. As it was she ran into the woods. Maybe to hide the change that had come over her. To this day, I still cannot believe what I saw take place in that girl. I had drank a little more than usual that afternoon and I'd like to think it was the Jack Daniels working his magic, but no; I know what I saw. I won't go into details but I've since learnt there are certain people in this town that can do this at will. If this is the result of their linage then maybe the Salem witch trials were not so hard to understand."

"What happened to this Abigail Potter?"

"Jack Potter and I were close friends. Before he died, which was two years after that incident, he asked me to promise I'd look after Abigail and keep her away from Tobias Fisher. I couldn't keep that promise the two ran away to Portland and got hitched. She and I are still close, I suppose in a way I replaced her dad. She usually comes to me with her problems."

"So they're both still here?"

"Not at the moment. The two of them joined Yarn's cult and left for San Francisco on some kind of mission. Abigail told me they were meeting up with another cult member, a man by the name of Dugan." Luke noticed another reaction as he said the name Dugan and waited for an explanation.

"Something very odd is going on here, Luke. The reason I reacted to the name Abigail Fisher is because that's the name of the girl that married my friend and partner, Neil Roster. Neil is a D.I. in the SFPD just as I was before I came here. I know you are probably thinking this Abigail can't be the same girl, but I can tell you that it was Charlotte Potter that introduced Neil to Abigail. Now I'm thinking if this Abigail is married to this Tobias Fisher then I'm guessing Neil's marriage was also a sham so what the hell's going on Luke." Luke's reaction to that was to stare at me in silence. I then exacerbated his speechlessness with, "Dugan, the man Abigail was to get in touch with in San Francisco, is here."

"What do you mean?"

"He's here in Peace with his wife. And I think they're as dangerous as Yarn."

"Are you sure?"

"Yes, Yarn brought him into the cell they had me locked in." Again Luke appeared deep in thought with a worried frown.

"What is it Lukas?"

"I've seen a couple in the town, a man and woman. Strangers I've not seen before. They arrived a few days ago and they're staying at Molly Prentice's lodging house. Molly is another one of Yarns cult. I asked Abigail to phone me while she was in San Francisco, just to let me know she's okay, but I've not had a call from either her or Tobias for over a month. If this Dugan has finished whatever business he's had in San Francisco then where is Abigail and why has she not been in touch. Knowing how close the bond is between Charlotte and Abigail, Yarn better hope no harm has come to her. Abigail was never a bad girl but once Yarn had Charlotte under his control it was inevitable that Abigail would follow. With regards to Aaron, he's bad seed. I've never trusted him."

With that, Luke poured himself another whisky and nodded at my empty glass. I declined his offer as I looked up at the clock. "Hell I've been here over an hour. Lukas, I want to thank you for your hospitality. The way I feel at the moment makes that lounger look very tempting but I've got to try getting my friend out of that cell tonight. I just hope Yarn thinks I'm long gone and won't be expecting me."

"Do what you must, son, and don't forget this." He took a rifle down from the wall and handed it to me with box of shells, then with a grin he said, "You'll forgive me if I don't offer up a prayer for you, whatever faults I may have, I hope hypocrisy isn't one of them."

309

Chapter 22 Voice from the grave

I could see the rain had eased up as I cautiously opened Luke's front door, but the night was just as black, which pleased me. The habit was still wet so I left it with Luke hoping my two tone shirt wouldn't make me too easy to spot. I melted into the shadows as best I could and made my way cautiously back to the church. My heart pounded as I opened the church door expecting any moment to be leapt upon by the mad monks of Peace. The thought of being locked up again got me thinking about my lock picks. They would probably search me if they get the chance to lock me up again. I took them out of my pocket and slipped them into my sock. The church was pitch dark inside and for a few seconds I stood listening for a sound, any sound, a footstep, a creak of shoe leather. I stepped inside rifle barrel first and inched my way in the dark towards the steps that I remembered led up to the altar. Listening, all the time listening. I pressed the hidden button at the back of the altar's woodwork and as the familiar whirring noise started I thought to myself if anything is going to kick off now the noise of that revolving altar is sure to be the cause. I pointed the rifle down at the widening gap in the floor, ready to blast anything remotely resembling a monk.

The whirring stopped, and as I gazed down at the tunnel's faint red glow a nasty little imp on my shoulder whispered negative thoughts in my ear like, Jimmy may already be dead and they may have taken revenge on him for your escape. For a few cowardly seconds I considered turning around and getting the hell out of there, but what would I tell Jenny, how could I even face her if I didn't at least try to get Jimmy out? I started down the steps toward the red glow, listening...all the time listening. I tried the door at the base of the steps, the one Luke said led to another secret entrance behind the church, it was still locked. There were other tunnels leading off the one I'd become familiar with. I had no way of knowing if, apart from the girls' dormitory, any of Yarns disciples slept down here. I kept going and reached what I remembered was Black's cell and quietly slid back the observation plate on his door. Black was lying on his bunk and appeared to be fast asleep. I closed the spy hole again and decided to attempt to get Jimmy out first and if that went well we'd recue Black as we made our escape. On reaching Jimmy's cell I put my ear to the door before chancing the inspection plate. I slid the plate across while pulling the metal picks from my pocket. Jimmy was still lying on the bunk but was now facing the wall. I found this a relief because it meant that if he could turn over then his nervous system was no longer affected by Yarn's debilitating drugs and he should be able to walk. It took only seconds for me to pick the lock. I entered his cell and immediately shook him by the shoulder. Two things happened. The man on the bunk turned to face me as I sensed movement from behind. I then felt, and heard, a loud thump and before the already dim light faded to black I saw what I thought was an illusion, the grinning face of Calvin Phipps.

~~~~~~~~~~

Detective Inspector Karen Sykes lay awake for hours worrying about the marshals arriving and the impending assault on Peace. Would they find Spencer alive? Would anyone in the little town of Peace still be alive when they finished their raid? She pictured dozens of heavily armed Oregon law officers storming the little town. She imagined them all being hyped up over rumours about witches and devil worshipers. Would one of them be nervous enough to pull the trigger? Her experience told her it only needed one nervous rooky with a twitchy trigger finger for mayhem to break loose. Her thoughts conjured up terrible newsreel pictures of the Waco siege, burning buildings and the thought of little children screaming with their clothes ablaze, and all because of the religious doctrine of some fanatic named Yarn. She tried to wipe it all from her mind. For the third time she looked at her watch. It was still only 1.30am. She laid back down for another attempt at sleep, then a high-pitched whine started somewhere in the distant reaches of her mind. Gradually the noise became louder until she recognised it as a car engine. As she listened to the sound her own experience with cars told her the vehicle was being driven hard in too low a gear. She quickly got dressed and knocked on Neil and Mick's door before opening it to find Neil just waking while Mick was already dressed but with only one leg in his pants.

"Kaz!" Mick yelled, blushing with embarrassment. "A lady shouldn't barge into a guy's bedroom uninvited," and then as an afterthought he added, "Unless she was hoping to get an eyeful?"

"I did see something," Karen said, winking at Neil; "but it wasn't enough to fill an eye."

Neil chuckled but was silenced by the sound of screeching tyres. The three stared at each other as if expecting the loud crash that followed. "Sounds like someone's up late, shall we go see." All three bundled outside to see a police patrol car just inside the camp's gate. It had obviously tried to turn into the camp entrance too fast. Its front fender was wrapped around the first tree inside the entrance. FBI agents, some in pyjamas and some in just underpants, were appearing from various cabins. Under the gate lights a girl could be seen behind the wheel struggling to open her door without success. As they hurried toward the black and white cruiser there was a sudden blast. The car's bonnet flew open and flames shot out from the engine compartment. This seemed to prompt haste from all directions. The tall agent reached the driver's door first and started tugging on the door handle. The deputy, wearing a dressing gown ran from his cabin and started wrestling with the rear passenger door but neither was having any success. Inside the car Jenny suddenly screamed and her arms went up to protect her face as flames shot out from the dashboard. As the three DI's reached the car Mick shouted at the two would be rescuers,

"The frame's buckled. Get out of the way." with that he suddenly produced a police thirty-eight from an ankle holster and aimed the gun directly at Jenny. He then motioned with his left hand for her to get down. Jenny needed no second prompting; she quickly hit the seat face down as the blast showered her with shattered glass. Immediately Mick and Neil pulled her bodily out through the shattered window.

"I thought I told you to hand over all your weapons," the deputy said to Mick as Karen and Neil lead the distressed girl towards Askey's camper.

"Lucky I forgot one." Mick said with a grin.

FBI men ran toward the burning cruiser with fire extinguishers as Alex Askey stood on the steps of his camper shouting orders to his men. As Karen and Neil reached him with the girl Karen said,

"She needs First-aid, Alex, and a stiff drink if you have any?" Askey saw the blood on Jenny's clothes and quickly ordered everyone else to wait outside before letting the two DI's help the girl in. He closed the door before fetching a first aid box and a half bottle of bourbon. Jenny had a gashed ankle caused by being dragged out through the cruiser's window, but Karen could see she was shaking and that her mental state was of greater concern than her injury. Karen put the bottle to Jenny's lips before setting about dressing her ankle, as she did she spoke quietly to calm the girl's nerves.

"What's your name, hon?"

"J-Jenny Blake." the girl stammered.

~~~~~~~~~

So here I am, back in that reoccurring nightmare: the a hole in the ground, only now I seem to have something the size of a small apple attached to the back of my head and it hurts like hell. I promised myself that if I got the opportunity I'd repay whoever put it there, and with more than an apple. But where was Jimmy? Was he still alive and did Jenny get away? When I came round I found the pocket lining of my pants had been pulled out and the lock picks were gone. They had obviously taken Luke's rifle and I felt that I was never going to get Jimmy out of this place without some kind of weapon. I could do no more but lie back and wait. After a while I heard a voice I recognized. It was the Bitch alias Winifred Howe alias April Dugan. I caught part of what sounded like an argument as they came passed my cell, and it went something like:

April-*"Christ, Andy, can't you do anything right. This has really fucked up our plan."*

Andrew-*"I'm telling you, April, it was there I'm certain of it. Someone has been in our room."* The voices faded leaving me wondering just what it was that had gotten her so mad.

Anyway I was now confident that even if it was Orville that came through the door, with the element of surprise, I could maybe trip him up, or grab his gun once they undone these cuffs. I don't know how long I lay there but I felt myself dropping off to sleep when I heard the inspection plate on the door suddenly slide open with a clank. Thinking this is it, this is my chance; I waited with my eyes shut, pretending to be asleep. I expected to hear the door open any second. If I had opened my eyes I might have seen whoever it was that fired the hypodermic dart into my neck.

I had underestimated my captives. They were not fool enough to chance injecting me at close quarters not while there was a chance I might get the better of them. I pulled the dart from my neck while eyes at the inspection slot watched patiently for their handiwork to take effect. They didn't have to wait long. It took about two minutes before my feet started to tingle. Giddiness forced me to lie back down and I'm guessing it took another minute or so before I'd lost all muscular control. Now only my thoughts, hearing and sight were functioning. I heard the door opening. I could not turn my head but what I saw out the corner of my eye filled me with dread. Two men placed what looked like a roughly fashioned wooden box, the size of a coffin beside my bunk. The jingle of keys told me my cuffs were being unlocked. Was this it then? Was this the way I was going out, unable to even put up a fight, possibly buried alive? Was the hole-in-the-ground horror that I experienced as a kid a foretaste of what fate had in store? My ghastly black thoughts were interrupted by a familiar voice.

"Grab his legs, Doc, we'll lift him in."

I know that voice! And who the hell was this Doc, I wondered. My thoughts were answered as a man moved into my line of sight. It was Kirby, the doctor that treated Ben Alden before he died—no! It can't be—that was the other voice! The second man now lifting my arms was Ben Alden the shrivelled thing I saw laying in that hospital bed, the man that was supposedly interred in the town cemetery. What had I been looking at in that hospital bed, was it someone wearing a mask? Maybe it was a dead body that I assumed was alive because Kirby said it was, but why the charade. Was it just to fool me or was there some other reason for such an elaborate farce; and what about his brother Don, was he part of this charade. There was no way of knowing. But of course that's why the hospital room was locked, it just never occurred to me at the time to ask Kirby about it. Maybe it was locked so nobody could walk in unescorted and question why a corps was left in a hospital bed. The Foxgrove loggers were really spooked; maybe one or two had been shown that shrivelled corps just as I was, knowing they would spread fear to the other workers. It was all contrived to keep non cult members away from the town. I remembered the strange chanting sounds I heard while at Pine Needle Camp and again after Alden's apparent demise...was that the reason...another frightener to keep the loggers away from the town?

"Is this necessary?" I heard Kirby say. "It's barbaric and why the urgency I understood the trial was going to be on Saturday."

"Aaron's had word there's going to be raid tomorrow and there's a lot of activity up in Pine Needle camp, that's why its got to be tonight. Strap his arms and legs in. We don't want him falling out on the way. Aaron wants this business over with before State Troopers get here."

Oh that's great, I thought to myself. The cavalry will probably get here about two days after I'm buried. I couldn't chase that thought from my mind. How does one condition one's mind to being buried alive if that was to be my fate?

"Why do I have to be there?" I heard Kirby say. "And why didn't you get Tollman to help you do this?" Kirby said as he strapped my arms to the inside of the box.

"Don't get all hoity-toity now doc, you took the oath and Aaron wants us all to take an active part in this. Eliminating a few of the cult's enemies now and then keeps them in line. And you know what Aaron's like, he will snuff anyone out without turning a hair if we don't toe the line. Anyway Aaron told us the town had been sacrificing their so called enemies for years. I don't know if that's true, but it shouldn't bother you; Aaron told me how many patients you eliminated before you joined us, so strap him in and we'll be on our way. The procession is lined up and waiting."

"Yes I know. I've seen Aaron issuing rifles?"

"Hell! He must be worried."

Now I was scared, was I to be buried alive, or shot? What was it that Kirby said was barbaric and just what was it time for? I stared into the blackness of Alden's eyes and read his enjoyment as he continued strapping me to the inside of the box. He tightened one strap about my chest while Kirby buckled the straps that secured my wrists to the sides of the box. Strange that I should feel a degree of comfort from this odd procedure, but it was the thought that if I were to be buried alive, my captors would surely not feel the need to strap me in a box. My reasoning, however, was short lived and fear became terror as a wooden lid was fitted over me. I was once again eight years old and trapped in a hole in the ground. Then there were more voices and the feeling of being lifted and carried awkwardly. I imagined my pallbearers struggling to manoeuvre my casket through the door and along passageways. I expected at some point for my casket to be tipped on end to enable it to be pulled up through the altar opening, but if it did I wasn't aware of it, so maybe there was another way out of the tunnels. Suddenly I felt cold draught in my eyes. The draught came from a gap where the rough wooden slats in the box didn't quite butt and I knew we were now outside in the open. This could mean they had used the exit Luke mentioned. I wondered if it was too late for this knowledge to be of any use to me. I was now hearing the murmur of voices and I felt my casket being placed down on a hard surface. I was sure I was among a large number of people. The murmur of voices died and was replaced by a single female voice I immediately recognised as Charlotte Potter. She spoke in a loud and contrived manner.

"Children of Peace, disciples of Lucifer, The master has spoken to Brother Aaron informing him that our community is about to have its faith tested. Government agents are amassing on the rim above our valley and we believe they intend raiding our town soon. They will attempt to take away your children and disband our community. This dire situation has been brought on by the intrusion of outsiders, nonbelievers that have set out to destroy Esor. They will not succeed, for you are the children of the forsaken one; the true deity that promises everlasting life. You have been given weapons and you will keep them by your sides at all times; if the marshals come you will be ready and the master will guide your aim. Meanwhile our immediate business is to deal with the traitors who have brought this strife among us. Today will be their day of reckoning. I therefore call on you to take up your weapons and follow me to the place of cleansing where the master's own creations will rid us of these non believers."

For some moments I heard excited whispering but I could not tell if the whispers were of dissent or approval. Gradually the chatter ceased and I felt movement. I knew by the sound that I was being pushed on some kind of wheeled vehicle. As we started to move I realised I was hearing the toneless dirge that I remembered from my first night at Pine Needle camp, but this time I heard the words and realised the significance of the first line;

For the enemies of the past the lake awaits.

As their monotonous dirge continued my mind was absorbed with three questions. One—Were there really government agents ready to raid Peace? Two—if so how did Yarn really find out? Three—what the hell were the master's creations.

~~~~~~~~~~

Karen could feel the young girl trembling as she bandaged Jenny's ankle.

"Don't worry Hon, you're safe now."

Askey, after shouting orders to his men to shift the burned out car clear of the driveway, Karen heard him thank Mick and Neil. He told them they could do no more and should use what was left of the night to get some sleep. He then closed the door and stood looking at Jenny.

"Is she going to be alright, Miss Sykes?"

Karen smiled at Jenny, "Sure she is."

"Is she capable of answering some questions?"

"Well I think she ought to get some sleep before..." "No!" Jenny cried out. "You must do something. People are going to die down there."

"Who's going to die, Miss Blake, and what were you doing driving a police cruiser—badly I might add."

Jenny Blake gave what answers she could to Alex Askey's questions. She explained the reasons for her presence in Peace. She told him about her boyfriend Jimmy Gardener and the fact that he was the investigating D.I. on a murder that took place in Witchville, Boston, Massachusetts. She told them that her friend Brenda Spinner was the murder victim and how she had been helping Jimmy with his investigation.

"But you must know your Jimmy Gardener has no jurisdiction here and what made him think the killer was here."

Jenny told them about the missing book, *Cargo of Hope,* and how it linked to the town of Peace and why they decided to take our vacation here on the off chance of finding him.

"Why didn't you pass your information on to the Oregon state police?"

"Jimmy didn't think we had enough evidence for them to spend time on it. We never even had a name to give them plus I was the only one who could identify the suspect."

"And have you..."

"Yes, and he's in that town and we now know his name is Aaron Yarn." Jenny noticed the glance between Karen and Askey. "You know about him?"

"He and his cult are the reason we are here," said Askey.

Jenny continued, "Yarn had us locked in a dungeon under the church. That place is like an underground maze and there are still people down there? I just hope they're still alive. I heard a girl or a young woman cry out. She sounded like she was in a lot of pain."

"So how did you escape," said Neil?

"The sheriff, he's not one of them. They had him locked up as well, but he managed to get us both out, but they..."

"Spencer Corwin? Have you seen him," Karen said excitedly.

"Spencer. Yes that's his name. Oh—of course Spencer told us he came from San Francisco, that's why you're here. Are you and he...?"

"Just a minute Miss Sykes," Alex Askey interrupted. "I understand your concern for this Spencer Corwin but I'm the official coordinator for this operation and I have allowed you and your two associates to be here because I feel we owe it to you for the time and effort you've put into this case. I'm sorry, however, but your personal interest will have to wait. You must allow me to conduct this interview in the national interest."

"Yes, sorry," said Karen.

"Okay, now Miss Blake we know that Yarn has been buying stolen guns. Can you tell us where he might be storing them? Have you seen any of these weapons?"

"No, but I have certainly heard some. They were shooting at Spencer and me after we escaped."

"I'm talking about fifty or more riffles."

"I don't know about that, it's possible; those tunnels are like a maze, so many doors down there, I suppose there could be guns down there. But I know there's a satanic cult and they have people locked in cells. Spencer found a school where they encourage underage kids to get pregnant."

"Where do you think these kids come from?" Karen asked.

"I imagine they are just opportune snatchings off streets. How many teens go missing across America every year? What I can't understand is why Yarn murdered my librarian friend back home and what his ultimate intentions are. I think he's seriously deranged and I'm worried about Spencer and Jimmy."

Alex Askey looked at Karen and could see she was itching to know more about Corwin. Okay Miss Sykes you wanted to ask Miss Blake about something."

"Yes what happened to Spencer after you escaped? You said they were shooting at you."

"Yes soon after we got out of the church they must have discovered our empty cells. They chased us and were firing at us but it was so dark and there is no street lighting. I think they were just firing at shadows in the hope of hitting us. They were some distance away when we reached Spencer's police car, but not enough for him to start the car and drive out of the alley where it was parked. Spencer told me to climb in the back and hide. He then led them into the woods giving me a chance to get away, but I didn't get the chance to tell him I had never driven a car before."

"What happened after he left you?"

"I don't know. He said he intended to double back and try to get Jimmy out, but I think that was easier said than done. You must do something, I'm sure Yarn don't intend to let them leave that town alive."

"Don't worry Miss Blake a contingent of state marshals will be here by first light and all will be taken care of. Now Detective Sykes, could you accommodate Miss Blake in your cabin. I think we could all use some sleep."

~~~~~~~~~

Jenny shared Karen's bed but they had not slept long before Karen was suddenly awakened, her heart racing. Neil had shaken her out of an unpleasant dream in which she was being pursued by crazed seventeenth century villagers wearing knickerbockers, buckled shoes and brandishing pitch forks.

"Neil! What the...What are you doing in our room?"

"Shh—listen..."

Karen held her breath for a few seconds and that's when she heard the voices: a slow melodious dirge that was repeated over and over. "Christ that sounds creepy; where's it coming from?"

"I don't know, but I think we ought to check it out, shall I wake Mick?"

"Yes and tell him to get dressed, he won't like it if we leave him out of this." Jenny then awoke and sat up,

"Karen what's that noise?" before Karen answered Mick came out of his room carrying his shoes and zipping his pants, "What's going on, Kaz and who's making that god-awful noise?"

"That's what we're going to find out." Neil, having dressed in a hurry, led the way out of the cabin door just as Alex Askey was about to knock. The tall FBI agent and police officer were with him.

"I take it you heard the chanting." said Askey

"Yes, we were coming to check it out. Where's it coming from."

"It's got to be the people from the town. We were just about to climb to the top of the hill and take a look."

On the ridge of the valley there was now a warm dampness in the air and the thick cloud cover that threatened a storm made the night exceptionally dark. The hill was steep and at one point Askey lost his footing and had to be helped to his feet. Mick was the first to reach the top followed by Neil and Karen. From here they could see a river below meandering off to a lake but the darkness was so complete that even the lake hardly glinted. The three detectives stood mesmerised by the melodious chant and the dozens of lights snaking through the forest below them. They waited for the deputy and Askey's, tall FBI shadow to help him reach the top.

"What the hell's going on down there?" said the deputy breathlessly. "Looks like some kind of religious ceremony. They seem to be heading toward Pike Lake."

"Sounds like you know this area pretty well, Deputy?" said Neil.

"I know some of its history I've lived in these parts most of my life. That building you can see on the edge the lake is an old English style tavern. I went there once when I was looking for some missing rental cars. The Inn's owner told me the lake had some kind of devil fish in it and the locals were afraid to go near the..." The deputy paused and appeared to be squinting in the direction of the lake.

"What's up?" Mick asked.

"Well maybe your eyesight is better than mine. Does the rear of the place appear to stretch out over the lake?"

Mick again glanced at the Inn and affirmed the deputy's observation.

"That's odd, owner of the place told me he was leaving because he couldn't make it pay, but unless my eyes are playing tricks, the place has more than doubled in size."

"Well what say we go down there and take a look," said Mick. I'm not afraid of fish unless it's a shark."

"I've decided it would be wrong to stop the three of you from going down there," said Askey. "If anything should happen to your friend before morning and I stopped you from helping him, I'd be to blame; but I must warn you, the Marshals will be here at first light. Their orders will be to arrest all the members of Yarn's cult. Now if they meet with armed resistance they have permission to shoot first. So I suggest you get out of there as soon as you find who you're looking for. You don't want to be there when those Marshals start shooting up the place. I'm sure you remember the scenes from Waco."

"That's exactly my thoughts Mr Askey," said Karen.

"Okay, come back to my camper and I'll give you your weapons, I just hope I'm doing the right thing."

"I appreciate your concern Mr Askey," Karen said, "We may already be too late but we've got to try. What about you, deputy. Are you going to wait for the marshals or...?"

"I'd rather wait for the marshals to get here but if anything happens to you three, I'll have some awkward questions to answer, like why I wasn't there. So yes, I'll tag along."

"One more thing," said Askey. "The Marshals are due to make their raid at 07:00 hours. The idea is to catch the town asleep so check your watches and be out of there before then because if any one discharges a gun when those guys are around they'll shoot first then ask questions. I'll give you each an FBI vest they might just save your skin."

Chapter 23 The courtroom

This was worse than my, hole-in-the-ground, nightmares. I felt like I was in my own funeral procession. I guessed I was being wheeled on some kind of handcart over rough terrain. Had my nervous system been functioning, I'm sure the ride would have been painfully uncomfortable. As it was, I felt nothing except a sensation of being bounced about. I remembered the meandering line of lanterns I saw from the top of Pine Tree hill and recalling the same dirge-like chant. There were gaps in the wooden slats of my container, but I saw no daylight, so concluded it was still night. Think positive I told myself, stay alert and you will find a way to escape this nightmare. I tried harder to move my limbs but apart from sight and sound, no other part of me had yet come to life mournful drone was not helping me to think. I thought about the mess I'd gotten Jimmy into and wondered if he was also part of this procession or Mat Black whom I now knew was a government agent. I wondered if Jenny had reached civilisation and phoned for help. If so, would anyone even believe her story?

As abrupt as it started the chanting and squeaking of wheels stopped. Then I was being lifted again before hearing the sound of many feet on creaking floorboards. We were inside a building, of that I was sure. I felt pressure easing from my back and hoped that it was a sign that the dart's effect was wearing off. Then I realised my container was being stood on end. I was at least pleased my bearers got it the right way up. I found that I was able to stand although straps still confined me to the wooden box. Then I heard a voice mumble what sounded like an order and someone removed the lid on my box and undid the straps on my legs and arms. I found myself being bundled through double doors that I remembered trying to open in the Pike and Heron Inn.

The numbness was still affecting me and I found myself being half walked, half dragged through what appeared to be a full courtroom. All eyes were on me as I was led towards the front of the court. Then I saw Jimmy and Mathew Black and felt at least relieved to know they were alive. They chained in an upright position in what I presumed was a prisoners enclosure. As the two men whom I recognised from the logging site pushed me into the same box I guessed we were in the new extension of the Pike and Heron. I concluded that this was not just a meeting place; it was where Yarn dealt with people that were either a threat to his cult or victims of his property stealing. I looked at Jimmy and Black and could see they had less physical movement than I had.

The whole court could be viewed from the prisoner's box. Facing us on the far side of the chamber was the jury enclosure. To our left was the spectator's area and to our right the judge's bench and witness box. As we waited for this farce of a trial to start I scanned the chamber. There among the front row of the spectator's area was Jake and Orville now out of uniform and wearing the same monk style Habit. Seven empty high backed chairs were positioned behind the bench. I assumed that this was the reason the court was waiting. As I looked around as far as my limited movement allowed, and my attention was drawn to the floor of the centre aisle where a large rectangular line or gap formed what I could only assume was a large trap door. Knowing we were above the lake a cold chill went through me. *He'll soon be fish food. The master's own creation will rid us of these non believers.* Now these words were beginning to mean something. I wondered what sinister secret the lake held. Most of what I saw before me had become clear. These people were Satanists who had come here to offer a sacrifice to their Deity. I now understood the building's ghastly function. It may have been fear that caused a reaction but I was suddenly aware that my fingers moved. Could my nervous system be coming back to life? I prayed that it was, as I felt I was running out of time. If I could not save myself I wanted to, at least, go out fighting. What I didn't understand was the need for the rifles.

Except for a few women spectators everyone sat with a rifle either across their lap or leaning against the seat in front. Was this something they always did on their night time jaunts or were they expecting unwanted visitors? Surely Yarn could not expect these simple people to survive a gunfight with federal lawmen, had he not learned anything from the Waco siege? Jake kept eying me with a now-who's-laughing kind of a smile, but Orville seemed reluctant to even look at me. As I scanned the congregation, it occurred to me that some of these people were among the strangest humans I'd ever seen. Inbreeding must have been populating Peace for centuries. I searched the faces and saw only hate filled eyes burning into me, but why now? After living among these people, murmuring good mornings and passing pleasantries on the street, what caused them to suddenly show this obvious hatred? Maybe they'd been hiding their true feelings? I assumed I was soon to find out. They sat mumbling to each other, and I heard the word Elders several times. I guessed they were waiting for someone to start the proceedings and I had no doubt Yarn and Charlotte would be among these so-called elders.

As my eyes scanned the congregation I spotted one of the men who had plied me with the foul drink, Sean Finnegan, next to him on the end of the row was Prudence Rider. I continued scanning the congregation trying to spot people I knew and hoping to find a friendly face but many had their cowls pulled low, like they were afraid to be recognised and I wondered if all of them were fully committed to Yarn and his cult. Maybe these were townsfolk that I'd become friendly toward. I scanned past those I could not clearly see but then I must have spotted one that compelled me to retrace a row of faces until my eyes halted. Now I knew I was not going insane, it was the face of the man who helped strap me in this box; Ben Alden. This induced me to scrutinise more closely the shadowy face of the cloaked figure beside him and this made me wonder if the dart in my neck had affected my mind because I found myself staring at another corpse: Cal Phipps. To the right of him, the man with the black and withered hand: Ben Alden's brother, Don. He caught me staring at him and his mouth distorted into a smile then mockingly he lifted the hand that had given me such a shock, it was perfectly normal and with it he gave a childish wave. His intention was to belittle me for being fooled by his ruse. It was obvious now that he had been wearing some kind of a Halloween glove.   I lifted my eyes to the next row and found myself staring at Amos Carrier, the boy that was supposed to have been blinded in a car accident. It was plain to see as the teenager glanced about the hall that there was nothing wrong with his sight. It was dawning on me that this whole affair from the moment I met Charlotte Potter was a farce, but why? Was it for the value of my house, retribution for breaking Yarn's legs or both? If those were the only reasons why the ridiculous pantomime played out by all these people? Maybe I had done something to make an enemy of a whole town if so, was it not enough to punishment me without murdering Lucy and our little girl. They had played with me like a cat plays with a mouse before the kill. Yarn made it clear that there could be no loose ends when claiming their ill-gotten properties.

Lucy and Avril were both gone, murdered by Yarn and his cult. Now I must concentrate on the here-and-now. I owed it to Jimmy and the promise I made to his girl to try to get him out of this mess. As long as I drew breath I would hold on to that thought and forget about things I couldn't change.

My attention was suddenly drawn to movement in the centre of the congregation. I saw Cal Phipps leaving his seat, I watched him as he came towards me. There was hate in his eyes as he carried his rifle menacingly across his middle. He stood on the steps of the enclosure so that our faces were level. He leaned toward me until his pock marked face was just inches from mine,

"You really have no idea what's going on have you, Corwin? You were staring at our faces wondering why some of us are not dead and buried. You might not be fully aware of why you are here and the reason you have become a hated enemy. I know Aaron told you it was for your property and his revenge for crippling him, but that's only part of it. My brother told you to check your name. Check your family tree, he said didn't he? You should have; you might have worked it out. Now it's too late but it will soon be over for you and for your friends here." With that, Phipps glanced to his left at Jimmy and Black. Phipps eyes were bright with madness as he continued taunting me. "I'm going to miss the games we played with you Corwin, but all good things must end. It's too risky keeping you around." As Phipps continued talking I could feel my fingers and toes tingling, signs of recovery. "Satan's pets will be fed soon and Aaron has promised that Satan himself will reward us. You see, everyone here has a reason for wanting to see you suffer, Corwin, as you will soon learn. As far as your two friends here are concerned it's just a matter of keeping things tidy, no one to tell the tale if you get my drift." He then directed his malicious taunting towards Jimmy. Jabbing him in the stomach with his rifle, he said,

"Did you know, Detective Gardner, Corwin helped your girl escape? Well never mind, we'll find her and when we do she'll make good breeding stock. I may take care of that myself. Then once she's served our purpose we'll have another fish feeding ceremony like this one." He then turned back to me saying, "Aaron has got this crowd baying for your blood Corwin simply by telling them about your linage, but even they don't know the full extent of his plan. Like you, they have such a surprise coming..." The muscles in my arms were coming back to life and Phipp's suddenly looked down and saw my right hand clenched in a fist as I tried wriggling it out of the strap. He turned to Orville, who was sitting close enough to hear everything Phipp's had said. "Tighten his straps, Orville, before the Elders get here."

Phipps returned to his seat as Orville approached me to carry out Phipp's instruction. There was a kind of sadness on Orville's face. Something in his manner told me he disliked being part of this gathering. I could now feel him adjusting the straps around my wrists and as he did I heard him mumble something but all I caught was the words "take me". Before he finished his task and sat back down I heard the sound of an engine getting louder and I recognized it as an outboard motor. The engine sound died and a few moments later I heard the creak of a door opening in the wall behind the bench. One after the other, six more cloaked figures entered and took their places in the high backed chairs behind the bench. The motor boat must have been moored at the end of the jetty. Yarn, in his red silken habit, was the last to enter, Except for him, the elders wore a dun coloured version of the same Habit. Even with their hoods on, I recognised them to be Mayor Cloyce; Joy Grey; Horace Ryder; Charlotte Potter; Andrew Dugan and his wife, April. They scuffed their chairs noisily as they took their places at the bench. As they took their seats Charlotte Potter remained standing and it was her voice that filled the hall.

"Brothers and sisters, most of you know why we are here. The prisoners you see before you are your enemies. Given the chance they would destroy your town, your religion and your beliefs. As you know we would normally hear words in their defence and a jury would decide their fate before sentence is carried out. Unfortunately circumstances have denied us the time. Marshals are at this very minute amassing in Portland and are expected to arrive in our town very soon." This brought an agitated and worried muttering throughout the congregation. Charlotte however continued with hardly a pause. "This," she said, "is why you have all been issued with weapons and you will keep them with you at all times. When you leave here tonight we will all assemble back at the church where you will be protected by our leader, Brother Aaron. Now I ask you to listen to what he has to say."

Then Yarn took the chair and as he spoke I could see adoration in the expression of his cult members. There was no denying Yarn had this audience eating out of his hand.

"Brothers and Sisters, I am pleased to announce that the rumours most of you have heard are true. We have among us a descendent of your most hated enemy: Jonathan Corwin." This caused an exited murmur among the congregation. "Yes Spencer Corwin is only one, but in time we will seek out many more of his linage and by eliminating each one we will appease the master and quell his anger for the murderous treatment of his loyal subjects back in the 17th century. You, my brothers and sisters are the descendents of those that escaped the persecution of Corwin and other such fiends. The master brought us to this place of safety, this place of Peace so that you can in time avenge the wrongs done to your ancestors. Those courageous pioneers of yesteryear will rejoice in their afterlife for the deeds we do here today. I was sent to you for just such a purpose, to point out the descendents of those so-called witch finders. Today we will please the master by offering him the souls of three enemies.

This seemed to animate the congregation some shouted "Crush them," while Cal Phipps's shouted "The lake awaits," encouraging their excitement. The angry cries lasted a few seconds then quickly abated due to what I guessed was a silent hand signal from Yarn. "Yes, Spencer Corwin will meet his end brothers and sisters, just as I have promised, but we now have the assistance of the Master himself for he has seen fit to bless us with the presence of his angels." Yarn then stared directly at me and I could have sworn those black evil eyes had a glint of red in them. Tonight, Corwin, you will witness the consequence of being an enemy of Satan." Yarns attention then went back to his audience.

"The first of our enemy to feel the wrath of Satan is a government agent, an infiltrator who came to Peace posing as a teacher in order to destroy your religion and your town."

"Brother Phipps and Brother Alden, make ready the master's pet's first course."

Pets—Angels! What the hell was Yarn talking about? I watched Phipps and Alden leave their seats and approach us. I tried with all my will to move my fingers and to my surprise they were coming to life, just. I felt that I might now be able to turn my head. I desperately wanted to see what Phipps and Alden were doing close beside me. If they were unbuckling the straps of Mathew Black it was taking a long time. I didn't quite know why but I felt it was important to give the illusion that I was still paralysed. Then the two appeared again and I understood why it was taking them so long. They had stripped the man almost naked. Mathew Black was still unresponsive because I could see his bare feet scraping the wooden floor as he was dragged upright towards the centre aisle. I heard a whirring sound as they stood him in the centre of what I was now convinced was a trap door. Then I saw the source of the whirring. A steel hook attached to a chain was being lowered from above. I saw Yarn make a sudden movement as the whirring stopped and I knew he was controlling the electric hoist. The hook had stopped a several inches above Mathew Black, who was still only semiconscious. Alden steadied him from falling as Phipps slipped his wrist straps over the hook. Yarn touched a control on his bench and the whirring raised Mathew until his feet were some four feet above the floor. Anger suddenly made me put more effort into freeing my hands and I unintentionally let out a grunt which captured Yarn's attention.

"That's it, Corwin, flex your muscles," he said. "This will speed the revival of your nervous system, thus enabling you to enjoy the excruciating pain the masters pets will inflict on you." Yarn then spoke directly to Prudence Rider who was sitting closest to the trap door. "Miss Rider, please summon the master's pets." With that he touched another control and the doors below Mathew Black quickly opened leaving him suspended above the open floor. I could now hear the gentle lapping of water.

Prudence also seemed to be in a trance as she left her seat and walked to the edge of the opening where she stood plucking small pieces of raw meat from a plastic bag and dropping them slowly into the lake.

I realised the position of the prisoners box had been purposely placed so prisoners could watch the sickening demise victims would suffer. Alden and Phipps had retaken their seats and as I glanced at them I was sickened by the excitement I read on their faces. Then I heard it, the water's lapping had become a sporadic splashing that became louder and more frequent. Black was obviously still paralysed. His body still appeared rigid and maybe that was a blessing because whatever horror was waiting below I imagined was going to inflict terrible pain before death brought him relief. The waters quickly changed from calm to turbulent and then to frenzied and that's when I saw it, one of Yarn's so called angels. It leapt up through the floor in an attempt to reach the feet of Mathew Black before dropping back with a huge splash. I realised then that Gabriel Proctors artistic interpretation of what I thought was a meant to be a pike was actually one of these ghastly creatures.

"It is time Prudence," said Yarn. "Your pets have had their hors d'oeuvres now it is time for their main course." Yarn once again reached across the bench for the control to lower the hoist. I expected to hear, again, the clack of an electrical solenoid, but instead a voice from the rear of the court shouted,

"Aaron Yarn! Stop this evil ritual." All heads turned and I, like the rest of the congregation, searched the faces at the rear of the hall. Then one of the cloaked figures stood up holding an antique Winchester rifle across his body. At that moment I realised it was

Lukas Plimpton. Luke threw back his hood saying, "Keep your hand away from that navy pistol and that control panel, Yarn, unless you want to lose it."

~~~~~~~~~~

The three San Francisco detectives used their hired Toyota pickup. They took the long and winding hill down into Peace while Deputy Murray followed in his police cruiser. It was around 1:00 am when they abandoned their vehicles discreetly on the edge of the town. There was no street lighting but clouds were clearing and on the spire of the church a black outline of an inverted cross stood out like a stark warning. Wearing their FBI labelled jackets and carrying torches, complements of Mr Askey, the four made their way toward the town centre. As they neared the church the only sound to be heard were cats bracing up to each other or mewing to be let in to their owner's houses.

"What the hell is that smell?" said Mick.

"Judging by the amount of cats around," Neil answered, "I'd say it was cats shit."

"Well that's a relief," Mick answered. "I thought you were getting nervous."

"Keep it serious, children," said Karen, smiling.

The four were still some hundred or so yards from the church grounds when Ken Murray announced, "This is it, guys, the path that leads to the Pike and Heron." They shone a torch up at the wooden signpost and saw the words "To the Lake 1/2 mile". The three men set off along the path leading into the woods they had not gone but a few paces when Mick realised Karen was missing. He looked back to see Karen stood gazing in the direction of the church.

Karen's attention had been drawn to the church and as she stood staring at its inverted cross protruding from the belfry. She suddenly shivered, recalling the happenings on her evening at Spencer's house.

"Are you coming, Kaz, or are you scared of the dark?" The sound of Mick's voice brought her back to the present.

"Nice one Mick, no I was just thinking it might be a better idea to take a look inside that church first. If that procession we saw started out there, it might be a good time to check out their meeting place. The girl said there were cells under the church and she thinks more people are locked up down there. This could be our chance to get them out."

"Sure, why not; what do you think deputy?"

"I suppose it's got to be worth a look. Two minutes later they were inside the church. Using their torches, they split up and started searching for a floor opening. Neil headed straight for the chancel, Mick checked out the high pulpit while Karen and the deputy shone their torches up and down the aisles looking for trap doors. Their searching lasted less than a minute before they heard a muffled yell followed by an ominous thump. Three torch beams all pointed to the chancel where Neil was last seen.

"Neil, where are you," Karen called out. Just then a torch beam shone upwards from the floor of the chancel before they heard Neil's distant reply,

"I think so." his voice sounded strained like he was in pain, "I'm okay but I may have sprained my ankle. There's an opening in the floor by the altar and I found it. Be careful, I don't want anyone falling on top of me."

The three reached the chancel and shone their torches into the opening. Neil was sitting at the bottom of a fixed ladder. His shoe was off and he was examining his ankle by torchlight.

"Christ Neil, that's some drop, why didn't you use the steps?" said Mick, as he grinned at Karen.

"Well Mick, it's only a ten foot drop and I didn't want to waste time so I thought it would be quicker to just fall in."

Karen and Murray were grinning while Mick had to turn his head and cover his mouth to stifle his laughter.

"Will you be able to go on, Neil," said Karen?

"I'll be okay it's just a sprain, but I'm thinking it'll be some size tomorrow. There's a passageway down here and there seems to be a red glow up ahead. If you're coming down you better hurry, we don't know how long it'll be before that procession gets back."

"Right, I better go first," Mick said. "Neil's going to need some help." Karen waited for Mick's head to drop below the first step before she started to follow him into the shaft. She had only reached the second step when a loud humming sound caused her to stop. She looked around to see the huge altar moving towards her. Estimating she would not get below floor level before being crushed, she quickly scurried back out. She and the deputy stood and watched, helpless, as the altar close the opening, thus sealing Neil and Mick inside.

"Well that's just great," Ken Murray said. "Now what do we do?" Before Karen could answer the humming started again and the floor started opening again.

"Sorry about that," Mick called up to them. "One of these steps activates a switch. Come down slowly and I'll tell you when to step over it."

As Mick helped Neil to his feet he said, "Neil, if I'd known you were such a clumsy fuck, I'd have suggested leaving you clamped in those town stocks until we were ready to leave." With Neil having Mick's shoulder to lean on, the four cautiously proceeded along the tunnel. Opening the first door they came to, they found a rack containing a dozen or so spare props to hold up the tunnel roof. They moved on to the next door. This happened to be a maintenance cupboard Neil couldn't believe his luck, among buckets and brooms, a pair of wooden crutches. Neil grabbed one and lowered the height to suit him. With Mick now relieved of Neil's weight the four moved faster, trying doors as they went until they came to one that emitted the sound of voices: young female voices, Karen grabbed hold of the door handle and was about to open it when Mick grabbed her arm.

"I don't think you should, Kaz," he whispered.

"Why the hell not, remember we also promised to look for the Cruikshank girl and those voices sound like girls."

"Mick's right Karen," said Neil. "Even if she is in there we can't take her with us until we finish what we came to do, find Spence." Karen nodded agreement and the four moved on passing several locked doors until they reached a T junction. They decided to split up Karen and Murray went left taking them down a slope to another level where they discovered a small room that resembled a chapel displaying satanic trappings. Another opening led down more steps to an even deeper level. It was here Karen and Murray found what they realised were the cells Jenny had mentioned. As they stepped inside the last of the dank and dingy cubicles, Murray said,

"Christ, Karen," Murray said, "What the hell has been going on down here?"

Karen was looking at a set of handcuffs hanging on the iron bed frame. "I don't know but it's worrying. I'm wondering if we are too late to help whoever has been locked in these cells."

Meanwhile Mick and Neil came upon another locked door. It had a frosted glass top panel with the ominous words *keep out* emblazoned on it. There was no light showing inside and Mick put his ear to the glass before showing a puzzled frown

"What is it?" Neil said.

"It sounded like water splashing." Mick said while trying the door handle. "There's no key hole so it must be bolted on the inside."

Neil put his ear to the door and also tried the handle, "I think we should break the glass," he said.

"What! Are you sure?"

Without repeating himself Neil turned his back to the door and smashed an elbow through the panel. "Yeah, I'm sure." Neil said grinning. Most of the glass fell in from one blow, the rest Neil cleared with his torch before reaching through and finding the bolt and light switch. The two stepped inside.

"Well I'll be..." Neil stood staring into the huge room as Murray and Karen suddenly appeared having heard the sound of breaking glass.

"We found some cells but their empty." said Murray, then staring at the smashed door panel, he asked, "What happened?"

"He did it, Deputy." said Mick, "I think you should arrest him, Deputy," Mick said grinning.

"Look Karen," Neil said ignoring Mick and moving aside for Karen to enter. "Remember what Gwyn told us about Yarn's experiments?"

Karen gazed about the room "A laboratory! Well equipped from the looks of it and aquariums, lots of them. Well what do you know?"

"Will someone let me in on the secret," said Murray following the others into the lab. "Is there something significant about fish tanks?"

"We may be about to find out, Deputy," Karen said as she stared at the swimming pool sized drum at the far end of the laboratory. "We can tell you this much, Aaron Yarn was sacked from a company in San Francisco for carrying out genetic experiments on the sly and we were told that whatever he was working on involved aquariums. Maybe we're about to find out just what he was working on."

They reached the first aquarium. "I don't know much about tropical fish," said Murray, "but I'd say that's too many fish for the size of this tank, look, there must be at least half a dozen dead fish on the bottom, what are they anyway?"

"Angel fish," said Mick, jubilantly.

"Sorry Mick, but they're not." said Neil.

"Okay posh boy, give us the benefit of your encyclopaedic knowledge."

"Tropical fish was a hobby when I was a boy. The live ones are Siamese fighting fish. They're also known as biting fish which could explain the dead fish on the bottom but I'm not sure what the dead ones are."

"And what about these?" said Murray, moving to a larger tank.

"Barracuda, only babies but unmistakable."

"And these?" Karen asked pointing to another tank.

"Well like I said I'm not an expert but they sure look like piranha." They moved along where the tanks were getting larger.

"Now I know that they are definitely pike" said Mick.

"Yes they are and have you noticed something all these species have in common?" Neil asked.

"No, enlighten us oh wise one," said Mick

"They are all aggressive predators and feeders."

"Yes and it makes me wonder just what Yarn is up to," Karen said. "Is this just a sideline like a hobby, or is it connected to this satanic cult of his?

"What do you make of that Karen?" Neil had spotted something of interest on a workbench lying beside a microscope. While Neil and Karen went to investigate, Murray and Mick moved on to the far end of the room where they became curious about the enormous circular galvanized tank. The tank measured least 7ft in height and its diameter was almost the width of the laboratory. Attached to its outside were four steps leading up to a metal observation platform. "Let's go take a look," Mick said, enthusiastically. The two climbed the grating-like steps onto the platform bringing the rim of the tank to waist height. The surface of the water came to a foot of so from the rim and while Mick stood back cautiously scanning the surface, Murray carelessly leaned over while searching its depth.

Meanwhile Neil and Karen became fixated on something in a stainless steel tray. "What the hell is that?" said Neil, staring at the saucer sized blob of pinkish flesh. "What do you think, Kaz; is it fish?"

Neil sniffed the sickly looking flesh "It doesn't smell like fish."

Karen picked up a set of stainless tongs and pulled some of the flesh to one side. "Oh shit, that looks like a human eye."

"Yes it seems like Yarn is still playing Frankenstein. I've seen enough, let's get those two and get the hell out of here." As they neared the tank Neil called up to them,

"Is there anything interesting in there, you two?"

Murray turned to them and while nonchalantly splashing the water with one hand, he said "The waters too cloudy and I don't think there's any...."

Murray didn't finish his sentence, but let out a terrifying scream. Mick just stood and stared in disbelief at the weird fish-like creature that had attached itself to Murray's arm by its shark-like teeth. In a fit of frenzy Murray tried shaking the creature off but in so doing he spattered some of his blood onto the water's surface setting off more activity in the tank. Neil immediately dropped his wooden prop and quickly climbed the steps. He grabbed hold of Murray and locked his arm under his to keep it still. "Mick, don't just stand there," Neil shouted. "Shoot the fucking thing!" Mick came out of his trance. He then struggled to reach his gun underneath the FBI tunic, and before he had time to take aim, a deafening blast echoed throughout the laboratory. A fearful scream came from the creature as its jaws opened and it fell against the rim of the tank before toppling into the water. Immediately the surface of the tank became like a boiling cauldron. Dozens of smaller creature's attacked the wounded fish. In seconds the creature was no more than a ragged skeleton. Mick and Neil turned to see Karen holstering her Beretta.

"Jesus Karen! You could have hit one of us!" said Neil.

"Yes, sorry about that, but I could see Mick struggling to get Murray's gun and I made a judgement. Either I take a chance on missing my target or watch Murray's arm get ripped off. Whatever that thing was, it had no intention of letting go. What do you think Deputy? Was I wrong?"

Murray looked at his arm as he tried to stem the blood still oozing from it.

"Right or wrong, Karen," he said, "you get my vote."

Karen Smiled, "Okay, I saw a first aid cabinet on the bench, let's get your arm wrapped up and get out of here. That shot could bring trouble."

~~~~~~~~~~

Luke Plimpton's eighty years did nothing to lessen the threatening presence he held over Yarns pseudo courtroom. Eyes turned from him back to the Elders in anticipation of a response from Yarn,

"Brother Lukas," Yarn answered with a smile that I felt was ninety percent bravado. "You rejected the chance to be a member of this cult and therefore you have no right to come here demanding..."

"I am not your dammed brother," Luke interrupted angrily. "And these people need to know just what kind of fraud they have running their town and just what your ultimate intentions are. I also demand that you tell me what has happened to Abigail Potter, a young girl these people have watched grow up in their town. Her father entrusted me with her care. Now tell this congregation where she is."

The anger in Luke's tone was obvious and Yarn appeared lost for words while Charlotte Potter appeared confused. The rest of the elders fidgeted uncomfortably. It occurred to me that Luke must still have carried some weight among these people to verbally attack Yarn in such precarious surroundings. I also had the feeling that since I left Luke's cottage he had learnt something more concerning his ward, Abigail Potter. What had he discovered to make him risk intruding on these armed fanatics and their psychopathic leader? The congregation was now muttering among themselves. Meanwhile I realised my nervous system was fast becoming functional. I could now turn my head without too much difficulty.

"People of Peace, listen to me." Luke announced, "There is an anger midst our community. This was not there before this man came to our hamlet. Abigail Potter has confided in me since her father died, and until now, no more than a week has passed without her contacting me..."

"Luke Plimpton," it was now Charlotte who interrupted Luke, "you have known me all my life and you know that, like yourself, I have always looked out for Abigail's well being. I'm sure Aaron would have told me if..."

"No, Charlotte," Luke shouted. "Like the rest of these people, you are under his control. And I've discovered why. You've been deceived by his lies and are most likely under the influence of his drugs right now."

It was at this point that Yarn made a sudden grab for his pistol. He was not sure how much the old man had discovered, and his intention was to silence Luke before the old man said too much but in his haste to grab his gun he tugged prematurely on the trigger. The deafening blast was followed by a scream causing the whole assembly to cower in their seats. The stray bullet had shattered the shoulder of a woman sat with her husband. Luke's reaction was to retaliate with less haste and before Yarn could perfect his aim Luke fired once hitting Yarn in the arm. Yarn dropped the gun back on the bench and the colour drained from his face. His pain became apparent as he sat rocking to and fro while mumbling some unintelligible incantation. Luke still held everyone's attention and thanks to Orville and the long sleeves on my flimsy shift, no one notice my facial contortions as I wrestled my hands free. Lukas then addressed the man now trying to pacify his injured wife. "Jacob, take your wife out of here now and get her to hospital." The man looked relieved as he helped his wife hobble past the congregation and through the double doors. Luke then addressed the Bench again.

"Charlotte, Ask the man Dugan where Abigail is." Charlotte looked confused and worried. She leaned forward to peer along the bench at Dugan and his wife. Both avoided Charlotte's stare and appeared decidedly guilty and uncomfortable. Charlotte put the question,

"Brother Dugan, you have just arrived from San Francisco. Do you know something about my cousin? Has something happened to her? Before Dugan could answer Yarn cut in angrily,

"I will answer your question, Plimpton, after which you will leave these premises hastily while you still can. Abigail and Tobias Fisher are living in San Francisco where they are working for the benefit of this community they are there to arrange the sale of properties that will benefit our community."

Luke cut in with, "Would that be the properties you've obtained by murdering the rightful owners, like you intend to murder the three innocent men you have brought here?" Luke then addressed the cloaked members around him. "People of Peace; wake up. You are being duped by this man and I believe you are all in danger. Revenge, anger, retaliation; all this aggression with which he has filled your minds belongs in the past. The people with whom this man is fuelling your anger have long since turned to dust. Can you not see the futility of your hatred? It has been rekindled by Yarn and not just through his preaching? For some time you have been subjected to his drugs. Have you not noticed a difference in yourselves and your neighbours since this man came to our hamlet? I have now discovered how he's been administering his concoction without your knowledge; it came to me as I watched..."

Luke's voice was muffled by a terrifying screech as a huge fish-like creature leaped out of the hatch to clamp its huge teeth onto the bag held in Prudence Rider's hand. It happened so fast I was left unsure of just what I had witnessed. Was this another illusion to attribute to Yarns drugs? No, the frightened look on some of the faces closest to the open floor and the terrified look on Blacks face told me others had seen it too. The incident left the congregation stunned. I don't believe Dugan saw the thing because he chose that very moment to lunge across the bench and grab Yarn's navy colt. This time Luke was caught napping and Dugan held him in his sights before Luke had even raised his riffle.

Yarn's eyes blazed as he yelled out with excitement, "Shoot him, Andy kill him now!"

"No!" Dugan shouted angrily. "The old man's right." With that Dugan grabbed his wife by the arm and pulled her to her feet. "We are getting out of here. We've had enough of your promises and I don't intend to be around when the Marshals come storming in here. Personally I hope they blow your fucking head off."

Now it appeared Andrew Dugan was running the show, or maybe Luke Plimpton, but things were getting interesting in a very scary way.

The wild splashing noise below the floor was becoming louder and I guessed the creatures were getting impatient for their main course: Mathew Black.

Charlotte Potter was still glaring at Dugan who had lost the look of fear now. He was waving Yarn's gun around while keeping his wife firmly between himself and the threat of Luke's riffle. Gripping April's arm he led her down from the Judges Bench and the two of them started to edge their way around the floor opening towards Prudence who appeared not to even notice the thing that almost took her hand off.

Suddenly there came a frightening screech as another creature leaped above the floor. I'm no great angler but recalling pictures of men holding up prize catches told me these beasts were upward of 40 to 50 lb. This time its mouth was open and its shark-like teeth struck enough fear in those sitting nearest the water that they hurriedly scuffled their chairs further away from the opening. The creature seemed intent on reaching Mathew Blacks bare feet dangling tantalisingly above the open trap. Its failed attempt was followed by a great splash as it fell back in the water, soaking Dugan and the closest cult members. The look on Dugan's face confirmed he'd seen it this time and for a few seconds he appeared mesmerized. This was Dugan's undoing. In those few seconds I saw Yarn give a discreet nod to someone in the congregation. Instantly a cloaked figure levelled a rifle at Dugan and fired. This started a riotous explosion of gunfire which resulted in wild panic throughout the hall. Everyone seemed to be moving in double quick time dropping their weapons and striping off their habits. Those unfortunate to have an end seat dashed for the exit doors while others tripped over the carnage of overturned chairs and discarded robes. Some tripped and trampled on others for whom they showed no regard. I watched one elderly woman fall and smash her teeth on a chair and as she tried to get up, men trampled over her as they fled.

The whole scene might have been hilarious had it not been frightening and surreal. The madness of it all had been started by a simple nod from Aaron Yarn to Calvin Phipps who had responded with an attempt to silenced Dugan. Phipp's thunderous shot echoed around the hall before it was followed by a second, third and fourth shot, from differing locations. The first: Phipp's shot hit Dugan in the chest like an invisible punch causing him to lurch backwards. Shock and pain showed on his face intensifying his grip on his wife's arm and pulling her off balance. April Dugan was no match for her husband's bulk and as she also tumbled towards open floor her last desperate act was to make a wild grab at the nearest thing she could reach, the wrist of Prudence Rider. Prudence was in no physical or mental state to resist April's hold on her and one by one the three plunged into the turbulent water. Only the sound of Horace Rider's hysterical voice yelling his daughter's name could be heard above the wild splashing and screams as the grotesque creatures dragged their long awaited meals below the fast reddening water. Less than a minute later from out of the floor opening came the sound of an outboard engine. I looked up at the bench guessing it would be deserted; it was.

~~~~~~~~~~

In the darkness below the end of the Inn's jetty, Mayor Cloyce started the little outboard engine. Having now witnessed the result of falling into this deadly lake, Joy Harris, Charlotte Potter and Horace Rider took great care stepping into the small boat. Meanwhile Yarn hurriedly closed and locked the rear entrance to the courtroom before joining those he considered his most dedicated and faithful followers. With his back to the others Yarn untied the mooring line. This was the moment Horace Rider chose to avenge the death of his daughter. Showing no regard for the danger lurking beneath the small boat, he sprang at Yarn in an attempt to push the big man over the side. Yarn, however, had read the hate Rider had directed at him seconds after Prudence had disappeared, and he was ready for just such an attempt on his life. The two men wrestled, and the boat pitched violently. Mayor Cloyce yelled and Joy Harris screamed while Charlotte held on to the sides of the boat expecting any minute that it would turn over. Then there was a great splash as Horace Rider finally fell into the water. Seconds later he surfaced and clung to the side of the boat, but try as he did, his thick serge cloak was now heavy with water and he could not find the strength to haul himself into the boat. Then the creatures were on him, biting, tearing at his legs until, with one gargled scream, his hands slid from the edge of the boat and Rider disappeared midst splashing ravenous mouths. Yarn yelled angrily at Cloyce to make for the shore. Cloyce quickly opened the throttle and the boat headed across the lake. As they neared the shore the dark shape of Aaron's Cadillac came into view.

"I'll drive you to the hospital," Joy Grey said to him, "you're losing a lot of blood."

"No! I want you to get to the town hall and destroy all paperwork. Cloyce, I want you to get to the church. Tell the Carrier boy to sound the warning bell. I want as many townsfolk as possible in that church. Kirby and the Alden brothers will be there and I want you all to knock on doors of those who refused to attend the church and tell them that Government agents will raid the town at first light. Tell them that if they want to survive they must get to the church before daylight. Charlotte will drive me to the Grange and fix my shoulder. Oh, and Sister Joy, tell Kirby and the Alden brothers to find Plimpton he will regret his interference.

~~~~~~~~~~

Yarn's Cadillac pulled into the Grange driveway and as Charlotte Potter applied the handbrake Yarn, now only semiconscious, lolled against her. Even by the car's dim interior lamp she could see how deathly pale he was and how his blood had soaked into his seat. She gazed at him. This was the tall overpowering handsome priest of her church, the man whom she had fallen so completely under the spell of when he arrived in the town. He was the one man she believed would understand when he discovered the secrets of Peace and not be afraid...but she had not found the courage to tell him. The right time or opportunity had not yet arisen.

Now as Aaron slumped against her, doubts crept into her mind. Doubts, about their strange platonic relationship, this was something she had once questioned him about. It had made him angry. He raved about how Satan controlled not only his body, but also his sexual emotions. He told her that when the master was ready she would experience pleasures she had never known before and she let it go at that, but she was still waiting. He talked to her about Satan as if his existence was new to her, but she had been born into a world where Satan was the only saviour. Aaron Yarn told her that she and he would share eternity together. He said Satan would demonstrate his gratitude for their loyalty to him. She had now convinced Yarn of her faith by taking part in Esor's human sacrifice rituals. Before Aaron came to her town she had never taken part in anything more extreme than sacrificing small animals; this was usually a rabbit or a chicken. Even then, the animal was given to a poor and deserving family in the village. Lukas Plimpton made their religion satanic in name only, and far from sinister, but Aaron changed that. He brought back Satanism the way it used to be. He put passion into his sermons, and took many villagers back to a time when punishing their enemies was the town's first commandment. He convinced them that over the years they had lost their way, that they had become unworthy of their own religion and that Lukas Plimpton's preaching was little better than mocking Satan. Aaron made the town believe that if they did not change their ways and follow his teachings they would know the real meaning of hell. Charlotte knew about the effects of Aaron's drugs, although Aaron always referred to them as the Masters Potion, maintaining that all experiments in his Lab were guided by Satan's hand. She remembered how Aaron had talked her into administering one of his concoctions regularly to Lucy Corwin, until Lucy became so convinced she was dying of a brain tumour she took her own life. Yes, Charlotte admitted to herself that she as good as committed murder for the love and belief in Aaron. But too many doubts were now creeping into her mind. There was Luke Plimpton's story about the town's water supply, had she also been a victim of it? She now asked herself.

Then there was the shock on the day she secretly explored the tunnels. Aaron had explicitly told her not to go down there unless escorted by him. But then, when he spent a fortnight away, she had found the locked dormitory she had listened at the door and heard the voices of young women, maybe even girls. Why were they there? Was this room Aaron's own personal little harem? Were those women the reason he had not shown any intimate desire towards her. She looked at the bandage around his head. It was obviously there to cover his left ear as she could see a small bloodstain that had soaked through it. He had told her he had gotten too close to one of his aquariums but she had her doubts. This last train of thought made her angry and the only consoling thought was that she, also, had secrets—secrets that she had kept from him, like the one she now suddenly remembered.

Easing Aaron back to an upright position and without waking him, she quietly opened her door and disappeared into the darkness at the side of the house. Ten minutes later she returned, got back in the car and shook Aaron. "Aaron, wake up we're here. You'll have to try walking. I can't carry you in the house and we must hurry if I'm going to dress that wound. Corwin has his belongings here and he may come back at any time." She struggled to get him up the porch steps, but eventually managed to sit him at the kitchen table. She put a full tumbler of water next to him. "You are lucky. The bullet missed the bone but you must drink as much as you can to replace the blood you've lost. We have got to get away from the town before..."

"Get away? No, I'm not leaving yet. I have to get back to the church the town will be waiting; I promised them I'd save them from the marshals."

"But by morning the town will be overrun with government marshals."

Yarn smiled "Indeed, let them come. They are in for a surprise."

"What do you mean? Aaron I'm afraid. I remember what happened in Waco when the marshals raided the place."

"Have faith Charlotte, This time it will be different."

"What do you mean—different—how?"

"Just fix the shoulder and drive me back to the town hall. I have some papers to collect. Then I want you to join the others in church, I will see you there. If Cloyce and Joy Harris have done as I asked the whole town should be at the church by the time you arrive. If they start getting anxious tell them they need not fear the marshals. I have the answer to their problem. You seem to be able to control the people, Charlotte...I've always wondered about that. You have some kind of influence over them and I'm not sure if it's trust or fear. One day you can explain it to me, but right now you must fix this wound and get me back to town.

~~~~~~~~~

The four gunshots that created the crazed panic inside the courtroom had only been seconds apart. The first had hit Dugan; the second shot oddly came from Dugan himself. In a desperate attempt to regain his balance his arms flailed outward and he involuntarily squeezed the trigger on Aaron's gun. His shot was accompanied by a loud cry of despair. I glanced around the hall before seeing Orville bespattered with his father's blood. Dugan's stray shot had hit Jake Tollman just above the ear and as Orville cradled his father's head in his arms panic took hold of the whole community. Then a third shot rang out. This again came from Luke Plimpton's old Winchester. Phipps had started to swing his weapon towards Luke, but the old man must have guessed he'd be Phipps's next target and fired before Phipps could take aim. Phipps's shot lodged itself harmlessly in a roof beam while Luke's bullet sent Phipps crashing across several chairs where he lay motionless. Women screamed and men discarded their weapons as they rushed for the exit to escape the madness. Even Ben Alden and Doc Kirby fled. The last sound that was heard from the fleeing cult was the sound of a distant voice yelling, *"It's the, marshals. Get to the church."*

It seemed everyone had one aim in mind, and that was to leave that place of murder and mayhem as fast as possible. Out of the few stragglers left in the hall I glanced to where Orville had been cradling Jake, but only the body of Jake sat slumped dead in his chair. Then my attention was distracted as another creature leaped through the open trap attempting to reach Mat Black. Fortunately the agent's injection had weakened. He swung his legs evading the creatures snapping jaws, but blood was running down his arms from the straps cutting into his wrists. I could tell his strength was waning, and I knew he was about to give up the fight. One snap of those huge jaws was about to cost him his life.

"Get to him, Spence!" It was Jimmy's voice. I turned to see Jimmy nearing normality his injections were wearing off. I wanted to release Jimmy's straps but Mathew Black took priority. With great effort I made it to the controls on the bench. There were just five push-buttons, four black and one red but no markings. I took pot luck and hit the first black button. The whirring started but to my horror Black started to descend. I quickly hit the red and stopped it. I found the right button to close the trapdoors before lowering Black down where he crumpled to a heap on the floor. The straps on his wrist were stopping his blood flow and as I relieved him of his straps and he croaked out a breathless, "thank you."

I was pleased to see Luke helping Jimmy, down from the prisoners' enclosure.

"I owe you, Sheriff, I was so sure my time was up," said Black.

"You and me both pal, but its Luke here that we have to thank, and call me Spence I think my time as sheriff is finished."

I collected three discarded robes and handed two to Matt and Jimmy. As we slipped them on I noticed Jimmy looking at me with fear in his eyes and I realised he'd not yet been told about Jenny and was probably afraid to ask.

"Jimmy, I think Jenny's okay," The relief on his face was unmistakable.

"How do you know? Where is she?"

"I'm not sure but I picked the lock on her cell and got her out of there. Three of Yarn's armed men chased us through Main Street in the dark, but I hid Jenny in my car and led the men into the woods. I heard her drive away that's when I then went back to try to get you out, but they were waiting for me. Anyway I think...I hope she got away before they could catch up with her. I told her to make for the Pine Camp."

The relief on Jimmy's face was something to see until a thought struck him, "But she can't drive?"

"Now you tell me!"

"Don't worry son," Luke cut in. "I saw her go and she was doing pretty good for a gal who can't drive. As long as that first gear holds out she should be in Portland by now. Hell that engine was screaming for help." That was the first time I saw Jimmy smile since he and I were caught climbing out of the tunnel; it was a welcome sight.

"She's not in Portland." The woman's voice came from the open doors at the entrance to the hall. I looked up and became embarrassingly emotional at the sight of three friendly faces smiling at me. And if my own limbs had been fully recovered I think I'd have run to embrace them. Jimmy, Mat and Luke looked on in wonder as I staggered the length of the court to welcome them.

"Hey Spence, you said you was gonna be a sheriff not a monk," said Neil, grinning.

"Yeah, it's a long story Neil. Hey Mick thanks for your support. I guess you must be with precinct 13 now?"

"Yes I think I was your replacement, and don't mention it Spence, I couldn't miss a show like this."

I then looked at Karen and ignoring any embarrassment I put my arms around her and kissed her long and hard.

"Hey, take it easy Spence, you're a married man said Neil."

"Apparently not, and neither are you, pal."

"Yeah we figured that much,"

Karen then said, "If we figured this Aaron Yarn right this is all about stealing property to fund his cult and whatever else his intentions are."

"Yes and I'm sorry to be the one to tell you, Karen, but you were right about your ex, Steve Sykes. He was another of Yarn's victims."

This brought a sadness to Karen's eyes and I thought she was about to cry, but she forced herself to take a deep breath, saying, "I expected as much—come on, let's meet your friends."

~~~~~~~~~~

I worked the introductions before we pooled our knowledge of Yarn's operations both here and in San Francisco leading up to my ex-colleague's presence here. Unfortunately Karen knew nothing of Luke's relationship to Abigail Potter and did not moderate her account of the circumstances in which his ward and her partner met their demise. I could see the hurt on Luke's face as did Neil and he changed the subject.

"We saw some of your cloaked brothers making for the hills as we got here," he said, "We tried to stop one outside but he took one look at the initials on my jacket and took off shouting something about marshals. One of them took a wild shot at us."

I could see Jimmy getting understandably impatient and finally he addressed Karen with,

"I heard you say my girl, Jenny, was not in Portland, do you know where she is?"

"You must be Jimmy," said Karen. "Yes she's fine, thanks to Mick and Neil here. They pulled her out of a burning car. Little cut on her leg is all. She's up at Pine Tree Camp. Now tell us about this place. It looks like a court room."

Lukas then explained, "That's exactly what it is," said Lukas. "Aaron Yarn had it built to make his barbaric executions appear lawful to members of his cult. First he brainwashed them with his preaching and the drugs he was secretly feeding them through the town's water supply. Of course the trials he held here were a farce. His objective was to steal property in order to finance what I believe is his ultimate goal and that is to cause the deaths of as many people as he can. You see he believes every death related to his doing is another soul collected for the master: his favoured name for Satan. You see, he believes that in return Satan will grant him everlasting life."

Neil then said, "We found a laboratory in the church tunnels. I guess that is where he concocts these drugs?"

"Not just drugs by all accounts" said Agent Black staring at the trapdoor that had taken three lives and so very nearly his own. "Have you seen the creatures in the lake below this floor? They're like no fish or mammal that I've ever seen."

"Christ," said Mike. "You're saying those things are in this lake?"

"So you've seen them?"

"Yes and where Yarn is rearing them. A Deputy who was part of our team got too close to the tank and had his arm almost chewed off."

"Yes," said Karen, "We strapped his arm up and he drove back up to Pine Needle Camp. I'm guessing these creatures function is to eliminate evidence, but there will be bones, and dragging the lake will tell how many victims are down there."

Karen then looked at her watch, "I've been told that in less than three hours, your colleagues, Mr Black, are going to storm the town. Initially they'll be looking for stolen weapons. As we now know, they'll find a lot more federal laws have been breached by Yarn than just stolen weapons. The point is if there's any resistance they have orders to use force and that could turn into a blood bath. Now if we don't want to be caught up in it we should get back up to Pine Camp."

"But there are young women in those tunnels," said Black, "I've heard voices."

"Oh hell—yes we heard them too but the FBI will have to deal with it."

"Yes, you people should go," said Luke but I can't go with you. I believe Yarn is still in the town and I know he's planning something. I have to stay."

"Luke, you'll excuse me if I say I don't give a damn about them," said Black. "Your people were quite happy to feed me to Yarn's pets."

"I understand," Lukas said "And no doubt you all feel the same, but Yarn's cult members are only part of the town and I'm convinced that their behaviour was influenced by Yarn's drugs. These are people I've known all my life. I have to get to the church."

"With that Lukas picked up his rifle and left. As I watched him hobble out I felt guilty that I had not offered to help him. The rest of us made our way back through the wooded shortcut and caught up with Luke just as he reached Main Street. The church bell was tolling and it seemed the whole town was answering its call by making their way to the church. No one appeared to take much notice of us. I suppose they were all well aware of Yarns cult, so our hooded cloaks were enough to render us insignificant. I felt another twinge of guilt as I watched Luke mingle with the crowd and head for the church. As Karen started to lead us back to the Toyota I hung back. Karen noticed,

"What are you doing Spencer? The marshals will be here soon. Do you want to be caught up in what could be another Waco?"

"No, Karen I'd rather be on my way back to San Francisco with you, but I can't abandon that old man he has saved my life twice.

Do me one last favour, will you; get Jimmy and the others back to Pine tree camp. I promised his girl I'd bring him back safe and he's in no condition to help or get there on his own and neither is Mathew Black, they've been through too much. I'll join you when this business is over."

I never waited for an argument and I was sure Karen was stoking up for one. I kissed her quickly on the cheek, turned and hurried after Luke. Due to his age I caught up with him just before he reached the churchyard gate.

"Sheriff, why are you still here?" He said as I reached him."

"I felt bad about leaving you to face whatever you intend to try alone. I also feel I should try to get those women out of the tunnel."

Luke smiled, shook his head and mumbled "Christians." He then said, "in that case, Sheriff, there is something I'd like you to do..."

Chapter 24 The Lift

As Luke pulled his hood low over his face and followed the last of the stragglers along the church path I made sure I wasn't being watched as I slipped away through the cemetery to the rear of the church. Luke told me the grave I was to look for was close to the back wall of the church, but to watch my step as it would most likely be left open. I was wishing I had borrowed Karen's torch, but there was a slight amount of light coming from the stained windows high above the back wall of the church and this was enough to stop me falling headlong down some twenty stone steps and into the short passage Luke had described to me. I looked down into that open grave and physically shivered. Thoughts of unmovable corrugated tin and dank earth returned to haunt me, but I was committed to doing what Luke had asked. I crept cautiously down the steps and into the darkness. On reaching the bottom I heard the faint sound of a door closing. Then I heard similar whining sound like the altar opening before all went quiet. With hands outstretched I felt my way forward until the faint glow of a light helped guide me to what Luke had described as Yarns one-man elevator. The light was coming through its glass panelled door. The tiny area inside the shaft looked no larger than a dumb waiter, but obviously wide enough to take a man. I pulled the door open to find an electric motor with a large power cable feeding it. The motor was geared to a spool of steel cables. Luke had asked me to try and disable it. I never quizzed his reasons but I figured he wanted close Yarn's escape route. I could hear the faint sound of a man's voice above me and I guessed Yarn was standing in his pulpit right now. My problem was how to sabotage the lift workings without making too much noise and warning Yarn I was down here. I had no tools to get at the electrics, not even a screwdriver. Then I suddenly remembered something Jimmy and I found behind one of the tunnel doors. I quickly moved on to where

Luke said I'd find a steel door. It was only a few yards further on and I found it was held shut by just one bolt. Once through this I found myself at the bottom of the steps that led down from the altar, just as Luke had described. My thoughts were now fixed on the putting that lift out of action as Luke had requested. It took me no more than four or five minutes to sabotage the lift to my satisfaction. The next task was to get those females out of there before the marshals arrived.

~~~~~~~~~~

It was years since the church had been so packed. Attendance to Yarns religious meetings had gradually dwindled of late until only his cult members continued to attend. Now, it appeared the warning sound of the church bell had a significant effect on the whole town. The seating area quickly filled and in the surrounding aisles people even jostled for standing room. The drone of so many nervous and worried voices was something unique in the church. The last of the townsfolk had arrived and two heavily built men closed the doors before lifting a huge beam into steel brackets, sealing the door from intruders. The murmur of two hundred or more voices then started to abate as the stern face of Aaron Yarn looked down from his pulpit and spread his arms demanding silence. In the belfry high above the rafters the bell suddenly stopped ringing as Aaron Yarn scanned the tightly packed hall. He quickly caught sight of Joy Harris, and his mood visibly darkened as she slowly shook her head indicating that Lukas Plimpton had not been found. He turns to the congregation.

"Citizens of Peace, I have summoned you here because your town and your earthly existence is about to end." Instantly the murmuring recommenced, while one man shouted,

"What do you mean," came a shout from somewhere in the crowd.

"I mean that government agents, state police and marshals are about to raid the town, and their violent methods for dealing with non Christian communities is renowned."

"But you have weapons, we saw them unloaded."

"Yes give us the means to defend ourselves and our town, another voice called out."

"That was my original intention," Yarn answered, "but members, who I believed were my most faithful followers have proved that you do not have the courage to stand up and fight to preserve your way of life." More mumblings of dissention followed as Yarn casually lifted his glass to quench his thirst.

"But we came because you said you would protect us," another man shouted.

"From the Marshals, yes, they will not harm you, because your souls are promised to..." Yarn paused, distracted by a single sheet of paper that drifting slowly down midst the crowded hall. Yarn watched it like he was mesmerized until an arm reached up from the crowded hall to grasp it. That was the moment he saw the face of Lukas Plimpton.

"Grab that man!" Yarn shouted, pointing at Lukas. "He's a traitor and an informant." Immediately, two cult members grabbed Luke by the arms. "Take him to the cells." The two men started to manoeuvre their way through the crowd toward the altar until Charlotte Potter ordered them to stop.

"Sister Charlotte," Yarn shouted, "Why do you countermand my order?"

"Charlotte ignored him as did Luke's two escorts as they complied with Charlotte's order. Yarn stood powerless as he watched Luke speak at length to Charlotte while handing her the paper in his hand.

"Charlotte!" Yarn shouted again, but Charlotte appeared to ignore him. Tears clouded her eyes as she read the words on the yellow edged page in her hand. The congregation waited before Charlotte finally turned to them, and held up the paper.

"My People, I have here a page torn from a copy of our sacred book, the page lists the last few names of witch finder informants, and among them is the worst traitor of all: Aaron Yarn." In that moment the whole congregation seemed to come alive with a clamour of threatening voices until Charlotte, again raised her hand. "There are also three words written across the page in blood, and I believe they were written as the last dying act of our own Abigail Fisher." She then held up the page, "those three words are, kill the Chemist." Again there came the clamour of angry voices.

Almost as if to emphasise the seriousness of her words, there came an alarming scream from high in the belfry rafters above them. This was followed by a sickening thud. All eyes turned towards the altar on top of which the gruesome sight of Amos Carrier's body lay. The black metal candelabra that had stood on the altars surface now protruded from the teenager's chest dripping with the boy's blood. The congregation, including Yarn, glanced first at the boy, then up at the tangle of wooden ladders and rafters. In that moment he realised that the rumours of shape shifting among Peace residents were more than just fanciful stories. High in the belfry's structure a huge figure moved slowly along the complex of rafters. Had it not been for the figures immense size and the tattered remnants of a habit hanging from its back, Yarn would not have known it to be Orville Tollman. His face had taken on rat-like features. As the creature moved slowly down toward the pulpit, Yarn glanced at the sea of faces below him and was disturbed by the expression on the faces of the local inhabitants. They were not showing fear at the sight of the beast, and some were actually smiling. Yarn recalled the crazed exchange of gunfire that took place no more than three hours earlier. He remembered how Jake Tollman died from a stray bullet. Even though he did not fire that fatal shot he knew Orville was seeking retribution for his father's demise. As Orville neared the pulpit Yarn could see the beasts red eyes looking directly at him. Desperation took hold of Yarn and he sought out faces in the crowd he believed would still follow his orders. He caught the attention of Kirby and Alden. "Quick, shoot the thing!"

The Alden brothers tried to comply and started to raise their rifles but they were over powered by non cult members. The beast was now less than twenty feet from the pulpit. As Orville made ready to pounce, Yarn reached down below the pulpit's balustrade and lifted up, what the congregation thought was some kind of rifle. Kirby, who had spent time as a medic in Vietnam, noticed a small flame near the barrel's end and the canister attached to the underside of the stock. Kirby recalled having to treat some of the victims of this terrible weapon. His immediate thought was to run, but fear paralyzed him at the thought that no one could run they were shoulder to shoulder, packed in like sardines in a can. Yarn aimed the nozzle of the M2 towards the creature above him. Seconds before Yarn pulled the trigger; Kirby found his voice and shouted,

"Run, he's got a flame thrower."

~~~~~~~~~

I had no idea of how much time I had to carry out the task Lukas had set me. Lukas guessed Yarn would attempt an escape after some kind of final showdown with the people of Peace and he had asked me to do one last thing before rescuing the females we knew were in the tunnel. I felt my way to the end of the short passage until I reached the steel door. I was pleased to find it held shut by just a single bolt and on the other side the red lights were still on. To my right were the steps leading to the altar just like Luke confirmed. It took me just one trip to retrieve what I needed to achieve Luke's request. I then made my way to the room where, earlier, Jimmy and I heard female voices. As I got there I heard the faint sound of a phone ringing and I remembered where the office was that I'd seen it. Curiosity got the better of me and I quickly made my way there. I picked up the receiver.

"Hello?"

"Mr Yarn?" said a man's voice.

"Er—Yes"

"My partner and I are up from Miami. I think you know what we've come for. We're at the Memaloose Airstrip right now and we're about to drive to the address on your correspondence: You called it the Pike and Heron. You would be wise to have our package ready when we get there."

I didn't get a chance to answer, the line went dead. Miami, Yes, I remembered hearing Yarns voice on my first visit to the tunnel and he mentioned the Mafia. Maybe his luck is about to run out without any help from me.

I made my way back to the women's room and put my ear to the door. All was quiet as I expected. I tried the handle, it was locked. I tapped lightly at first, but getting no answer I banged harder. A light appeared under the door. Then a female voice answered angrily,

"If that's you Phipps you can fuck off. You're not coming in. We've barricaded the door."

I answered "Listen, you don't know me, but my name is Sheriff Corwin. Can you tell me how many of you are in there and how you came to be here?"

There was a pause while I heard other female voices and I guessed they were debating whether I was genuine.

"There are four of us and we're locked in here." said the same voice. "We came to Peace in answer to an advert for teachers but we discovered what they were teaching kids, and refused to be a part of it. Hell that Aaron guy is a sick fuck. Next thing we know we wake up in this shit hole. We all have a similar story."

"I see—I guess you must be the language teacher." I heard a giggle before I said, "look I've come to get you out of there and we don't have much time."

"You say you're the law—you better not be another one Aarons rapists."

"I'm not, and I get the picture. Clear away whatever you've put against the door. I'll try to break it in." With that I heard what sounded like a whispered argument, then furniture being scraped across a floor.

"Alright it's clear."

"Okay, move away from the door." With that I used the width of the tunnel to use what little momentum I could muster and hoped the door was as flimsy as it looked. I hit it shoulder first and for once was glad of my weight; wood split with a crack and the lock gave way. I found myself in a room staring at three young women, all looking decidedly apprehensive. Then before I could ask where number four was, for the second time in a few hours my lights went out. I don't think I was unconscious for more than a few moments though, because when I came round I was lying where I fell, and looking up at four young women. One was holding a heavy wooden base of a table lamp.

"You fucking hit me?" I said, like I was telling her something she didn't know.

"Now who's the language teacher? And I'll hit you again if you don't tell us who you are and what you're doing here."

"I told you I'm the sher...oh I see," I realised I was still wearing a habit.

"Yes we don't get too many monk-type sheriffs drop in here. If a man comes in here wearing one of them, it usually means one of us is going to get dragged in there," she said, pointing to another door.

"Hit him again and you'll get something worse."

I looked around and was glad to see Karen leaning against the broken door jamb with a Beretta in her hand. I should have been annoyed that she put herself in danger but under the circumstances I was pleased to see her. It didn't take much to convince the four that we were on the level, Karen's FBI vest made it easy and we managed to get some answers from them. I asked their names. Judy was the one with the colourful vocabulary and the make-do cosh, the others were, Alex, Bev, and Irene. I looked around and counted six beds. There were two more doors inside the room, one of which had to be a toilet. The women were all attractive and I guessed between twenty five and thirty five.

"So what's behind those doors?" I asked Judy.

"That one's a toilet and the other is...," she acted embarrassed to complete the sentence. "We call it the rape room. It's just an eight by eight room with a bed. Anyway when they we discovered what was going on at their school I tried to leave. I asked the kids about their parents and they looked at me like I was an alien. None of them could remember their parents."

"Yes I tried asking them that," interrupted Bev, "and the kids reported me; next thing I remember was waking up in here."

"The same goes for Irene and me," said Alex "The strange thing is have started to forget things since they put us down here. What is this place anyway it always smells musty."

"That's because you're under ground," said Karen.

Judy turned to the others; "There, I told you it had an earthy smell didn't I."

"Yes, we all have a similar story," Alex said. "That beast they call Aaron and his friends started coming down here and..." she struggled to find the right words before her tears won through. As the others tried to comfort her I said.

"It doesn't matter. I think I can guess what Yarn and his thugs have been up to."

"Yarn? Is that the one they call Aaron?" Judy asked.

"Yes why?"

"He hasn't been back down here since he tried to drag a young girl into that room. She almost bit his ear off. He went out of here with blood pouring down his face and screaming like a big kid."

"That explains something. What happened to the girl?"

Judy looked at the other girls and was slow answering, "We think they drowned her in that lake. I heard that pig, Arden, whisper to Phipps, something about the girl being fish food; what did he mean by that?"

Karen and I looked at each other before I said, "You don't want to know." I then glanced at the water jugs by the side of their beds and remembered Luke's words before asking,

"Where do you get your water?"

"That spiteful Harris woman brings it. We have a toilet but there's no tap in there. The water she brings tastes funny, but she hits us if we don't drink it."

"That may be the cause of your memory being cloudy. Any longer down here and you'd probably forget your own names."

"I suspected the water," said Irene. "We tried rebelling," said Irene. "Like the night we all purposely messed our beds. It stopped those bastards coming in here to abuse us. But now before lights out, Harris makes us stay on the toilet until we go. I'm sure the sick bitch likes to watch us."

"I get the picture," I said, "and don't worry I think your memories will come back. Look, It'll be daylight soon and these tunnels are about to be raided by government agents so we've got to get you out of here now. Where are your clothes?" they looked at me with a blank stare before Alex said,

"We've only got dressing gowns and slippers."

"Okay put them on and stay close behind each other; the tunnels are like a maze and I don't want anyone taking a wrong turn.

~~~~~~~~~~

At that moment Yarn pulled the trigger of the M2 flame gun. Blazing napalm roared upwards to momentarily silence the panicking congregation. They unwittingly stopped to stare up at the spectacular sight as if it were a firework display. Flames and burning chemicals just missed Orville, sending him scurrying off into the darkness of the belfry again. Much of the chemicals clung to the woodwork setting it ablaze. The congregation, however, unmindful that gravity would bring much of the burning wax back to earth, were caught gazing upward. Screaming chaos ensued as the burning chemicals descended on them, sticking to their skin, hair and clothes.

Meanwhile, Yarn, content that Orville was no longer a threat, turned his attention back to the nave. He noticed two male cult members climbing over injured and burning bodies to try reaching the oak doors. Before the two had time to lift the heavy wooden beam from its brackets, Yarn pulled the trigger on the M2 again. Flames roared, spreading a blanket of burning wax across the crowd. This not only set the two men ablaze, but many more villagers. Yarn's eyes took on a look of madness as he trained the blazing jet at everything combustible including the wooden pews and the door itself. Above the crackling of burning wood and the vociferous furore of panic the sound of Yarns manic laughter could still be heard as People ran in circles bumping into each other and setting ablaze those who had escaped Yarns aim. Others tried rushing the steps of his pulpit in an attempt to climb up and disarm him, but he turned the flame gun on them setting them and the base of the pulpit on fire. Then out the corner of his eye, Yarn saw more movement close to the altar. It was Doc Kirby, and the brothers: Ben and Don Alden, trying to reach their last hope of escape. Before Kirby could press the button that would open the altar, flames engulfed the three of them. After watching them perish, Yarn gazed around at what he regarded as his great achievement. Bodies were piled three high in places and Yarn was now finding the heat unbearable himself as flames now licked the underside of his lectern. He made one final scan of the nave and was amazed to see Charlotte Potter and Lukas Plimpton still standing amid the flames. They were not screaming or crying out in pain, but just staring at him. The sight unnerved him and he quickly pulled the trigger on the flamethrower once more, emptying the last of its deadly chemical in their direction before throwing the empty weapon over the balustrade. He then opened a hidden panel on the woodwork and pressed a button.

~~~~~~~~~~

We had just left the women's dorm when the low voltage lights started to flicker before dying completely.

"That's never happened before," I said, switching on the torch.

"Spence, I can smell smoke," said Karen.

"Yes, and if it's what I think it is, we better move fast. Okay everyone better grab each other's hand so no one gets left behind or takes a wrong turn, we have to move fast."

As we neared the metal door beside the altar steps the smoke was denser and we heard faint yet vociferous and disturbing cries coming from above us. "What's up there?" I'd never known Karen to show fear, but she did now as I said,

"We're below the church chancel now, Kaz, and by those sounds I'd say the church was on fire so we better keep moving, if the church roof falls, it could collapse this tunnel. Just pray no one has closed that grave stone."

~~~~~~~~~~

Aaron Yarn pressed his elevator button but when his platform jerked to a halt after dropping only a few inches, the look of smug satisfaction on his face changed to one of panic. But then came another jolt and the platform started to descend again and he breathed easy again until a loud crack from above made the platform shake. He looked up to see a burning rafter collapse raining sparks and hot ash down on him. The lift came to a halt almost a foot short of its normal docking level but he ignored the fault and vacated the lift and the tunnel in much haste. His one concern was to get to his room at the Pike and Heron before getting driving as far away from Peace as possible before the Marshals could find him. The mystery of the elevator's malfunction was of little interest to him, especially knowing he would never use it again.

~~~~~~~~~~

I pushed the metal door open and ushered the women along the stretch of tunnel leading to the open grave stone. We got as far as the elevator and I was disturbed to find the glass-panel door was open. The lift platform had been lowered which meant my attempt at sabotage had failed. The wooden crutch that I'd used to jamb the cable spool had snapped and was sticking out from under the platform. As I stared at it a burning piece of timber fell through the, now, open shaft to glanced off my shoulder. As I looked up I could see that the pulpit was on fire above. Yarn had got away and I was doubly worried that he may have closed the grave, but a few yards further along the tunnel we saw the glow of the church fire coming through the open grave and I knew we were going to make it. We dodged hot embers, burning timber and falling masonry as we climbed out and made our way to the main entrance of the church. The double doors were still closed and a crowd of townsfolk, those who had refused to be drawn by Yarns warning, some cried while others appeared dumbfounded and confused. Then from within the crowd we heard someone call out before seeing Neil shouldering his way toward us.

"Thank God," Neil said as he reached us. Then smiling a greeting at the girls he then said, "I thought you were both in there. Have you seen Mick?" As he spoke another loud crash sounded within the flames, sending a great flurry of sparks swirling into the night.

"No, didn't Mick go back to the camp with you?"

"Yes. We dropped Jimmy and Mat off at the camp, but that's when we saw the fire. Thinking you and Karen might be caught up in it, we drove back down here."

"So where is he?" said Karen.

"I don't know. As I was parking the car Mick jumped out and disappeared into the dark. I hope he never ran into the church. If he did..."

We looked at each other then at what was left of the church, none of us wanting to voice our thoughts. Eventually I broke the silence with.

"It looks like Yarn has got away. Neil did any cars pass you on the road like a dark green Cadillac?"

"Only one car passed us, but it was coming down the hill into the town."

Karen noticed the four girls were shivering. "Say can we discuss this after we get these ladies up to the camp."

"Yes I think the authorities better take over now. I figure Yarn must have gone through Cranford to miss going past the camp. He's probably half way across Idaho by now."

~~~~~~~~~

In the first glow of dawn Yarn's car arrived at the Pike and Heron all was silent around the lake except for the occasional splash as one of his masters pets leaped from the water. Not a light could be seen from outside the Inn and the entrance door had been left open. Yarn stepped cautiously inside the door, while wishing he still had the navy colt that was now lying at the bottom of the lake with whatever his genetic creations had left of the Dugan and all the others. Relieved however that a dozen marshals were not waiting to leap out at him, he made his way up to his room where he quickly stripped off. He then washed and shaved off his beard before discarding the bandage around his head, and covering his jagged ear with a first aid plaster. Content that his appearance was sufficiently altered. He donned a shirt and jeans before prizing up a floorboard to reveal a revolver and a stack of fifty dollar bills which amounted to a hundred thousand dollars. It was money that was meant for the Miami branch of the Mafia. Now, however, he decided he would need that money himself to make a new start. He slipped the gun in his belt. He then organised half the bills neatly at the bottom of holdall before packing his clothes and personal papers on top. The other fifty thousand he wrapped in a plastic carrier bag. In the midst of doing this he thought he heard the sound of a car door closing. He went quickly to the window but saw no car parked outside. Nerves, he told himself. He then reached up to the top of his wardrobe to retrieve a leather briefcase containing the deeds to three houses. With the two cases and the parcel of bills he crept silently down the stairs and out to the car where he loaded the two cases in the trunk and stashed the parcel under his seat. He was about to drive away when he remembered the book: Cargo of Hope locked in the drawer of the judicial bench. He knew it was valuable maybe more so than the money. He re-entered the Inn and crept quietly toward the doors of the court room. A strip of light shone at the bottom of the door, but that didn't surprise or concern him. After what had taken place a few hours earlier he couldn't imagine anyone taking the time to turn out the lights. But still he took the gun from his belt and put his ear, (the good one), to the door before opening it. He then opened the door and stepped inside. He glanced nervously around the hall before a sound directed his attention to a man sitting in his judicial chair.

"Mister Aaron Yarn, I believe," the man said, while nonchalantly spinning a coin on the top of the bench.

"Who are you?" said Yarn pulling the gun from his belt.

"I think you know who I am but you can call me Mr C lets say its short for collector. I told you not more than two hours ago on the phone, I'm from Miami."

The penny dropped and Yarn suddenly knew he was in trouble although he didn't remember such a phone call. He made a quick calculation as he weighed up the man's size. Guessing Mr C to be close to three hundred pounds Yarn believed he could easily get to his car which was right outside the Inn, and be well on his way before...he heard click behind him and turned to find the doors now closed and an even larger man facing him with a snub-nosed .38mm in his hand. Yarn knew his plan was scuppered.

"I hope you weren't thinking of leaving before settling your bill Mr Yarn, said C. There's a little matter of a hundred thou that you owe for a small arsenal we delivered to you."

"Yes, but I explained that funds were short because house sales were down and that I'd square things all in good time."

"No, Mr Yarn. The only good time is the time agreed in the agreement and that time has passed. The gentleman standing behind you is Anthony and I want you to do as he asks because he can be very short tempered with clients who don't cooperate." Yarn looked back at Anthony who was sliding a leather belt from around his waist, if waist was an appropriate description of its enormous girth.

"Put your palms together and hold them out," Anthony said, taking Yarns gun. Yarn complies and watches the big man wind the belt around his wrists before buckling the ends tight. He then prods Yarn to move towards the bench until they are both stood on the trapdoor.

Mr C then said, "I've noticed an interesting panel of buttons on this bench, Mr Yarn and I believe I've got the hang of their functions. It really makes one wonder what kind of a set up you've been running in this town. There's this button for instance."

There came a loud clack and Yarn heard the familiar sound of the chain and hook descending from above. It was a sound that once thrilled and exited Yarn, but now all he felt was fear and a trickle of sweat running down his face. Then, like the big man knew exactly what was expected of him, Anthony forced Yarn's arms up to slip strap over the hook. Then there came another loud click as Mr C reversed the chain's motion until yarn's feet were a few inches off the floor.

Sweat started to run down Yarns face as he thought about the sequence of buttons on that panel and what horror waited beneath the floor. "Ok, you win," Yarn said. "There's a holdall in the trunk of my car. It contains half the money I owe you." Mr C nodded to Anthony who left the courtroom to return seconds later with the holdall which he promptly opened. He then proceeded to scatter Yarns clothes and personal belongings about. Finding the money he quickly checked the amount before returning a positive nod to C who then smiled at Yarn as he reached across the bench toward the control panel. Before he reached the second button Yarn cried out in desperation...,

"Wait!" Mr C stopped and waited for yarn to speak

"Look I can pay the rest with interest. Just give me two weeks. If you kill me the family is out of pocket, surely that can't make sense."

"Who said I was going to kill you? You paid half of what you owe, so I only intended to half drown you."

"But you don't understand; if you open that trap door I'll die."

Mr C stared at the trap door then at Yarn as if he was contemplating what Yarns words could possibly mean. Then he withdrew his arm from across the bench and stood up.

"Okay Mr Yarn, you have another two weeks to come up with the rest of the cash. But I should warn you, if you try to run we'll find you no matter where you go or how long it takes." With that he and Anthony started to walk toward the double doors.

"Wait! You can't leave me like this."

"Sure we can. Consider it punishment for bringing us all the way up here and wasting our time."

"But if no one finds me I'll die, then how will you get the rest of your money."

"Don't worry you'll be found. I have it on good authority that this town is about to be raided, and by all the activity going on at the Pine Needle campsite, that will be pretty soon. Don't forget now, two weeks."

Yarn heard the entrance door of the Inn slam and a feeling of relief came over him, but as Anthony's belt was slowly cutting off his circulation with increasing pain. As he hung there he tried to console himself with the knowledge that he still had fifty thousand dollars under the seat of his car and two property deeds including Corwin's signed legal papers, strewn on the floor below him. They would at least get him out of trouble with the Miami Family.

Just then, for no apparent reason, the metal hook started to rotate turning him slowly around. And as his view of the bench was lost he heard the sound of the judicial chairs being moved and shuffled as if court was coming to order behind him. Then as the hook approached its 360 degree turn, he saw, or imagined he saw, the bench fully occupied with Charlotte Potter sitting in the centre chair. In the other six judicial seats were Jake and Orville Tollman, Mayor Cloyce, Joy Harris, Miss Proctor and Horace Rider.

At first Yarn was sure that this illusion, this manifestation was brought on by the stress of being threatened by two hired killers. Then he remembered the glass of water that he drank in the church, Yes he thought, anyone could have stolen the drug from his room or his laboratory. He shut his eyes, and shook his head hoping they would disappear, but on opening them they were still there. "Get out of my head," He yelled hysterically, "None of you are real. I sent you to the master, you're all dead."

The seven faces at the bench were solemn and as Charlotte stretched across the bench toward the control panel Aaron heard the familiar thump of a sliding bolt below the trap door. The floor below him dropped away and a cold draught of air embraced him as the hook start to rotate again. Aaron Yarn slowly descended as a hundred familiar faces that he last saw being consumed by fire now commenced to chant. *for the Enemy of Peace the lake awaits.*

Chapter 25 Ghost town

I awoke this morning looking up at a familiar ceiling. It felt good to know I was back in my own home although it had never felt so empty with Lucy and Avril both gone. I ate a slice of toast while I sifted through a pile of postal ads until I eventually got to the letter that brought me to my old precinct. As I entered the DI's office Karen gave me a smile that would set any guy up for the day, while Neil gave me the thumbs up.

I gazed around the DI's office looking to wave hello to Mick O'Donnell but forgetting that he had disappeared in that creepy town of Peace.

I entered the CDI's office and stood looking across the same desk I stared across on the day I was offered a position as Sheriff of Peace; Christ, where the hell was my mind on that day.

What I'm looking at is a new shiny plaque. It reads Captain Trevor Crouch.

"Spencer Corwin, you're wondering why my letter asked you to come see me. Well we'll come to that but can I first ask why you have not returned to the department. After all, you must know your colleagues have returned to their jobs? Oh, bad luck about McDonnell, by the way. It looks like he must have bought it in that church. DI Roster told me what happened."

"Yes, but I'm pleased that you've taken Neil and Karen back, they're good cops and I'm not saying that just because they're my friends; but it was different for me, you see, unlike them, I didn't just go AWAL, I actually quit."

"No you didn't!"

"Sorry?"

"According to our records you're still on the payroll. Wages are still being paid into your account. That's why I've asked you to come see me. I need to officially wind up your employment; that is if it's what you want."

"I don't understand, are you saying..."

"I'm saying you never handed your resignation to anyone in an official capacity. You are still officially a detective inspector in the SFPD unless you want me to terminate your employment. You see the department feels that they have to take some of the blame for what happened to you as they employed Dugan in the first place. Somehow his background went unnoticed. Did you know he and his wife rubbed shoulders with the Manson Family?"

"No but it doesn't surprise me."

"Dugan made the rank of CDI this made it easy to get rid of Danvers then get his wife to sit in this chair and play chief for a while. Then once they had you in their net. She disappeared."

"How come you know all this?"

"The FBI investigated the whole setup. Before I disciplined your colleagues, I spent a morning at the federal building over on Turk Street. A couple of agents filled me in on the caper you were all tangled up in. A guy named Black filled me in on the whole operation, he said you and your friends had saved his life. Oh, and he said to tell you the tunnels have been filled in and that they dragged the lake. They found the remains of twenty five victims and almost the same amount of cars before laying submersible charges in the lake. Apparently one of the Marshals was attacked by something in there but they wouldn't elaborate. Not sure why they had to set charges but he said it would make sense to you. Anyway, I've been going over your records and as cops go yours is pretty good. Can I ask what your plans were if you did not intend to come back to the dept?"

"I'm not sure, I thought about starting a private detective agency."

"You're reading too many who-done-it's, Corwin." With that he pulled open a drawer before pushing my old gun and badge towards me. "You want them or not?" Before I could answer, his phone rang. He picked it up...

"I thought I told you to hold my..." he looked at me as I heard the faint sound of a voice on the handset before the captain came back with,

"Yes okay but he's here. Do you want to tell him yourself?" With that came a click and the captain stared at the receiver like it had just said a bad word. "It appears I have to give you another important message. You must go without delay to the cottage in the woods."

"Did the caller give a name?"

"It sounded like Plimpton."

"That's impossible."

"I'm sure that's what he said."

The cottage in the woods; this was the kind of strange event that I hoped I'd heard the last of when I left that crazy town. I was convinced Lukas Plimpton was dead, that he had perished in the church fire, yet I had told no one about my visit to Luke's cottage and it was the only cottage in woods that I had ever seen.

"Hell, I have to go back to Peace."

"Does that mean you know what this is about?"

"No, but I know this man Lukas, and if he says it's important it's important,"

Crouch gave a sigh then dropped my gun and badge back in his drawer "Corwin, I'll give you a week to come back and collect them, after that their gone for good, understand?"

"Yes Sir and thanks." On my way out I intended to break my date with Karen and explain why, but she was not at her desk so I asked Neil to explain to her that I had to find out why a dead person, using the name Lukas Plimpton was urging me to go back to Peace.

~~~~~~~~~~

"Neil, where's Spence?

"You just missed him."

"Hell! I thought he might have stayed long enough to say goodbye. Did he mention our date tonight?"

"Yes he said he won't be able to make it and he asked me to make his apologies, Kaz, but he said he'd make it up to you."

"He'd better! Did he say why he can't make it?"

"You won't believe it. Apparently he got a call from that old man Lukas Plimpton. He's catching a flight back to Peace."

"Oh Christ I thought he had seen enough—but Spence said the old man went into the church, how could..."

"Exactly, but there's something else that's been bothering me, Kaz; do you remember...

~~~~~~~~~

Although I wasted no time arranging a flight and getting to the airport, my flight was delayed due to bad weather. It was now twelve hours since I left Captain Crouches office, and I calculated that if I'd taken the Jeep and driven, I could have got to Peace at least an hour sooner. My stomach was in knots as my flight neared the Memaloose air strip but not because of the flight. The voice on the phone had told CDI Crouch his name was Plimpton and with all the strange happenings I'd experienced in Peace and believing Luke had perished in the fire, I was dreading what kind of surprise Peace had in store for me. At the airstrip I found myself hiring the same Toyota pickup that Karen had hired.

The guy told me how pleased he was that the FBI had found his missing hire cars at the bottom of Pike Lake. It apparently allowed him to claim the insurance on them.

By the time we landed the weather had calmed and I made good time on the fifty mile trip to Peace. I stopped the car at the top of the last hill. Pine Needle Camp had closed for the winter now, but looking through its barred gates I could see the burnt out wreck of my old cruiser and I smiled at the thought of Jenny driving all the way up here in first gear. I know Jimmy was disappointed that he didn't get to see Yarn pay for the murder of the east coast librarian. I promised, however to call him if there was any news as to Yarn's disappearance.

I slipped off the handbrake and cruised down the hill. I had no idea why, but I had butterflies in my stomach as I turned into Main Street, although not in a bad way. For the first time in this place I felt at ease. It seemed odd seeing the wide open space at the end of the street that now gave way to beautiful bright sunlight instead of the dark monstrosity with the inverted cross on its apex.

For no other reason than to stretch my legs I parked up at the entrance to the street and started to walk. The town seemed deserted. I reached the general store to find its front door wide open; I stepped inside and called out. "Hello!" there was no answer. The thick dust on the floor was obviously come from the church fire but looked like it had been there for a hundred years. I came away, but before I had reached the end of the boardwalk the oddest thing occurred. I heard a sound from behind me. I turned around to see Alvin Stokes the general store's proprietor. Alvin was sweeping dust out of his shop door, but I was certain he had passed me to enter the church on the night of the fire. I continued towards the path that led to the lake when a woman villager, followed by her cat, crossed the road and started to pump water from the towns well into a wooden bucket, yet I was led to understand that the FBI had filled the well in having found the water contaminated by Yarn's drugs. I then heard children laughing. I looked toward the nursery to see several infants playing. I suddenly felt that all the strange happenings that I had experienced in that town were starting again. It was like the town was coming alive.

~~~~~~~~~~

I entered the path that led to the lake and set about looking for Luke's cottage in the woods, although just who or what I expected to find there, I had no idea. After seeing Alvin Stokes maybe it could actually be Lukas Plimpton, but would he be flesh and blood?

Reaching the woods I tried retracing the circular route that I took when pursued by those rifle toting monks. I was hoping I'd eventually come across the clearing that surrounded Luke's cottage. As I weaved in and out of the trees I realised it was the first time I'd been in these woods in daylight. I was puzzled to see several large bundles of woven twigs entwined with matted hair and old rag. Was it possible I asked myself? I was suddenly reminded about Luke's story of Abigail Potter and the shape shifting phenomenon. Then I had an uncomfortable feeling I was being followed or at least watched. I came across the path where I started. I'd come a long way to get this far, however, and I wasn't about to give up just yet. That cottage had to be there. I started out again this time taking a bigger sweep. Suddenly there it was, just as I remembered it, with its thatched roof. It appeared deserted as I picked up the knocker and dropped it to produce a single clonk. After repeating the action twice more and getting no answer I pushed the door and to my surprise it opened with little effort.

"Hello!" I called, and received the silence I expected. "Lukas?" I called as I edged my way along the short passage and into the little room where I had listening with interest to Luke's fascinating take on religion and his town's history. The room was as I remembered it except for the range that now contained just grey cold ash instead of a welcoming fire. I wandered into another passage. There was a door facing me at the end. I assumed this would lead into a rear yard, but there was a door either side of the passage. I opened the first to find a small kitchen, but before I had time to try the second door which I assumed to be a bedroom, a voice said,

"So you came, Mr Corwin. I'm glad."

I turned to see Lukas standing at the open front door. "Lucas, you're alive! How is that possible? I don't under..."

"Come and sit awhile Mister Corwin. You obviously have a few questions."

I stepped back into the cosy room again and that's when I got a second surprise. As Luke stood at his cabinet pouring two whiskeys I noticed the range that contained just ashes less than two minutes ago was bright red with burning coals. Luke saw me looking at it with my mouth open and he smiled. As I sat he said,

"I suppose I have a lot of explaining to do and I'll admit I wasn't very open with you the last time you sat in that chair."

"You probably saved my life that night. I'll not complain about anything you may or may not have told me. I'm just glad I have the chance to apologise for letting Yarn escape; now I'm afraid we don't know where he is."

"Don't concern yourself with Aaron. The government agents took away many human bones dragged from the lake. I can assure you Aaron Yarn's were among them."

"You killed him?"

"Let's just say his master's pets, of which he helped create, did the deed. Individuals like Aaron arrive here every so often. They are sent to try us, tempt, if you like."

"I don't understand?"

"Well the events in this town have been much like the events described in Exodus 32. You know the story of the Israelites and the golden calf. How they were led astray by the brother of Moses: Aaron. Ironical don't you think; another Aaron?"

I nodded, "Sure I would think everyone knows the story."

"As I said I was not completely open with you before. I told you the town had always worshiped Satan. That was not true. The town rejected Satan after their church had been destroyed; Most of the town regarded it as a message from a higher God, and by rejecting Satan they were given a gift. Aaron Yarn however learning of the town's history and being a Satanist himself, he was determined to curry favour with the devil and turn things back to the way they were. He was here to do the devils work. The inverted cross above the church and the stained glass windows: Yarn paid for that to be done, and through his drugs and his preaching he enticed the weaker people back into their old ways, these are—were the members of his cult. God annulled their gift, and they became mortal again."

"This gift..."

"Yes of lasting life. I told you I was the priest here before Aaron Yarn came. What I didn't tell you, was how long before he came here. The reason was because I didn't know how you would react to the truth.

"And that being?"

"That I came here with the first settlers as did Charlotte potter, and many others."

I let that sink in before my mouth broke into a grin.

"Yes, sure you did Luke, but I hope you haven't too many more surprises because my space ship is waiting for me outside."

"Mock if you like Spencer Corwin, but before you leave this valley again, you will come to believe what your logic denies."

"Well you could start by telling me how you evaded the flames in that church?"

"Can you be sure that I did? Anyway it's not important but I can tell you that only Aaron Yarn's disciples, his outsiders if you like, and the worst of the town's apostates actually perished in that fire."

"What about Orville, did he..."

"Remember we talked of Abigail Potter and her strange affliction? Orville also had the same gene and he suffered in the fire but he will survive."

"What about Charlotte Potter?"

"She could have saved herself by renouncing Yarn. She realised at the end what Yarn was, but I think she wanted to pay the price not just for her part in Yarn's scheme, but for the loss of her cousin, Abigail. I know Charlotte was saddened by the death of your wife. She fed her drugs as directed by Yarn but never foresaw Lucy taking her own life."

"You know about Lucy?"

Lukas finished his drink, smiled and stood up, "Charlotte tried to atone for her allegiance to Yarn as you will come to understand Mister Corwin."

"But you still haven't told me why you brought me here?"

"Yes, there is a loose end to this Aaron Yarn affair and it is a matter that you must deal with. To do this you will need to go back to the Grange once more before leaving the valley."

Luke then finished his drink, stood up and offered his hand. It was a polite way of saying our meeting was at an end.

I closed Luke's cottage door behind me and walked across the clearing to the path on the edge of the woods; It was here I saw the wife of Mister Stokes the general store keeper, she was picking mushrooms. Missus Stokes was one of the few villagers that had always been civil and friendly towards me.

"Morning Missus Stokes, I hope they're not poison mushrooms you're picking"

"Morning Sheriff. Oh no, those with the red caps are the dangerous ones. Would you like some I've got more than I need?"

I thought it strange that the woman made no mention of the serious events that had taken place in the town like the church fire or government marshals banging their doors in the early hours of the morning or the evacuation of dozens of kids from the nearby school.

"No thank you, Missus Stokes but maybe Lukas would like some."

"Who?"

"Lukas Plimpton, the old man that lives..." I turned to point at Luke's cottage but there was nothing but more trees.

"Sounds like you've seen the watchman. Not many outsiders have had that privilege."

"The watchman," I queried?

"Yes, he's the angel that watches over our village. I've even heard it said that he used to be a preacher in our church many years ago but it must have been before my time."

~~~~~~~~~~

My mind was doing cartwheels as I slipped behind the wheel of the Pickup, started the car and pulled away. Before I reached the end of Main Street I glanced in the mirror which caused me to slam my foot on the brake. Needing to be sure of what I'd seen, I got out and stared back along Main Street. Many more people were now milling about and that in itself was enough to unnerve me, but there at the end of the cul-de-sac in all its splendour stood Peace church with the sun glinting off its, now, orthodox cross.

~~~~~~~~~~

I got back in the pickup and I pulled away I wondered if Lukas had slipped me something in that drink, but then dismissed the thought. As I drove up to the front of The Grange two things caused me to use caution, one was seeing a car that I didn't recognise. It was parked on the grass verge behind a hedgerow that fronted the lawn and therefore unseen from the house. The second, and more head-scratching mystery, was the double garage was open which I had never seen before and never been given a key to. I parked the Toyota behind the mystery car and walked quietly up the drive and into the garage where I stood looking around it. Apart from a bench and a bunch of woodworking tools on a wall rack, the place was empty. I don't know why, but I was about to close it when I noticed the metal was dented and the lock was broken. I left the door open, turned and walked back to the front of the house and climbed the veranda steps. I had no key but when I tried the door it opened. I was expecting to see a shambles, but all seemed in order except the kitchen. Corn flakes were all over the floor but nothing else appeared out of place. I checked each room treading quietly as I went, expecting with every step to discover the reason Lukas had sent me here. I found nothing amiss in the bedrooms. My clothes were still in the wardrobe, my razor still in the bathroom. After checking the kitchen it only left the lounge. I was now wondering if Lukas was mistaken or just playing some kind of game. I crossed the room to glance out of the window when I was startled by a voice from behind me.

"Hello Spence."

I turned to see Mick O'Donnell sitting in my high backed arm chair. I had walked past him, thinking the room was empty. On the occasional table beside him was a briefcase and resting on his lap with his finger on the trigger was the antique Winchester rifle that Lukas had handed me the night Jenny Blake and I were chased by Yarn's mad monks. It didn't need a high IQ to work out that O'Donnell was the loose-end that Lukas spoke of, or that the Irish D.I was somehow mixed up with Dugan and Yarn. I tried to act cool,

"Hello Mick what are you doing here and what's with the briefcase and rifle?"

"Well the briefcase is for me and the rifle is for you."

"Okay, are you just going to shoot me or do I get to know why?"

"Truth is I was just going to shoot you, but I'm curious as to why you should turn up here at this particular time. Have you been tailing me?"

"No, I had no idea you were here."

"So did you come looking for this?" He said patting the briefcase on the table.

"Nope, what is it?"

"Fifty thousand dollars and a couple of prime pieces of realty, one of which is yours I'm sure there was a lot more cash but I guess the mob got to Yarn first. Lucky for me they never searched his car. It took me a while to find it."

"How long have you been part of Yarns set up?"

"Pretty much from the beginning," he said boastfully. "In fact I bumped off the first property owner and guess who gave that ex DCI a nudged on the station platform."

Now I knew O'Donnell could not let me walk away. "I don't think you've thought this through, Mick. If Karen and Neil see my property up for sale they'll smell a rat and realise that rat is you." I saw the slight smirk on O'Donnell's face disappear and I recognised the look of a man unbalanced. I braced myself expecting to feel the awesome power of the Winchester "If you get rid of me you'll have to go after Karen and Neil. They know as much as me, and if they don't, they'll figure it out. They won't stop until they tie you to my disappearance." As I said this the door that I'd left ajar was now slowly opening and I had to force myself not to look at it lest it gave Mick the warning he may need.

"I'll climb that fence when I come to it. If I have to get rid of them I will, but you still haven't told me why you followed me here. Did I slip up somewhere?" Then to my surprise Karen was standing inside the door with her Beretta pointing at the back of Mick's chair.

"Yes you did Mick and you won't be getting rid of anyone." She said.

Mick had his back to Karen and must have guessed she'd be holding a gun on him and that his chance of getting the better of her was slim at best. But what he attempted was probably his best chance of changing his luck. He suddenly threw himself to the floor while twisting his body and firing the Winchester in the general direction of the door. His aim was high. A large chunk of plaster from above the door peppered the floor carpet as two more shots came, this time from Karen's gun before Mick lay still.

~~~~~~~~~~

Karen was shaking. It was the first time she had to shoot someone while looking directly at them. I helped her into a chair and remembered the bottle of scotch I bought after losing Avril. I fetched it and put the drink in her hand before saying. "I don't know why you came here Karen but I'm sure glad you did."

Karen was staring at the body as she said. "He asked if he had slipped up, Spence. He did, and it was more than once. It was Neil that brought it to mind. Mick apparently made some remark about locking Neil in the town's medieval stocks when we first got here, but Neil said at that point they had not seen or known about them. That got me thinking and I remembered the time Jenny Blake drove your cruiser into that tree. I rushed into Mick's room to wake him and Neil was just waking but Mick had his shirt on and one leg in his trousers. He said he had heard the crash and was getting dressed but I remember thinking nobody moves that quick. Then later when we got into the Toyota to drive into peace I remember thinking the cab was warm yet it was hours since we arrived at the camp."

"I see where you're coming from Karen. I remember it bugging me as to how Yarn knew about the Marshals imminent raid on the town. It seems you were on the right..."

A sudden thump on the ceiling above caused Karen and I to stare at each other with a, *what the hell was that,* look on our faces. Karen drew her gun while I picked up Mick's rifle. I led the way as we crept out into the hall and slowly climbed the stairs. At the top of the stairs Karen and I split up. We each searched bedrooms, wardrobes and under beds before meeting back on the landing. Karen shrugged and I looked at her and shook my head.

There was one other place that we had not checked and we were standing right beside it: the airing cupboard. I pointed at the door as I voiced,

"No, there's no body up here Karen. Maybe It was a bird on the roof, come on lets go." I motioned for Karen to go down the stairs while I waited at the hinge side of the closet door rifle at the ready. Karen knew the score. She went to the front door, opened it then slammed it loud enough for anyone in the house to hear. Seconds passed before the airing cupboard door slowly started to open. In a flash I grabbed the door handle and flung it open. This not only startled the young lady whose hand was gripping the edge of the door but flung her headlong onto the landing floor and the box of cornflakes that she was holding under her arm went all over the floor.

The girl appeared to be filthy dirty and her dress was torn. As Karen ran back up the stairs I asked the girl "Who are you and what are you doing here?"

Before the girl could answer Karen made it to the landing. She took one look at the girl and said, "Could you possibly be..."

"I wasn't stealing," interrupted the girl nervously. "I only came in the house to get this," she said holding out a bar of soap, "but we were hungry. The soap slipped out of my hand; you must have heard it."

"Are you Gina?" said Karen.

The girl looked puzzled. "Yes, how did you..."

"Gina, your mother is going to be so happy to know you're safe. Where have you been?"

"We've been here all the time. Charlotte told us Aaron would kill us if he knew we were here. She hid us but she stopped bringing us food and we got hungry."

"Was it you who broke the garage door Gina?" I said.

"Yes but only because..."

"It doesn't matter Hon. Why do you think Aaron Yarn wanted to kill you?"

"I found out he murdered my step father. I tried to stick a dagger in him at one of his initiation services, but one of his so called disciples grabbed me before I could get to him."

"You said we, so how many are we?"

"Just the two of us; Aaron tried to rape my friend but she bit a piece of his ear off. He ordered her to be taken to the lake; I don't know why but anyway Charlotte hid us both."

~~~~~~~~~

My mind went into overdrive. Did I dare raise my hopes and believe my little girl could still be alive? Maybe this was what Lukas meant when he said Charlotte tried to atone for all the wrongs she did.

~~~~~~~~~

"Good for her," said Karen, "so, you've been hiding in the garage I take it the garage is where Charlotte was hiding you?"

"Yes. Come with me, I'll show you."

Karen and I followed Gina out to the garage where she led us to a large cardboard box containing a bunch of discarded household items. We shifted the box to reveal a large metal plate with a hinged handle.

I'd had my fill of secret trap doors, but as I took hold of the handle my heart pounded with apprehension. And I thought of Luke's words: I tugged on the handle and a section of the floor came up and we found ourselves gaping at a single camp bed and peeking out from under its covers, my daughter's frightened eyes.

Also by this Author

Angels of the mud
A historic thriller set in the streets of Old Portsmouth.

The Dormant Gene
A Psychological thriller
A promiscuous teenager's twin babies are abducted setting the scene for a thrilling chase across the US.

Fifteen Twisted Tales
A bunch of short stories from fairy tales to scary tales
And all designed to surprise or keep the reader guessing

www.ingramcontent.com/pod-product-compliance
Lightning Source LLC
Chambersburg PA
CBHW070627180626
46817CB00006B/2071